Bella Rosa Marriages

FIONA HARPER
PATRICIA THAYER
JENNIE ADAMS

MILLS & BOON

First published in Great Britain 2013
by Mills & Boon, an imprint of Harlequin (UK) Limited,
Eton House, 18-24 Paradise Road, Richmond, Surrey TW9 1SR

BELLA ROSA MARRIAGES © by Harlequin Enterprises II B.V./S.à.r.l 2013

The Bridesmaid's Secret, The Cowboy's Adopted Daughter and Passionate Chef, Ice Queen Boss were published in Great Britain by Harlequin (UK) Limited.

The Bridesmaid's Secret © Harlequin Books S.A. 2010
The Cowboy's Adopted Daughter © Harlequin Books S.A. 2010
Passionate Chef, Ice Queen Boss © Harlequin Books S.A. 2010

Special thanks and acknowledgement are given to Fiona Harper, Patricia Thayer and Jennie Adams for their contributions to THE BRIDES OF BELLA ROSA series.

ISBN: 978 0 263 90553 3
ebook ISBN: 978 1 472 00126 9

05-0513

Harlequin (UK) policy is to use papers that are natural, renewable and recyclable products and made from wood grown in sustainable forests. The logging and manufacturing processes conform to the legal environmental regulations of the country of origin.

Printed and bound in Spain
by Blackprint CPI, Barcelona

THE BRIDESMAID'S SECRET

BY
FIONA HARPER

As a child, **Fiona Harper** was constantly teased for either having her nose in a book or living in a dream world. Things haven't changed much since then, but at least in writing she's found a use for her runaway imagination. After studying dance at university, Fiona worked as a dancer, teacher and choreographer before trading in that career for video editing and production. When she became a mother she cut back on her working hours to spend time with her children, and when her littlest one started preschool she found a few spare moments to rediscover an old but not forgotten love—writing.

Fiona lives in London, but her other favourite places to be are the Highlands of Scotland and the Kent countryside on a summer's afternoon. She loves cooking good food and anything cinnamon flavoured. Of course, she still can't keep away from a good book or a good movie—especially romances—but only if she's stocked up with tissues, because she knows she will need them by the end, be it happy or sad. Her favourite things in the world are her wonderful husband, who has learned to decipher her incoherent ramblings, and her two daughters.

PROLOGUE

NO ONE else must see the contents of this letter, Scarlett! Give it only to Romano.

Her older sister's words echoed through her head as Scarlett ran through the woods on the outskirts of Monta Correnti, her long dark hair trailing behind her. Jackie would be cross if she knew Scarlett had peeked at the sheets of the scrawled, tear-stained writing, but one corner of the envelope flap had been a little loose and it had been too tempting.

Before she went to the piazza to find Romano and give it to him, she had to show Isabella, her cousin and partner in crime. This was way too big a secret to keep to herself. Although she and Isabella were both the same age, Isabella was the eldest in her family and always seemed to know what to do, how to take charge when anyone needed her.

It was totally different in Scarlett's family. She was the youngest of the three sisters. The one who was always left out of important discussions because she 'wouldn't understand'. She was fed up with it. Just because Jackie was four years older she thought it was okay to boss Scarlett around and make her do her errands, which wasn't fair. So just this once Scarlett was going to do things her way, to *make* it fair.

There were too many hushed voices and whispered insults in her family already, and no one would tell her why.

She was heading for a small clearing with a stream running through it at the bottom of the hill. No one else knew about this spot. It was her and Isabella's secret. They would come here to talk girl-type stuff, when Isabella could get away from looking after her nosey little brothers. They would build camps out of branches and leaves, and make up secret codes and write in their diaries—which they always let each other read. Sometimes they would whisper about Romano Puccini, the best-looking boy in the whole of Monta Correnti.

That was another thing that wasn't fair!

Just as Scarlett had decided she was old enough to notice boys and develop her first crush, Jackie had got in there first—as always. Jackie had been seeing Romano for weeks and weeks! Behind Mamma's back as well. Just wait until Isabella found out!

Scarlett's breaths were coming in light gasps now and the small sigh she let out was hardly noticeable. So Romano only had eyes for bossy old Jackie! Scarlett hated her for it. At least she did when she remembered to.

A flash of pink sundress through the trees told Scarlett that Isabella was in the clearing already. They'd whispered their plans to meet earlier, in the piazza outside their parents' restaurants.

As Scarlett burst into the clearing Isabella looked up. Her raised eyebrows said it all. *What are you in a flap about this time, Scarlett?*

Scarlett just slowed to a walk and held the letter out to Isabella, her arm rigid.

Isabella shrugged as she took the envelope and pulled three sheets of paper out of it. But she wasn't sitting and shrugging and rolling her eyes at Scarlett for long. Once she'd read the first page she was on her feet and joining in the *flapping*.

After all the exclamations, they stood and stared at each other, guilty smiles on their lips.

'Oh, my goodness!' Isabella finally whispered. 'Jackie and Romano! Really?'

This was the reaction Scarlett had been hoping for. She nodded. She'd hardly believed it herself when she'd read all that mushy stuff Jackie had written to Romano! Okay, some of it hadn't exactly made sense, but she'd got the general gist. She nodded to Isabella to keep reading.

Isabella didn't need much encouragement. She quietened down and carried on, stopping every now and then to ask Scarlett to decipher her sister's handwriting.

When she'd finished she looked up. This time there were no guilty smiles. There was no *flapping*. The look on Isabella's face wiped away the giddiness Scarlett had been experiencing and the spinning feeling moved swiftly to her stomach.

'What are you going to do?' Isabella asked.

Scarlett frowned. 'Give the letter to Romano, of course.'

Isabella shook her head. 'You can't do that. You need to show this to Aunt Lisa!'

A noise of disbelief forced its way out of Scarlett's lips. 'Do you *know* what Mamma will do if she finds out? Jackie will be in *so* much trouble!'

Isabella looked at the sheets of paper between her fingers, now looking less than pristine and just a little crumpled. 'It's too big a secret.' The letter made a crinkling noise as she tightened her grip.

Scarlett suddenly had a nasty feeling about this. Isabella wouldn't, would she? She wouldn't take the letter to Mamma herself? But then she saw the glint of determination in her cousin's eyes and knew that Isabella just might take the matter into her own hands.

If that happened, not only would Jackie suffer their mother's wrath, but Scarlett would be in big trouble herself. Jackie had a temper every bit as fiery as Mamma's. Scarlett snatched for the letter.

Isabella was fast, though, too used to dealing with a pair of rambunctious younger brothers to be caught off guard, and Scarlett only managed to get a grip on one bit of paper. They pulled at either end of the sheet. Isabella was shouting that Scarlett needed to let go, because she wasn't going to tell. Just as the words were starting to make sense to Scarlett, as the page was on the verge of ripping in two, Isabella released it. The sheets of pink writing paper and matching envelope flew into the air.

Both girls froze and watched them flutter slowly towards the ground.

Just before it landed in the dirt, one wayward sheet decided to catch its freedom on a gust of air. It started to lift, to twirl, to spin. Suddenly Scarlett was moving, jumping, reaching, trying to snatch it back, but it always seemed to dance out of her fingers just as she was about to get a hold of it.

Now Isabella had finished collecting up the rest of the paper, she was trying to get it too. The wind heaved a sigh and the piece of paper fluttered tantalisingly close. Scarlett jumped for it. Her fingers closed around it.

But then Isabella collided with her and she found herself crashing onto the damp earth of the stream bank. She hit the ground hard and every last bit of air evacuated from her lungs, and she momentarily lost the ability to control her muscles. The page saw its chance and eased itself out of her hand and into the waiting stream.

Isabella started to cry, but all Scarlett could do was watch it float away, the ink turning the paper a watery blue, before it disappeared beneath the surface.

She pulled herself up and brushed the dirt off her front. 'Stop it!' she yelled at Isabella, who was sobbing. And before she could dampen the rest of the pages with her silly crying, Scarlett pulled them from Isabella's fist and tried to smooth them out.

'Page three is missing! Page three!' She glanced back towards the stream, her face alive with panic.

Oh, why couldn't it have been page two, with all the love-struck gushing and rambling? Romano would never have noticed. But it had been page three—the one with the *really* big secret.

'What are we going to do?' Isabella said quietly, dragging a hand over her eyes to dry her tears. More threatened to fall, but she sniffed them away.

Scarlett shook her head. 'I don't know.'

The icy fear that had been solidifying her limbs suddenly melted into something much warmer, much hotter.

This was all Jackie's fault! Why couldn't she have taken the letter to Romano herself? Why had she involved her baby sister in the first place? Didn't she know that was a stupid thing to do? According to everyone else, Scarlett couldn't be trusted with anything!

She turned to Isabella, her mouth pulled thin. 'We can't give the letter to Romano like this.' Jackie would just have to do her own dirty work and talk to him herself. 'And Jackie will kill me if I tell her what I did. There's only one thing we can do.'

Isabella started to sniff again, mumbling something about it all being her fault, but Scarlett wasn't listening; she was staring at the gurgling waters of the stream.

Slowly, she walked back to the very edge of the bank. Between thumb and forefinger, she lifted another page high and then, in a very deliberate motion of her fingers, let it go. Another page followed, then the envelope. It seemed an almost solemn procedure, as if she were scattering dirt on a coffin. Thick, funereal silence hovered in the air around them as they held their breath and watched Jackie's secret float downstream.

No one else must see the contents of this letter, Scarlett.

Now no one ever would.

CHAPTER ONE

THE air conditioning of the limo was functioning perfectly, but as Jackie stared out of the tinted window at the rolling hills, at the vineyards and citrus groves, she could almost feel the sun warming her forearms. It was an illusion. But she was big on illusions, so she let it slide and just enjoyed the experience.

The whole process of coming home would also be an illusion. There would be loud exclamations, bear hugs, family dinners where no one could get a word in—not that it would stop anyone trying—but underneath there would be a wariness. There always was. Even the siblings and cousins who didn't know her secret somehow picked up on the atmosphere and joined in, letting her keep them at arm's length.

They became her co-conspirators as she tried to deny her Italian side and laced herself up tight in Britishness—the one thing her father had given her that she treasured. She had learned how to shore herself up and keep herself together, but then Jackie always excelled at everything she did, and this was no exception.

She hadn't called ahead to let the family know what time she was arriving. A limousine and her own company were preferable at present. She needed time to collect herself before she faced them all again.

It had been a couple of years since she'd been home to

Monta Correnti. And when she did come these days, it was always in the winter. The summers were too glorious here, too full of memories she couldn't afford to revisit. But then her older sister had chosen a weekend in May for her wedding celebrations, and Jackie hadn't had much choice. It seemed she hadn't been able to outrun the tug of a big Italian family after all, even though she'd tried very, very hard.

She turned away from the scenery—the golds and olives, the almost painful blue of the sky—and picked up a magazine from the leather seat beside her. It was the latest issue from *Gloss!* magazine's main rival. Her lips curved in triumph as she noted that her editorial team had done a much better job of covering the season's latest trends. But that was what she paid them for. She expected nothing less.

The main fashion caught her attention. Puccini—one of Italy's top labels. But she hadn't needed to read the heading to recognise the style. The fashion house had gone from strength to strength since Rafael Puccini had handed the design department over to his son.

With such a man at the helm, you'd expect the menswear to outshine the women's collections, but it wasn't the case. Romano Puccini understood women's bodies so well that he created the most exquisite clothes for them. Elegant, sensuous, stylish. Although she'd resisted buying one of his creations for years, she'd succumbed last summer, and the dress now hung guiltily in the back of her wardrobe. She'd worn it only once, and in it she'd felt sexy, powerful and feminine.

Maybe that was why the house of Puccini was so successful, why women stampeded the boutiques to own one of their dresses. Good looks and bucketloads of charm aside, Romano Puccini knew how to make each and every woman feel as if she were as essentially female as Botticelli's *Venus*. Of course, that too was an illusion. And Jackie knew that better than most.

She frowned, then instantly relaxed her forehead. She

hadn't given in to the lure of Botox yet, but there was no point making matters worse. Although she was at the top of her game, Editor-in-chief of London's top fashion magazine, she was confronted daily by women who wore the youthful, fresh-faced glow that she'd been forced to abandon early. Working and living in that environment would make any woman over the age of twenty-two paranoid.

Her mobile phone rang and, glad of the distraction, she reached into her large soft leather bag to answer it. The name on the caller ID gave her an unwanted spike of adrenaline. Surely she should be used to seeing that name there by now?

'Hello, Kate.'

'Hey, Jacqueline.'

Her own name jarred in her ears. It sounded wrong, but she hadn't earned the title of 'mother' from this young woman yet. Maybe she never would.

'Is there something I can help you with?'

There was a pause. A loaded sixteen-year-old pause.

'Are you *there*? In Italy?'

Jackie's gaze returned to the view beyond the tinted windows. It whipped past silently, the insulation of the limousine blocking out any noise from outside. 'Yes. I left the airport about twenty minutes ago.'

There was a sigh—which managed to be both wistful and accusatory—on the other end of the line. 'I wish I could have come with you.'

'I know. I wish you could have too. But this situation…telling my family…it needs some careful handling.'

'They're my family too.'

Jackie closed her eyes. 'I know. But it's complicated. You don't know them—'

'No, I don't. And that's not my fault, is it?'

Jackie didn't miss Kate's silent implication. Yes, it was her fault. She knew that. Had always known that. But that wasn't going to help calm her mother down when she announced that the child she'd handed over for adoption sixteen years ago had recently sought her out, that she'd been secretly meeting with that daughter in London for the last few months—especially when it had been her mother's iron insistence that no one else in the family should ever know. To a woman like Lisa Firenzi, image was everything. And a pregnant teenage daughter who'd refused to name the father of her baby didn't fit in the glossy brochure that was her life.

Jackie hadn't even been as old as Kate when it had happened. Back then, every day when she'd come down the stairs for breakfast, her mother had scrutinised her profile. When she hadn't been able to disguise the growing swell of her stomach with baggy T-shirts, she'd been quietly sent away.

She'd arrived in London one wet November evening, a shivering fifteen-year-old, feeling lost and alone. The family had been told she'd gone to stay with her father, which was true. He'd been husband number two. Lisa had managed to devour and spit out another husband and quite a few lovers since then.

So, not only had Jackie to reconcile her mother to the fact that the dirty family secret she'd tried to hide was now out in the open, but she had to break the news to her uncle and cousins—even Lizzie and Scarlett, her sisters, didn't know. She was going to have to handle the situation very, very carefully.

Lizzie's wedding would be the first time she and all her sisters and cousins had been together in years and she couldn't gazump her sister's big day by turning up with a mystery daughter in tow, and it wouldn't have been fair to drop Kate into the boiling pot of her family's reactions either. Jackie had absolutely no idea how they were going to take the news and the last thing her fragile daughter needed was another heap of rejection.

She drew in a breath through her nostrils, the way her

Pilates instructor had taught her. 'I know, Kate. And I'm sorry. Maybe next time.'

The silence between them soured.

'You're ashamed of me, aren't you?'

Jackie sat bolt upright in the back seat. 'No!'

'Well, then, why won't you let me meet my uncles and aunts, my cousins—my grandmother?'

There was no shyness about this girl. She was hot-headed, impulsive, full of self-righteous anger. Very much as her biological mother had been as a teenager. And that very same attitude had landed her into a whole heap of trouble.

'Family things…they're difficult, you know…'

A soft snort in her ear told Jackie that Kate didn't know. That she didn't even *want* to know. Jackie only had one card left to play and she hoped it worked.

'Remember how you told me your mum—' Your mum. Oh, how that phrase was difficult to get out '—found it difficult when you told her you wanted to find your biological mother, even though you weren't eighteen yet? It was hard to tell her, wasn't it? Because you didn't want to hurt her, but at the same time it was something you needed to do.'

'Yes.' The voice was quieter now, slightly shaky.

'You're just going to have to trust me—' Sweetheart. She wanted to say *'sweetheart'* '—Kate. This is something I need to do first. And then you can come on a visit and meet everyone, I promise.'

Just like every other girl of her age, Kate was rushing at life, her head full of the possibilities ahead of her, possibilities that dangled like bright shiny stars hung on strings from the heavens. They tempted, called. If only she could make Kate see how dangerous those sparkly things were…how deceptive.

Something in her tone must have placated her newly found daughter, because Kate sounded resigned rather than angry when she rang off. Jackie slid her phone closed and sank back into the padded leather seat, exhausted.

She hadn't realised how hard the reunion would be, even though she'd been waiting for it since she'd put her name on the adoption register when she'd been twenty. When she'd got the first call she'd been overjoyed, but terror had quickly followed. She and Kate had had a tearful and awkward first meeting under the watchful eye of her adoptive mother, Sue.

Kate had been slightly overawed by Jackie's high-fashion wardrobe and sleek sports car. Sue had taken Jackie aside after a few weeks and warned her that Kate was dazzled by the fact her 'real' mum was Jacqueline Patterson, style icon and fashion goddess. *Don't you dare let her down,* Sue's eyes had said as she'd poured the tea and motioned for Jackie to sit at her weathered kitchen table.

Jackie was doing her best, but she wasn't convinced she could make this work, that she and Kate could settle into a semblance of a mother-daughter relationship. They'd gone through a sort of honeymoon period for the first month or two, but now questions and emotions from the past were starting to surface and not everything that was rising to the top was as glossy and pretty as Jackie normally liked things to be.

Once she told her mother, Kate's grandmother, the cat would be out of the bag and there would be no going back. But Jackie had no other option. She wanted…*needed*…to have her daughter back in her life, and she was going to do whatever it took to make a comfortable space for her, no matter how hard the fallout landed.

The limo swung round a bend in the road and Jackie held her breath. There was Monta Correnti in the distance, a stunningly beautiful little town with a square church steeple and patchwork of terracotta tiled roofs seemingly clinging to the steep hillside. It was currently a 'hot' holiday destination for Europe's rich and notorious, but it had once been Jackie's home. Her only *real* home. A place filled with memories, yellow and faded like old family photographs.

Before they reached the town centre, the limo branched off to the left, heading up a tree-lined road to the brow of the hill that was close enough to look down its nose on the town but not near enough to feel neighbourly.

The road to her mother's villa.

Jackie tided the magazines on the back seat, made sure everything she needed was in her handbag and pulled herself up straight as the car eased through gates more suited to a maximum-security prison than a family home.

Romano opened the tall windows of his drawing room and stepped onto the garden terrace. It all looked perfect. It always looked perfect. That pleased him. He liked simple lines, clean shapes. He wasn't a man who relished anything complicated or fussy. Of course, he knew that perfection came at a cost. None of this happened by accident.

In his absence, the low hedges of the parterre had been clipped by an army of gardeners, the gravel paths raked and smoothed until they were perfectly flat and unsullied by footprints. The flowers in the vast stone urns had been lovingly weeded and watered. And the attention hadn't been confined to the garden. Every inch of the Puccini family's old summer home was free from dust. Every window and polished surface gleamed. It was the perfect place to retreat from the grime and noise of Rome in the summer months. And Romano enjoyed it so much here he'd recently decided to keep it as his main residence, even in winter, when Lake Adrina was filled with waves of polished pewter and the wind was less than gentle.

Palazzo Raverno was unique, built by an ostentatious count in the eighteenth century on a small island, shaped like a long drawn-out teardrop. On the wider end of the island Count Raverno had spared no expense in erecting a Neo-gothic

Venetian palace, all high arches and ornate masonry in contrasting pink and white stone. It should have looked ridiculously out of place on a tranquil wooded island in the middle of a lake—but somehow the icing-sugar crispness of the house just made it a well-placed adornment to the island. From what he knew of the infamous count, Romano suspected this had been more by accident than design.

And if the palazzo was spectacular, the gardens took one's breath away. Closer to the house the gardens were formal, with intricate topiary and symmetrical beds, but as they rolled away to the shore and reached to the thin end of the island they gave the impression of a natural Eden.

Romano could resist it no longer. His wandering became striding and he soon found himself walking down the shady paths, stopping to listen to the soft music of the gurgling waterfall that sprang out of a rockery. He didn't plan a route, just let his feet take him where they wanted, and it wasn't long before he arrived in the sunken garden.

The breeze was deliciously cool here, lifting the fringes of the drooping ferns. Everything was green, from the vibrant shades of the tropical plants and the dark glossiness of the ivy, to the subtle sponginess of the moss on the walls of the grotto.

It was all so unbearably romantic. The island was the perfect place for a wedding.

Not his wedding, of course. He smiled at the thought. Nobody would ever be foolish enough to think the day would come when he'd pledge his body and soul to one woman for eternity.

A month or two, maybe.

He sighed as he left the leafy seclusion of the sunken garden and walked into the fragrant sunshine of a neatly clipped lawn. From here he climbed a succession of terraces as he made his way back towards the house. The days when this island had been a playground for the idle rich were long gone. He had work to do.

However, he was whistling when he headed into the ground-floor room he'd converted into a studio to collect the paperwork for his afternoon appointment. When a man had a job that involved dressing and undressing beautiful women, he couldn't really complain, could he?

Before Jackie's stiletto-heeled foot could make contact with the driveway, her mother flew out of the front door and rushed towards her, her arms flung wide.

'Jackie! There you are!'

Jackie's eyes widened behind her rather huge and rather fashionable sunglasses. What on earth was going on? Her mother never greeted her like this. It was as if she were actually overjoyed to see—

'You're late!' Her mother stopped ten feet shy of the limo and her fists came to rest on her hips, making the jacket of her Chanel suit bunch up in a most unappealing manner.

This was more the reception Jackie had been anticipating.

Her mother looked her up and down. Something Jackie didn't mind at all now she knew her mother could find no fault with her appearance, but once upon a time it had sent a shiver up her spine.

'I don't believe I mentioned what time I—'

'The other girls arrived over an hour ago,' her mother said before giving her a spiky little peck on the cheek, then hooking an arm in hers and propelling Jackie inside the large double doors of the villa.

What girls?

Jackie decided there was no point in reminding Mamma that she hadn't actually specified a time of arrival, only a date. Her mother was a woman of expectations, and heaven help the poor soul who actually suggested she deviate from her catalogue of fixed and rigid ideas. Jackie had come to terms with the fact that, even though she was the toast of

London, in the labyrinthine recesses of Lisa Firenzi's mind her middle daughter was the specimen on a dark and dusty shelf whose label read: Problem Child.

Although Jackie hadn't seen her mother in almost a year, she looked the same as always. She still oozed the style and natural chic that had made her a top model in her day. She was wearing an updated version of the classic suit she'd had last season, and her black hair was in the same neat pleat at the back of her head.

The excited female chatter coming from her mother's bedroom and dressing room alternated between Italian and English with frightening speed. Three women, all in various states of undress, were twittering and cooing over some of the most exquisite bridal wear that Jackie had ever seen. In fact, they were so absorbed in helping the bride-to-be into her wedding dress that they didn't even notice Jackie standing there.

Lizzie, who was half in, half out of the bodice, looked up and spotted her first, and all at once she was waddling across the room in a mound of white satin. She pulled Jackie into a tight hug.

'Your sister finally deigned to arrive for the dress fitting.'

Jackie closed her eyes and ignored her mother's voice. Dress fitting? Oh, that was what Mamma had her knickers in a twist about. She needn't have worried. Jackie had sent her measurements over by email a couple of weeks ago and she knew her rigorous fitness regime would not have allowed for even a millimetre of variation.

'We all know Jackie operates in her own time zone these days, don't we?'

Ah. So that was it. Mamma was still irritated that she hadn't fallen in with her plans and arrived yesterday. But there had been a very important show she'd needed to attend in Paris, which she couldn't afford to miss. Her mother of all people should understand how cut-throat the fashion industry was. One minor stumble and a thousand knives would be ready to welcome her back as a sheath.

She wanted to turn round, to tell her mother to mind her own business, but this was neither the time nor the place. She wasn't about to do anything to spoil the frivolity of her sister's wedding preparations. She squeezed Lizzie back, gently, softly.

'It's been too long, Lizzie!' she said in a hoarse voice.

As she pulled away she tried to file her mother's remark away in her memory banks with all the others, but the words left a sting inside her.

'Here, let me help you with this.' She pulled away from Lizzie and walked round her so she could help with the row of covered buttons at the back. The dress was empire line, gently complementing Lizzie's growing pregnant silhouette. And true to form, the bride was positively glowing, whether that was the effect of carrying double the amount of hormones from the twins inside her or because she was wildly in love with the groom Jackie had yet to meet, she wasn't sure. Whatever it was, Lizzie looked happier and more relaxed than she'd ever been. If it was down to Jack Lewis, he'd better know how to keep it up, because Jackie would have his hide if he didn't.

'Thanks. I knew there was a reason why we had a fashion expert in the family,' Lizzie said, smiling as she pulled her long dark hair out of the way.

Jackie concentrated on the row of tiny silk-covered buttons that seemed to go on for ever. 'This dress is exquisite,' she said as she reached the last few. Which was amazing, since it had to have been made in mere weeks.

Jackie stood back and admired her sister. Getting a dress to not only fit somebody perfectly, but complement their personality was something that even cold, hard cash couldn't buy, unless you were in the hands of a true artist.

Isabella and Scarlett came close to inspect the dress and mutter their appreciation. Jackie turned, a smile of utter serenity on her face, and prepared herself to greet her fellow bridesmaids.

Isabella first. They kissed lightly on both cheeks and Isabella rubbed her shoulder gently with her hand as they traded pleasantries. Jackie kept her smile in place as she turned to face her younger sister. They kissed without actually making contact and made a pretence of an embrace.

She and Scarlett had been so close once, especially after Lizzie had gone to university in Australia, when it had just been the two of them and she'd felt like a proper big sister rather than just Lizzie's deputy. She'd even thought vainly that Scarlett might have hero-worshipped her a little bit.

But that had all changed the summer she'd got pregnant with Kate. Scarlett had never looked at her the same way again. And why should she have? Some role model Jackie had been. Who would want to emulate the disaster area that had been her life back then—Jackie in tears most of the day, Mamma alternating between ranting and giving her the ice-queen treatment?

Not long after that Scarlett had moved away too. She'd followed in Lizzie's footsteps and flown halfway round the world to live with her father. They'd never had a chance to patch things up, for Jackie to say how sorry she was to make Scarlett so ashamed of her. No more late-night secret-sharing sessions. No more raiding the kitchen at Sorella, one of them rifling through the giant stainless-steel fridge for chocolate cake, one of them keeping guard in case the chef spotted them.

Now they talked as little as possible and met in person even less. Jackie released Scarlett from the awkward hug and took a good look at her. They hadn't laid eyes on each other in more than five years. Scarlett hadn't changed much, except for looking a little bit older and even more like their mother. She had the same hint of iron behind her eyes these days, but the generous twist of the mouth Jackie recognised from their childhood tempered it a little.

Of course, Lizzie was far too excited to notice the undercurrents flowing around amidst the tulle and taffeta.

'Come on, girls! You next. I want to see how fabulous my bridesmaids are going to look.'

Scarlett and Isabella had already removed their dresses from their garment bags. They were every bit as stunning as Lizzie's. She'd been told that all three dresses would be the same shade of dusky aubergine, but she hadn't realised that they would vary in style and cut.

Isabella's was classic and feminine, with a gathered upper bodice, tiny spaghetti straps and a bow under the bustline, where the empire-line skirt fell away. Scarlett's was edgier, with a nineteen-thirties feel—devoid of frills and with a deep V in the front.

Jackie appointed herself as wardrobe mistress and zipped, buttoned and laced wherever help was needed. When she'd finished, Isabella handed her a garment bag.

Jackie hesitated before she took the bag from her cousin. It had been a bad idea to help the others get dressed. Now they had nothing else to do but watch her strip off. She clutched the bag to her chest and looked for the nearest corner. Isabella and Scarlett just stood there, waiting.

Then she felt the bag being tugged gently from between her fingers. 'Why don't you use Mamma's dressing room?' Lizzie said as she relieved Jackie of the bag and led her towards a door on the other side of the room. 'You can freshen up a little from your flight, if you need to.'

Jackie sent her sister a grateful look and did exactly that.

Lizzie had been the only one she'd confided in about her body issues. It had started not long after she'd given Kate away. At first, eating less and exercising had been about getting her shape back before she returned to Italy, removing all evidence that her body had been stretched and changed irrevocably. Mamma had been pleased when she'd met her off the plane, had complimented her on her self-discipline. But back in Italy she'd been confronted with the sheer pleasure of food, the sensuality of how people ate, and she'd shied away from it. Somewhere along the line the self-denial, the discipline, had become something darker. She'd sought control. Punishment. Atonement.

She'd liked the angles and lines of her physique and, when she'd finally escaped Monta Correnti at eighteen and moved to London to take the position of office assistant at a quirky style magazine, she'd fitted right in. Her new world had been full of girls eating nothing but celery and moaning that their matchstick thighs were too chunky.

It had taken her quite a few years to admit she'd had a problem. To admit that the yellowish tinge her skin had taken on had been more than just the product of her Italian genes, that the sunken hollows beneath her cheeks weren't good bone structure and that it hadn't been natural to be able to count her ribs with such ease.

Quietly she'd got help. Putting the weight back on had been a struggle. Every pound she'd gained had been an accusation. But she'd done it. And now she was proud to have a body that most women her age would kill for. It was meticulously nourished on the best organic food and trained four times a week by a personal trainer.

Even though she knew she looked good, she still didn't want to be gawped at without her clothes on. It was different when she was in her cutting-edge designer suits. Dressed like that she was *Jacqueline Patterson*—the woman whose name was only uttered in hushed tones when she walked down the corridors of *Gloss!* magazine's high-rise offices. Remove the armour and she became faceless. Just another woman in her thirties with stretch marks and a Caesarean scar.

With the dressing-room door shut firmly behind her, Jackie slipped out of her linen trouser suit and went through the connecting door to Mamma's en suite to freshen up. As she washed she could hear her cousin catching Lizzie up on all the latest Monta Correnti gossip, especially the unabridged story of how Isabella had met her own fiancé.

When Jackie felt she'd finally got all the traces of aeroplane air off her skin, she returned to the dressing room and removed her bridesmaid's dress from its protective covering.

Wow. Stunning.

It reminded her of designs she'd done in senior school for the class play of *Romeo and Juliet*. Like the other dresses, it was empire line, with an embroidered bodice that scooped underneath the gathered chiffon at the bust and then round and up into shoulder straps.

Not many people knew enough about fashion design to see the artistry in the cutting that gave the skirt its effortlessly feminine swell. Nor would they notice the inner rigid structure of the bodice that would accentuate every curve of a woman's torso but give the impression that it was nature that had done all the hard work and not the fine stitching and cutting. She took it off the hanger and undid the zip. As she stepped into the dress there was a knock at the door that led back out into the bedroom.

'Everything okay in there?' Lizzie's voice was muffled through the closed door. Jackie smiled.

'Almost ready,' she yelled back, sliding the dress over her hips and stopping to remove the bra that would ruin the line of the low-cut bodice.

She'd been right, she realised as she started to slide the zip upwards. If her instincts were correct, this dress was going to fit like the proverbial glove. She doubted it would need any alteration at all.

As she got to the top she ran into problems with the zip. Despite all the yoga and Pilates, she just couldn't get her arms and shoulder sockets to do what was necessary to pull it all the way up.

'Lizzie? Isabella? I need a hand,' she yelled and dipped her head forwards, brushing her immaculately straightened hair over one shoulder so whoever rushed to her aid had easy access to the stubborn zip.

There was a soft click as the door opened. The thick carpet hushed the even footsteps as her saviour came towards her.

'If you could just…' She wiggled her shoulders to indicate where the problem was.

Whoever it was said nothing, just stepped close and set about deftly zipping her into place. For a second or so Jackie let her mind drift, wondering if it would look as dreamy as it felt when she raised her head and looked into the full-length mirror, but then she realised something was out of balance.

The fingers brushing her upper back as they held the top of the bodice's zip together didn't have Scarlett's long, perfectly manicured fingernails. Lizzie was already getting too big with the twins to be standing quite this close and, at five feet five, Isabella was a good inch shorter than she was. This person's breath was warming her exposed left ear.

Jackie stilled her lungs. Where fingers touched bare back, the pinpricks of awareness were so acute they were almost painful.

The person finished their job by neatly joining the hook and eye at the top of the bodice and then stepped back. Jackie began to shake. Right down in her knees. And it travelled upwards until her shoulders seemed to rattle.

Even before she pushed her hair out of her face and straightened her spine, she knew the eyes that would meet hers in the mirror would be those of Romano Puccini.

CHAPTER TWO

HIGH in the hills above Monta Correnti was an olive grove that had long since been abandoned. The small stone house that sat on the edge of one of the larger terraces remained unmolested, forgotten by everyone.

Well, almost everyone.

Just as the sun's heat began to wane, as the white light of noon began to mellow into something closer to gold, a teenage girl appeared, walking along the dirt track that led to the farmhouse, a short distance from the main road into town. She looked over her shoulder every couple of seconds and kept close to the shade of the trees on the other side of the track. When she was sure no one was following her, she moved into the sunlight and started to jog lightly towards the farmhouse, a smile on her face.

She was on the way to being pretty, a bud just beginning to open, with long dark hair that hung almost to her waist and softly tanned skin. When she stopped smiling, there was a fierce intensity to her expression but, as she seemed to be joyfully awaiting something, that didn't happen very often. She rested in the shade, leaning against the doorway of the cottage, looking down the hill towards the town.

After not more than ten minutes a sound interrupted the soft chirruping of the crickets, the gentle whoosh of the wind in the branches of the olive trees. The girl stood up, ramrod straight, and looked in the direction of the track. After a couple of seconds the faint buzzing that an untrained ear might have interpreted for a bee or a faraway tractor became more distinct. She recognised the two-stroke engine of a Vespa and her smile returned at double the intensity.

Closer and closer it came, until suddenly the engine cut out and the grove returned to sleepy silence. The girl held her breath.

Her patience ran out. Instead of waiting in the doorway, looking cool and unaffected, she jumped off the low step and started running. As she turned the corner of the house she saw him jogging towards her, wearing a smile so bright it could light up the sky if the sun ever decided it wanted a siesta. Her leg muscles lost all tone and energy and she stumbled to a halt, unable to take her eyes from him.

Finally he was standing right in front of her, his dark hair ruffled by the wind and his grey eyes warmed by the residual laughter that always lived there. They stood there for a few seconds, hearts pounding, and then he gently touched her cheek and drew her into a kiss that was soft and sweet and full of remembered promises. She sighed and reached for him, pulling him close. Somehow they ended up back in the doorway of the old, half-fallen-down cottage, with her pressed against the jamb as he tickled her neck with butterfly kisses.

He pulled away and looked at her, his hands on her shoulders, and she gazed back at him, never thinking for a second how awkward it could be to just stare into another person's eyes, never considering for a second what a brave act it was to see and be seen. She blinked and smiled at him, and his dancing grey eyes became suddenly serious.

'I love you, Jackie,' he said, and moved his hands up off her shoulders and onto her neck so he could trace the line of her jawbone with his thumbs.

'I love you too, Romano,' she whispered as she buried her face in his shirt and wrapped herself up in him.

Jackie hadn't actually believed that a person could literally be frozen with surprise. Too late she discovered it was perfectly possible to find one's feet stuck to the floor just as firmly as if they had actually grown roots, and to find one's mouth suddenly incapable of speech.

Romano, however, seemed to be experiencing none of the same disquiet. He was just looking back at her in the mirror, his pale eyes full of mischief. '*Bellissima*,' he said, glancing at the dress, but making it sound much more intimate.

She blinked and coughed, and when her voice returned she found a sudden need to speak in English instead of Italian. 'What are you doing here?'

Romano just shrugged and made that infuriatingly ambiguous hand gesture he'd always used to make. 'It is a dress fitting, Jacqueline, so I *fit*.'

She spun round to face him. '*You* made the dresses? Why didn't anyone tell me?'

He made a rueful expression. 'Why should they? As far as anyone else is concerned, we hardly know each other. Your mother and my father are old friends and the rest of your family thinks we've only met a handful of times.'

Jackie took a shallow breath and puffed it out again. 'That's true.' She frowned. 'But how…? Why did you…?'

'When your mother told my father that Lizzie was getting married, he insisted we take care of the designs. It's what old friends do for each other.'

Jackie took a step back, regaining some of her usual poise. 'Old friends? That hardly applies to you and I.'

Romano was prevented from answering by an impatient Lizzie bursting into the room. Still, his eyes twinkled as Lizzie made Jackie do a three-sixty-degree spin. When she found herself back at the starting point he was waiting for her, his gaze hooking hers. *Not old friends,* it said. *But old lovers, certainly.*

Jackie wanted to hit him.

'It's beautiful!' Lizzie exclaimed. 'Perfect!'

'Yes. That is what I said,' Romano replied, and Jackie had to look away or she'd be tempted to throttle him, dress or no dress.

'Come and show the others!' Lizzie grabbed her hand and dragged her outside for Isabella and Scarlett to see. Isabella was just as enthusiastic as Lizzie but Scarlett looked as if she'd just sucked a whole pound of lemons. What was up with her? She just kept glowering at Jackie and sending daggers at Romano. Somebody or something had definitely put her nose out of joint.

The fitting was exhausting for Jackie. Not because her dress needed any alterations—she'd been right about that—but because she kept finding herself watching Romano, his deft fingers pinching at a seam as he discussed how and where he would make alterations, the way his brow creased with intense concentration as he discussed the possibilities with the bride-to-be, and how easily he smiled when the concentration lifted.

She'd spent the last seventeen years studiously avoiding him. It was laughable the lengths she'd gone to in order to make sure they never met face to face. Quite a few junior editors had been overjoyed when she'd sent them on plum assignments so that she wouldn't have to cross paths with that no-good, womanising charmer.

How could she chit-chat with him at fashion industry parties as if nothing had ever happened? As if he'd never done what he'd done? It was asking too much.

Of course, sometimes over the years she'd had to attend the same functions as him—especially during London fashion week, when she was expected to be seen at everything—but she had enough clout to be able to look at seating plans in advance and position herself accordingly.

However, there was no avoiding Romano now.

At least not for the next twenty minutes or so. After that she needn't see him again. Her dress was perfect. No more fittings for her, thank goodness.

Her mother chose that moment to sweep into the room. She gave Romano an indulgent smile and kissed him on both cheeks. Jackie couldn't hear what he said to her mother but Mamma batted her eyelashes and called him a 'charming young man'.

Hah! She'd changed her tune! Last time Lisa Firenzi had seen her daughter and Romano Puccini within a mile of each other, she'd had no compunctions about warning Jackie off. 'That boy is trouble,' she'd said. 'Just like his father. You are not to have anything to do with him. If I catch you even *talking* to him, you will be grounded for a month.'

But it had been too late.

Mamma had made Jackie help out at Sorella that summer, to 'keep her out of trouble'. And, if her mother had actually had some hands-on part in running the restaurant rather than leaving it all to managers, she would have known that Jackie and Romano had met weeks earlier when he'd come in for lunch with his father.

Of course she'd paid him no attention whatsoever. She'd seen him hanging around the piazza that summer, all the girls trailing around after him, and she hadn't been about to join that pathetic band of creatures, no matter how good-looking the object of their adoration was. But Romano had been rather persistent, had made her believe he was really interested, and, when she'd noticed that he hadn't had another girl on the back of his Vespa in more than a fortnight, she'd cautiously agreed to go out on it with him.

She should have listened to her mother. 'Like father, like son,' Lisa had said at the time. Jackie had always known that her mother and Romano's father, Rafe Puccini, had known each other in the past, but it wasn't until she'd moved to London and heard all the industry gossip that she realised how significant that relationship had been. By all accounts they'd had a rather steamy affair.

Look at her mother and Romano now! They were laughing at something. Her mother laid a hand on his upper arm and wiped a tear from under her mascara, calling him an 'impossible boy'. That was as much as Jackie could take. She strutted off to the dressing room and changed back into her trouser suit, studiously ignoring her reflection in the mirror. She didn't even want to see herself in his dress at the moment.

Keep a lid on it, Jacqueline. In a few minutes he'll be gone. You won't have to see him again for another seventeen years if you don't want to.

When she emerged, smoothing down her hair with a hand, her mother was just finishing a sentence: '…of course you must come with us, Romano. I insist.'

Jackie raised her eyebrows and looked at the other girls. Scarlett stomped off in the direction of the en suite, while Isabella just shrugged, collected up her clothes and headed for the empty dressing room.

'Give me a hand?' Lizzie asked and turned her back on Jackie so she could help with the covered buttons once again. As she worked Jackie kept glancing at her mother and Romano, who eventually left the room, still chatting and laughing.

'What's going on?' she muttered as she got to the last couple of buttons.

Lizzie strained to look over her shoulder at her sister. 'Oh, Mamma has decided we're all going to the restaurant for dinner this evening.'

Jackie kept her focus firmly on the last button, even though it was already unlooped. 'And she's invited Romano?'

Lizzie nodded. 'He's been spending a lot of time at the

palazzo in the last few years. He comes into Monta Correnti regularly and eats at both Mamma's and Uncle Luca's often.'

Jackie stepped back and Lizzie turned to face her.

'Why?' Lizzie said, sliding the dress off her shoulders. 'Is that a problem? That she's invited Romano?'

Jackie smiled and shook her head. 'No,' she said. 'No problem at all.'

She looked at the door that led out to the landing. Would her mother be quite as welcoming, quite as chummy with him, if she'd known that Romano Puccini was the boy who'd got her teenage daughter pregnant and then abandoned her?

She'd always refused to name the father, no matter how much her mother had begged and scolded and threatened, too ashamed for the world to know she'd been rejected so spectacularly by her first love. Even a knocked-up fifteen-year-old had her pride.

Jackie picked up her handbag and headed for the door. It still seemed like a good plan. There was no reason why her mother should ever know that Romano was Kate's father. No reason at all.

Refusing an invitation to dine with five attractive women would not only be the height of bad manners but also stupidity. And no one had ever accused Romano Puccini of being stupid. Infuriatingly slippery, maybe. Too full of charm for his own good. But never stupid. And he'd been far too curious *not* to come.

He hadn't had the chance to get this close to Jackie Patterson in years, which was odd, seeing as they moved in similar circles. But those circles always seemed to be rotating in different directions, the arcs never intersecting. Why was that? Did she still feel guilty about the way their romance had ended?

That summer seemed to be almost a million years ago. He sighed and took a sip of his wine, while the chatter of the elegant restaurant carried on around him.

Jackie Patterson. She'd really been a knockout. Long dark hair with a hint of a wave, tanned legs, smooth skin and eyes that refused to be either green or brown but glittered with fire anyway.

Yes, that had been a really good summer.

He'd foolishly thought himself in love with her but he'd been seventeen. It was easy to mistake hormones for romance at that age. Now he saw his summer with Jackie for what it really had been—a fling. A wonderful, heady, teenage fling that had unfortunately had a sour final act. Sourness that obviously continued to the present day.

She had deliberately placed herself on the same side of the table as him, and had made sure that her mother had taken the seat next to him. With Lisa Firenzi in the way, he had no hope of engaging Jackie in any kind of conversation. And she had known that.

Surely enough time had gone by that he and Jackie could put foolish youthful decisions behind them? Wasn't the whole I'm-still-ignoring-you thing just a little juvenile? He wouldn't have thought a polished woman like her would resort to such tactics.

And polished she was. Gone were the little shorts and cotton summer dresses, halter tops and flip-flops, replaced by excellent tailoring, effortless elegance that took a lot of hard work to get just right. And even if her reputation hadn't preceded her, he'd have been able to tell that this was a woman who pushed herself hard. Every hint of the soft fifteen-year-old curves that had driven him wild had been sculptured into defined muscle. The toffee and caramel lights in her long hair were so well done that most people would have thought it natural. He'd preferred it dark, wavy, and spread out on the grass as he'd leaned in to kiss her.

Where had that thought come from? He'd seen it in his mind's eye as if it had happened only that morning.

He blinked and returned his attention to his food, an amazing lobster ravioli that the chef here did particularly well. But now he'd thought about Jackie in that way, he couldn't quite seem to switch the memory off.

The main course was finished and Lizzie's fiancé appeared and whisked her away. Isabella disappeared off to the restaurant next door and when Lisa was approached by her restaurant manager and scuttled off with him, talking in low, hushed tones, that left him sitting at the table with just Jackie and Scarlett. He made a light-hearted comment, looking towards his right at Jackie, and saw her stiffen.

This was stupid. Although he didn't do serious conversations and relationship-type stuff, there was obviously bad air between them that needed to be cleared. He was just going to have to do his best to show Jackie that there were no hard feelings, that he could behave like a grown-up in the here and now, whatever had happened in the past. Hopefully she would follow his lead.

He turned to face her, waited, all the time looking intently at her until she could bear it no longer and met his gaze.

He smiled at her. 'It has been a long time, Jackie.'

Jackie's mouth didn't move; her eyes gave her reply: *Not long enough.*

He ignored the leaden vibes heading his way and persevered. 'I thought the March issue of *Gloss!* was particularly good. The shoot at the botanical gardens was unlike anything I'd ever seen before.'

Jackie folded her arms. 'It's been seventeen years since we've had a conversation and you want to talk to me about *work*?'

He shrugged and pulled the corners of his mouth down. It had seemed like a safe starting point.

'You don't think that maybe there are other, more important issues to enquire after?'

Nothing floated into his head. He rested his arm across the back of Lisa's empty chair and turned his body to face Jackie, ready to engage a little more fully in whatever was going on between them. 'Communication is communication, Jackie. We have to start somewhere.'

'Do we?'

'It seemed like a good idea to me,' he said, refusing to be cowed by the look she was giving him, a look that probably made her employees perspire so much they were in danger of dehydration.

Now she turned to face him too, forgetting her earlier stiff posture, her eyes smouldering. A familiar prickle of awareness crept up the back of his neck.

'Don't you dare take the high ground, Romano! You have no right. No right at all.'

He opened his mouth and shut it again. This conversation had too much high drama in it for him and, unfortunately, he and Jackie seemed to be, not only on different pages, but reading from totally different scripts. He looked across the table at Scarlett, to see if she was making sense of any of this, but her expression was just as puzzling as her sister's. She looked pale and shaky, as if she was about to be sick, and then she suddenly shot to her feet and dashed out of the restaurant door. Romano just stared after her.

'What was that all about?' he said.

Jackie, who was obviously too surprised to remember she was steaming angry with him, just frowned after her disappearing sister. 'I have no idea.'

He took the opportunity to climb through the chink in her defences. He reached over and placed his hand over hers on the table top. 'Can't we let the past be the past?'

Jackie removed her hand from under his so fast he thought he might have a friction burn.

'It's too late. We can't go back, not after all that has happened.' Instead of looking fierce and untouchable, she looked very, very sad as she said this, and he saw just a glimpse of the young, stubborn, vulnerable girl he'd once lost his heart to.

'Why not?'

Suddenly he really wanted to know. And it wasn't just about putting the past to rest.

She looked down at his hand on the tablecloth, still waiting in the same spot from where she'd snatched hers away. For a long time she didn't move, didn't speak.

'You know why, Romano,' she whispered. 'Please don't push this, just…don't.'

'I don't want to push this. I just want us to be able to be around each other without spitting and hissing or creating an atmosphere. That's not what you want for Lizzie's wedding, is it?'

She frowned and stared at him. 'What on earth has this got to do with Lizzie's wedding?'

Didn't she know? Hadn't Lizzie or Lisa told her yet?

'The reception… Lizzie wanted to have it at the palazzo. She thought the lake would be so—'

'No. That can't be.' She spoke quietly, with no hint of anger in her voice, and then she just stood up and walked away, her chin high and her eyes dull, leaving him alone at the table, drawing the glances of some of the other diners.

This was not how most of his evenings out ended—alone, with all the pretty women having left without him. Most definitely not.

Back at the villa, Jackie ignored the warm glow of lights spilling from the drawing-room windows and took the path round the side of the house that led into the terraced garden. She kept walking, past the fountains and clipped lawns, past the immaculately groomed shrubs, to the lowest part of the garden, an area slightly wilder and shadier than the rest.

Right near the boundary, overlooking Monta Correnti and the valley below, was an old, spreading fir tree. Many parts of its lower branches had been worn smooth by the seats and shoes of a couple of generations of climbers.

Without thinking about the consequences for her white linen trousers, Jackie put one foot on the stump of a branch at the base of the trunk and hoisted herself up onto one of the boughs. Her mind was elsewhere but her body remembered a series of movements—a hand here, a foot there—and within seconds she was sitting down, her toes dangling three feet above the ground as she stared out across the darkening valley.

The sun had set long ago, leaving the sky a shade of such a deep, rich blue that she could almost believe it possible to reach out and sink her hand into the thick colour. The sight brought back a rush of homesickness, which was odd, because surely people were only supposed to get homesick when they were away, not when they came back. It didn't make any sense. But not much about this evening had made sense.

She'd expected Romano to be a grown-up version of the boy she'd known: confident, intelligent, incorrigible. But she hadn't expected such blatant insensitivity.

She closed her eyes and tried to concentrate on the sensation of the cool night breeze on her neck and cheeks.

Thank goodness she hadn't given into Kate's pleading and let her daughter come on this trip. If Romano could be so blithe about their failed relationship all those years ago, she'd hate to think how he might have reacted to their daughter.

If only things had been different…

No. It was no good thinking that way. Time had proved her right. Romano Puccini was not cut out to be a husband and father. The string of girlfriends he'd paraded through the tabloids and celebrity magazines had only confirmed her worst fears. Maybe, if he'd settled down, there would have been some hope of him regretting his decision to disown his firstborn. Maybe a second child might have melted his heart, caused him to realise what he'd been missing.

A huge sigh shuddered through her. Jackie kicked off her shoes and looked at her toes.

And Romano had made her miss all of those moments too. Without his support she'd had no choice but to go along with her mother's wishes. How stupid she'd been to believe all those whispered promises, all those hushed plans to make their parents see sense, the plotting to elope one day. He'd said he'd wait for ever for her. The truth was, he hadn't even waited a month before moving on to Francesca Gambardi. One silly spat was all it'd taken to drive him away.

For ever? What a joke.

But she'd been so in love with him it had taken right up until the day she'd handed her newborn daughter over to stop hoping that it was all a bad dream, that Romano would change his mind and come bursting through the door to tell her he was so sorry, that it was her that he wanted and they were going to be a proper family, no matter what his father and her mother said.

Well, she'd purged all those silly ideas from herself about the same time she'd tightened up her saggy pregnancy belly. It had taken just as much iron will and focus to kill them all off.

'Jackie?'

It was Scarlett's voice, coming from maybe twenty feet away. Jackie smiled. She'd never quite got used to the Aussie twang that both her sisters had developed since moving away. It seemed more prominent here in the dark.

'Up here.'

'What on earth are you doing up there?'

Scarlett walked closer and peered up at her, or at least in her general direction. She'd only just left the bright lights of the house behind and her eyes wouldn't be accustomed to the dark yet.

'Come up and join me. The view's lovely,' she said.

'I know what the view looks like.' Scarlett stared up at the tree. 'You're being silly.'

That was altogether possible, Jackie conceded silently, but

she wasn't going to admit that to anyone. Scarlett folded her arms and stared off into the distance.

'What? You're not going to tell me I had too much wine at dinner?' Jackie said.

Scarlett just shook her head, the movement so small Jackie guessed it was more an unconscious gesture than an attempt at communication. She had that same can't-quite-look-at-you expression on her face that she always wore in Jackie's presence. It made Jackie want to be twice as prickly back. But it became obvious as she continued to observe her sister that Scarlett hadn't taken into account that Jackie had been out here long enough to get her night vision and could see her sister's features quite clearly. After a few seconds the hardness slid out of her expression, leaving something much younger, much truer behind.

'No. I'm not going to tell you that.' Her voice was husky but cold.

Jackie stopped swinging her legs. She knew that look. It was the one Scarlett had always worn when she'd heard Mamma's footsteps coming up the stairs after she'd done something naughty. Was Scarlett…was she *hiding* something?

Just as she tried to examine Scarlett's face a little more closely, her sister turned away.

'Mamma wants us all in the drawing room for a nightcap. She says she's got some family news, something about Cristiano not being able to come to the wedding.'

Jackie swung herself down off the branch in one fluid motion and landed beside her sister. She supposed they'd better go and make peace with their mother. Mamma hadn't been best pleased when she'd returned from her powwow with the restaurant manager to find that all her illustrious dinner guests had deserted her.

CHAPTER THREE

DESPITE the lateness of the hour, Romano stripped off by the edge of the palazzo's perfect turquoise pool and dived in. Loose threads hung messily from the evening he'd left behind and in comparison this felt clean, simple. His arms moved, his muscles bunched and stretched, and he cut through the water. Expected actions brought expected results.

But even in fifty laps he couldn't shake the sense of uneasiness that chased him up and down the pool. He pulled himself out of the water, picked up his clothes and walked across the terrace and through the house, naked.

Once in his bedroom he threw the floor-to-ceiling windows open and let the night breeze stir up the room. But as he lay in the dark he found it difficult to settle, to find any trace of the tranquillity this grand old house usually gave him.

More than once during the night he woke up to find he'd knotted the sheet quite spectacularly and had to sit up and untangle it again before punching his pillow, lying down and staring mutely at the inky sky outside his windows.

When dawn broke he gave up trying to sleep and put on shorts, a T-shirt and running shoes and set out on an uneven path that ran round the perimeter of the whole island. When he'd been a boy, he'd always thought the shape of Isola del Raverno resembled a tadpole. The palazzo was on the wide end, nearest the centre of the lake, and the long thin end reached towards a promontory on the shore, only a few hundred metres away. As he reached the 'tail' of the island he slowed to a jog, then came to a halt on the very tip. He stood there for quite some time, facing the wooded shore.

Monta Correnti was thirty kilometres to the west, hidden by rolling hills.

He'd waited here for Jackie once. His father had been back in Rome, either dealing with a business emergency or meeting a woman. Probably both. When he and his father had spent the summers here, Papa's presence had been sporadic at best. Romano had often been left to his own devices, overseen by an assortment of servants, of course.

He'd hated that when he'd been young, but later he'd realised what a gift it had been. He'd relished the freedom that many teenagers yearned for but never experienced. No wonder he'd got a reputation for being a bit of a tearaway.

Not that he'd ever done anything truly bad. He'd been cheeky and thrill-seeking, not a delinquent. His father had indulged him to make up for the lack of a mother and his frequent absences and, with hindsight, Romano could see how it made him quite an immature seventeen-year-old, despite the cocky confidence that had come with a pair of broad shoulders and family money.

Perhaps it would have been better if Papa had been stricter. It had been too easy for Romano to play the part of a spoiled rich kid, not working hard enough at school, not giving a thought to what he wanted to do with his life, because the cushion of his father's money and name had always been there, guarding his backside.

He turned away from the shore and looked back towards the palazzo. The tall square tower was visible through the trees, beautiful and ridiculous all at once. He exhaled, long and steady.

Jackie Patterson had never been just a fling, but it made things easier if he remembered her that way.

She'd challenged him. Changed him. Even though their summer romance had been short-lived, it had left an indelible mark on him. Up until then he'd been content to coast through life. Everything had come easily to him—money, popularity, female attention—he'd never had to work hard for any of it.

Meeting Jackie had been such a revelation. Under the unimpressed looks she'd given him as she'd waited tables at her mother's restaurant, he'd seen fire and guts and more life in her than he'd seen in any of the silly girls who had flapped their lashes at him in the piazza each day. Maybe that was why he'd pursued her so relentlessly.

Although she'd been two years his junior, she'd put him to shame. She'd had such big plans, big dreams. Dreams she'd now made come true.

He turned and started to jog round the remaining section of the path, back towards the house.

After they'd broken up, he'd taken a long hard look at himself, asked himself what he wanted to make out of his life. He'd had all the opportunities a boy could want, all the privileges, and he'd not taken advantage of a single one. From that day on he'd decided to make the most of what he had. He'd finished school, amazing his teachers with his progress in his final year, and had gone to work for his father.

Some people had seen this as taking the easy option. In truth he'd wanted to do anything *but* work for the family firm. He'd wanted to spread his wings and fly. But his mother had died when he'd been six, before any siblings had come along, and the only close family he and Papa had were each other. So he'd done the mature thing, put the bonds of family before his own wishes, and joined Puccini Designs with a smile on his face. It hadn't been a decision he'd regretted.

He'd kept running while he'd been thinking and now he

looked around, he realised he was back in the sunken garden. He slowed to a walk. Even this place was filled with memories of Jackie—the most exquisite and the most intimate—all suddenly awakening after years of being mere shadows.

Did she ever think of the brief, wonderful time they'd had together? Had their relationship changed the course of her life too? Suddenly he really wanted to know. And more than that, he wanted to know who Jacqueline Patterson was now, whether the same raw energy and fire still existed beneath the polished, highlighted, *glossy* exterior.

Hopefully, the upcoming wedding would be the perfect opportunity to find out.

'What's up, little sister?'

Jackie put down the book she was reading and stared up at Lizzie from where she was sitting, shaded from the morning sun by a large tree, her back against its bark. 'Nothing. I'm just relaxing.'

Lizzie made a noise that was half soft laugh, half snort. 'Jackie, you're the only person I know who can relax with every muscle in their body tensed,' she said as she carefully lowered herself down onto the grass.

Jackie took a sideways look at Lizzie's rounded stomach. Carrying one baby had been hard enough. She couldn't imagine what it would be like to have two inside her.

Lizzie was smiling at her. An infuriatingly knowing, big-sister kind of smile.

Okay, maybe trying to do the usual holiday-type thing wasn't such a great idea. She found relaxation a little…frustrating. She kept wanting to get up and *do* things. Especially today. Especially if it distracted her from remembering the look in Romano's eyes last night when he'd reached for her hand across the table.

He'd made her feel fifteen again. Very dangerous. She

couldn't afford to believe the warmth in those laughing grey eyes. She couldn't be tempted by impossible dreams of love and romance and for ever. It just wasn't real. And he shouldn't be able to make her feel as if it were. Not after all that had happened between them.

The nerve of the man!

Ah, this was better. The horrible achy, needy feeling was engulfed by a wash of anger. She knew how to do anger, how to welcome it in, how to harness its power to drive herself forwards. Who cared if it left an ugly grey wake of bitterness that stretched back through the years? She was surviving, and that was what counted.

Being angry with Romano Puccini was what she wanted, because without the anger it would be difficult to hate him, and she really, really needed to hate him.

Jackie exhaled, measuring her breath until her lungs were empty. This was better. Familiar territory. Hating Romano for rejecting her, for abandoning her and their daughter.

How could the man who had left her pregnant and alone, a mere girl, flirt with her as if nothing had happened?

'You're doing it again.'

Jackie hurt her neck as she snapped her head round to look at her sister. She'd half forgotten that Lizzie was sitting there and her comment had made Jackie jump. 'Doing what?'

'Staring off into space and looking fierce. Something's up, isn't it?'

'Yes.' The word shot out of her mouth before she had a chance to filter it. Lizzie leaned across and looked at her, resting her hand on Jackie's forearm.

'No…' Jackie said, wearing the poker face she reserved for fashion shows, so no one could tell what her verdict on the clothes would be until it was printed in the magazine. 'It's nothing.'

Why had she said yes? It wasn't as if she'd been planning

on telling Lizzie her problems, certainly not in the run-up to her wedding. She looked at her sister. The poker face started to disintegrate as she saw the warmth and compassion in Lizzie's eyes.

Could she tell Lizzie now? It would be such a relief to let it all spill out. Over the years, her secrets had woven themselves into a corset, holding her in, keeping her upright when she wanted to wilt, protecting her from humiliation. Seeing Romano last night had tightened the laces on that corset so that, instead of giving her security, it made her feel as if she were struggling to breathe. Suddenly she wanted to rip it all off and be free.

But it wasn't the time to let go, even if her sister's open face told her that she would understand, that she would comfort and not condemn. Already Lizzie was tapping into her maternal side, helped along by the buzzing pregnancy hormones. It brought out a whole extra dimension to her personality. She was going to be an excellent mother, really she was.

The sort of mother you have never been. May never be.

A shard of guilt hit Jackie so hard she almost whimpered, but she was too well rehearsed in damage limitation to let it show. Just as an underwater explosion of vast magnitude happening deep on the ocean floor might only produce a small irregularity on the surface, she kept it all in, hoping that Lizzie couldn't read the ripples on her face.

She smiled back at her sister, squinting a little as she faced the morning sun. 'It's just wedding jitters.'

Lizzie's concerned look was banished by her throaty laugh. 'I thought it was me who was supposed to get the jitters.'

Jackie saw her chance and grabbed it, turned the spotlight back where it should be. 'Have you? Got any jitters?'

Lizzie shook her head. 'No. I've never been more certain of anything in my life.' She went quiet, gazing out over the gardens, but the look on Lizzie's face wasn't fierce or hard; it was soft and warm and full of love. Jackie envied her that look.

She leaned in and gave her sister a kiss on the cheek. 'Good.' This was about as expressive as communication got in their family. But Lizzie got that. She knew how pleased her little sister was for her.

Lizzie began to move and Jackie stood up to lend her a hand as she heaved herself off the slightly dewy grass. 'Why don't you get rid of those jitters of yours by going into town with Mamma and Scarlett? They're planning to leave shortly.'

'Maybe.'

As she watched Lizzie walk away Jackie decided against the idea of joining her mother and other sister on their jaunt. A morning in the company of those two would give her grey hairs.

Going into Monta Correnti, however, taking some time to re-discover her home town, to see whether it still matched the vivid pictures in her head, now that was a plan she could cope with.

Exploring Monta Correnti was fun, but it didn't take more than an hour or so, and Jackie soon returned to feeling restless. She kept wandering anyway, and ended up in the little piazza near the church, outside Sorella.

It was late morning and Scarlett and Mamma were probably inside, having a cool drink before they decided what they were going to eat for lunch. She really should go in and join them.

But beautiful smells were coming from Uncle Luca's res-taurant next door and, despite the fact she'd sworn off carbs, she had a hankering for a simple dish of pasta, finished off with his famous basil and tomato sauce.

So, feeling decidedly rebellious, she sidestepped her mother's restaurant and headed for Rosa. Uncle Luca was always good for a warm welcome and she wanted to pump him for more information on all of Isabella's brothers. This year had certainly been a bombshell one for her extended family. So much had happened already. First, there had been the shocking announcement that Uncle Luca had two sons living in America that nobody had known about. Isabella had been trying to get in contact, but she wasn't having much luck. The family had thought that sending invitations to Lizzie's wedding might help break the ice, but Alessandro had declined and Angelo hadn't even bothered to reply.

Personally, Jackie wasn't too optimistic about Isabella getting any further with that. This family was so dysfunctional it wasn't funny. But she understood the need to heal and mend, to ache to bring forgotten children back into the fold.

She also wanted news of Isabella's little brothers. She didn't know if Valentino was in Monta Correnti at the moment or not, but it would be great to catch up with him before the hustle and bustle of Lizzie's wedding. She also wanted to find out the latest news on Cristiano. Mamma had announced last night that he'd been injured at work, fighting a fire in Rome, and was currently in hospital. Of course, Mamma had made it all sound totally dramatic, even though he'd only suffered minor injuries. Jackie would have preferred an update straight from her uncle, minus the histrionics, hopefully. Cristiano wasn't going to make it to the wedding either, which was such a pity. She'd always had a soft spot for him.

The entrance to Rosa was framed by two olive trees in terracotta pots. Jackie brushed past them and stood in the arched doorway, looking round the restaurant. The interior always made her smile. Such a difference from Sorella's dark wood grain and minimalist decor.

Everything inside was a little outdated and shabby, but, somehow, it added to the charm. There was a tiled floor, wooden tables and chairs in various shapes and styles, fake ivy climbing up the pillars and strings of garlic and straw-covered bottles hanging from the ceiling. Locals knew better than to judge a restaurant's food by its decor. Sorella, next door, was where the rich visitors and tourists ate, but Rosa was where the locals came, where families celebrated, where life happened.

At this time of day, the restaurant was deserted, but not silent. There was a hell of a racket coming from the kitchen. A heated argument seemed to be taking place between two women, but Jackie couldn't identify the voices above the banging of pots and pans and the interjections of head chef Lorenzo.

Unfortunately his fierce growling was not having the desired effect, because nobody shot through the kitchen door looking penitent. However, she heard someone enter the restaurant behind her.

Jackie had never been one for small talk. She didn't chat to old ladies at bus stops, or join in with the good-natured banter when stuck in a long queue. Perhaps it was her upbringing in Italy. When things went wrong, she wanted to complain. Loudly. So she didn't turn round and make a joke of the situation; she just ignored whoever it was. For a few seconds, anyway.

'*Buon giorno.*'

The warm tones, the hint of a smile in the voice, made her spine snap to attention. She licked her lips and frowned.

'Are you stalking me?' she said, without looking round.

Romano had the grace not to laugh. 'No. I came to see Isabella, but I won't lie—I was hoping I would run into you this morning.'

She didn't dignify the pause that followed with an answer.

'Jackie?'

She took a deep, calming breath, opening her ribs and drawing the air in using her diaphragm, just as her personal trainer had taught her. It didn't work. And that just irritated her further. She'd bet the man standing behind her didn't have to be *taught* how to breathe, how to relax.

He wasn't standing behind her any more. While she'd been on her way to hyperventilating he'd walked round her until she had no choice but to look at him.

'I would like to talk with you. I believe we have some things to discuss, some mistakes from the past to sort out.'

Now she abandoned any thoughts of correct breathing and just looked at him. That, of course, was her big mistake. The expression on his face was so unlike him—serious, earnest—that she started to feel her carefully built defences crumbling.

What if he actually wanted to acknowledge Kate after all these years? What if he really wanted to make amends? Could she let her pride prevent that?

No.

She couldn't do that to her daughter. She had to hear him out.

As always, Romano had sensed the course of her mood change before it had even registered on her face.

'Have lunch with me,' he said.

Lunch? That might be pushing it a bit far. She opened her mouth to tell him so, but the kitchen door crashed open, cutting her off.

'We have to, Isabella!' Scarlett said, marching into the dining area, looking very put out indeed. 'What if she talks to him again? What if—?'

'I don't think it is the right time,' Isabella countered in Italian. 'After the wedding, maybe.'

Scarlett, as always, was taking the need for patience as a personal affront. 'After the wedding might be too late! You know that.'

Isabella's hands made her reply as she threw them in the air and glared at her cousin. 'You're so impulsive! Let's just wait and see how things—'

It was at that moment that she spotted Jackie and Romano, her view half blocked by a pillar, both staring at her.

'—turn out,' she finished, much more quietly, and gave Scarlett, who was still watching Isabella intently, a dig in the ribs. Scarlett turned, eyes full of confusion, but they suddenly widened.

'Jackie!' she said warmly, smiling and rushing over to give her a hug. Jackie stayed stiff in her embrace. It felt awkward, wrong. But she had to give Scarlett credit where credit was due—she was putting on a wonderful show.

'Isabella and I were just talking…'

That much had been evident.

Scarlett paused, her gaze flicked quickly to the ceiling and back again. 'We're planning a surprise hen party for Lizzie and we want to drag you out to lunch to help us organise it!'

Isabella looked at Scarlett as if she'd gone out of her mind.

Isabella voiced Jackie's very thought. 'I don't think Lizzie—'

'Nonsense!' Scarlett said with a sweep of her hands. 'And there's no time like the present. You don't mind, do you, Romano?'

Romano didn't really have time to say whether he minded or not, because Scarlett grabbed Jackie's elbow and used it as leverage to push her back out into the sunshine, while Isabella followed.

Yep, thought Jackie, rubbing her elbow once she'd snatched it back, Scarlett was getting more and more like their mother every year.

Once they were clear of the tables and umbrellas out front of the restaurant, Jackie turned and faced them. 'You two are deranged!'

Isabella looked at the cobbles below her feet, while a flash of discomfort passed across Scarlett's eyes. 'We need to talk to you,' she said. 'Don't we, Isabella?' She hung a lead weight on every word of that last sentence.

Jackie looked towards the restaurant door, not sure if she was annoyed or relieved that her chance meeting with Romano had been unexpectedly hijacked. She looked back at her cousin and her sister in time to see a look pass between them. Isabella let out a soft sigh of defeat.

'I suppose we do. But we need to go somewhere private,' she said. 'Somewhere we won't be interrupted or overheard.'

The three of them looked around the small piazza at the heart of Monta Correnti hopelessly. Growing up in a small town like this, you couldn't sneeze without the grapevine going into action. And, this being Italy, the grapevine had always had its roots back at your mamma's house. She'd be waiting with a handkerchief and a don't-mess-with-me expression when you got home.

That was why Jackie and Romano had gone to such lengths to keep their relationship secret once their respective parents had warned them off each other. They'd been careful never to be seen in public together unless it was when Romano and his father had eaten at Sorella on one of Jackie's waitressing shifts.

Scarlett stopped gazing around the piazza and put her hands on her hips. She fixed Isabella with a determined look. 'I know one place where we won't be disturbed.' She raised her eyebrows and waited for her cousin's reaction.

'You don't mean…?' Then Isabella nodded just once. 'Come on, then,' she said and marched off across the old town's market square. 'We'd better get going.'

A low branch snapped back and hit Jackie in the face. She lost her footing a little and gave her right ankle a bit of a twist. Nothing serious, but she'd been dressed for a stroll around town and a leisurely lunch, not a safari.

'Sorry,' called Scarlett over her shoulder as she tramped confidently down the steep hill.

Jackie said nothing.

What had started off as a brisk walk had turned into a full-on hike through the woods. Her stomach was rumbling and she was starting to doubt that food was anywhere in the near future. What kind of shindig was Scarlett planning for Lizzie that involved all this special-forces-type secrecy?

Eventually the trees thinned and the three women reached a small, shady clearing at the bottom of the hill with a small stream running through it. Jackie smoothed her hair down with one hand and discovered far too many twigs and miscellaneous seeds for her liking. When she'd finished picking them out, she looked up to see Isabella and Scarlett busy righting old crates and brushing the moss and dirt off a couple of medium-sized tree stumps.

As she looked around more closely Jackie could see a few branches tied together with twine lying on the floor, obviously part of some makeshift construction that had now collapsed. A torn blue tarpaulin was attached by a bit of old rope at one corner to the lower branch of a tree while its other end flapped free.

Scarlett sat herself on the taller of the two tree stumps and motioned with great solemnity for Jackie to take the sturdiest-looking crate. Isabella took the other crate, but it wobbled, so she stood up and leaned against a tree. Jackie suddenly wanted to laugh.

It all felt a bit ridiculous. Three grown women, sitting round the remains of an ancient childhood campfire. She started to chuckle softly, but the shocked look on Scarlett's face killed the sound off while it was still in her throat. She looked from her sister to her cousin and back again.

'So… What's this all about? You're not planning something *illegal* for Lizzie's hen do, are you?'

Scarlett looked genuinely puzzled and every last trace of hilarity abruptly left Jackie at that point. Despite the summer sun pouring through the leafy canopy, she shivered.

'It's you we need to talk to,' Isabella said. 'The party was just an excuse.'

Scarlett looked scornful at Jackie's tardiness to catch on. 'Can you imagine what Lizzie would do if we planned a night of debauchery and silliness? Not very good for her public image.'

Not good for anyone's image, Jackie thought.

Scarlett stood up and looked around the clearing. 'This was our camp. Isabella and I used to come here to share secrets.'

'I remember how close you both were—joined at the hip, Uncle Luca used to joke. It was such a shame that you fell out. I thought—'

'Jackie! Please? Just let me talk?'

The hint of desperation in her sister's voice sent cold spiralling down into Jackie's intestines.

'This is difficult enough as it is,' Scarlett said, and stood up and ran a hand through her hair. She looked across at Isabella.

'There's no easy way to say this,' Isabella continued. She pushed herself away from the trunk of the tree she'd been leaning on and started pacing. Jackie just clasped her hands together on her knees and watched the two women as they walked to and fro in silence for a few seconds, then Scarlett planted her feet on the floor and looked Jackie squarely in the eye.

'We know your secret.'

Although her mouth didn't open, Jackie's jaw dropped a few notches. Her secret? Not about Kate, surely? They had to mean some other secret—the anorexia, maybe. Her eyes narrowed slightly. 'And what secret would that be, exactly?'

The leaves whispered above their heads, and when Isabella's answer came it was only just audible. 'About the baby.'

An invisible juggernaut hit Jackie in the chest.

'You know I…? You know about…?'

Their faces confirmed it and she gave up trying to get a sentence out.

But exactly how much did they know? All of it? She stood up.

'You know I was pregnant when I went away to live with my father?'

They both nodded, eyes wide.

'You know I gave the baby up for adoption?'

Isabella nodded again. 'No one told us, but it was kind of obvious when you came home the following summer without a baby.'

Oh, Lord. They knew everything. She sat down again, but she'd chosen the wrong crate and it tipped over, leaving her on her hands and knees in the dirt. Both Isabella and Scarlett rushed to help her up. She was shaking when she grabbed onto their arms for support.

They got her to her feet again and she met their eyes. There was no point in trying to hide anything now.

'My daughter—Kate—contacted me a couple of months ago. We've met a few times—'

'Kate?' The strangled noise that left Scarlett's mouth was hardly even a word. Jackie watched in astonishment as her normally feisty, bull-headed little sister broke down and sobbed. 'You had a little girl, a little girl,' she whimpered, over and over.

Jackie was stunned. Not just by Scarlett's reaction, but by the outpouring of emotion; it must mean that, on some level, Scarlett didn't despise her as much as she'd thought. She'd always seemed so indifferent.

'I'm so sorry,' Scarlett finally mumbled through her tears. Jackie turned to Isabella, hoping for an explanation, but Isabella wasn't in a much better state herself.

A thought struck her. 'You can't tell anyone about Kate!' she said quickly. 'Not yet.'

My goodness, if this was going to be the reaction to the news, she'd been right to decide to keep her mouth shut until after the wedding.

'It's okay,' she added, taking a deep breath. 'Things are going to be okay. Kate and I are getting to know each other. Things are going to work out, you'll see. So don't be sad for me—be happy.'

She'd hoped she sounded convincing, but she'd obviously missed the mark, because Scarlett and Isabella, who had been in the process of mopping up a little with a few tissues that Isabella had pulled from her pocket, just started crying even harder. Jackie stood there, dumbfounded, as they sat down on the two tree stumps looking very sorry for themselves indeed.

And then another thought struck her. One that should have popped into her head at the beginning of this surreal 'lunch', but she'd been too shocked to even think about it.

'How?'

Both the other women went suddenly very still.

'How did you find out? Did Mamma tell you?'

They both shook their heads, perfectly in time with each other. If she weren't in the middle of a crisis, Jackie would have found it funny.

'Then how?'

Scarlett looked up at her, her eyes full of shame. She didn't even manage to maintain eye contact for more than a few seconds and dropped her gaze to the floor before she spoke.

'The letter.'

What letter? What was Scarlett talking about? Had Mamma written a—

White light exploded behind Jackie's eyelids. She marched over to Scarlett's tree stump and stood there, hands on hips, just as she would have done when she'd been a stroppy fifteen-year-old, and *made* her sister look at her.

'You read the letter? *My* letter?'

Scarlett bit her lip and nodded.

'How dare you! How dare you! How—'

She was so consumed with rage she couldn't come up with any new words. Not even wanting to share a woodland clearing with the other two women, she strode over to the stream, as far away from them as she could possibly get without getting tangled up in trees, and stared into the cool green tranquillity of the woods.

Another thought bubbled its way to the surface. She turned round and found them twisting round on their tree stumps, watching her.

'Then you know who...'

Isabella swallowed. 'Romano.'

Jackie covered her mouth with her hand. This was worse than she'd imagined. Hen nights involving L-plates, obscene confectionery and tiaras would have been a walk in the park compared to this.

She exhaled. It all made sense now—why they'd freaked out when they'd seen her and Romano together back at the restaurant. But why had they dragged her away? Why tell her now?

'We didn't ever tell anyone else,' Isabella added hastily.

Jackie breathed out and sat down on the crate—the good one—and looked at her sister and her cousin.

They knew. And that had been her secret mission this visit, hadn't it? To tell everyone. Did it really matter if Scarlett and Isabella had known all along? Probably not. It would just be one difficult conversation she could cross off her list. They'd actually done her a favour.

Her anger had faded now, and she even managed a tiny smile. 'I was planning on telling you all after the wedding, anyway. Kate would really like to meet her aunts and uncles and I think it's time this secret came out into the open.'

Why weren't Scarlett and Isabella looking more relieved? They were still folded into awkward positions on their tree stumps. She decided to lighten the atmosphere.

'The least you two can do after all this is help me break the news to Mamma. I think you owe me!' And to let them know she was rising above it, dealing with the past and moving on, she gave them a magnanimous smile.

'You don't understand,' Scarlett said, rising from her stump, her forehead furrowing into even deeper lines. 'There's more.'

More? How could there be more? She'd told them everything. There were no more secrets left to uncover.

CHAPTER FOUR

SCARLETT gulped and cleared her throat. 'The letter... I brought it here to show Isabella.'

Jackie felt her core temperature rise a few notches.

'You have to remember—' Scarlett shot a glance at Isabella '—we were only eleven...'

Jackie's voice was low and even when she spoke. This was the tone that made her staff run for cover. 'What else, Scarlett? You did give my letter to Romano yourself, not pass it to someone else to give to him? If someone else knows—'

Isabella, who'd been unable to stand still for the last few moments, jumped in. 'It was my fault. I wanted to tell Aunt Lisa at first...' She trailed off at the look on Jackie's face. 'I didn't!' she added quickly.

'We fought,' Scarlett said, her voice gaining volume but at the same time becoming toneless, emotionless. 'Isabella had hold of the letter and I tried to snatch it away from her. It just seemed to leap out of my hands...'

They ripped the letter a little? Got it dirty? *What*? Jackie willed Scarlett to say either of those things. *Just a little smudge. No harm done.* But she could tell from the look of pure desolation on Scarlett's face that the fate of her letter had been much worse.

'What happened to it?' she asked, and her voice wobbled in unison with her stomach.

Scarlett didn't say anything but her gaze shot guiltily towards the stream innocently bubbling over the stones, and lingered there.

'*No!*' It was barely a whisper, barely even a sound. Suddenly Jackie needed to hold something, to cling onto something, but nothing solid was within easy reach. Everything was moving in the breeze, shifting under her feet.

Tears started to flow down Scarlett's cheeks again. 'I'm so sorry, Jackie. I'm so sorry…'

Jackie tried to breathe properly. *Her letter to Romano had ended up in the stream?* Thinking became an effort, her brain cells as slow and thick as wallpaper paste. She knew it was awful, her worst nightmare, but she couldn't for the life of her seem to connect all the dots and work out *why*.

'I didn't realise at the time what I'd done,' Scarlett said, dragging the tears off her cheeks with the heels of her hands. 'I didn't realise what it meant, that Romano was even the father… It was only later, when you and Mamma were shouting all the time.' She hiccupped. 'And then she sent you away. I knew I'd done something bad, but it wasn't until I was older, that I put all the pieces together, and understood what it all meant for you and Romano.'

Romano.

The letter had been for Romano.

Work, brain. Work!

She looked at the stream.

And then the forest upended itself. She didn't faint or throw up, although she felt it likely she might do either or both, but the strength of the revelation actually knocked her off her feet and she found herself sitting on the hard compacted earth, her bottom cooling as its dampness seeped into the seat of her trousers.

She closed her eyes and fought the feeling she was toppling into a black hole.

Oh, no… Oh, no… Oh, no.

The truth was an icy blade, slicing into her. Adrenaline surged through her system, making clarity impossible. She had to do something. She had to go somewhere.

Jackie staggered to her feet and started to run.

Romano didn't know.

Romano had never known.

There was a knock at the bedroom door. Jackie hadn't been moving, just lying spreadeagled on the bed staring at the ceiling, but she held her breath and waited. When she heard footsteps getting quieter on the landing she let the air out again slowly, in one long sigh.

From her position flat on the bed she could hear voices murmuring, the occasional distant chink of an ice cube. Mamma must have opened the drawing-room doors that led onto the terrace. She glanced at the clock. Ah, cocktail hour. Vesuvius could erupt again and Mamma would still have cocktails at seven.

But there were no Manhattans or Cosmopolitans for Jackie this evening, just an uneasy mix of truth, regret and nausea, with an added slice of bitterness stuck gaily on the edge of the glass.

A migraine had been the best excuse she'd been able to come up with when she'd arrived back at the house, uncharacteristically pink, sweaty and breathless. And to be honest, it wasn't far from the truth. Her head *did* hurt.

Mamma had moaned in her sideways way about self-indulgence, but she hadn't pushed the issue, thank goodness. She was far too busy to deal with her middle daughter. Nothing new there, then.

No way was Jackie going downstairs tonight. Mamma and Scarlett would be more than she could handle in her present state of mind. No, she wouldn't leave this room until she had pulled herself together and done the laces up tight.

Now the threat of interruption had diminished she hauled herself off the bed and looked around her old bedroom. If she squinted hard she could imagine the posters that had once lined the walls, the piles of books on the floor, the certificates in frames.

Of course, none of it remained. Mamma wasn't the kind to keep shrines to her darling daughters once they'd flown the nest. She'd redecorated this room the spring after Jackie had moved to London for good. In its present incarnation, it was an elegant guest room in shades of dusky lavender and dove grey.

Jackie caught herself and gave a wry smile.

Here she was, undergoing the most traumatic event since giving birth, and all she could think about was the decor. What was wrong with her?

Nothing. Nothing was wrong with her.

It was just easier to notice the wallpaper than it was to delve into this afternoon's revelations.

Uh-oh. Here came the stomach lurching again. And the feeling she was stuck inside her own skin, desperate to claw her way out. She steadied herself on the dressing table as her forehead throbbed, avoiding her own gaze in the mirror.

Everything she'd believed to be true for the last seventeen years, the foundation on which she'd forged a life, had been a lie.

She stood up and walked across the room just because she needed to move. She couldn't get her head round this. Who was she if she wasn't Jacqueline Patterson, a woman fuelled by past betrayal and life's hard knocks? Possibly not the sort of woman who could have climbed over a mountain of others, stilettos used as weapons, to become Editor-in-chief of *Gloss!* And if she weren't that woman, then she had nothing left, because work was all she had.

Romano didn't know.

He'd never known.

She closed her eyes and heard a gentle roaring in her ears.

Would that have changed things? Would he have stood by her after all, despite the fact they'd been so young, despite the argument that had sent them spinning in different directions? A picture filled her mind and she didn't have the strength to push it away: a young couple, awake long after midnight, looking drained but happy. He kissed her on the forehead and told her to climb back into the bed they shared, to get some sleep. He'd try and rock the baby to sleep.

No.

It wouldn't have been like that, couldn't have been. They couldn't have lost their chance because of a few sheets of soggy paper.

She had to be real. Statistics were on her side. She was more likely to have been a harried single mother, burned out and bored out of her mind, while her friends dated and went to parties and were young and frivolous.

Yes. That picture was better. That would have been her reality. She had to hang onto that. But the tenderness in the young man's eyes as he looked over the downy top of the baby's head at its mother wouldn't leave her alone.

She walked towards the window but kept back a little, just in case any of the family were milling on the terrace with their cocktails. She stared off into the sunset, which glowed as bright as embers in a fire, framing the undulating hills to the west. Tonight the sun looked so huge she could almost imagine it was setting into the crystal-clear lake that lay behind those hills. Where Romano probably was right now.

All these years she'd hated him. For nothing. What a waste of energy, of a life. Surely she must have had something better to do with her time than that? Maybe so, but nothing came to mind.

Slowly, quietly, she began to feel the right way up again. Get a grip, Jacqueline. You're not a terrified fifteen-year-old now; you're a powerful and successful woman. You can handle this.

Romano wasn't the monster she'd needed to make him in her imagination. And he probably wasn't the boy-father of her fantasies either. The truth probably lay somewhere in between.

She had to give him a chance to prove her wrong, to find out what the reality would be. He had a daughter on this planet, one who was hungry to know who she was and where she came from.

Jackie walked away from the window and sat back down on the edge of the bed. This changed all her plans. She couldn't tell her family about her daughter's existence yet. She had to tell Romano first. It was probably a bit late for cigars and slaps on the back, but he needed to know that he was a father.

Warm light filtered through the skylights in Romano's studio, dancing across the walls as tiny puffy clouds played hide-and-seek with the sun, daring him to come out and play. That was one of the downsides of having a home office in a home like his. Distractions, major and minor, bombarded him from every direction. One of the reasons he'd accepted Lizzie's wedding invitation was that it had given him a perfect excuse to spend two whole weeks at the palazzo. The plan had been to use the free time running up to and after the festivities to think about the next Puccini collection.

Just as he'd managed to dismiss the idea that the sky was laughing at him for sitting indoors working on a day like this, his mobile rang. He stood up with a growl of frustration.

He didn't recognise the caller ID. 'Hello?'

There was a slight pause, then a deep breath. 'Romano?'

He stopped scowling and his eyebrows, no longer weighted down with a frown, arched high.

'It's Jackie,' she said in English. 'Jackie Patterson.'

It wasn't lack of recognition that had delayed his reply, but surprise. After all these years her voice was still surprisingly familiar. It was her reasons for calling that had stalled him.

Why, when she'd been at pains to avoid him at all costs for the last couple of days—including that ridiculous show of some 'secret' lunch with Isabella and Scarlett—had she called him? As always, Jackie Patterson had him running in circles chasing his own tail. It was to his own shame that he liked it.

He smiled. 'And to what do I owe the pleasure?'

There was a pause.

'I believe you owe me lunch.'

He might be laid-back, but he wasn't slow. She hadn't actually agreed to lunch before she'd been whisked away.

He let it pass. If thirty-two-year-old Jackie was anything similar to her teenage counterpart, the starchy accusation was only the surface level of her remark. With Jackie, there were always layers. Something that had both bewitched him and infuriated him during their brief summer fling. Her about-face could only mean one thing: Jackie wanted something. And that also intrigued him.

'So I do,' he said, injecting a lazy warmth into his voice that he knew would make her bristle. Jackie might like to play games, rather than come straight out and say what she thought and felt, but that didn't mean he was going to lie down and let her win. The best part of a game was the competition, the cycle of move and counter-move, until there was only one final outcome. 'Do you want to go to Rosa?'

'No,' she said, almost cutting the end of his sentence off. 'Somewhere…quieter.'

Romano smiled. 'Quieter' could easily be interpreted as *intimate.*

'Okay,' he said slowly, letting her lead, letting her think she was in control.

He racked his brains to think of somewhere nice… *quiet*… to take Jackie. He doodled on a pad as he came up with, and rejected, five different restaurants. Too noisy. Bad food. Not the right ambience…

He looked out of the window, at the shady lawns and immaculate hedges. 'You want to talk? In private?'

'Yes.'

Did he detect a hint of wariness in her voice? Good. Jackie was always more fun when she was caught off guard. She always did something radical, something totally unexpected. He liked unexpected.

'Come to the island, then,' he said. 'We'll have all the quiet we want. We'll eat here.'

There was a sharp laugh from Jackie. 'What? *You* can cook?' Her response reminded him of the way he'd used to tease her until she just couldn't take it any more and had either walloped him or kissed him. He'd enjoyed both.

He laughed too. 'You'll just have to accept my invitation to find out.'

There was a not-so-gentle huff of displeasure in his ear.

He waited.

'Okay.' The word was accompanied by a resigned sigh. 'You're on.'

Jackie was on time. He hadn't expected anything less. She parked a sleek car on a patch of scrubby grass near a little jetty on the shore of Lake Adrina, just south of Isola del Raverno. He had been waiting in a small speedboat tied at the end of the rough wooden structure. The gentle side-to-side motion lulled him as he watched her emerge from the car looking cool and elegant.

She had style—and that wasn't a compliment he assigned easily.

She was dressed casually in a pair of deep turquoise Capri pants and a white linen halter-neck top, which she immediately covered with a sheer, long-sleeved shirt the moment she stepped into the sunshine. Her hair was in a loose, low ponytail and the honey highlights glinted gold in the midday sun. Bewitching. She pulled a large pair of sunglasses down from the top of her head to cover her eyes and it only added to the effect, making her seem aloof and desirable at the same time. He'd always been a sucker for forbidden fruit.

There was no doubt in his mind, though, that when she'd got dressed for this meeting, she'd thought very carefully about the 'look' she wanted to create. The clothes said: *Think of me as any other woman—down-to-earth, non-threatening, relaxed*. Romano was intrigued with her choice, why she'd felt the need to dress down when most other women would have dressed up.

He stood up, vaulted out of the boat and walked towards her. She didn't smile, and he liked her all the more for it. A smile would have been a lie. He was very good at reading women, their bodies, the silent signals their posture and gestures gave off, and as he watched Jackie walk towards him the signals came thick and fast—and all of them contradictory.

Greeting people with visible affection, even if little or no emotion was involved, was part of their world and, almost out of reflex, they leaned in, he kissed her on the cheek and took her hand. He'd done it a thousand times to a thousand different women at a thousand different fashion shows, seen her do the same from across the room, but as he pulled away a wave of memories as tall as a wall hit him.

She smelled the same. Warm. Spicy. Feminine.

And suddenly the hand in his felt softer, more alive, as if he could feel the pulse beating through it, and his lips, where they had touched her cheek, tingled a little.

Up until now the idea of embarking on a second summer fling with Jackie Patterson had been a mentally pleasing idea rather than a physical tug. He sensed that afterwards he would be able to erase the niggling questions about their romance that surfaced every few years from his subconscious, only to be swiftly batted down again. A rerun now they were older and more sensible would soothe whatever it was that jarred and jiggled deep down in his soul, wanting to be let out. But this time they would end it cleanly. No fuss, no ties.

As he ushered her into the small speedboat he realised that his only half-thought-out plans had moved up a gear. Now he didn't just want to get close to Jackie again to put ghosts to rest; his body wanted her here and now. But it wouldn't do to rush it. While she was all cool glamour on the surface, underneath she was awkward and nervous. Skittish. If he wanted to take Jackie to his bed, he was going to have to see if he could peel back some of those layers first.

He smiled. Not many men would guess what warmth and passion lay behind the glossy, cool exterior. But he knew. And it made the anticipation all the sweeter.

There were several mooring sites on the island and he chose the one that gave them a walk through the lush gardens to the palazzo. Jackie didn't say much as she walked in front of him, looking to the left and right, a slight frown creasing her forehead as she climbed the sloping steps from terrace to terrace. Now and again he saw her eyelids flicker, the very bare hint of colour flare in her cheeks, and he knew she was remembering the same things he was—memories of soft naked flesh, cool garden breezes that carried the scent of flowers. Heat and fulfilment.

It was here that they'd first made love, one night when his father had been away. He'd managed to invent an excuse to send the housekeeper and cook off for the evening—making sure they'd prepared food before they'd left, of course—and he and Jackie had spent the evening eating at the grand six-metre-long dining-room table, sneaking sips of his father's best vintage wine and pretending they were older and more sophisticated, free to love each other without remark or interruption.

He hadn't intended to seduce her. He'd just wanted some time alone with her far away from prying eyes, somewhere nicer than a dusty old run-down farmhouse. She'd been too young, and he'd been holding himself back, but that night…when they'd taken a walk in the gardens after dinner and she'd turned to him, kissed him, whispered his name and offered herself to him with wide eyes and soft lips, he hadn't been able to say no. Not when she'd purposely played with fire, done things that she knew got him so hot and bothered that he could hardly think straight.

But he couldn't regret it.

It had been intoxicating, and for the rest of the summer they'd lived in a blissful, heated bubble where the only thing that had mattered was time they could spend alone together. Foolish, yes. Forgettable, no.

They reached the large terrace with the parterre and giant urns. He watched her amble round a few paths, stooping to brush the tops of the geometric hedges and leaning in to smell the flowers dripping over the edges of the stone ornaments. This time it would be different. An adult affair, free from all the teenage angst and complications. He had a feeling it would be just as memorable.

On a large patio around to the side of the palazzo a table was set with linen and silver, a cream umbrella shading the waiting food. He led her to it. Crisp white wine was chilling in a bucket of ice, a dish on a stand stood in the middle of the table. She lifted her sunglasses for a moment and he noticed her eyebrows were already raised. He knew what she was thinking.

'I had a little help,' he said, not being able to resist teasing her, even though he'd prepared most of the meal himself. He liked cooking. It was just another way to be creative, and the results brought such pleasure, if the right amount of time and precision was lavished upon a dish. And he was all for pleasure, whatever the cost.

'Would you prefer to sit in the sun? I can remove the umbrella.'

She shook her head. 'I don't do sun. It's aging.'

He shrugged and pulled her chair out for her and she sat down, her eyes fixed on the domed cover over the central dish. He whipped it away to reveal a mountainous seafood platter: oysters, mussels, fat juicy prawns, squid and scallops, all stacked high on a mound of ice. Jackie forgot for a second to wear her mask of composure. He'd remembered well. She loved seafood.

'Wow.'

'See? I can cook.'

For the first time since he'd zipped her up in her mother's dressing room, she smiled. 'You don't really expect me to believe you prepared all this?' She swept a hand across the table. 'Even the salads?'

He handed her a serving spoon and nodded towards the platter. 'Any fool can shred a lettuce or slice a few tomatoes and drizzle a bit of oil and vinegar on them.'

She fixed him with a sassy look. 'It seems that *any fool* did.'

Warmth spread outwards from his core. He'd always loved her acerbic, dry sense of humour. Jackie was funny, intelligent, and with a quirky prettiness that had fascinated him; she'd been his favourite summer fling. His last, actually. After that he'd had other things to concentrate on. Learning the ropes at Puccini Designs, proving he wasn't a waste of space. It wasn't until success had come that he'd returned to finding women quite so distracting. And by then he'd been older, and summer flings had had their day.

Lunch was pleasant. He almost forgot that he'd sensed Jackie had a secret agenda for their meeting. They talked about work and what was new in the fashion world. She listened with interest as he bounced a few ideas for the next collection off her. Jackie Patterson deserved to be where she was. She knew her stuff. Not one person he'd ever come across in the length of his career had ever dared to suggest she was a success because her mother had once been a famous model. Quite the reverse, actually.

Lisa's prima-donna tendencies had been legendary. No one who'd been in Jackie's company for more than five seconds would accuse her of being anything but highly focused, knowledgeable and professional. He was so taken with getting to know her again that he almost forgot his own secret agenda.

'How long are you staying in Monta Correnti?' he asked as he served her second helpings of almost everything from the platter, hoping that she wasn't going to announce some urgent meeting back in London straight after the wedding.

She swallowed the scallop she'd been chewing. 'Two weeks. Mamma convinced me to take a holiday since Scarlett would be visiting.'

He nodded, too preoccupied with his own calculations to fully register the heat that suddenly burned in her eyes and died away. Two weeks would be perfect. Long enough to seduce her—it was his turn this time, after all—but not long enough to tie them together for life.

When they'd finished eating, there was a natural lull. They sat in silence, staring out at the lake, which was showing off for them, flipping its waves into frothy white crests. Out of the corner of his eye he noticed a subtle shift in Jackie's posture, felt rather than heard her take in a breath and hold it. He moved his head so he could look at her.

For a moment she was motionless, but then she pushed her sunglasses back onto her head and stared at him. He blinked and refused to let his muscles tighten even a millimetre.

'Romano…'

She broke off and looked at the lake. After a long, heavy minute, she turned to him again. 'I…I wanted to talk to you about something.'

Although they'd been talking Italian all this time, she switched into English and the consonants sounded hard and clunky in comparison. He stopped smiling.

'Would you consider an exclusive fashion shoot for *Gloss!,* timed to come out the day after the new Puccini collection is revealed?'

He opened his mouth and nothing came out. For some bizarre reason he hadn't been expecting that at all.

But that was Jackie Patterson all over. She had a way of overturning a man's equilibrium in the most thrilling manner. It was a pity he'd forgotten how that excitement was always mixed with a hint of disorientation and a dash of discomfort. Didn't mean he liked it any less.

This could be the perfect opportunity to keep close to Jackie for the next few days, easing that frown off her forehead, making her relax in his company until she remembered how good they'd been together instead of how messily it had ended.

'It's a possibility,' he said and gave her a long, lazy smile. 'But let's save the details for later—say, drinks tomorrow evening?'

CHAPTER FIVE

IT WAS just as well that Jackie knew the road to Monta Correnti like the back of her hand, because she wasn't really concentrating on her driving as she travelled back to her mother's villa. Just as well she'd only drunk half a glass of wine at lunch too. Romano had her feeling light-headed enough as it was and she'd decided she needed her wits about her if she was going to tell him what could be the biggest piece of news in his whole thirty-four years on this planet.

Only, it hadn't quite turned out that way, had it?

She'd chickened out.

Jackie sighed as she made her way up the steep hill, hogging far too much of the road to be polite.

She'd thought she'd been ready for it, thought she'd been ready to open her mouth and change his life for ever.

What she hadn't counted on was that, without the benefit of almost two decades of hate backing her up, Romano's effect on her would be as potent as ever. He'd always made her a little breathless just by standing too close, just by smiling at her. It had got her completely off track. Distracted. She'd do well to remember the mess she'd ended up in the last time she'd given in to that delicious lack of oxygen.

All the chemistry she was feeling probably didn't have anything to do with her. He couldn't help it, just exuded some strange pheromone that sent women crazy. While Romano had built a solid foundation and long-lasting reputation in his professional life he wasn't the greatest in the permanence stakes, and she'd started panicking that he'd be a bad father, that he wasn't what Kate needed.

Jackie muttered to herself as she took a hairpin bend with true Italian bravado.

What did she know? Did she have any more 'permanence' in her life? The truth was, after Romano, she'd never really let anyone get that close again. Oh, she'd had relationships, but ones where she'd had all the power. They'd dragged on for a couple of years until the men in question had realised she never was going to put them ahead of her work, and when they'd left she'd congratulated herself for having the foresight not to jump into the relationship with both feet.

Jackie slowed the car and pulled into a gravelly lookout point near the top of the hill. She switched off the engine, got out and walked towards the railing and the wonderful view of the lake.

She'd wanted to run, to get as far away from him as possible. Was that why she'd chickened out of telling Romano the truth? Was she once again thinking of herself, of keeping herself safe, of keeping the illusion of perfection intact?

No. She'd been scared, but not for herself—for Kate. She'd imagined all the different scenarios, all the different reactions he might have. Would Romano be angry? Horrified? Ambivalent?

What if she scared Romano off by dropping this bombshell? It was too sudden, too much, after seventeen years of silence. She wouldn't get a second go at this. It had to be right the first time.

She swallowed and gripped the wonky iron railing for support, but instead of staring at the majesty of Lake Adrina, she just stared at her feet.

Her heart might just break for Kate if Romano didn't want to have anything to do with her. She knew what it was like to lose a man like that. It hurt. Really hurt. And Kate might hate her for doing it all wrong and scaring him away. She couldn't have that.

Lunch had been good, but it had only been a starting point. They had to build on the fragile truce they'd started to mesh together. Whether they liked it or not, she and Romano would be for ever linked once he knew the truth.

So she'd invented a reason to keep him talking to her, to keep them seeing each other. They needed to get to know each other again. Then she could work out a way of telling him about Kate that wouldn't send him running.

She'd just have to ignore the glint of mischief deep in those unusual grey eyes, forget about the fact her body thought it was full of adolescent hormones again when she clapped eyes on him. At least Romano hadn't tried anything; he'd been the perfect gentleman, even though she was sure there'd been a hum of remembered attraction in the air. Thank goodness they were older and wiser now and both knew it would be a horrible mistake to act on it.

When Jackie finally drove through the gateposts of her mother's villa, she spotted Scarlett sitting on the low steps that led to the front door, watching her rental car intently as she swung it round and parked it beside her mother's sports car. She pressed her lips together as she switched off the engine. She knew that look. Scarlett was in the mood for a showdown and Jackie *really* wasn't.

She got out of the car and tried to ignore Scarlett, but as she neared the steps Scarlett stood up and blocked her path.

'What?' she said with the merest hint of incredulity in her voice. 'Have you been waiting for me here all afternoon?'

Scarlett returned her stare. 'Basically.'

Jackie shook her head and moved to pass her sister. Stubborn wasn't the word.

'Please?' Scarlett said, just as they were about to brush shoulders.

It wasn't the tone of her voice—slightly hoarse, slightly high-pitched—that stopped Jackie in her tracks, but the desperation in her sister's eyes. Neither of them spoke for a few seconds, and Jackie found it impossible to look away or even move.

'Okay,' she finally said.

Scarlett nodded, a flush of relief crossing her features, and set off towards the garden at breakneck pace. Instead of heading for the table and chairs on the terrace, or the spacious summer house, Scarlett kept marching downhill through the gardens. Without even glancing back over her shoulder at Jackie, she launched herself at the old tree and swung her leg over one of the thicker, lower branches.

'I thought we might as well talk on your territory,' she said.

Jackie just stared at her. This week had to be the most bizarre of her entire life.

Scarlett smiled at her—not her usual bright, confident grin, but a little half-smile that reminded Jackie of the way she'd looked when she'd stuck her head round Jackie's bedroom door and had asked her to read her a bedtime story when Mamma had been too busy.

'I can't believe I'm doing this.' Jackie hoisted herself up onto 'her' branch again. 'I thought you said this was silly,' she said, shooting a look across at Scarlett, who was now sitting quite merrily astride a branch, swinging her legs.

'It is.'

Jackie grunted and pulled herself upright and straddled the branch so she could look at Scarlett.

'We always used to come here to whisper about things we didn't want Mamma to know,' Scarlett said. She picked at a scrap of loose bark on the branch in front of her, then studied it intently for a few seconds. 'Are you going to tell her?' she said, not taking her eyes off the flaking bit of tree she was destroying.

Jackie waited for her to meet her gaze.

'I have to. It's all going to come out into the open shortly.'

Scarlett nodded.

Jackie drew in a breath and held it. 'But I have to tell Romano first.'

A look of pain crossed Scarlett's features. 'I'm so sorry, Jackie. I should have told you earlier…'

Jackie kept eye contact. Scarlett didn't shrink back; she met her gaze and didn't waver.

'Yes, you should have,' she eventually replied.

Scarlett sighed. 'It was easier to pretend it had all been some horrible nightmare once I'd moved to the other side of the world. I thought I could run from it, pretend it hadn't happened… But as time went on, I realised the true implications of my actions and I…' her chin jutted forward '…I chickened out. I'm sorry.' She shrugged one shoulder. 'What can I say? The gene for self-preservation is strong in our family.'

Jackie exhaled. She knew all about chickening out, all about desperately wanting to let the truth out but not being able to find the right word to pull from the pile to start the avalanche.

It was much harder than she'd anticipated to stay angry at Scarlett. Just yesterday she'd thought this fierce sense of injustice would burn for ever. But these weren't just pretty words to smooth things over and keep the family in its disjointed equilibrium. Scarlett's apology had been from the heart. After all that had passed between them, could they use this as a starting point to building their way back to what sisters were supposed to be?

'At least I understand why you hated me all these years.' She'd done it herself many times—made an error of judgement and turned her fury on the nearest victim rather than herself. A trick they'd both learned from their mother, she suddenly realised.

She wanted to say she was sorry too, for disappointing Scarlett, for setting up the series of events that had forced her to leave her home and live with her father, but she couldn't mimic Scarlett's disarming honesty. The words stuck in her throat.

In one quick movement Scarlett swung herself off her branch and landed on the same one as Jackie, side on, so both her legs dangled over one side. Her eyes were all pink but she hadn't surrendered to tears yet.

'Is that what you thought? That I hated you?'

Jackie felt the skin under her eyebrows wrinkle. 'Didn't you?'

'No!' The volume of her reply startled both of them. 'No,' she repeated more quietly.

'But…'

Now the tears fell. 'I didn't leave because of you, Jackie. I left because I couldn't live with myself.' Scarlett hung her head and a plop of salty moisture landed on her foot. 'When you came back from London you looked so different, so sad… I couldn't face seeing you like that. So I did what any self-respecting little girl would—I ran away and told myself it wasn't my fault.'

Jackie hadn't thought the pain could get any worse. She'd only ever thought about how she'd felt, how she'd been wronged. Emotionally, she'd never matured past fifteen on this issue, too concentrated on her own wounds to see the others hurting around her. It was as if she'd only just woken up from suspended animation, that she could suddenly see things clearly instead of through a sleepy fog of self-absorption.

Romano had a daughter he didn't even know existed. He'd missed all those years; he'd never be able to get them back.

And Scarlett had carried the scars of this terrible secret round with her all her life. It had affected their relationship, Scarlett's relationship with their mother…everything.

Jackie's eyes burned. She closed her lids to hide the evidence and grabbed at the sleeve of Scarlett's blouse, using it to pull her into a hug. They stayed like that just resting against each other, softening, breathing, for such a long time.

'I was too proud,' Jackie whispered. 'I should have gone to Romano myself, but I took the coward's way out. I shouldn't have dragged you into it, Scarlett.'

Scarlett pulled back and looked at her, eyes wide. 'You mean that? You forgive me?'

Jackie had to stop her bottom lip from wobbling before she could answer. 'If you can forgive me.'

Scarlett lunged at her, tightening the hug until it hurt. Unfortunately it caught Jackie off guard and she lost her balance. Scarlett let out a high-pitched squeak and it took a few moments for Jackie to register what that meant. Uh-oh. They clung even tighter onto each other as the tree slid away from them and they met the ground with a *whomp*, leaving them in a tangle of arms and legs.

'Ow,' said Scarlett, and then began to laugh softly.

Jackie wasn't sure whether she was moaning in pain or laughing along with Scarlett. The pathetic noises they were making and their fruitless attempts to separate their limbs and sit up just made them laugh harder.

'Girls?'

Their mother's voice sliced through the late-afternoon air.

Scarlett and Jackie held their breath and just looked at each other. Unfortunately this prompted an even more explosive fit of the giggles, and Lisa found them crying and laughing helplessly while trying to wipe the dirt off their bottoms at the foot of the old pine tree.

The boy slowed his Vespa to a halt at the back of the abandoned farmhouse and cut the engine. Everything seemed still. He looked up. The sky was bright cobalt, smeared with thin white clouds so high up they were on the verge of evaporating, and there was the merest hint of moisture in the air, a slight heaviness that he hadn't noticed while the wind had been buffeting him on his moped. Now he was motionless, he felt it cling to his skin and wrap around him.

Wasn't she here? Why hadn't she come running round the side of the farmhouse at the sound of his arrival as she usually did?

Frowning slightly, he jogged round the old building calling her name. No one answered.

He found her sitting on the front step, her back against the rotted door jamb, her long legs folded up in front of her. She didn't move, didn't look at him, even though she must have heard him arrive.

'Jackie? What's the matter?'

He sat down on the step beside her and she swiftly tucked her legs underneath herself. Her long dark hair was pulled into a high, tight ponytail and combined with the coldness in her hazel eyes it made her look unusually severe.

'I'm surprised you managed to drag yourself away,' she said, looking up, her tone light and controlled. 'I thought you'd be down in the piazza still, letting that Francesca Gambardi make eyes at you.'

Romano turned away. He was getting tired of this. Ever since they'd spent the night together almost three weeks ago Jackie had been acting strangely.

Oh, most of the time she was her normal, fiery, passionate self—a fact he was capitalising on, since they didn't seem to be able to keep their hands off each other for more than a few seconds at a time—but every now and then she just went all quiet and moody. And then she'd come out with some outrageous statement. Just as she had done a few moments ago. His head hurt with trying to figure it all out.

He sighed. 'We were just talking.'

Jackie humphed. 'Well, you seem to do a heck of a lot of *talking* with Francesca these days!'

He felt unusually tired and old when he answered her. 'There's nothing wrong with talking to a friend and, besides, I was only in the piazza because I was waiting for a chance to ask you to meet me here. Which I did. And you came. So I can't see what the problem is.'

She rolled her eyes and Romano felt his habitually well-buried temper shift and wake. 'What more do you want me to do?'

Jackie's answer was so fast it almost grazed his ears. 'Tell her you're not interested!'

'I *have* told her! She keeps asking me why, wanting a reason. I can't very well tell her it's because I'm seeing you. The news would be all over town in a flash and we'd never be able to see each other again. So, until we can convince our parents to take us seriously, I'm just going to have to let Francesca talk and I will pretend to listen.'

'How very convenient for you. Sounds like you've got the perfect excuse to flirt with whomever you want and still have me on the side.'

There was a hint of grit in his voice when he replied. 'It's not like that.'

She knew it wasn't. How could she believe he'd spend every moment he could making love with her, whispering promises, making plans, and the next moment be chasing around after girls like Francesca? Did she really believe him capable of that?

Jackie's silence, the thin line of her mouth told him all he needed to know.

He stood up and walked away. Only a few paces, but hopefully far enough from her distracting presence to let him think.

'You're not being logical,' he said.

Jackie jumped to her feet. 'I'm as logical as the next girl!'

That was what he was worried about.

She put her hands on her hips, looked at him as if she wanted to melt the flesh from his bones with just her stare. Jackie always had the oddest effect on him. Instead of making him cower, it made him want to stride over to her and kiss her senseless, persuade her she was everything he wanted.

He was on the verge of doing just that when she shot his plan full of holes by marching over to him and poking him in the chest with one of her fingernails. 'I don't need your so-called logic when I've got eyes in my head. You like her, don't you? Francesca?'

He shoved his hands in his pockets and walked swiftly back towards the farmhouse and went inside, hoping the cool air would improve his mood.

Jackie had fooled him.

At best the rest of the world saw him as a financial drain on his famous father, at worst a spoiled brat who knew no limits and respected no authority. He'd always thought that Jackie was the one person who credited him with more depth than that—more than he did himself even. So it stung for her to accuse him like this, it stung. It was the worst insult she could have flung at him.

It was a pity that just a few short months ago she would have been right. He'd been all those things. But that was before he'd met her, before she'd challenged him to join her in seeing who he could be if he was brave enough. But he'd obviously failed her, and that hurt.

There was a noise behind him and he looked over his shoulder to find her standing in the doorway, backlit with dust and sunshine and looking anything but penitent.

'This is stupid,' he said, sounding steelier than he'd meant to.

Instead of agreeing with him, softening and running to him and throwing her arms around him as he'd hoped she would, she just lengthened her spine and looked down her nose at him.

'Hit a raw nerve, did I?'

He didn't even bother answering her and she took a few steps towards him. 'Francesca is a very pretty girl, isn't she?' She blinked innocently and her voice was suddenly all syrup and silkiness.

He didn't know what kind of game she was playing but he had a feeling he'd lose, whichever tack he took. She went on and on, asking him over and over again, until he began to think she *wanted* him to agree with her, that on some level his capitulation would give her satisfaction, and eventually he got so cross with her incessant prodding that he walked over to her and gave her what she wanted.

'Yes. Okay? Francesca is very pretty.'

There. That had shut her up.

Jackie seemed to shrink a little, wither, as her eyes grew round and pink.

'You like her better than me,' she said, her voice husky.

Romano ran his hand through his hair, sorry he'd let her goad him into agreeing with her. He loved her, he really did, but if he'd known that taking their relationship to the next level would have opened this Pandora's box of female emotions, he might have resisted and sat on the lid a little longer.

She hadn't been ready for this. Neither had he.

Suddenly a summer of sweet, stolen kisses and innocent eye-gazing had morphed into an adult relationship, full of complications and blind alleys.

'I see you're not denying it,' she said, her voice colder than ever.

That was it. Romano didn't lose his temper very often, but when he did…

His thoughts were red and bouncing off the inside of his skull, searing where they touched. Perhaps this wasn't all worth it. Perhaps he would be better off with a girl like Francesca—a simple girl who wouldn't tax him the way this one did. This jealousy of Jackie's…it was ugly. And he was just furious enough to tell her so.

'At this precise moment in time, I'm starting to think you are right.'

The look on Jackie's face—pure horror mixed with desolation—warned him he'd gone too far, crossed a line. It wouldn't help to tell her that he hadn't jumped over it willingly, that she was the one who'd given him an almighty shove.

'In that case,' she said, backing away, walking heel-to-toe in an exaggerated manner, 'I never want to see you again.'

And then she turned and sprinted out of the farmhouse, leaving him only one option. It didn't take him long to catch up with her, despite those long toned legs.

'Jackie,' he yelled, when he was only a few metres away, that one word a plea to cool down, to see sense.

She stopped dead and turned around. 'I mean it. If you try to call me, I'll slam the phone down. And if you come to the house, I'll set the dog on you!'

His burst of laughter didn't help her temper, but surely when he explained she'd see the funny side and it would pop this bubble of tension. Then they could walk hand in hand to the bottom of the grove and spend the rest of the afternoon making up.

She was still glaring at him, but he stepped forward, brushed her cheek with his thumb. 'Your mother's dog is a miniature poodle,' he said, a join-me-in-this smile on his face. 'What is he going to do? Fluff me to death?'

It was at that moment that he realised he'd stupidly taken one of those blind alleys he'd been trying to avoid. Jackie was not amused by his observation in the slightest. She called him a few names he hadn't even known were part of her vocabulary then set off down the dirt track. As she passed his Vespa, she gave it a hefty kick with her tennis shoe and it fell over.

Romano didn't bother following.

There was no salvaging the situation this afternoon. He might as well get his Vespa vertical again and take off on a ride to clear his head. Jackie would calm down eventually—she always did—and then he would go and see her and they would both say sorry and things would get back to normal.

Jackie couldn't help thinking about Romano as she slid into her bridesmaid's gown. As Scarlett helped her zip it up it wasn't her sister's fingers she felt at her back, but his. Wearing his gown, knowing he had designed the ridiculously romantic bodice with her in mind, made her feel all fluttery and unsettled. And as the thick satin brushed against her skin she was reminded of what it had felt like to feel the tips of his fingers on her shoulder blades, the weight of his hands around the small of her waist, the tease of his thigh against hers…

'There,' Scarlett said as she did up the hook and eye at the top of the zip. 'I'm just going back to my room to get my bag. I'll meet you downstairs.'

Jackie just nodded. She needed to snap out of this, really she did.

There was no point in thinking about…remembering…Romano that way. Romantically, they were explosive. An unstable force. But what Kate needed right now were parents who could stand in the same room without tearing each other to shreds, and she knew from personal experience just how destructive bad parental relationships could be.

No, Kate needed security, stability. *Sensible, supportive co-parent* was the only relationship she wanted with Romano these days.

Jackie leaned towards the mirror on the dressing table and checked her make-up. It hadn't helped that in the last couple of days she and Romano had been in constant contact. But that had been the plan, hadn't it? They'd talked on the phone, had coffee together, another lunch. Conversation had mainly revolved around business, but she'd felt she'd accomplished what she'd set out to. They had the beginnings of a friendship, one that she hoped would survive the bombshell she was about to drop.

It was time to tell him.

Not today, of course. Tomorrow. She'd have to catch him at the wedding reception and arrange a meeting, somewhere far away from her family's straining ears.

'Jackie?' Scarlett yelled for her as she ran past her bedroom door and headed down the staircase.

'Coming,' she called back and grabbed both her wrap and her bag. She ran as quickly and elegantly as she could in heels to meet the rest of the bridal party, which had now assembled in the wide marble entrance hall. She slowed as she reached the last couple of stairs.

'Lizzie, you look absolutely perfect. Glowing.'

A slight blush coloured her elder sister's cheeks just adding to the effect.

'Well, it's good to know I'm glowing, especially as these two—' she paused to rub her tummy '—have been having a two-person Aussie rules football match inside me since five a.m.! I'm absolutely exhausted.'

Jackie kissed her on the cheek. 'You're not glowing *in spite* of those beautiful boys, but *because* of them.' She sighed. 'You have so much to look forward to…'

She hadn't meant to say that. Her mouth had just done its own thing. Her mouth never did its own thing. She was always in control, always careful about what she said and what she projected, and she was horrified to have heard her voice get more and more scratchy, until it had almost cracked completely as she'd trailed off.

Lizzie *did* have so much to look forward to. And it had suddenly hit her again that she'd missed all those things with

Kate. Moments she wished she'd witnessed, had treasured, instead of giving them to someone else for safekeeping. Moments she would never get back.

Scarlett rested a hand on her shoulder, gave her a knowing squeeze.

'Are you okay?' Lizzie asked, ruining her 'glow' a little with a concerned frown.

Jackie instantly brightened, glossed up. 'Of course. Absolutely fine. Just the…you know…emotion of the day getting to me.'

At that her mother gave a heavenwards glance. 'Not everything is about you, Jackie.'

A couple of months ago, maybe even a couple of days ago, she would have bristled at that remark, stored it away with the others to be brought out as ammunition at some time in the future, but today she turned to face her mother and did her best to stop her eyes glinting with pride and defiance.

'I know that, Mamma,' she said quietly. 'Believe me, I finally get it.'

CHAPTER SIX

THE wedding ceremony at Monta Correnti's opulent court-house was simple and moving. The way Jack Lewis looked at his new bride as he slid a ring on her finger brought a tear to almost every eye in the place. And then they were whisked away in limousines and a whole flurry of white-ribboned speedboats to Romano's island for the rest of the celebrations. Jackie's heart crept into her mouth and sat there, quivering, as the boat neared the stone jetty just below Romano's over-the-top pink and white palazzo.

Only close friends and family had been at the courthouse. Now a much larger guest list was assembling for a religious blessing and reception in the palace and formal gardens of Isola del Raverno.

Jackie tried not to think about Romano, but the conversation she knew they must have the following day was looming over her.

Today wasn't about that. Wasn't about her. Her mother had been right, even if only accidentally. During the winding journey from Monta Correnti to Lake Adrina, she'd thought hard about her mother's words. For as long as she'd been able to remember, even before she got pregnant with Kate, everything had been about her. Being a middle child, she'd felt she had to fight for every bit of attention, had learned to be territorial about absolutely everything, even though Lizzie and Scarlett hadn't been treated as favourites in any way.

And she'd never let go of that need to be the hub of everything, of needing the adulation, position…supremacy.

Until she'd rediscovered her lost daughter, she hadn't realised she'd had any of those sacrificial maternal feelings, hadn't let herself remember what she'd buried deep inside. She hadn't ever let herself feel those things, not even when she'd been carrying Kate. It had been easier to bear the idea of giving a piece of herself up if she imagined it to be nothing but a blob—a thing—not even a human being. Of course, all that clever thinking had fallen apart the moment Kate had come silently into the world, in the long moments when Jackie had been helpless on an operating table with doctors and midwives hurrying around and issuing coded instructions to each other. She'd felt as if her heart had stopped, but the monitor attached to her finger had called her a liar.

When Kate had finally let out a disgruntled wail, Jackie had begun to weep with relief, and then with loss. She hadn't had the right to care about this baby that way. She'd decided to give that right away to someone else, someone who would do a better job.

And somebody else had done a better job. She didn't know if that was a blessing or a curse. Whichever way she'd thought about it, it hurt.

She'd caused all of it. All of this mess.

The boat hit the jetty and jolted her out of her dark thoughts. She grimaced to herself. So much for today not being all about her. She'd spent the ten-minute ride to the island submerged in self-pity.

Today is not the day, she told herself. You can do it tomorrow. You'll tell Romano and then you'll have plenty of reasons to feel sorry for yourself—and for him.

* * *

The wedding breakfast was held in the palazzo's grand ballroom—the late count's pride and joy. 'Ostentatious' didn't begin to do it justice. There was gold leaf everywhere, ornate plasterwork on every available surface and long mirrors inserted into the panels on the walls at regular intervals. Totally over-the-top for casual dining, but perfect for an elegant wedding. Perfect for Lizzie's wedding. And she looked so happy, sitting there with her Jack, alternately rubbing her rounded belly through the flowing dress and fiddling with the new gold ring on her left hand as she stared into his eyes.

Jackie tried to keep her mind on the celebrations, but all through the afternoon she would catch glimpses of Romano—talking to some other guests with a flute of champagne in one hand, or walking purposefully in the shadows, checking details—and it would railroad all her good intentions.

Perhaps it would be better if she just got it over and done with, went and sought him out. Then she wouldn't be seeing him everywhere, smelling his woody aftershave, listening for his laugh. Every time her brain came up with a false-positive—when she'd thought she'd detected him, but hadn't—her stomach rolled in protest. It brought back memories of morning sickness, this uncontrollable reaction her body was having. She pushed the heavy dessert in front of her away.

In the absence of dry crackers and tap water, what she really needed was some fresh air. She needed time on her own when she wasn't expected to chit-chat and smile and nod. At the very least she owed it to her cheek muscles to give them a rest.

The meal was over, coffee had been served and the cake had been cut. Jack and Lizzie were making a round of the room, talking to the guests. No one would notice if she slipped out for a few moments. If anyone missed her, they'd just assume she'd gone to powder her nose.

But escape was harder than she'd anticipated. She was only a few steps from the double doors that led onto the large patio when her mother swept past, hooked her by the crook of her arm and steered her towards a huddle of people.

'Rafe?' her mother said.

Rafael Puccini looked very distinguished with his silver-grey hair, dressed in an immaculate charcoal suit. Even though he must be a few years over sixty, he still had that legendary 'something' about him that made women flock to him. He turned and smiled as her mother herded her into their group, and she couldn't help but smile back.

'Jackie asked me a while ago about those sunglasses of yours…you know the ones.' Her mother waved a hand and tried to give the impression she didn't give a jot about the subject of their conversation.

Jackie didn't react. Everyone knew that her mother had been Rafe Puccini's muse back in the Sixties. His *Lovely Lisa* range of sunglasses were modern classics, and were still the best-selling design in the current range.

What had surprised her was her mother's sudden mention of the glasses. She'd asked her—oh, months ago—about finding some vintage pairs for a feature for *Gloss!* Normally most of what she said to Mamma tended to go in one ear and out the other. If anything was retained, it usually had a wholly 'Mamma' slant to it, and was often completely inaccurate.

Rafe took her mother's hand and kissed it. 'Certainly I know which glasses you mean. How could I forget something inspired by those sparkling eyes?'

If Kate had been here, she'd have made gagging noises. Jackie wasn't actually that far from it herself. She'd met Romano's father many times before, of course, and had often seen him in full flirt mode, but never with her own mother. Lisa wagged a disciplinary finger at her old paramour, smiling all the while.

Well, she'd been fishing for a compliment and she'd hooked a good one. Why wouldn't she be pleased?

Just as Jackie broached the possibility of buying or borrowing some of the vintage sunglasses, Romano materialised for real.

Fabulous. The last thing she needed was her eagle-eyed mother picking up on a stray bit of body language and working out there was some sort of undercurrent between her and Romano. Mamma was very good at that. That was why Jackie had such excellent posture. Being able to snap to attention, give nothing away, had been her best survival mechanism as a teenager. As for today, she was just going to have to extricate herself from this cosy little group and try and catch up with him on his own later.

That plan was also a little tricky to execute. Rafe and her mother greeted Romano and drew him into the conversation. Jackie had no choice but to stand and smile and hope against hope that Lizzie would send for her to fulfil some last-minute bridesmaid's duty.

As the discussion turned towards hot new designers to watch, Jackie's attention moved from the outrageous flirting on the part of the older generation to the interaction between father and son. She'd never thought of Romano as being particularly family-oriented. He didn't have those heavy apron strings most Italians had to tie them to their families. But there was a clear bond between him and his father these days. Quick banter flowed easily between them, but it never descended into insults or coarseness. They both had the same mercurial thought patterns, the same sense of humour.

Jackie became suddenly very conscious of the lack of even

polite conversation between her and her mother. They didn't know how to relate to each other without all their defences up, and the realisation made her very sad.

If only she could work out how Romano and his father did it, she might be able to analyse and unpick it, work out how to reproduce it with Kate.

The need to have more than an awkward truce with her daughter hit her like a sledgehammer. She was so tense around Kate, even though she tried not to be. But the knowledge that she'd failed her daughter pounded in her head during their every meeting, raising the stakes and making her rehearse and second-guess everything she said and did. And the feeling that it was all slipping through her fingers just added to the sense of desperation every time they were together. And the more desperate she got, the harder it seemed to be natural.

She wanted her daughter to like her. *Needed* her daughter to like her. Maybe even love her one day.

Sudden jabs of emotion like this had been coming thick and fast since she'd reconnected with Kate and, to be frank, she was feeling more than a little bruised by all the pummelling she was giving herself. She'd never had to keep such a lid on herself, do so much damage control to keep the illusion of omnipotence in place.

She made sure none of her inner turmoil showed on her face, pulled in some air and slowly let it out again without making a sound.

Back in the here-and-now, she joined the conversation again, but even that was difficult. She could feel Romano watching her. She tried not to look at him, tried to let her eyes go blurry and out of focus if she needed to glance in his direction, but it was as successful as trying not to scratch a mosquito bite. Eventually she had to give in, and the more she did it, the more she needed to do it again.

Even when she managed a few moments of victory and maintained eye contact with Rafe or her mother, she could sense his gaze locking onto her, pulling her. Her skin began to warm. The outsides of her bare arms began to tingle.

She made the mistake of glancing at him for the hundredth time and, instead of the warm sparkle of humour in his eyes, they were smouldering. Her mouth stuck to itself.

How stupid she'd been to think she'd been safe from that look, that the delicate friendship they'd been threading together had wiped it from existence. It hadn't diluted its power one bit. Romano wasn't looking at her like a friend. He was looking at her as if he wanted to…

No. She wasn't going to go there.

One problem with that, though: she wasn't sure that she wasn't returning that look, measure for measure.

It was just as well he'd decided that today was the day he was going to make his move. The way Jackie looked in that dress—his dress—made it impossible to wait any longer.

When he'd first spotted her walking through the gardens with the rest of the bridal party, he'd actually held his breath. It looked perfect on her. Exactly as he'd imagined it would when it had been nothing more than a fleeting image in his head and a quick sketch on the page. Exactly the same, but at the same time so much more.

She brought life to his design, made it move, made it breathe.

Of course he'd seen hundreds of his ideas translated into fabric and stitching before, but not one had had this impact on him. Not one. It was more than just the fit. Jackie's dress— the romantic bodice, the gently flaring chiffon skirts—brought out a side of her he'd thought she'd lost.

Jacqueline Patterson, Miss Editor-in-chief, was attractive in a slick, controlled kind of way, but now…now she was all curves and softness. So feminine. From the coiled hair at the back of her head with the soft ringlets framing her face, to the tips of her satin sandals. All woman.

His woman.

That thought snapped him back to the present pretty fast, to the conversation his father and Lisa and Jackie were having about sunglasses.

Hmm. He'd never had the desire to *own* the women who wore his creations before, or the women who flitted through his life. They were on loan—as was he. Nothing permanent. Nothing suffocating. Nothing…meaningful.

Must be an echo. Of things he'd felt long ago. Maybe once he'd dreamed of having and holding for ever. But he'd been so young. Naive. And he knew Jackie well enough to know she was far too independent to be anyone's trophy. She'd always been that way. Seventeen years ago he hadn't been worthy of that prize, and she'd let him know in no uncertain terms. Just as well he wasn't interested in that this time around.

And, with his current agenda fresh in his mind, he immersed himself again in the conversation that had been flowing round him.

It was time. The fact he was letting his imagination run away with him only served to highlight how bright his desire for her was. But he still needed to act with finesse, with respect and patience. It was that instinct that had kept him hovering on the fringes of the wedding celebrations, holding back until he felt in control of himself, be close to her without dragging her into the garden.

His father turned to Jackie. 'Ah, your glass is empty, my dear. Let us find you another.'

Before Jackie could answer her mother piped up, mentioning the need to have a stiff word with the head waiter, and their parents disappeared with a nod to say they'd be back in only a few moments.

Jackie smiled at him. Actually smiled. And it was real—not

that perfect imitation she normally did. Once again he felt a tug deep inside him. Not yet, he told himself. Running headlong into this will only get you kicked in the teeth, and you will walk away with nothing. Play this right and you'll have a summer affair hot enough to give you your own private heatwave.

'He's quite something, your father, isn't he?' she said with an affectionate glance over her shoulder. 'I was too young and too in awe of him when I used to serve you at Sorella to realise what a charmer he is.'

He smiled back, carefully, tactically. 'I don't think that's stopping your mother from falling for it again.'

'Now that's a scary thought.' She looked behind her again to where her mother was tearing strips off one of the catering staff, while his father smoothed any ruffled feathers with a smile and a wink. It was an odd kind of teamwork, but strangely effective.

Jackie took a long look at their parents, then turned to look at him. She raised her eyebrows. 'Do you think history will repeat itself?'

A sudden burst of heat filled his belly. He didn't glance over at their parents, but kept his gaze concentrated on Jackie. 'I'm counting on it,' he said, his voice coming out all rough and gravelly.

Jackie, being Jackie, wasn't swept away by one simmering look and loaded comment, but she laughed gently. He took it as a point scored.

'I see he has taught you all of his tricks,' she said.

Although he was tempted to laugh with her, he moulded his facial muscles into a look of mock-seriousness. 'Oh, I think the old dog has had a bit of an education from me too.'

She laughed again. 'You're incorrigible.'

Now he flashed her a smile, timing it to perfection. 'So I've been told. Come on.' He looked towards the open doors, only a few feet away, that led onto the terrace '*Andiamo!*'

Jackie followed his gaze and then they were both moving, both picking up speed and heading for the delicious coolness of the shady edges of the garden. He grabbed two glasses of champagne from a waiter's tray as they made their escape, and it struck him that he hadn't needed to drag her to get her to go outside with him after all. They hadn't even touched.

Not yet, anyway.

This is ridiculous, Jackie thought, as she ignored the pain on the balls of her feet and jogged in her high heels. They fled across the terrace, out of the view of the wedding guests inside the grand dining room and down a shady path. Romano was so close behind her she could hear his breath, practically feel it in the little ringlets at the nape of her neck.

When they'd reached relative safety, beyond a curve in the path, she gave in to the nagging fire in her feet and stopped. Romano just grinned at her and handed her a glass of champagne.

'You hardly spilled a drop! That's an impressive skill.'

Romano took a step closer. 'Oh, you have no idea of the skills I've picked up since we were last together.'

A slight rumble in his voice caused her to flush hot and cold all over. Just the thought that Romano might be better at some things—other things—was not good for her equilibrium. She steadied herself on the wooden rail that followed the path downhill and looked out to where the lake was sparkling at them through the trees.

What are you doing? You can't behave like this. Not with Romano. Not now. Not ever.

She closed her eyes briefly, took a sip of champagne and opened them again. How could she have let herself start thinking this way, feeling this way? Her daughter's whole happiness hung in the balance and she'd forgotten all about that, had been too busy being selfish, letting herself relive the unique buzz of attraction that still hummed between her and the man standing just a few short steps away.

She decided to start walking again, because standing there in the shadowy silence, feeling his gaze resting softly on her, was somehow too intimate. She had to break this strange feeling that had encapsulated her. It was as if she and Romano were trapped in a bubble together, with the rest of the world far, far away. She had to find a way to pop it before she did something stupid.

Her stiletto would be perfect. She took a step away from him, hoping that the heel of her shoe would be sharp enough to cut through the surface tension and let reality flood back in. He followed her and, if anything, the skin surrounding them, joining them, just bounced back and thickened.

She kept walking and didn't stop until she'd realised her subconscious had led her to the one place on the island that she'd really wanted to avoid.

The sunken garden was as beautiful as it had always been, full of ferns, some dark and woody, some small and delicate in a shade of pale greenish-yellow that was almost fluorescent. There was something timeless about this garden. The memory of the dark, waxy ivy that had worked its way up and around every feature was still fresh in her mind. The grotto still beckoned silently, promising secrecy and shelter in its cocoon-like depths.

She tried to keep the memories, and the man she was here with, even her own desires, at bay with her next words. It was time to stop getting carried away and ground herself in reality, in the sticky, complicated present, not some half-remembered adolescent fantasy.

'I... I wanted to ask you if you were free tomorrow,' she said, without looking him in the eye. That would be far too dangerous. 'There's something important I need to discuss with you.'

She heard—no, felt—Romano move closer.

'Look at me, Jacqueline,' he said in a low, husky voice.

She licked her lips. She didn't want to look at him, but *not* looking at him would be an admission that she was feeling weak, that he was getting to her, and she needed to give at least a semblance of control. She inhaled and met his gaze.

He was wearing that lopsided smile he'd always had for her. The one that had turned her heart to butter.

'We both know that we have talked the idea of the Puccini shoot for *Gloss!* to death over the last few days.' His fingers made contact with her wrist, ran lightly up her forearm. 'We're both adults now.'

Jackie decided she had need of a fire extinguisher. She didn't trust herself to say anything helpful, so she just kept looking at him. Had she blinked recently? She really didn't know.

'So…' he continued, 'let's not play games as we did when we were younger. If we want to spend time together, we should just say it is so. There is no shame in it.'

Jackie tried hard to deny it, but he shook his head.

'Don't lie to me. I can see it in your eyes.' He dipped his head closer, until she could almost taste him in the air around her. 'I know we both want this.'

Heaven help her, she did.

She didn't push him away when he dragged his lips across hers, so gently it was as if they were barely touching. Too gently, teasing, so her nerve endings went up in flames. More so than if he'd started off as hot and hungry as she'd half-wished he would.

Boy, Romano could kiss.

He'd always been able to kiss. But he was right. There was new skill here too. Enough to make her forget her own name.

Romano had disposed of his champagne glass—she hadn't noticed when or how—and now his hands were round her waist, pulling her closer to him. She needed to touch him, hold him, but her own glass was still dangling by its stem from her right hand. They were right beside one of the water features and she felt with the base of the glass for a flattish patch on the knobbly surface of the pool's edge. She hardly registered the plop a second or two later, too busy running her hands up Romano's chest, relishing the feel of him.

She kept going all the way up his body until she could weave her fingers through the deliciously short hairs at the back of his head. Still kissing her, he let out a gruff moan from the back of his throat. She smiled almost imperceptibly against his lips.

This was the wonder of Romano Puccini. He made her feel beautiful and feminine and alive. Not by wading in and taking control, dominating, but by acknowledging her power, meeting her as an equal, making her feel sexy and confident.

Romano's lips moved from hers. He kissed a line from her chin down to the base of her neck, then along her collarbone to her shoulder, nipping the bare skin there gently with his teeth.

Jackie just clung to him. She hadn't known how much she'd missed this. Missed him. Hadn't realised that subconsciously she'd been waiting to feel his lips on her skin again for almost two decades. How could she have denied herself so long? Why had she thrown this away?

'Jackie…' His breath was warm in her ear. 'I want you. I *need* you.'

He was whispering her name in that way that had always made her melt, but it was another name that suddenly crystallised in her consciousness, freezing out all other thoughts and sensations.

Kate.

In a split second what had been hot and tingly and wonderful between them seemed nothing more than an undignified grope in the bushes. And it was selfish. So selfish.

She pushed Romano away. Or maybe she pulled herself out of his arms—she wasn't quite sure. He blinked and looked at her, his eyes hooded and clouded with confusion.

'We can't do this,' she said in a shaky voice.

He reached for her and she was too numb to react fast enough. He breathed in her ear, knowing just what he was doing, before whispering, 'What's to stop us?'

Jackie prayed for strength, prayed for a clear head. She couldn't lose herself like that again. She needed to focus on the reason she needed to get close to Romano, and it certainly wasn't *this* reason. It was about Kate. It was all about Kate. But then his lips found hers again and she almost went under.

'No,' she said softly, firmly, and she grabbed his chin with her hand, doing whatever she had to do to stop him.

He sighed and gave her a wistful look. 'I thought we said we weren't going to play games.'

Part of her softened, found his cheeky confidence charming. Another part of her took umbrage. He was too sure of himself. Too sure he could have her if he wanted her.

'I'm not playing games,' she said, looking him in the eye, refusing to waver.

'Good,' he said, wilfully misunderstanding her.

Jackie felt like wilting. They could do this all day, go back and forth, back and forth. Romano was as persistent as she was contrary, and she feared she might eventually weaken. That would do lasting damage to her plan to build a solid relationship with him, the kind of relationship that would give Kate stability and confidence in them as parents. Unfortunately, there was only one way she could think of to shock Romano out of seducing her amidst the ferns.

'The reason we can't do this,' she said, 'is that there's something you don't know. Something important.'

He froze. 'You're not married?'

She shook her head and the smile returned, saucier than ever. '*Buono.*' And he went back to placing tiny little teasing kisses on her neck.

It was no good. Romano had obviously decided she was

playing along with him, albeit in a very 'Jackie' way. He stopped what he was doing and straightened, one eyebrow hitched high, but paused when his lips were only a few millimetres from hers. She had to do this now.

'There's something you don't know about that summer we were…together.'

He was too close to focus on properly, but she sensed him smiling, felt him sway just that little bit closer. 'Oh, yes?'

'When I left for England that autumn, after our summer, I was…'

Oh, Lord. Did she really have to say it? Did she really have to let the words out of her mouth?

'I was pregnant.'

CHAPTER SEVEN

I WAS pregnant.

Those words had the combined effect of a cold shower and a slap round the face for Romano. His arms dropped to his side and he stepped back.

She had to be joking, right? It had to be some unfathomable, Jackie-like test. He searched her face as she stood there with all the flexibility of an ironing board, her eyes wide and her mouth thin.

'You mean…you…and I…?'

She bit her lip. Nodded.

Now, Romano was a man who usually liked to indulge in the elegant use of language, but at that moment he swore loudly and creatively. Jackie flinched.

He looked at her stomach. After making that dress he knew her measurements to the millimetre, had crafted it to hug them. There was no hint. Fewer curves, even, than when he'd…than when they'd…

A million questions flooded his mind, all of them half finished. And then the awful truth hit him.

'You had a… You lost it?' he said, unable to work out why a solid wall of grief hit him as he uttered those words.

She shook her head, and the sorrow reared its head and

became an ugly, spitting monster. He clenched his fists, spoke through his teeth.

'You *got rid* of it?'

The look of pure horror on her face was more than enough of an answer. He didn't need to hear the denial she repeated over and over and over. But that meant…

It couldn't.

He'd never heard mention of a child…a family…in all the years he'd worked in the same gossip-fuelled industry as Jackie. She was a private person, sure enough, but could that fact have slipped by him unnoticed?

He turned in a circle but came back to face her.

Of course it could.

When had he ever been interested in colleagues' pictures of pink-faced, scrunched-up newborns? He tuned out every single conversation about their children's ballet recitals and football games, preferring to amuse himself with statistics of a different kind. Cup sizes, mainly.

He looked around his sunken garden, at the grotto, which now seemed less like a lovers' nest and more like a crime scene.

'Romano?'

He looked back at her, confused. The soft, vulnerable expression she'd worn only moments ago had been replaced with something much harder.

'You have a daughter,' she said, voice as flat as if she'd been reading random numbers in the phonebook.

A baby? He had a baby?

He backed away, and, when he could go no further, sat down on a low, mossy wall.

No. Don't be stupid. It had been such a long time ago. She was a girl by now. Almost a woman. He stood up again, suddenly fuelled by another revelation.

'You kept this a secret from me? Why?'

There was a flicker of discomfort before Jackie resumed

her wooden expression. 'I tried, but—' she looked away '—it's complicated. I'll explain in a minute, when you've calmed down a bit.'

When he'd…?

This woman had been sent to test him to the limits. All these years she'd kept this from him. All these years she'd preferred to bring up their child on her own rather than involve him. Who gave her the right to make such decisions?

And why had she done it?

The answer was a sucker-punch, one from his subconscious: she hadn't believed him ready or capable to take on that responsibility, hadn't even entertained the thought he might be able to rise to the challenge. Just as she hadn't deemed him worthy of her love. Inside his head something clicked into place.

'Is that why you ended it? Refused to see me? Or take my calls?'

She inhaled. 'No. I didn't know then. I only realised…later.'

Then why hadn't she told him later? The words were on his lips when he remembered he already knew the answer. He matched Jackie's stance, returned ice with ice as he looked at her.

'Where is she now?' He looked to the terraced garden above them, back to the house. 'Is she here?' His stomach plummeted at the thought, not from a fear of being trapped, he realised, but in anticipation.

'She's in London.'

London. How many times had he been in that city over the last seventeen years? It was a massive place, with a population of millions, and the chances of having walked by her in the street were infinitesimal, but he was hounded by the idea he might have done just that.

'Does she know about me? Does she know who her father is?'

At that question, the inscrutable Jackie Patterson wavered. 'No.'

He closed his eyes and opened them again. Even though he'd had the feeling that would be her answer, it felt like a karate kick in the gut.

'What about the birth certificate? You can't hide it from her for ever. One day she'll find out.'

To his surprise, Jackie nodded, but the words that followed twisted everything around again and sent him off in an even more confusing direction.

'I didn't tell anyone who her father was. Not even Mamma. The birth certificate has my name alone on it.'

Romano sucked in a breath. That was it, then. He was nothing more than an empty space on a form. All these years trying to prove himself, trying to get the world to understand he was something in his own right, and that was what this woman had reduced him to. An empty box.

Jackie came a little closer, but not so close that she was within touching distance. He didn't have any more words at the moment, so he just looked at her. Her hands were clasped in front of her, her fingers so tense he could clearly see the tendons on the backs of her hands.

He came full circle again. 'Why?' he whispered. 'Why have you never told me?'

'I thought I had.'

Her answer turned his pain into anger. And when he was angry his usual good humour became biting and sarcastic. 'That's funny,' he said, aware that the set of his jaw was making it blindingly obvious he was anything but amused, 'because I think I would have remembered that conversation.'

Jackie walked over to a low stone bench and sat down, staring at the floor. Reluctantly he followed, sensing that keeping close, pushing her, would be the only way to uncover more facts.

As he sat there staring at the fountain bubbling away she told a ridiculous story of lost letters, secret rendezvous and missed opportunities. She told him she'd waited at the farm-house for him. Waited for him to turn up—and dash her hopes, he silently added, because, surely, that was what she'd expected.

'Why didn't you try to reach me again when I didn't show up? You had no way of knowing if I'd been prevented from meeting you there.'

Jackie leaned forward and covered her face with her hands. For a long time the only sound she made was gentle, shallow breathing.

'I wondered about that at first,' she said through her hands, and then she sat up and looked at him. 'I waited for hours, way past when I should have been back home. Just in case you were late. And I would have come back day after day until I saw you. I wanted to believe you were coming.'

The look of exquisite sorrow in her eyes tugged at him. It felt as if she were pulling at a knot of string deep inside him, a knot that was just about to work itself loose. He refused to relax and let it unravel.

'I thought you knew me better than that, Jackie. If I'd got the letter, of course I would have come.'

She made a tiny little noise and he couldn't tell whether it was a laugh or a snort. 'And you would have done…what?'

'I don't know.' He frowned. 'We would have worked something out.'

Jackie stopped staring straight ahead and turned her whole body towards him. 'You're not saying that you would have stood by me?'

'Yes.'

'No!' She blinked furiously. She spoke again, softer this time. 'No.'

'You can't know that!'

He would have stood by her. He would have. At least that was what the man he was now wished he would have done.

'Think about this, Romano! You're saying you would have wanted to keep her, that you would have put a ring on my finger and we have had our own little teenage Happy Ever After?'

He looked deep inside himself, saw a glimmer of something he'd hoped he'd find. 'Maybe.'

Instead of her laughing in his face, Jackie's eyes filled with tears, but she didn't let a single one fall, not even as her hands shook in her lap. 'Don't be ridiculous. You're just daydreaming.'

He jumped up, started pacing. All this sitting around, keeping everything in, was far too British for him. He needed to move, to vent.

'Is that so hard to believe? Am I that much of a disappointment?'

Jackie opened her mouth to answer, but there was a sudden rustling and the sound of voices further up the path. Without thinking about how or why—maybe it had been the memories of all that sneaking around in the past—Romano grabbed Jackie by the arm and manhandled her into the shelter of the grotto, silencing her protests with a stern look. This was one conversation neither of them wanted to have overheard.

He was close to her again now, pressed up against her, her back against the wall of the grotto. If they stayed in exactly this position they couldn't be seen from most of the sunken garden. She was rigid, all of the soft sighing, the moulding into his arms, over and done with. Just as well. Any desire to *fling* with Jackie Patterson had completely evaporated.

But how much worse would it have been if she'd told him afterwards? She'd been right to put a stop to what had been going on. However, that one small mercy in no way balanced out her other sins.

'It's Lizzie and Jack,' she mouthed at him, obviously recognising the voices.

He nodded and tilted his head just a little to get a better view, hoping that the happy couple weren't looking in his direction. He was lucky. Bride and groom were too wrapped up in each other to spot an inconsistency in the shadows at the far end of the garden.

Lizzie laid her head against Jack's shoulder and let out a loud sigh. He stroked her back, kissed her hair. Romano and Jackie weren't the only ones who had needed a bit of fresh air. He hoped, however, that the newly-weds' walk was going to turn out better than his had done.

Jack and Lizzie wandered briefly round the sunken garden, hand-in-hand, stopping every now and then to kiss, before moving on down the path towards the small beach.

Romano stepped out of the grotto as they disappeared out of view and stayed there, staring at the spot where he'd last seen a flash of white dress.

They seemed so happy.

From his short observation of the bride and groom, they were a wonderful complement for each other. They had so much to look forward to: their honeymoon, starting a new life together, raising the twins Lizzie was carrying and building their own little family.

He realised he was outrageously jealous, which surprised him. He'd never expected to want all of that. He'd got on quite well since the death of his mother without feeling part of a traditional family, and he'd never guessed he'd harboured a longing for it, preferring to keep his relationships light, his ties loose.

How ironic. He could have had it all along. *He* could have been the man in the morning suit looking captivated by his fresh-faced bride. *He* could have been the one looking forward to seeing his child born, to rocking her when she cried and, when she was older, scaring the monsters away from under her bed. But now, when he realised how much he wanted those things, those moments were gone, never to be salvaged.

They'd been stolen from him by the woman steadying herself against the grotto wall with wide-spread hands, looking as much like an out-of-her-depth teenager as he'd ever seen her.

The sight drew no pity from him. He wouldn't allow it. Instead he looked away.

Marry her? Have a Happy Ever After with her? Right at this moment it was the last thing he wanted to do. In fact if he never saw her again he'd be ecstatic. But that wasn't an option. She was his sole link to his daughter. A daughter he could still hardly believe existed.

He spoke without looking at Jackie. 'What's her name?'

'Kate,' she said blandly.

Kate. Very English. Probably not what he would have chosen, given the chance. But he hadn't been given the chance—that was the point. He wanted to shout, to punch, to...do *something* to rid himself of this horrible assault of feelings. Normally he could bat negative things away, dissolve them with a joke or distract himself—usually with something female and pretty—but this just wouldn't go away and he didn't know how to handle it.

Facts. Stick to facts.

'Kate,' he echoed. 'Short for Katharine?'

She didn't answer. He let out a rough sigh. How could she still be playing games with him after what she'd revealed? How did she have the gall to make him work for the answers?

Because she's Jackie. She sets tests. You have to prove yourself to her over and over and even then she'll never believe you.

He swivelled round and looked her in the eyes, knowing that the lava inside was bubbling hard, even though he was desperately trying to keep a lid on it. Instead he let its heat radiate in his stare, let it insist upon an answer.

She swallowed. 'I suppose so. I'm not sure.'

Was a straight yes or no so hard to come by? Suddenly, it

was all too much for him. He couldn't do this now. He needed time to think, to breathe. One more of her cryptic answers and he was going to lose it completely.

'Fine. If that's the way you want to play it, I'll go.'

She looked shocked at that. He didn't care why.

'But don't think you've heard the end of this,' he added. 'You owe me more. And you can start paying tomorrow with answers. Facts. Details. Call them what you want, but I will have them.'

Jackie got over her surprise and pushed herself away from the wall of her grotto with her hands so she was standing straight. She fixed him with that flesh-melting stare he remembered so well. He refused to acknowledge the ripple of heat that passed over him in response.

'Don't you dare act all high and mighty about this, Signor Puccini! You and I both know you weren't ready for fidelity and commitment back then.'

That lid he'd been trying to keep tightly on? It popped.

But he was aware Lizzie and Jack might well still be within earshot and he didn't have the luxury of using the volume he would have liked to. He did the next best thing and dropped his voice to a rasping whisper.

'You have no right to judge me. No right at all. You don't know what I would have done, how I might have reacted. Who do you think you are?'

Jackie marched out of the grotto and for a moment he thought she was going to leave him standing there, all his anger unspent, but she got halfway up the garden and then turned back and strode towards him.

Of course. She always had to have the last word. Well, let her. It still wouldn't make what she'd done right.

'Who do I think I am? I'll tell you who I think I am!' Her face twisted into something resembling a smile. 'I'm the poor, pathetic girl who waited at the farmhouse all afternoon for you, scared out of her wits, feeling alone and overwhelmed.'

She wasn't making any sense.

'You know I didn't get your letter,' he said. 'You can't blame that on me.'

She took her time before she answered, her eyes narrowing, faint glimmer of victory glittering there. 'I saw you, Romano, that afternoon.'

Saw him? What was she talking about? He'd thought the whole point had been that he *hadn't* turned up.

'When I finally gave up waiting, I walked back up the track towards the main road, and that was when I saw you.' She waited for him to guess the significance of her statement, but all he could do was shrug. 'I saw you drive past on your Vespa with…*her*. With Francesca Gambardi!'

Ah.

He'd forgotten about that.

So that was the afternoon he'd finally given in to Francesca's pestering, had agreed to take her out on his *bella moto,* as she'd called it, because he'd hoped her presence would make him forget the crater Jackie had left behind when he'd finally got the message she'd wanted nothing more to do with him.

It hadn't been one of his finest moments. Or one of his best ideas.

And it hadn't worked. Francesca hadn't been enough of a distraction. Every time she'd looked at him, every time she'd brushed up against him, he'd only been plagued by the feeling that everything had been all wrong, that it should have been Jackie with her arms around his waist as they whipped through the countryside, that it should have been Jackie sidling up to him as they'd stopped to look at a pretty view. In the end, he'd taken Francesca home without so much as a kiss. A first for him in those days.

Jackie was way off base, thinking he'd had something going with Francesca, but he remembered how insecure, how jealous she'd been of the other girl, and he knew how it must have looked to her. But if she'd only asked, only would have deigned to talk to him, she would have known the truth. He'd acted foolishly, yes, but she hadn't behaved with any more maturity.

'And that was why you didn't bother telling me you were carrying my child? Because you saw me with another girl on the back of my Vespa? Jackie, that's a pathetic excuse.'

The smug look evaporated and she looked as if she'd been slapped across the face with the truth of his statement. Her jaw tensed. It didn't take her long to regroup and counter-attack.

'But I thought you'd read my letter, remember? I thought you knew I was pregnant, that I was waiting for you to discuss our future. And when you rode past the farmhouse—our special place—with that girl pressing herself up against you...well, it sent a message loud and clear.'

Okay, things might not be as black and white as he'd thought.

It was all so complicated, so hard to keep track of who knew what and when. Jackie had always been hot-headed and quick to judge and while he didn't like her reaction to the situation he could understand it, understand it was the only way she could have acted in that moment. What he didn't understand was why that one, unlucky coincidence, when he'd driven past with Francesca, had decided everything, had defined both their futures.

'But you didn't think to ask me? To find out for sure? Maybe not right then, when you were still angry, but what about the next month or the one after that? What about when the baby was born, or when you registered her? On her first birthday? On *any* of her birthdays? Hasn't she asked questions? Doesn't she want to know?'

Jackie just stared at him.

Maybe his daughter took after her mother. Maybe Jackie had brought her up to be as hard and self-obsessed as she was. Unfortunately he could imagine it all too easily. The elegant flat in one of the classier parts of London, the two of them being very sophisticated together, eating out, going to fashion shows. What he couldn't imagine was them laughing, making daisy chains or having fun.

He sighed. Jackie had always been such hard work, had always kept him on his toes. What would it be like if he had two such women to placate? It would leave him breathless.

He'd drifted off, almost forgotten Jackie was there. Her voice pulled him out of his daydream…nightmare…whatever.

'I did think of you when she was born, in the days following…' She paused, made a strange hiccupping noise. 'And don't think that every birthday wasn't torture, because it was. But by then it was too late. It had already been done. And I wouldn't have turned back time if I could have done. It would have been selfish and wrong.'

His first reaction was to stoke his anger—she was talking in riddles again—but the weighty sorrow that had settled on her, making her shoulders droop, diluted his rage with curiosity.

'What do you mean "it was too late"?'

Jackie looked up, puzzled. 'She'd gone to her new family—the people who adopted her.'

The words didn't sink in at first. He heard the sounds, even knew what they represented, but, somehow, they still didn't make sense. He walked away from her, back towards the grotto and stuck his hand—shirtsleeves and all—into one of the chilly black pools, just because he needed something physical, something to shock his body and brain into reacting.

It worked all right. Suddenly his brain was alive with responses. Unfortunately, the temperature of the water had done nothing to cool his temper. He flicked the water off with his hands and dried them on the back of his beautifully crafted, mortgage-worthy suit.

'You're telling me that, rather than raise our daughter yourself, rather than telling me—her father—of her existence, that you gave her away to *strangers*? Like she was something disposable?'

He marched up to her, grabbed her by the shoulders.

'Is that what it was like, Jackie? She didn't fit into your nice, ordered plans for your life, so you just put her out of sight…out of mind?'

Jackie's jaw moved, but no sound came out. She had gone white. And then she wrenched herself free and stumbled out of the garden on her high heels, gaining speed with every step.

For a man who lived his life in the shallows, Romano experienced the unfamiliar feeling of knowing he'd gone too deep, said too much, and he didn't know how to deal with that. There wasn't a quip, a smart remark, that could save the situation. He was in open water and land was nowhere in sight.

Jackie had disappeared along the path and into the small patch of woodland that hid the sunken garden from the island's shore.

The path. The one that led down to the beach.

Oh, hell.

He sprinted after her, even though he couldn't rationalise why stopping her from bumping into Jack and Lizzie was so important. In his mind she deserved all she got. He told himself he was speeding after her to stop her putting a huge dampener on the wedding and ignored the pity that twinged in him every time he thought of how much she would hate anyone—especially her adored older sister—to see her in such a mess.

It didn't take long to catch her up, only twenty steps away from where the trees parted and she would have a full view of the shingle beach.

'Jackie!' It wasn't quite a shout, wasn't quite a whisper, but a strange combination of the two.

She faltered but didn't alter her course. He was closer now and put a restraining hand on her arm, spoke in a low voice. 'Not that way.'

All of her back muscles tensed and he just knew she was getting ready to let rip, but then they heard a rumble of low laughter from the direction of the water's edge and she jolted in surprise.

'This way,' he said, as quietly as possible, and led her through the trees in the opposite direction, heading for the narrow tip of the island, away from the house, where they would be less likely to be disturbed by wandering wedding guests. They reached a clearing with a soft grassy bank and she just seemed to lose the ability to keep her joints locked. Her knees folded under her and she sat down on the grass with a thud.

'It wasn't like that at all,' she said, enunciating each word carefully. 'You don't know…'

It took Romano a couple of seconds to realise she was continuing the conversation she'd walked out on as if no time had passed. And that wasn't the only strange thing that had happened. He no longer wanted to erupt. He didn't know why. Maybe he'd experienced so many strong emotions in the last half-hour that he'd just run out, had none left. He sat down beside her.

'So tell me what it *was* like.'

He knew his request didn't sound exactly friendly, but it was the best he could do under the circumstances.

She kicked off her shoes and sank her bare feet into the grass. Even the shade of her toenails complemented her outfit. So *Jackie*…

She hugged her legs, drew them up until she was almost in a little ball, and rested her cheek on her knees. Her face was turned in his direction, but her eyes were glazed and unfocused.

'I wanted to believe you'd come,' she said in a voice that reminded him of a little girl's. 'I wanted to believe that it would all turn out right, but I truly didn't think it was ever going to happen.'

Another nail in the coffin. Another confirmation from her

that he was a loser. He ought to get angry again, but there was something in her voice, her face, that totally arrested him.

Honesty. Pure and unguarded.

It was such a rare commodity where Jackie was concerned that he decided not to do anything to scare it away. He needed answers and she was the only one who could provide them.

'Mamma was so cross when I told her I was pregnant that I thought she was going to break something.'

One corner of his mouth lifted. Yes, he could well imagine the scene. It wouldn't have been pretty.

'She insisted that adoption was the only way. How could I argue with her? I couldn't do it on my own.'

'What about your father?'

She snorted. 'He might be a blue-sky-thinking entrepreneur, but he's smart enough to do what Mamma tells him to do.' She blinked, looked across at him as she lifted her lashes again. 'I don't think he knew what to do with me. He's good with big ideas and balance sheets, but not so great with the people stuff. I think he wanted the problem to just go away. It was as much as he could manage just to let me go and live with him until the baby was born.'

Romano didn't say anything. He'd always thought of Jackie as being just like him—a child of a wealthy family, secure in the knowledge of her place in the world. He'd even envied her the sisters and the multitude of cousins compared to his one-parent, no-cousin family. His father hadn't been perfect, but he'd always shown him love, and that had made Romano too sure, too cocky, when he'd been young, but he realised that Jackie had never had that.

One loving parent—however unique he might be—had to be better than two clueless ones. His father would never have forced him to do what Jackie's parents had made her do. Yes, her mother had been the driving force, but her father had to take responsibility too. He'd let her down by omitting to stand up for her, to fight for her, to do anything he could to make her happy. That was what fathers were supposed to do.

That was what *he* was supposed to do now.

Jackie lifted her head from her knees. 'Once I was too big to keep it a secret any more, Mamma packed me off to London to live with Dad, and you know what?' She rubbed her eyes with the heels of her hands and took a long gulp of air.

'What?' he said softly. No longer was he trying just to keep her talking, aiming to get dates and times and details from her. He really wanted to know.

'When I went to live with him, he never even mentioned my pregnancy, even though I was swelling up in front of his face. He just…ignored it. It was so weird.' She shook her head. 'And when I came home from the hospital without…on my own…the only emotion he showed was relief.'

She hugged her knees even tighter and rested her chin on top of them. He could see her jaw clenching and unclenching, as if there were unsaid words, words she'd wanted to say to her father for years, but never had.

She'd been so young. And so alone.

He didn't have a heart of stone. He would have been a monster if he couldn't have imagined how awful it must have been for her. And she'd only told him bare details.

There wasn't anything he could say to change that, to make it better. For a long time they sat in silence.

'What was it like?' he finally said. 'The day she was born?'

Jackie frowned. 'It rained.'

He didn't push for more, sensing that the answer he wanted was coming, he just needed to give her room. The sun had started to set while they'd been in the clearing and, through the trees, the sky was turning bright turquoise at the horizon, and the ripples on the lake glinted soft gold. The temperature must have dropped a little, because Jackie shivered.

Not a monster, he reminded himself, and pulled his jacket

off and draped it around her shoulders. The sleeves hung use-
lessly by her sides.

When she spoke again, she went on to describe a long,
complicated labour that had ended in a distressed baby and
an emergency Caesarean section. All the half-formed ideas
of cute newborns sliding easily into the world were blown
right out of the water. Real birth, it seemed, was every bit
as traumatic as real life. And she'd done it all on her own,
her father away on a business trip and her mother still in
Italy keeping up at the façade, lest anyone suspect their
family's disgrace.

'What was she like? Kate?'

Jackie's face softened in a way he hadn't thought possible.
'She was perfect. So tiny. With a shock of dark hair just like
yours and a temper just like mine.'

He wanted to smile but he felt strangely breathless.

A single tear ran down her cheek. 'She's amazing,
Romano. Just so…amazing.'

He sat up a little straighter. 'You've met her?'

She nodded. 'She started looking for me a few months ago
and we've been meeting up, trying to establish a bond.' She
pulled a face. 'It's not been going very well.'

Well, if she had Jackie's temper, that was hardly surprising.

He watched Jackie as she stared out into the gathering
dusk, not sure he'd ever seen her like this before, with all the
armour plating stripped away.

'I was going to tell my family after the wedding,' she said.
'She wants to meet them, find out where she comes from. And
then Scarlett told me about the letter and I realised I had to
tell you too—tell you first. But I was going to do it after
today, to avoid all…this.'

You stupid fool, he told himself. All this time you thought
she was coming on to you and all she was doing was paving
the way for the truth to come out.

'What are we going to do?' she said, with equal measures of fear and uncertainty in her eyes.

He stood up and offered her his hand. She took it, and he pulled her to her feet and waited while she slid her feet back in her shoes.

He stared at a cluster of trees, looking for answers.

Honesty deserved honesty.

'I don't know,' he said, 'but it's time we went back to the party and faced everybody.'

CHAPTER EIGHT

JACKIE felt as if her skin were too thick, as if sensations from the outside world couldn't quite get through. She was floating and heavy all at the same time. The details of the walk back towards the terrace were fuzzy; she didn't remember which path they took, or any of the sights and sounds. Just before they emerged from the trees and into the open, she stopped, pulled at Romano's shirtsleeve.

'Here. You'd better have this back.'

She started to slide his jacket from her shoulders, but he hooked the collar with a finger and pulled it back up. 'Keep it. You look cold.'

She *was* cold. Ever since Romano had said those things to her in the grotto, she hadn't been able to ignore the shivering deep, deep inside. Sometimes it worked its way outwards and she had to clench her teeth to stop them rattling, but it all felt a little disconnected from her, as if it were happening to someone else.

'But—'

'What's the point, Jackie?'

'I…'

She didn't know. Just that it seemed the right thing to do, to hide the fact she'd been in the garden with Romano. The need to keep everything about their relationship under the radar had become a habit she'd never thought to break.

'We don't have to keep it a secret that we went for a walk in the garden,' he said, taking her by the hand and leading her forwards. 'Who cares if anyone sees us together? Your family will know all there is to know soon.'

Jackie nodded, because she recognised the need for response of some kind. Her brain wasn't working fast enough to keep up. Romano's words seemed to make sense. Why hadn't she thought about this before? Somehow in the confusion of recent days she hadn't connected the fact that telling her family also meant that they would know about Romano, that they would all know the secrets she had kept to herself for seventeen years.

Seventeen years.

That was more than half of her life. She'd hated Romano, believed him to be heartless and superficial, for all that time. But now the truth was out. Her secret had been revealed. Wasn't she supposed to feel free? Lighter? But she was too numb to feel anything but the pressure of Romano's fingers on her hand and the warmth spreading all the way up her arm.

In their absence the party had spilled outside. The tall glazed doors that led from the ballroom onto the patio had been thrown open and guests were wandering through the upper terraces, champagne flutes in hands. The large paved area where she and Romano had lunched the other day had been cleared of furniture and planters, and a swing band played while couples danced.

She tugged on Romano's hand, not really knowing why. Just that she didn't want to throw herself headlong back into the party. She didn't know what to do now, how to behave. How could she just go and rejoin her family as if nothing had happened?

He squeezed her fingers lightly and nodded towards the palazzo.

Good idea. Perhaps there was somewhere quiet inside where she could sit and recover.

Despite the fact she was still wearing his jacket, nobody took any notice of them as they weaved their way through the neatly clipped bushes. Romano walked slightly ahead, his face serious but not forbidding.

He'd surprised her by taking her news incredibly well. Too well—he was handling it much better than she was, even though she'd had more time to adjust to recent revelations. Under normal circumstances, doing better than Jackie Patterson at anything simply wasn't allowed, but at this moment she was heartily relieved.

They were only a matter of steps from one of the entrances to the ballroom when she spotted her mother inside, heading their way. Jackie suddenly veered in another direction, following the curve of one of the low hedges. Their hands were still joined and she took Romano with her. He let out a grunt of surprise, then muttered something about quick thinking. Jackie was looking directly ahead but with all her attention behind her as she strained to pick out her mother's footsteps, as she waited to hear her name in that shrill voice.

Just as they reached the edge of the dance floor it came.

'Jackie?'

She kept going. There was no way that she could deal with her mother in her present state. The only fireworks planned for this evening were the ones that Jack and Lizzie had arranged, and she'd very much like to keep it that way.

'Jacqueline!'

She should have known that she'd need a more sophisticated plan than just trying to outrun Mamma.

'Sorry, Lisa,' she heard Romano say beside her as he slipped his jacket off her shoulders and pulled it away. Jackie didn't see how he disposed of it. '*Jacqueline* promised me a dance. You don't mind, do you?'

And then he took her in his arms and spun her away. When the motion had taken her one hundred and eighty degrees and they were disappearing into the crowd, she looked back to see her mother standing there, holding Romano's jacket, with her mouth open.

'I can't believe you just did that!'

Romano smiled his twinkly smile. 'What was it that you called me? Incorrigible?'

A soft laugh escaped her lips. 'I never thought I would say this, but I'm very glad that you are.'

He turned again with some nimble footwork and her mother disappeared from view.

'Glad to know I have a redeeming feature,' he said softly so only she could hear. 'I've been trying very hard to develop one.'

She smiled and laid her head against his shoulder. It hadn't been a conscious decision, but something she'd done on autopilot. How strange that after all this time being in Romano's arms felt as easy and comfortable as it always had done. She really ought to put some distance between them, try to maintain a little bit of self-respect, but she couldn't quite bring herself to reverse her mistake. It was too much of an effort to pull away from him and balance on her own two feet again.

Romano wasn't helping. He slid his arms around her waist and pulled her close, rested his cheek against her temple.

The song changed. In fact it might have changed more than once, but Jackie didn't notice. She just moved side-to-side, round-and-round, enjoying the luxury of having someone to lean on, if only for a few snatched moments. She'd spent her whole life making sure she stood high and lonely on her self-created pedestal, and now she realised that it had left her unspeakably tired.

Romano didn't say anything as they danced; he just held her. There was something wonderfully comforting about a man who knew how to be strong, solid…still. They silently danced like that for what seemed like hours and she was grateful for the chance to have time to absorb and assimilate the afternoon's events.

She tried to pack it all away neatly in her brain, but one question refused to be properly silenced and stowed.

Why hadn't she made more of an effort to talk to Romano about the fact they were bringing a new life into the world? Just one attempt in all that time seemed juvenile. Had she really believed him to be the villain of the piece, an evil seducer of young girls, who cared for no one but himself and never faced the consequences of his actions?

Yes and no.

She'd believed it because she'd needed to believe it. Not believing that had been far too dangerous an option. Hatred had helped her shut the door on him, pull up the drawbridge and keep herself safe. Second chances would have meant giving him access, giving him the opportunity to hurt her all over again, and she couldn't have had that, because any further rejection would have involved Kate too. Self-righteous anger had been the path of least resistance—the coward's way out. She'd taken it without a second thought, without even really understanding her own motivations or the long-term consequences.

But you were fifteen…

No excuse.

She'd been old enough to make a baby and that meant she'd needed to accept the responsibility that went with it. And despite her best efforts she'd failed, had chosen a course of action she wasn't sure now had been the right one.

Could she have made a go of it with Romano?

The truth was she'd never know. They might have survived. They might have been awful teenage parents—children trying to bring up a child of their own. Perhaps it was better for Kate that her adoptive parents had been so stable and sensible. They obviously loved her a great deal.

More than you?

She shut her eyes against that thought. Whichever way she answered it, it made her stomach bottom out.

'I think it's safe now.'

Jackie raised her head from Romano's shoulder. She felt so lethargic. 'Huh?'

'Your mother. She's gone. I think I saw her talking to your uncle.'

Well, that didn't make sense. Mamma and Uncle Luca were hardly on chatting terms.

Romano stopped moving and Jackie looked up at him. 'That means we can stop now,' he said, looking down at her.

Was it wrong that she didn't want to stop? That she wanted to stay here, warm in his arms, and not have to face the world again?

She knew the answer to that one.

Of course it was wrong. It was weak. She let her hands slide from where they'd been resting against his chest and stepped back. All the easy warmth that had flowed between them suddenly evaporated. She didn't know what to say, how to leave gracefully.

In the end she decided to do what she did best and attack the practical angle. Inter-personal stuff was so much harder. She brushed herself down, straightened her hair. 'I think we should talk tomorrow, once we've both had time to think.'

Romano gave her an odd look. 'I agree,' he said slowly. 'Jackie? Are you okay?'

She straightened her shoulders. 'I'm fine. Just tired. You know…'

His mouth creased into a sort of combined grimace and smile. 'I will call you in the morning.' And then he nodded once and walked away.

Jackie blinked. What had she done to Romano? He'd lost all his charm and polish. She'd never seen him take leave of a woman without kissing her on the cheek, or saying something witty to make her laugh and then watch him as he walked away.

Jackie decided to find somewhere quiet to sit and fend off the migraine she felt developing before it took hold.

As she made her way through the wedding guests in the ballroom, heading for one of the smaller rooms, she spotted her mother and Uncle Luca deep in conversation, just as Romano had said. She passed behind her mother, but stayed out of her peripheral vision so she could slip by unnoticed. As she did so she caught a snatch of their conversation.

'I appreciate your honesty,' her uncle was saying.

She heard that little intake of breath her mother made when she was finding a subject difficult. 'I mean it, Luca. I am truly sorry I ruined your birthday dinner by causing a scene. It was extremely bad manners.'

Jackie paused, hovering on the balls of her feet. She'd heard all about her mother's outburst from Lizzie—how Mamma and Luca had got into a terrible fight and then she had told the whole of his unsuspecting family of the twin half-brothers they'd never known had existed. What was it with this family? Surely life would have been much easier for them all if they could have put their pride aside and just accepted each other, *loved* each other. Wasn't that what families were supposed to do?

And then her mother's words actually registered.

Holy…something or other. Had her mother just apologised? Wonders would never cease! Or maybe it was just the prosecco talking. Mamma had knocked plenty back this afternoon.

'What's done is done,' Luca said, his palms upturned in a gesture of resignation. 'I didn't like the way the news came out, but it was well past time for my family to know about

Alessandro and Angelo. It needed to be said. There are too many secrets in this family.'

Jackie wanted to laugh out loud. You don't know the half of it!

But you should. You all should.

Jackie filled her lungs with air and moved slightly to the left so her uncle could see her, but he was too deep in conversation to register her presence at first.

'How can we be strong as a family if we are splintered like this?' he said, taking Lisa's hands in his. 'It's time to put the old grudges to sleep, time to stop the fighting.'

Her mother sighed. 'We've been warring for so long that sometimes I forget how it all started.'

Uncle Luca laughed and kissed her on the cheek, much to her mother's surprise. 'We have war, yes, but that is because we have passion. Let us use that to build rather than to destroy.'

Jackie smiled. Uncle Luca always did get very flowery with his speech when he'd had a few.

'It is a new era,' he added. 'Valentino and Cristiano and Isabella now know about their brothers and I am feeling the need to mend things instead of fortifying them. There is a subtle difference, you know.'

Much to her surprise, her mother nodded. 'I know. Having my girls together again has me feeling that way too, even if I am not convinced we can learn to do things differently. There are some wounds that just don't want to heal, no matter how well we bandage them up.'

Uncle Luca shrugged. 'We can but try.'

Her mother gave the smallest of nods and began to look around. This was Jackie's cue to scuttle away before she was noticed, but she did the unthinkable and took a step forward to stand beside her uncle, putting herself right in the firing line. Uncle Luca gave her a kiss and hug.

'Beautiful as always, *piccolo.*'

She smiled and shook her head. 'Uncle Luca, you're full of it, but I love you anyway.'

'We've been talking about family,' he said. 'Talking about coming together, all Rosa Firenzi's children and grandchildren—as it should be. We need to unearth the roots of the secrets that have grown within us and choked us.'

There he went again. But this time Jackie didn't smile. There was too much truth in what he said.

'I agree,' she said, and turned to face her mother. 'And in this new spirit of unity and openness, I have something I really need to tell you.'

Even though Jackie slept hard and deep that night, she still woke up feeling as if she'd been clubbed about the head with a cricket bat. She crawled downstairs and found Scarlett in the kitchen.

'You're looking fabulous this morning,' Scarlett said with a broad smile on her face.

Jackie just grunted. As always, Scarlett was looking perfect. 'I told Mamma,' she added, by way of explanation.

Scarlett grimaced. 'And you survived? How did you manage that?'

'I don't know,' she replied, shaking her head slightly. 'It wasn't at all what I'd expected. She was very calm, which was worrying, because either she's had a complete personality transplant or it means there's going to be a delayed reaction.'

'Good luck with that.'

'Thanks.' Jackie walked over to the coffee machine and kept her voice matter-of-fact. 'And I told Romano.'

Her sister didn't say anything.

'Sorry,' Scarlett said from behind her. 'But I thought you just said you'd told Romano.'

Jackie turned round. 'I did. Yesterday. At the wedding.'

'At the…? Wow!'

Jackie nodded. 'I know. I hadn't planned on it, but it was the only way to stop him…never mind.'

Scarlett's eyebrows had almost disappeared into her hairline. 'Oh, really?'

'Let's not go there,' Jackie said, trying her best to make her cheeks cool down. 'Let's just say that things took an…interesting…turn. I hadn't planned on letting it all out on Lizzie's wedding day, but situations arose that warranted full disclosure.'

Scarlett burst out laughing.

'What?' Jackie said, a little cross after her great efforts to remain dignified about the whole thing.

'Just listen to yourself!' Scarlett said. 'As soon as anything becomes remotely emotional, you start getting all wordy and businesslike. You're just like—'

'Don't you dare say it!'

But it was too late. The word had slipped out while Jackie had been ranting.

'—Mamma,' Scarlett finished.

'I am nothing like Mamma. You're the one who looks most like her.' Jackie countered.

Scarlett shrugged. 'What can I say? I've come to terms with the similarities between us. Doesn't mean I like it, but at least I'm not in denial.'

Jackie steadied herself by taking a sip of coffee. 'Don't be ridiculous!' she muttered. 'I'm nowhere near being in denial—about that or anything else.'

'Darling,' Scarlett said before sauntering out of the room, 'denial is your middle name.'

'Rubbish!' Jackie called out after her. 'You haven't a clue what you're talking about.'

She couldn't have.

Jackie wasn't wrong about this. She was rarely wrong about anything.

Oh, yes? Or is it just that you've made sure that you're top of the heap, that yours are the opinions that count, so you never have to deal with being wrong? It's too difficult.

Rubbish, she repeated to herself. One mistake. That was all she'd made in her life. Sleeping with Romano when she hadn't been old enough for that kind of relationship. Okay, and there was the letter. She should have talked to Romano herself. She'd been big enough to admit that to herself—and him—already. And, of course, there was the whole thing about her not getting in contact with him ever since. She knew that was wrong now.

See? Scarlett didn't know what she was talking about. She was capable of admitting her mistakes. She'd just unearthed an extra two. Denial? Hah!

She'd matured since she'd met Kate again. She was ready to turn around and face the past she'd been running away from for so long. That didn't sound much like denial, did it?

What about Romano?

What about Romano? she asked herself in a haughty tone. Things are going well there, too. He hasn't disowned Kate. Early days, but it's all good.

What about how you feel about him?

She closed her eyes, but the question just reverberated round the inside of her head, so she opened them again. I don't love him, she told herself. I'm attracted to him, yes, I can admit that, but that's all there is to it.

See? No denial at all. She was being brutally honest with herself.

But that attraction wasn't a factor in her plan. The only relationship she wanted with Romano was as co-parent. No time for distractions or repeating any of the silliness of yesteryear. They would have to work as a team, think up strategies, come up with a plan for blending their lives with Kate's seamlessly.

You're getting all wordy and businesslike again.
Oh, shut up, she told herself.

The only place they could think to meet nearby where they wouldn't be interrupted was the old farmhouse. Jackie drove her rental car as far up the dirt track as it would go, then walked the rest of the way.

On the surface, it was exactly the same. But then she looked more closely. The olive trees looked even knottier and had grown tall and spindly. Some had fallen or been damaged in storms or high winds and had never been repaired or cleared away. The roof of the farmhouse had almost gone completely and every window was broken. In the cracks in the masonry, weeds and wild flowers had found sanctuary and were busy pushing the stones apart as they anchored themselves better.

She found Romano sitting on the low step by the front door. He was looking at the ground, shoulders hunched, his elbows rested on his knees and his hands hanging limp between his bent legs.

She'd always thought Romano untouchable, capable of dissolving anything negative with a wink or a dry comment, but he looked...broken.

She'd done this.

Why hadn't she tried harder, told him sooner? It all seemed so stupid now, her reasons—her justifications—for keeping their lives separate. She hadn't been thinking of Kate at all, even though that had been a big part of her rationalisation. She'd been selfish, keeping herself protected and pretending she was being altruistic.

But you were fift—
No. No more excuses. You were wrong. Live with it.
'Romano?'
He looked up, smiled. But the eyes didn't twinkle the way they ought to. They were cold and grey and still.

'I want to meet her.'

Jackie nodded and sat down next to him on the step, mirroring his pose. 'Of course you do.'

Of course he did. Why had she expected anything else? This was Romano. Didn't she remember what he was like? Yes, he was full of froth and bluster, but underneath there was so much more. The boy she'd known had carefully hidden his softer, more sensitive side from the world, but he'd revealed all of it to her. Yet she'd only chosen to remember the surface. The lie.

And she knew all about lies. For the first time, she wondered why Romano stuck with his, why he persisted in letting everyone think he was shallow, feckless. Even in a few short days she could see that he'd surpassed the man she'd hoped he'd become. Oh, he'd never lose that infuriating charm—and she wasn't sure she'd want him to—but he was honest and caring, committed and trustworthy. A man worth knowing. A man worth—

No. Co-parents, remember? Focus, Jacqueline.

'When? I'll have to talk to her parents—'

'*We're* her parents.'

He sounded cross. She could understand that.

'I know. But this is complicated.'

He looked across at her, one eyebrow raised. She put her hands up in the air, palms out.

'Yes…okay! *I* made it complicated. I accept that.'

Romano snorted, the kind of snort that said: *What's new…?*

'But it doesn't change anything,' she added. 'We'll have to tread carefully.'

Romano stood up and walked away. 'To hell with treading carefully.'

'For Kate,' she added softly. 'Don't do it for me. Do it for her.'

He turned and nodded, and his expression softened a tad. 'Okay. For Kate.'

He walked back towards her and offered her a hand. Jackie

looked at it. He'd done the same many times before. Then she looked at the half-dilapidated farmhouse and the neglected olive grove. Some things could never be the same. She mouthed her thanks, but pushed herself up on her own. He shoved his hand in his jeans pocket.

'I have booked us flights back to London in the morning.'

Jackie's eyes bulged. Tomorrow?

'That's too soon! I need to talk to Sue—her adoptive mother. I thought we said—'

'And I agreed,' he said, his brows bunching together. 'But if I have to wait, I would rather be in London.'

She could understand that too.

'Okay.' She exhaled. It seemed to have been an awfully long time since she'd done that. 'What time do we fly?'

CHAPTER NINE

THE sun drifted softly between the leaves of the olive tree Jackie was propped up against and tickled her cheeks. Her lashes fluttered and then she opened her eyes. It was a perfect afternoon. A gentle breeze flowed round her occasionally and she felt utterly relaxed.

'Hey there, sleeping beauty…'

She shifted against the warm body underneath and behind her and smiled gently. 'Yeah, right. If "beauty" means "the size of an elephant".'

He leaned forward, placed his hands, fingers spread wide, on the curved mound of her stomach. 'You're beautiful…both of you.'

She sank back into him and sighed. 'What did I do to deserve you?'

She waited for an answer, but none came. After a few minutes she realised she wasn't as comfortable, that something hard was sticking into her back, just below her left shoulder blade. She sat up, all the sleepy languor gone, and turned around. The only thing behind her was the twisted trunk of the ancient tree.

Carefully she hoisted herself to her feet, resting a hand on the trunk of the tree when things got dicey, when the seven months' worth of baby growing inside her made it too difficult.

'Romano?'

Nothing. She heard nothing save the sound of the clouds bumping by and the sun warming the dry grass in the meadow.

'Romano!' Louder now, with an edge of panic to her voice.

She began to run—well, waddle—as fast as she could, every step making her feel heavier and heavier. She called his name once more and listened for his reply.

Silence.

No…wait!

She could hear something. Just at the edges of her range of hearing, a familiar rumble…

A Vespa!

She began to half waddle, half run again, supporting her stomach underneath with splayed hands, searching, calling…

Soon it got dark and it began to rain. Not the warm, heavy drops of a summer storm, but cold, icy drizzle that chilled her skin and sank into her flesh. There were no meadows and olive trees now, only grey paving slabs and narrow brick alleyways. And the rain, always the rain. She began to shiver.

Where was he? Where had he gone?

She kept looking, no longer running, just loping along as best she could, putting one foot in front of the other, through dirty puddles and potholed backstreets. It seemed to take hours to find somewhere she recognised.

Did she know this street? The trees reminded her of the ones near her father's house, but the buildings were wrong— too small, too dirty. And not a single one had a light on.

Another shiver ran through her and she instinctively reached for her bump, a habit she'd developed in the last few months, a form of self-comfort.

But her fingers found nothing but fresh air.

Now she was grabbing at her stomach with both hands, but it was saggy…empty…the hard, round proof of the life inside her gone.

'No,' she whispered as her legs buckled under her. And then the whisper became a scream.

'No!'

Jackie, although her eyes were still closed, breathed in sharply and tensed. Romano lowered the paper he was reading and turned to watch her, lying rigid in the half-reclined seat.

'It's just turbulence,' he murmured, watching the movement below her closed lids and guessing she'd just woken up. 'The captain mentioned a while ago that the descent into Gatwick might be a bit bumpy.'

While he'd been talking she'd opened her eyes. She looked very sad, almost on the verge of tears.

'I'm sorry it hasn't been a smoother journey.'

Jackie nodded. And then she looked away, turned to the window.

Romano straightened in his seat and stared straight ahead. He sensed that Jackie was finding his smooth composure irritating. Even he was finding it irritating, but he didn't seem to be able to snap out of it. What was the alternative? Lose his temper? Have a breakdown? He would be meeting his daughter for the first time in a few days and the last thing he needed was to be a nervous wreck. What good would that do anyone?

On the other hand, he wasn't sure he wanted to be the same old, skating-on-the-surface Romano. He wanted to change, be better. Learning he'd been a father for the last sixteen years had caused him to look back on that time with fresh perspective.

He'd been successful professionally, yes. But the rest of his life? Full of ugly holes, a wasteland—which was odd, because he'd always thought he'd been having so much fun. Why had he never seen this desolation before?

Ah, but you saw it a long time ago. Jackie showed you.

He shifted in his seat and frowned.

But he'd done something about that, changed since then. He'd matured, hadn't he? He'd stopped living the life of a poor little rich kid and had learned how to work for a living.

Work. Is work life?

Oh. Now he got it. He'd channelled his newfound sense of responsibility into his professional life, but not much had spilled over into his private life. True to form, he'd been so shallow that it had taken him seventeen years to see that. And once again, it had been Jackie Patterson that had held the mirror up to his face.

He turned just his head, the leather of the headrest squeaking against his ear, and looked at her.

It was Jackie who had caused him to look deep inside himself as a teenager. At first he'd been horrified by the casual arrogance he'd seen, but she'd not let him stop there, she'd brought out the nobler virtues that had been rusting away in the dark—honesty, courage, love. Things he'd thought he had lost for ever after the death of his mother.

He'd cried right up until the funeral, but after that he'd become numb. When he'd thought of her, he'd been unable to produce a single tear. He'd been so upset about that he'd just stopped thinking of her, worried he was a bad person for not being able to feel anything more.

It had been a horribly short time before his father had started disappearing regularly, being photographed with one woman after another, but Romano hadn't judged him. He'd known that his father had adored his mother, and that this had just been his way of distracting himself from the grief he'd been too afraid to feel.

A cold churning began in his stomach, nothing to do with aeroplane food. *Like father, like son,* Lisa Firenzi had once said to him. She'd meant it as a compliment, but suddenly another layer of his life was ripped back, exposing the unflattering truth.

He'd let his guard down once, briefly—for Jackie—and when she'd walked away without a backward glance, so he'd thought, he'd done what he'd always done. Instead of asking himself why, of being brave enough to keep trying until he'd made her listen to him, he'd given up, run from those awful feelings of not being good enough to stay around for. And he'd kept himself busy with pretty young things like Francesca Gambardi, distracting himself.

He'd been seen out and about with the cream of the fashion world, A-list celebrities. Women who had everything. And yet he hadn't wanted *everything* from even one of them. Where Jackie had been high-maintenance, abrasive, complex, he'd chosen to date bland, interchangeable blondes who would sit at his feet and worship. No threat there. He'd been safe.

He'd also been incredibly bored.

At the time he'd told himself not to be so stupid, told himself he was reaching for a fantasy that didn't exist, and that he might as well enjoy the moment. Despite his best efforts, he'd never been able to convince himself he was in love.

Jackie sighed softly and pulled her seat belt a little tighter. The plane was rocking now as they descended through a thick layer of cloud. She glanced across at him and when she found him looking back at her she averted her gaze and pulled the duty-free magazine from the pocket on the back of the seat in front of her.

Only her.

He'd only ever loved one woman.

Did that mean she was the love of his life? The one he was fated to be with?

He let out a gentle huff of a laugh. His friends would never let him live it down if they knew he was thinking like this.

He really hoped he was wrong. If Jackie had been 'the one', then his chances of finding anything close to a fulfilling love life in the future with someone else were zero. And that was a scary thought. He couldn't live his life looking over his shoulder, believing his one chance was behind him, getting farther and farther away with each passing year. No wonder he'd not wanted to consider this before. It had been much more comfortable to pass her off as a fling and kid himself that the chance to have what his mother and father had had was still in his future.

She'd become a speck in the distance, a grain of sand that irritated and niggled now and then. Not any more. They were slap-bang in the middle of each other's lives now, joined for ever—but not in the naïve way they'd imagined when they'd been young and in love.

What did it mean? Was this a second chance or a cruel joke? He was slightly terrified by either option.

Getting involved with Jackie again would be…complicated. But if that wasn't his fate, it didn't seem fair that he'd been woken up to the truth only to make him ache for chances lost. He'd have preferred to stay happy and ignorant in the shallows if that were the case.

No. No, he wouldn't.

Somehow he knew the mix of emotions that was finally breaking through the crust of numbness was necessary. Kate didn't need a father who would only provide money, status and a million opportunities to have too much too soon. She needed a man who could be there for her, who could communicate his love without flashing his credit card. And he wanted to be that man.

Love.

Normally that word made him itchy.

But when he thought about the girl he was yet to meet, who didn't even know he existed, warmth flooded every vein and filled his chest to bursting point.

He loved his daughter. He always would. Strangely, the realisation didn't bring panic, but relief.

The captain announced it would be another twenty minutes

before they were able to land. A collective sigh of frustration travelled through the cabin.

Jackie held hers in.

She held everything in.

She felt very similar to how she did when a bee or a wasp was buzzing round her. She knew she needed to be still, calm, but the effort of doing so made her feel as if she were going to implode. Even in the wider business-class seats, she felt crowded. Romano was too close and she couldn't switch her awareness of him off, no matter how hard she tried to ignore it.

That stupid dream was lingering in her subconscious, flavouring the atmosphere, making her want things she shouldn't, ache for things that were impossible.

She'd dreamt about him every night for the last week, ever since he'd done up her zip and given her the tingles. Had that only been a week ago? She felt as if she'd aged a decade since then.

She turned that thought around and made it work for her.

Act your age, Jacqueline. You're a mature woman in control of your emotions. You're too old for silly fantasies and fairy tales. You've got to stay focused, strong. For Kate's sake.

Think of Kate.

She shifted her hips slightly under her seat belt and angled herself to face Romano. 'I got a text from Kate's adoptive mum, Sue, before we boarded. She was responding to the message I left.'

Romano looked completely relaxed, even with his feet planted squarely on the floor and his arms on the arm rests of his chair. Most people would look rigid in that pose, but Romano just looked as if he owned the world and was slightly bored with it. If there hadn't been a spark of interest in those grey eyes, she'd have wanted to slap him.

'Kate's finished all her exams,' she continued, 'so she doesn't have any school at the moment. Sue's going to see if she wants to meet up with me tomorrow, but she stressed it was totally up to Kate and she wasn't going to push it if Kate had other plans.'

Romano blinked and his lids stayed closed just a nanosecond longer than they needed to. 'What about me?'

Jackie cleared her throat, tried to make herself sound as neutral as possible. 'I think we need to minimise the shock factor.'

No, the overwhelming first meeting loaded with fears and expectations hadn't gone brilliantly for her and Kate. Too much pressure on them both. And it had set the tone for subsequent meetings, a tone that was doing its best not to fade away. She wanted to spare him that. After all she'd done, it was the least she owed him.

'What does that mean?'

'I don't think we should tell her straight away. I'll take her out for the day. You can come along, and she can get to know you a bit first.'

Romano still lounged in his seat, but there was something about the set of his shoulders now that gave him away. That spark in his eyes had turned cold.

'So…who do you introduce me as? Your boyfriend?' His eyebrow hitched ever so slightly, making an innocent suggestion sound all rakish and inappropriate. Jackie felt the familiar slap-or-kiss reflex and her cheeks got all hot and puffy. He was doing it on purpose, to get a rise out of her, making her pay for her unwanted suggestion.

'No. Of course not.'

'No,' he said, a dry half-smile on his lips. 'Stupid idea. Who would believe anything so…what do you always say? Ah, yes. *Ridiculous.*'

The eyebrow dropped and his mouth straightened as the ever-present lopsided quirk evaporated. Her breathing stalled for a heartbeat and then kicked in at double speed.

This man was the darling of the gossip mags for his seductive charm, his devil-may-care attitude but, when the devil *did* care, he was twice as devastating. Knowing this, seeing what everyone else usually missed, was what had got her into trouble the last time. She didn't want to see it now.

'What about us? What are *we*, Jackie?'

His voice was all soft and rumbly. Her throat suddenly needed moisture. She reached for the glass of water perched on the arm of her chair and then remembered that the stewardess had cleared it away.

'There is no *us*,' she managed to say after swallowing a few times.

His eyelids lowered a fraction; the shoulders bunched a little further. 'We have to have some kind of relationship,' he said. 'We have a daughter together.'

'I know that. Don't you think I know that?' She heard the shrewish tone in her voice and made herself breathe, consciously relaxed her vocal cords before she tried again. 'We're…co-parents. That's all.'

The infuriating smirk was back. 'That sounds very formal. This isn't a business merger. You know that too, yes?'

She folded her arms across her stomach. 'It's the best I could come up with,' she snapped. 'Stop making fun of me. This isn't easy for either of us, and you're taking this out on me by being all…by making me feel all…' She shook her head, gave a half-shrug. 'You know what you're doing, Romano.'

He dismissed the whole thing with a slight pout of the bottom lip and an imperious wave of the hands.

They both straightened in their seats and stared straight ahead. For the longest time, as the plane circled and circled, he didn't say anything then, just as the jet straightened and began to lower again, making her ears feel full and heavy, he spoke. His voice was quiet, all the bravado gone.

'Do you think she'll like me?'

With just that one question, walls inside Jackie that had been built and firmly cemented into place years ago crumbled like icing sugar. She'd never heard such self-doubt in his voice before, such sadness. It broke her heart.

She didn't have to force the smile that accompanied her next words. 'Of course she will.'

He looked across at her without moving his head much, just his eyes. That hooded, sideways glance reminded her so much of the boy who had made it his mission to be cool, no matter what. The boy she'd lost her head and her heart to. The air turned cold in her lungs.

'Everybody does,' she added, keeping the smile in place, even though her mouth wanted to quiver.

He broke the moment with a subtle shift of his features and she knew he had his mask back in place while hers was still sliding.

'That is true,' he said, pretending to be serious, but covering his real vulnerability with a twinkle and a smile in his eyes. 'I am me, after all.' But what he said next just confused her further, because she couldn't tell if he was mocking her or in earnest. 'You don't.'

She didn't leap to agree with him the way she knew she should have done and, for the life of her, she didn't know why. The only option was to follow his lead and descend into razor-sharp humour.

'Maybe that's because I'm a world-class bit—'

He covered her mouth with the tips of three fingers, leaned in close enough to make her pulse race and shook his head.

'You might be able to fool the rest of them,' he said, glancing over his shoulder and then locking his gaze back onto hers, 'but you can't fool me.'

Waiting. He'd never liked it. Now he absolutely hated it.

He wanted to meet Kate.

His every waking moment was spent anticipating this

moment, and the more he waited, the more he started to think he'd be the worst father in the world and should probably just get back on a plane to Naples and do the kid a favour.

But he couldn't leave.

He sat down on the edge of the hotel bed and stared at his shoes. It should have made him laugh that he could actually see tracks in the carpet from this angle. Not that he'd worn it away. It was just his pacing had brushed the pile into a wide stripe.

When Jackie had first told him about his daughter he'd been furious. It had been easy to be angry; everything had been black and white, right and wrong, but now he'd been living with the knowledge for a while he was only too aware that anger had been the first of so many emotions he'd experienced.

He stood up again. It was all so complicated. Multi-layered. Confusing.

Jackie's actions—her choices—that had seemed so wrong to him, now were much more understandable. He knew the same gut-wrenching fear of rejection, the same awful sense of impending failure, had pushed and pulled her too.

He'd forgiven her.

That might seem odd to some, especially as revenge and ret-ribution were coded into his genes, but from the moment she'd collapsed onto the grass and told him of the rainy day when Kate had come into the world in that strange monotone voice of hers, he hadn't been able to stop his heart going out to her.

At the moment his generosity annoyed him. He wanted to be cross with her, cross that she'd scuttled back to her house and had left him to his thoughts while he'd booked into a nearby hotel. He needed her to distract him.

Because distracting him she was.

The phone rang and he was relieved to hear her voice on the other end of the line. Meet up for dinner to finalise plans for tomorrow? Sure.

He filled up the hour before dinner by having a shower and

at eight o'clock sharp he met Jackie at some overpriced restaurant close to both her flat and his hotel in Notting Hill. One look at the menu told him he was going to order an unpromising appetiser just so he could send it back and vent some of this nervous energy that was eating him alive.

As soon as they'd ordered, Jackie got straight down to business. It was as if the London air had breathed fresh starch into her.

'I thought we could either go to this new art gallery I've heard good things about, an exhibition on Chinese music or a walking tour of Churchill's London. What do you think?' she asked without even cracking a smile.

'That's the sort of things you do with Kate when you take her out?'

Jackie nodded, but was distracted by a movement near the kitchen, which heralded the arrival of their appetisers.

'How about I pick the venue?' he said. 'It's the least you can let me do, if I am going to ride shotgun.'

Jackie's mouth tightened and her eyebrows puckered. 'But you hardly know London—'

'I know it well enough,' he said, refusing to blink or even look away. 'I've been here plenty of times—for business and pleasure.'

'Oh…okay.' She kept scowling as the waiter placed a dish of seared scallops in front of her. Romano studied his calamari with disappointment. It looked much better than he'd expected.

The waiter had only retreated a few steps when Jackie called him back. 'I can't possibly eat these,' she said, shoving the plate back at him. 'They're horribly overdone. Bring me something else.'

That was when Romano began to chuckle. All the tension rolled out of him in wave after wave of laughter. Jackie just stared at him as if he'd lost his mind. Perhaps he had. Tomorrow was the most important day of his life and he was acting like an idiot.

'You are not as English as you make out,' he finally explained when he was able to get a word out.

'Of course I am,' Jackie said, lifting her chin. A tiny twitch at the corner of her mouth gave her away.

As they continued their meal Romano realised he hadn't watched Jackie eat in the last week. Once she'd attacked her food with passion, now she measured it out with meticulous cuts, removing any trace of fat or sauce or flavour. He eyed the steamed vegetables she'd requested to go with her plain grilled fish suspiciously. Why did he know she was going to order nothing but black coffee for dessert? How had he guessed that she'd leave half of her meal picked over but not eaten?

Because he'd seen this behaviour before.

Suddenly it all made sense.

He could see it so clearly, as if he'd known her during the time when she'd punished her body, when she'd denied herself life and pleasure. It didn't take much imagination to fill in the blanks of the years he'd missed. He could tell she wasn't in the grip of it any more, but the ghosts of old habits lingered.

He wanted to tell her that she hadn't needed to do it to herself, that she was the bravest, strongest, most maddening woman he'd ever met. That she ran circles around the doe-eyed, physically interchangeable *girls* that seemed to be everywhere these days. Her sharp humour, her quick mind—and, yes, her giving heart—set her apart, but he doubted she'd believe him.

And that was when it hit him like a steel-capped boot to the solar plexus.

It didn't matter what had happened in the past. He still wanted her.

No. He wasn't ready to admit that yet.

He focused back on her half-finished food. This was her coping mechanism. So what was she coping with? What was she finding hard to deal with?

'You're nervous,' he said as the waiter cleared away their plates.

She'd been folding up her serviette and she paused. Without answering, she carried on, folding it into perfect squares—once, twice, three times. And then she laid it on the table and smoothed it flat.

He pushed harder. 'Why?'

She looked up at him, moving only her eyes and keeping her head bowed. 'Tomorrow.'

'About me? You think I'll blow it? That I won't be up to scratch?'

She exhaled and everything about her seemed to deflate a little. 'I don't want to think that way, but I'd be lying if I didn't say I'd worried about it once or twice.'

Thanks, Jackie. That's the way to put a man at ease.

She shook her head. 'I'm more worried about me than I am about you.'

He frowned. 'I don't understand.'

'It's not been going well, Romano. Kate and I…' She gave a hopeless little shrug. 'We can't seem to find any common ground. I'm worried that she's slipping away from me. Again.'

Just the panic at the thought of the same thing happening to him was enough to erase any lingering indignation that her less-than-subtle but totally honest answer had caused. They didn't need coffee. He signalled for the bill.

'*Andiamo*,' he said.

Jackie just nodded.

A few minutes later they were walking down the street, the warm, slightly humid air of the summer evening hugging them close. Jackie didn't seem to be thinking about where she was going, but her feet were taking her in the direction of her tall white house and he kept pace beside her.

He took her hand and she let him.

They were the only two people in the world who felt this way at this precise moment. Both of them waiting, fearing, dreaming of what might happen in the morning, their fate resting in the hands of a stranger. Yet that stranger was their daughter.

Somehow the skin-to-skin contact, their fingers intertwined, communicated all of this. They didn't need to speak. The silence continued until they were standing on Jackie's doorstep.

She turned, her back to the door, and looked somewhere in the region of his chest. 'I can't lose her again,' she whispered. And then the tears fell.

Romano was momentarily stunned. He'd seen Jackie cry before, of course, but this was different. Each bead of moisture that slid down her face was alive with heartbreaking desperation. Until a few days ago, he wouldn't have understood that, but now he did. She couldn't give up now. He wouldn't let her.

He rested his hands on her shoulders, pulled her a little closer. 'You won't.'

She looked up into his face, eyes burning. 'You don't know what it's been like.'

He wanted to say something, but the words weren't in his head yet. He knew what she was like deep down inside, how she loved freely and passionately and completely. He knew she had it in her to win her daughter's heart.

He moved his hands up her neck, held her face gently and stroked her cheeks with the sides of his thumbs. 'You can do this, Jackie. You have so much to give—if only you'd let yourself.'

She blinked another batch of tears away and stared back at him. *Do you think so?* her eyes said. *Really?*

He started to smile. *Really.*

This was the Jackie he'd missed all these years, this unique woman full of contradictions and fire. Finally she'd peeled the layers back and he could see the woman he'd loved. The woman he still loved—God help him.

He sealed the realisation with a kiss, bending forward, pressing his lips gently against hers. It reminded him of their first kiss ever: tender, slightly hesitant, as if they both could hardly believe it was happening. This kiss was far sweeter than the hungry ones they'd shared in the grotto, because it joined them. They weren't just 'co-parents' any more; they were Romano and Jackie—nothing more, nothing less—two souls that were meant to be together.

Full of romance and drama as teenagers, they'd seen themselves as a modern-day Romeo and Juliet. Now, as he held her close against him, as he felt her warm breath through the cotton of his shirt, he hoped with all his might that their tragedy would end up better. He wasn't sure he could lose either her or Kate again.

He kissed her again, losing himself in her softness, in the feel of her slender frame within his arms. Every soft breath from her lips pulled him deeper. He knew he was lost now. He might as well admit it.

She broke the kiss and shifted back a little to look at him. He just drank her in, letting his eyes communicate what his mouth was on the verge of saying.

'I—'

She quickly pressed her fingers to his lips, mirroring the gesture he'd made on the plane.

'Don't say it,' she whispered, looking not angry but very, very frightened.

'I want to,' he said plainly, unable to keep the beginnings of a smile from his lips.

Jackie just looked pained. 'Then you're more of a fool than I am.'

He knew this wasn't going to be easy; he'd been prepared for that, but something in her tone made his insides frost up.

'You feel the same way. I know you do.' The smile uncurled itself from his mouth and left.

She shook her head. 'It's just chemistry, Romano. Echoes of long ago. We couldn't make it then, how are we supposed to make it now?'

He threw his hands upwards in lieu of an answer. He didn't know how or why; he just knew.

'We were kids back then,' she said, stepping to the side and walking back down the garden path a little. 'We weren't ready for that kind of relationship.'

'We're not kids any more.'

'I know. I know.' She clasped her hands in front of her and straightened her back. 'But I don't think we're any more ready for it now than we were then.'

'What you mean is—*you're* not ready.'

'Neither of us are ready. I don't want—'

'Save it, Jackie!' Unfortunately, he knew only too well what she didn't want. Him.

'It wouldn't work,' she said, looking and sounding infuriatingly calm. 'You know that, deep down.'

'Then what was all this about?' he said, walking up to her and invading her space, reminding her of just how close they'd been a few moments ago.

'Like I said—chemistry.'

Oh, she really knew how to send him skyrocketing.

He clenched and unclenched his fists. 'So what you're saying is, I'm good enough for a—' he was really proud that he managed to find a milder English idiom than the first that had come to mind '—for a roll in the hay, but I'm not good enough for anything permanent? And you call *me* shallow?'

Jackie got all prim and prickly on him. 'I'm not saying that at all!'

Somehow the fact he had her all flustered too made him feel better, but the glow of triumph only lasted for a few seconds and then he was feeling as if he needed to burst out of his skin again.

He moved closer and closer to her, walked round her and kept going, so she backed up until she was pressed against her front door and had nowhere to go.

'Then maybe I should be the man you think I am and give you what you want,' he said with a devilish twinkle in his eye, his lips only millimetres from hers.

If she'd looked fierce, or frightened, he would have walked away as he'd intended to, but he saw her pupils dilate, heard the little hitch of breath that told him he wasn't entirely wrong, so he kissed her instead. Hard and long and hot. And he pulled back before she had a chance to push him away, while her fingers were still tangled in his hair and her chest was rising and falling rapidly.

The name she called him wasn't nice.

He shrugged. The contrary kid in him rejoiced in having her confirm her assessment of him, even if he knew it was no longer the truth. If she couldn't see it, then it was her loss.

He walked back down the path and swung the black iron gate wide. 'I'll be here at nine with a car to pick you up,' he said. 'Wear comfortable shoes.' And then he strode away into the falling darkness.

CHAPTER TEN

JACKIE opened the lock with fumbling fingers and crashed through her front door. Once she'd run up the stairs and shut herself in the sanctuary of her bedroom, she sat on the end of the bed, knees clamped together, back straight, and stared at the warm angled patterns the street lamp was making on the wall through the plantation shutters.

She had not seen that coming.

She *should* have seen it coming.

Ever since she'd told Romano about Kate, he'd changed. She'd thought he'd stopped thinking about her that way, had thought that the way the air fizzed every time he was close was a totally one-sided thing.

Why? Why did he want this?

Why did he want *her*?

She didn't get it, really she didn't. She'd just been grateful that they'd been getting along, while she tried to puzzle out why he didn't hate her more.

She closed her eyes.

Had he really been going to say what she'd thought he'd been going to say?

Her head automatically started to move side to side. That couldn't be right. He couldn't feel that way after all she'd done to him. It had to be the emotion of the moment. He was caught up in a whirlwind of feelings about meeting his daughter for the first time, and she'd got sucked in by accident. When he came back down to earth, he'd realise it was all a mirage.

And yet that kiss…

Her insides felt like ice cream that had just met with a blowtorch. It had been much more than chemistry. She'd lied about that. But she'd had to. She'd had to push him away.

It was the right thing. For her. For Romano. For Kate. She was certain of that.

She opened her eyes again and forced herself to move, forced herself to switch on the light, close the shutters and take a shower. And as she stood there under the steaming jet she asked herself one more question.

Why did doing the right thing always have to hurt so much?

She was giving him the silent treatment. Frankly, he didn't blame her. Things always went wrong when he lost his temper. Why else had he spent most of his life making sure he didn't care too deeply about anything, if not to save himself from these extremes of emotion? It never ended well.

Look at what he'd done: Jackie was sitting on the opposite side of the limo's back seat, almost pressed against the door.

And they'd been making such progress. They'd begun to enjoy each other's company again. Now she thought him an insensitive idiot.

She was right.

All he wanted to do was crawl back under his security blanket of quick wit and smooth banter and forget the whole thing had ever happened. He was nervous enough as it was and he didn't need his heart jumping about as if it were riding a pogo stick inside his chest.

His gaze dropped to her shoes and he felt a familiar tickle of temper down in his gut. Four-inch heels in fire-engine red. They looked fantastic with the skinny jeans, a floaty bohemian top and coloured beads—a look he hadn't expected to ever see her in, but was working for her. Why the change?

Ah, yes. It was part of her costume for today, just as she'd dressed down to come to lunch on the island. She was making sure she looked fun and funky and carefree, dressed in the sort of thing that might appeal to a teenage girl. When was Jackie going to learn that wearing the right accessories didn't change anything?

They travelled out of central London, past some really grotty areas and then into the leafier suburbs. The car slowed then stopped down an ordinary road filled with semi-detached houses. He glanced over to where Jackie was easing herself elegantly from the car.

And then his heart stopped.

Standing on the doorstep of the house they'd pulled up outside was a young girl with long dark hair and eyes just like his mother's.

Jackie stepped out of the car and smiled. Kate gave a half-wave and a grimace and turned to shout inside that she was going. As Jackie reached the garden gate Sue appeared and gave Kate a kiss and a hug. Jackie ignored the squeeze of her heart as she saw how easy they were with each other.

'I hope you don't mind, but I brought a friend with me.'

What Romano was to her couldn't exactly be quantified, but that was as specific as she wanted to get. She glanced over her shoulder and frowned. Where was he? She could have sworn he'd been right behind her.

She gave Kate and Sue a nervous smile. 'I'll be with you in just a second.'

She turned round just late enough to see Kate roll her eyes and give her mum a weary look.

Romano was nowhere to be seen. She walked back down the path and opened the limo door. It was empty.

Where—?

On instinct she straightened and looked down the road. He was twenty feet away, staring at a neatly clipped privet hedge. She opened her mouth to call him over, but then she noticed the way his hand shook as he turned his back to her and leant on a fence post. He ran his spare hand through his hair then dropped it to his face. Even from the back she could tell he'd just dragged his palm across his eyes.

The wall of ice she'd built that morning disappeared into a steaming puddle.

She walked forwards until she was hidden by the next-door neighbour's hedge, called his name softly and held out her hand. His shoulders shuddered as he took a breath and then turned round. The brave smile he'd forced his face into was her undoing.

Of course she loved him too.

How could she not?

But that didn't change the fact that it was the worst possible thing in the current situation. He walked towards her and she bit her lip, nodded. She understood. Right from the bottom of her heart she felt his pain, because it was her pain too.

He took her hand, kissed her knuckles, placed it back down by her side and looked in the direction of Kate's house, hidden as it was behind a wall of green shiny leaves. She admired his courage, knew why he'd chosen not to hang onto her. Everyone had their pride.

Side by side they walked back to the limo. Kate had ambled down the path and now was staring at Romano with open curiosity.

Jackie took a breath. 'Kate? This is Romano—a friend of mine. He's coming with us. Is that okay?'

Kate tipped her head on one side. 'Suppose so.'

As they climbed into the car she turned to him.

'Are you her boyfriend?'

Jackie held her breath.

Romano made a rueful face. 'No. I am not her boyfriend.'
And then he smiled. 'She won't let me be.'

It was probably the most mortifying thing he could have
said, but he had such a way with him that it seemed light and
funny. Kate even gave a one-sided smile in return.

'So where are we going?' Jackie asked, eager to be
included in the conversation.

Romano looked very pleased with himself. 'The zoo.'

Both Jackie and Kate spoke at the same time, an identical
note of incredulity in their voices. 'The zoo?'

Inside Jackie wilted. Kate was sixteen, not six! This was
going to be a disaster.

'Everybody loves the zoo,' he said, the trademark Romano
confidence now completely back in place. Jackie folded her
arms and gave him a *'we'll see'* kind of look.

As they drove through the London streets, back in the direction of the city centre, Kate yabbered away to Romano, obviously deciding he was a safer option than her biological
mother. Jackie willed her to keep going. She wanted Kate to
like him. Wanted her to accept him.

Which was most unlike her. Normally, she wasn't that
generous.

Every now and then she caught Romano's eye over the
top of Kate's head. If she'd thought there'd been a sparkle
before, it had only been a foreshadowing of the light she
saw there now.

Isn't she amazing? his eyes said. Look what we made!

She couldn't help but sparkle back in agreement.

Jackie rested against the solid glass of one of the enclosures
in the ape house and took the weight off her feet. She looked
down at her shoes. Stupid choice. She'd known it when she'd
put them on. They'd been payback for that last kiss, the one
that had left her both angry and pulsing with desire. She'd

wanted to show him that it hadn't meant anything, that he couldn't tell her what to do.

As always, her hot-headedness had backfired on her. Romano was having a blast of a time with Kate, running all over the place, while Jackie hobbled along behind them. She was the only one smarting from her so-called defiant gesture. She sighed as she eased her hot, slightly swollen foot from its patent leather casing and wiggled her toes.

A sudden pounding behind her made her jump so high she left her shoe behind as she propelled herself forwards and away from where the glass had reverberated behind her. She spun round to see a large black chimpanzee glaring at her and baring its teeth.

Of course Romano and Kate fell about laughing.

But she couldn't work herself up to quite the pitch of indignation she'd have liked to. Not when those two laughs sounded so similar and so infectious that she almost joined in.

Romano walked across to where her shoe was lying, picked it up and handed it to her. She jammed it back on her foot. It complained loudly.

'I'm hungry,' Kate said.

'I think it is time to eat,' Romano said, looking at his watch. He looked down at Jackie's feet. 'I saw picnic tables under some trees over there. Why don't you two sit down and I'll get us something?'

Jackie sent him a look of pure worship. How she was going to get through the rest of the afternoon, she didn't know, but at least half an hour or so off her feet might help.

Kate pointed out a free picnic table and jogged towards it while Romano headed off in the direction of one of the zoo's cafés. Jackie trailed behind her daughter and plonked herself down with very little elegance when she reached the rough wooden structure, so desperate was she to shift weight off her feet and onto her bottom.

Kate played with the table, tracing the ridge of some blocky graffiti carved into it with her fingernail. 'He's okay, isn't he?' she said, without looking up.

'Yes,' Jackie said, a little too wistfully for her own liking.

Kate kept her head bowed slightly, but raised her eyes to look at Jackie from under her long fringe. 'And he's definitely not your boyfriend?'

Jackie glanced over her shoulder towards the café. She couldn't make out Romano in the crush inside.

'No.'

'Why not?'

Jackie didn't really want to answer that, but she was aware this was the first conversation Kate had initiated with her all day and she didn't want to jinx that.

'It's complicated,' she finally said.

Wrong answer.

Kate's expression hardened. 'You always say that.'

'Normally because it's true,' she answered with a sigh. 'Life *is* complicated.'

Kate went back to running her finger over the graffiti and the silence congealed around them. Then the finger stopped and Jackie heard Kate inhale.

'Mum—I mean Sue—says things are usually simpler than I make them.'

Jackie just smiled. Maybe there was some common ground here after all. When Kate looked up and saw her smiling, she looked shocked at first, but then the beginnings of a curl appeared on her lips too.

Oh, what Jackie wouldn't give to just vault over the table and pull that girl into her arms. But she was painfully aware that any such gesture might be rejected, so she made do with smiling all the wider.

There had been another first. Kate normally always referred to Sue as 'Mum'; the fact she'd adjusted that, had used her name as well, was a tiny concession to Jackie that she hadn't missed. Maybe Romano would be good for the two of them. If he and Kate got on, it might help somehow. For the first time in weeks Jackie thought her relationship with Kate was starting to go in the right direction. She had hope, and she clung onto it as if it were a life raft.

Romano returned with a tray of ominous-looking food-stuffs. He placed it in the centre of the picnic table. Jackie looked warily at the cardboard cartons and cups that didn't look like skinny, decaff, no-foam lattes. Something cold, fizzy and sweet seemed to be lurking inside.

'Burgers and chips?' she said, trying to sound unfazed.

'Cool.' Kate dived right on in.

Jackie didn't do burgers and chips. In fact she couldn't even remember the last time she'd eaten junk food. She almost said as much, but she managed to stop herself. A comment like that would probably earn her another black mark from Kate.

'Not hungry?' Romano said, with just a glimmer of mischief in his eyes.

Ah. She got it now. Payback for the shoes.

She grabbed one of the square cartons and flipped its lid open. A waft of warm meat hit her nostrils. Romano and Kate were already making great inroads into their lunch, loving every bite. Jackie, however, felt as if she were on one of those high-diving boards, teetering on the edge.

She looked into her carton again.

As fast food went this wasn't too repulsive. The bun wasn't soggy. The lettuce and tomato looked crisp and fresh. She picked the burger up with both hands and held it in front of her, elbows resting on the table.

She'd show Romano Puccini she wasn't afraid of a bit of meat and a few carbs! Without hesitation she sank her teeth into it, taking as big a bite as she could. Now all she had to do was keep it down. She chewed and took another bite.

Actually, this was okay—she'd forgotten how nice a little bit of fat with her meat could be.

After a short while, she became aware of someone watching her.

'What?' she said to Romano, mouth still slightly full.

He shook his head and smiled, then pushed a container of chips her way. Jackie wavered for a second. Oh, well, might as well put on a good show. She grabbed a handful and put them in the lid of her open burger box. She'd regret this next week when she saw her personal trainer, but at the moment she just didn't care.

Just so Romano didn't think he'd had a complete victory, she shoved the sticky, fizzy drink back in his direction. 'I draw the line somewhere,' she said, but couldn't help grinning afterwards. He just laughed.

It wasn't long before they were clearing away. Unfortunately the end of lunch meant she was going to have to stand up again. Something she was not looking forward to. Romano went to dispose of their rubbish and then disappeared. She and Kate just looked at each other in bewilderment when after five minutes he hadn't returned.

'Do you think he's been eaten by a lion?' Kate asked, a little hint of sarcasm in her voice.

Jackie laughed. 'No. I reckon he could sweet-talk most creatures out of having him for supper, especially the female ones.'

Just as she said this Romano appeared round the corner of the café, a brown paper bag from the zoo gift shop in his hand.

Kate stood up and put her hands on her hips. 'Where have you been?'

Jackie shut her mouth. She'd been about to say and do exactly the same thing.

'On an errand of mercy,' he said and produced an ice cream for Kate, which she eagerly accepted. But then he reached into the bag and pulled something else out—the ugliest pair of flip-flops that Jackie had ever seen. They were luminous turquoise and had plastic shells and starfish all over them. He handed them to her.

She kicked her shoes off and slid them on. Heaven.

'I could kiss you,' she said as she plopped her heels into the waiting paper bag and took it from him.

Kate paused from licking her ice cream. 'Why don't you? Sue says it's rude not to say thank you when you get a gift.'

The look on her face was pure innocence, but Jackie wasn't fooled for a second. Still, Kate was actually talking to her, joking with her, and she wasn't going to spoil that now, and she was ridiculously grateful for the garish footwear. She stood up and gave Romano a quick, soft kiss on the cheek.

'Thanks.'

Kate smiled.

Jackie didn't miss the way his arm curled round her waist and how it didn't seem to want to let her go when she tried to step away again.

'What's next?' she said brightly. 'Snakes or elephants.'

'Both,' Kate and Romano said in unison.

Jackie couldn't remember when she'd enjoyed an afternoon as much. They wandered round Regent's Park Zoo, pointing things out to each other and having increasingly inane conversations that made them all laugh. She wondered how they looked to other people.

Could people tell they were a family? Did they blend in and look like the other adults and children? It would be wonderful if they did. Maybe, if they looked like that on the outside, they could feel like that on the inside too one day.

She and Kate hadn't got along this well in weeks—if ever. And Romano…

Jackie was starting to anticipate the moments when he'd move closer to get a better view of something, when their hands would 'accidentally' brush. He'd been so wonderful, so... perfect. He made her believe she could be that way too—at least when she was with him. She needed him. Needed him for herself and for Kate. If only she could snap her fingers and have him appear out of thin air every time she met with her daughter. It would help their relationship mend so much quicker.

And maybe, when things were finally on a better footing with Kate, they could revisit the idea of being more than just co-parents. She hardly dared hope it would work between them, but she wanted to believe it might, that maybe second chances existed after all.

Just as the heat bled out of the day Romano called for the car and they all piled inside. After the initial chatter about the day out, they fell into silence, then Kate began to ask Romano about where he lived, who his family were. Jackie listened with a smile on her face as she gazed out of the windows.

Kate was sitting in the middle seat, between her and Romano, and Jackie was suddenly aware of a lull in the conversation. She turned to find Kate looking at her, brain working away at some complex internal question. Without saying anything she transferred her gaze to Romano.

'You're my dad, aren't you?'

Jackie held her breath. Why on earth had she thought they could keep this anonymous? A girl as sharp as Kate was always going to guess, was always going to be one step ahead. She too looked at Romano, willing him to give the perfect answer, even though she was pretty sure there wasn't one.

Romano's face split into the biggest grin yet. It was totally captivating. 'Yes,' he said simply. 'And I'm very proud to be so.'

There *was* a perfect answer! And it wasn't so much in the words as in the delivery. Kate rewarded Romano with a matching smile. 'Cool.'

But over the next few minutes the smile faded, more questions arrived behind her eyes. She turned to Jackie.

'So why didn't you tell me about him right at the start? Why did you say all those things about not needing to know, about how it wasn't the right time?'

Uh-oh. She needed an injection of Romano's effortless charm. Quick. Jackie sent him a pleading look. He gave a rueful smile, and she knew he'd have helped her if he could have done, but this was her question and hers alone. She only hoped she could pull her answer off with as much panache as he had done.

She frowned. How did she say this? She didn't want to tell Kate that she'd thought Romano hadn't wanted her—that would be too cruel. So she started to tell a story. A story about a girl younger than Kate who had unexpectedly found herself pregnant, and her sadly inadequate attempt to deal with the situation. Kate's eyes were wide and round as she listened and as she got deeper into the story Jackie found she couldn't look at her daughter, that she had to concentrate on the fingers endlessly twiddling in her lap instead.

Before she'd finished all she had to say, they arrived at Kate's home. None of them made a move to get out of the car. Jackie kept talking, afraid that if she stopped, she might never have the courage to start again. And then finally there was silence. All was laid bare. She held her fingers still by clasping her hands.

The air in the back of the limousine was thick with tension. Jackie's heart thudded so hard she thought she could feel little shock waves reverberating off the windows with each beat. She looked up.

Kate was crying. Large fat tears rolled down her cheeks. Jackie reached for her, reached to brush them gently away. 'Sweetheart—'

'Don't!'

Kate sprang away from her, back against Romano, her mouth contorted in a look of disgust. Jackie would never, ever forget that look.

'Don't you dare call me that! Don't *ever* pretend that you

care! You couldn't even be bothered to name me. You left that up to Sue and Dave!'

Jackie dropped her hand. Her mouth was open, but she was frozen, unable to close it, unable to do anything.

'You! This was all your fault! All of it!' Kate broke off to swipe at her eyes. Her voice dropped to a whisper. 'You ruined our lives. All of our lives. I…'

Don't say it, Jackie silently begged. Please, don't say it.

'I hate you. I never want to see you again.'

She made a move for the door and Romano clambered out of her way. He reached for her, laid a hand on her arm. 'Kate, please?'

She shook her head. 'Sorry, Romano.'

And then she marched up the garden path and disappeared past a shocked-looking Sue into the house.

Jackie just sat there, numb. Just like that, her whole world had caved in around her. She really, really wanted to blame Romano, but she knew she couldn't. Kate had been speaking the truth. It *had* been all her fault. How could she foist the blame on anyone else?

'She doesn't mean it,' Romano said as he climbed back into the car.

Jackie's eyes were fixed on the back of the driver's seat. 'Just like I didn't mean it when I said I didn't want to see you again? I think you'll find she meant every word.'

'Then you do what I didn't do. Keep trying. Never give up. Don't be a coward like I was and take the easy way out.'

The tiniest of frowns creased Jackie's forehead. She smoothed it away with her palm. 'The easy way out?' she echoed quietly.

Romano nodded. 'Pretending you don't care. Distracting yourself with other things so it doesn't hurt so much.' He let out a dry, short laugh. 'In my case, distracting myself with other girls.'

Jackie felt her shoulders tense. 'I don't want to know how

many girls you had to sleep with to get over me, especially not as Francesca Gambardi was first in the queue.'

Romano's arm shot out and he captured her face in his hand. 'Look at me.'

The tension worked its way up from her shoulder and into her jaw. Reluctantly she let him manoeuvre her face until she was looking at him.

'I *never* slept with Francesca. I didn't even kiss her. How could I have? After all that we had?'

She wanted to spit and shout and tell him he was a liar, but the truth was there in his eyes. She nodded and tears blurred her vision.

'You changed me, Jackie. Knowing you made me a better person.'

She started to laugh. That had to be the funniest thing she'd ever heard. As if she had that kind of power! Why, if she could do such miracles, she'd wave a magic wand and make her mother love her, she'd wiggle her nose and Kate would come skipping into her arms.

'Stop it!'

The laugh snagged in her throat. She'd never heard Romano speak that way before and it shocked the hilarity right out of her. She'd never seen him look so fierce.

'You were wrong about me and Francesca. Just allow for the fact that you might be wrong about this too?'

She nodded. Mainly because she knew it was the expected response. She was such a liar. Even when she kept her mouth shut she kept on lying—to him, to herself, to everyone.

'Can you take me home?' she asked, sinking back into the seat and kicking the stupid flip-flops off so they disappeared under the passenger seat. 'I'm starting to get a headache.'

Once again, because of her own stupid decisions—the same stupid decisions—she'd lost her daughter.

Kate refused point-blank to have any contact with Jackie. Texts went unanswered. Calls ignored. If Jackie got creative and dialled from a number Kate wouldn't recognise, she put the phone down on her.

At least she was still in contact with Romano.

Apparently the whole drama had only served to increase the bonding process between father and daughter. They'd been calling each other every day. Romano had even been to the house to see her again.

Jackie knew this because she demanded daily updates. Each evening they'd meet up to pick apart what had happened that day. Romano was unswerving in his belief that Kate would come around eventually. He was deluding himself. He'd even told her he was staying in London until it was all sorted, to which she'd replied that he'd better find himself a nice flat, because the hotel bills would bankrupt him.

By Sunday of that week she'd had enough of torturing herself. A call had come in from the office to say there was an emergency meeting of all the different editors-in-chief of the various international *Gloss!* editions in New York that Monday and Jackie had no reason to tell them to take a hike. Her job wouldn't exactly be on the line if she didn't go, but it wouldn't look good. And with her personal life flushed down the pan, she might as well hold onto the one area that *was* working out.

She was busy throwing things into a suitcase when the doorbell went. She heard her housekeeper let someone in. Moments later there were footsteps on the stairs, then Romano appeared at her bedroom door. She flipped the lid of her case closed, bizarrely ashamed of her haphazard packing, and turned to face him. 'How did it go today?'

He did one of those non-committal gestures that involved both hands and mouth.

'That good, huh?'

'She is a fiery young woman, not too different from another young woman I used to know.' He raised his eyebrows. 'Give her time. All her life she's wanted to know who we were, and it's nothing like the fairy tale she invented for herself. It's been a shock.'

Jackie marched over to her wardrobe and threw the doors open. She didn't know what she was looking for.

'Well, it's all worked out rather nicely for you.'

Romano ran a weary hand over his face and said something gruff in Italian before he answered her properly.

'With two such women! I should be sainted.'

'You do that,' she said, then pulled a black suit from the rail, only to throw it back in again two seconds later.

Romano sat down on the armchair near her dressing table. 'Jackie?'

She peered round the wardrobe door at him. 'Yes?'

'I have something to tell you. Good news, I think.'

She clutched the blouse she was holding to her chest and walked towards him. 'You do?'

'Kate has asked to come with me back to Italy to meet my father, and Sue has agreed—as long as she comes too.'

Of course Sue had agreed. With Jackie she'd been like a Rottweiler, but with Romano...

'She thinks it will help Kate come to terms with all that has happened recently,' he added. 'She hopes that meeting my family—and yours—will help Kate put it all in context. I agree.'

Jackie crushed the silk blouse so hard she feared she might never get the wrinkles out again. 'You want to take her to meet my mother?'

Romano nodded.

A short, hard laugh burst from her mouth.

He dropped his voice, laced it with honey. 'I was hoping you would come too.'

Oh, yes. That would be really popular.

'It's impossible.'

He stood up and walked towards her, and his easy, graceful stride momentarily mesmerised her. What would it be like to just walk into a room and have people react that way…to love you, to adore you? She'd never know. And in truth she really didn't care. There was only one person she wanted to impress and she doubted very much that walking anywhere, anyhow, was going to accomplish that.

He tugged the blouse from her claw-like hands and put it on the bed, then he ironed her fingers out with his and closed his hands round hers. 'Nothing is impossible. Look at us. For years…nothing. And now—'

She began to shake her head.

'No, Jackie. I know you feel it too. What we thought was dead is very much alive.'

She pulled her hands away. 'You're starting to sound like Uncle Luca. Pretty words aren't going to solve this, Romano.'

Jackie opened her case up again and threw the crumpled blouse inside. Romano started to say something, but then stared at her and closed his mouth.

'What are you doing?'

She went and picked the black suit up from the floor of the wardrobe, then folded it clumsily into the case. 'Packing.'

He frowned. 'But you were packing *before* I came in. Why?'

'I'm going to New York. Work. Tomorrow morning.'

CHAPTER ELEVEN

WAS she insane?

Who was thinking of work at a time like this? This was family! And if Jackie handled this badly now she might never be able to repair the damage. Wasn't she even going to try?

He had the feeling that Kate was testing her mother, stretching the fragile bond between them to its utmost. The worst thing Jackie could do now was to disappear. He needed to persuade her to change her mind—and not just for Kate's sake, but for his own.

He'd never expected to want a family, had never been sure he'd know what to do with all that permanence, all those expectations. But now he had one, he'd found himself rising to the challenge. The idea of loving someone, of pledging himself to one woman, come what may, didn't scare him any more. He wanted that adventure.

'You can't go.'

Jackie paused from collecting together an armful of products from a drawer in her dressing table. 'I have to.'

He walked over to her, took each item out of her hands one by one and put them on the dressing table. 'No. You need to come with me, with Kate, to Italy. You need to come home.'

Jackie had her weight on the balls of her feet, rocking

backwards and forwards slightly, as if she was getting ready to run. 'There's no point. Not now.' She didn't add the words *not ever*, but Romano heard them inside his head.

She was giving up. Locking herself up tight inside her pride.

But Jackie wasn't arrogant, or full of hot air. Quite the opposite. Pride was her life jacket, her air bag—emotional bubble-wrap. She used it as protection, and as such it was extremely effective.

Even if there hadn't been a trip to New York, she'd have found an excuse not to come with him. And it was this mindset that was dangerous. He had to shake her out of it, show her that there was a better way. He wanted her to learn how liberating it could be to knock down the walls, to feel the breeze on her soul and be *seen*.

But Jackie wasn't thinking about breeze and walls and souls. She was packing.

Romano knew of only one sure-fire way to claim her full attention, so he decided to play dirty. He waited until she brushed past him on her way to putting more 'stuff' into her case, pulled her into his arms and kissed her.

When he finally felt the tension melt from her frame, he pulled back and looked at her. 'I still love you, Jacqueline. Come with me.'

Jackie went white. Instead of reassuring her, his words only seemed to spook her further. He kissed her forehead and drew her back against him, letting her ear rest against his chest so she could hear the steady thump of his heart. And then he just held her.

'Be brave,' he whispered. 'There is still a chance for you and Kate. And for us. Be patient. There will be healing.'

Jackie, who had been breathing softly against him, went still, and then she wriggled out of his embrace and stepped away. On the surface she was all business and propriety, but he could see the war inside shimmering in her eyes.

'You're going all Italian on me again, saying things you don't mean, getting caught up in the moment…'

A corner of his mouth lifted. 'You know that's not true.'

She moistened her lips by rolling one across the other. 'It doesn't matter if it is or if it isn't—' she shook her head and backed away further '—because I don't love you back.'

The words hit him in the chest like a bullet, even though he knew they were only blanks, empty words designed to scare, with no real impact, no truth to them. She must have seen this in his eyes as he gathered himself together, ready to make another assault of his own.

'Don't flatter yourself,' she said, raising her chin and looking at him through slightly lowered lids.

So this was how it was going to be. Once again Jackie was going to abandon everything that was real in her life in order to keep herself safe.

He wasn't going to beg, but he wasn't above one last attempt at making her see sense—for their daughter's sake.

'Don't do this,' he said.

Jackie picked up the items he'd put back on the dressing table and placed them in strategic points in her half-full case. 'I have to.'

Her voice didn't wobble, but he knew that was only down to supreme effort on her part. He knew this was breaking her heart, but he had to keep pushing. He wanted her to believe in Kate the way she hadn't been able to believe in him all those years ago.

It was useless. As each second passed he watched her use all her strength to board herself up. His compassion for her evaporated in a sudden puff.

He walked away from her, right to the bedroom door, and back again. 'I never thought you a coward, Ms Patterson, but that is what you are.' He shook his head. 'She deserves more than this from you. A lot more.'

Jackie met his gaze, jaw tense, eyes narrowed. 'You think

I don't know that? I can't believe it's taken you all these years for you to work out I'm just not up to it.'

His hands made an explosive gesture, like lava gushing out of a volcano. What was it with this woman? She was so stubborn! So blinkered! It was so…familiar. He took a moment to assimilate that thought. So very familiar.

'If it makes you happy to pretend that's the way it is, fine! Why bother risking anything when you have your wall of denial to hide behind? You know, sometimes you are just like your mother.'

'Get out!'

Jackie was holding a shoe in her right hand. Her fingers were tensing and flexing around the rather sharp heel and he sensed he might need to duck at any second. He kept himself ready but folded his arms across his chest.

'I am not going anywhere until you agree to come to Italy with me.'

'Fine!' She tapped the heel of the shoe on her upturned palm, then tossed it on the bed. Then she pivoted round and headed for her bathroom. The door slammed hard enough to get an answering rattle from the hefty front door downstairs. 'I'm taking a shower,' she yelled through the door. 'And if you are here when I get out, I'll be calling the police!' The sound of drumming water drowned out anything he might say in response.

Impossible woman! He let out a huff of air and scratched his scalp with his fingertips. Think, Romano. He was loath to beat a retreat, but if he stayed and fought Jackie would just dig deeper trenches, hide herself in her iron-clad excuses.

So he would go. But he wasn't giving up entirely. A good soldier knew that when frontal assault wasn't possible, guerrilla tactics were occasionally necessary.

First, he tore a page from a pad by the telephone and wrote down the details of the flight to Naples in the morning. There was still a ticket with her name on it. All she had to do was check in at London City Airport and the seat on the plane was hers. Secondly, he took a moment to retrieve a couple of items he'd spotted in the bottom of Jackie's wardrobe and placed them in her case.

With one final look at the bathroom door he walked out of the room, out of Jackie's house and back to his hotel. He had some packing of his own to do.

Jackie had such a migraine coming on by the time she emerged from the shower that she took a couple of tablets and crawled into bed, not even bothering to move the case that filled half of it. She'd work round it.

But sleep wouldn't come.

The accusation Romano had flung at her ran round her head, screaming, making her temples throb.

Why, when anyone wanted to get close, did she push them away? It was a reflex she didn't have any control over. Where had that come from?

It didn't take long for her subconscious to provide a clue. She saw herself as a child, sitting halfway up the old pine tree, shivering in the dark. The memory of the cold air on her skin, the prickle of the needles against her arms was very clear. What was less clear was the reason for the tongue-lashing Mamma had given her, but she recalled the look on her mother's face, the one that said once again she hadn't lived up to expectations, that her best just wasn't good enough.

She'd sat up in that tree for hours and had promised herself that whenever she got told off in the future, she wouldn't cry and try to cuddle Mamma again, because that only made her crosser. No, from then on she'd decided she wouldn't make a sound, wouldn't shed a tear. She'd show Mamma she could be a good girl. Even if Mamma didn't believe it, she'd save herself a few smacks for 'making a fuss'.

So when her mother had finally found her late that evening,

Jackie had calmly climbed back down to the ground and had taken her punishment without even a whimper.

Somewhere along the line—probably not long after her father had been kicked out—Mamma had decided she was 'difficult'. The label had stuck, even though Jackie had tried a hundred times to peel it off and prove her mother wrong. Why could she never see that? Why was she always so sure she was right?

How did you deal with someone like that? Trying to change their mind was like trying to stop the earth and start it spinning in the other direction.

With these hopeless thoughts in her head, Jackie set her alarm for six-thirty and drifted off into a tense sleep. But the spinning didn't stop. It carried on through her dreams, shaking loose everything she held to be true, turning her over and over until she wasn't sure which way was up.

Kate came and stood next to Romano as he helped the driver load cases into the boot of the car.

'She's not coming, is she?'

He put an arm round his daughter and squeezed her to him. 'I don't know.'

Kate sagged against him. 'It's all my fault. I shouldn't have said those things. I was horrible and I don't even know why I did it! It's just sometimes, all this stuff is boiling up inside and it all comes out.'

He placed a hand on each of her shoulders and turned her towards him. 'Family…' he said, and added an arm gesture that encompassed the English he couldn't remember. 'This is not easy for any of us. Family is so…so…'

What was the word he was after? It was right there on the tip of his tongue.

A small wry smile curled the edge of Kate's mouth. 'Complicated?'

Romano nodded. '*Sì. Complicato.*'

He shut the boot of the taxi and opened the door for his daughter. What more could anyone say?

An hour before the alarm went off Jackie opened her eyes.

Oh, hell. Romano was right. She was just like her mother.

Why her brain had processed this unfortunate realisation during the night and had decided to wake her with it was a mystery. She rolled over onto her other side and kicked something hard.

Ouch.

Her case.

It was a sign. She might as well catch up on the packing she'd forgone last night. She didn't have to be at Heathrow until ten, but it always made her feel better once her case was all zipped and padlocked and sitting obediently by the front door.

Coffee first. She slid on some dark pyjama bottoms and an old T-shirt.

Once her coffee was made she went back upstairs and decided she would have to completely redo her case. She didn't even remember what she'd chucked in there last night while she'd been rowing with Romano.

As she walked back into the bedroom she noticed a scrap of paper on the dressing table. She didn't remember leaving anything there so she leaned over to get a better look.

Flight number and time. Destination. Airport.

But not her flight. Not her destination.

She turned her back on the note and walked over to the bed, took a large slurp of coffee, then rested the mug on the bedside table.

Unpacking and reorganising the emotions that were fermenting inside her just have to wait until later. After New York, probably. There was no way she was going to risk breaking down at the airport or on the plane. Right now she needed something mundane to keep her distracted. Packing a suitcase sounded like the perfect job.

She flipped the lid of her case open and squinted at the contents.

Really?

What had she been thinking packing that blouse? It was so last season.

She tugged it out, intending to get it back on a hanger as soon as possible, but something underneath it in the case caught her eye.

The ugliest pair of flip-flops she'd ever seen.

Eye-piercing turquoise with plastic shells and sea creatures on them.

Gingerly, she reached out and traced a bright orange seahorse with the tip of a nail. It wasn't enough. She picked the flip-flops up and hugged them to her. The soles pressed against her T-shirt, stamping zoo dirt onto her chest.

She didn't cry; she wouldn't let herself.

Unravelling was for later, remember?

So she peeled the flip-flops away from herself and placed them neatly on the floor, a good distance from the rest of her packing, just in case she was tempted. Then she stared straight ahead.

She needed to order a taxi.

It had slipped her mind last night and if she didn't get on the phone soon, she'd have a terrible job getting to the airport in time. Mechanically, she reached for the phone.

Romano stood with Kate and Sue at the check-in desk. For the first time in his life he envied the people flying economy. There were no queues to delay his party at the business-class desk and he'd gladly have put up with non-existent leg room and a snotty kid kicking the back of his seat if it meant just a few more minutes before they went through security.

He knew he was being stupid, but he'd made a silent bet with himself that she'd appear before they passed through the metal detector and X-ray machines. It was getting closer and closer to their flight departure time, and once they went through into the interior of the airport he knew the chances of Jackie appearing were slim.

The check-in clerk handed him back his passport and boarding pass and he felt the last shred of hope slip from his grasp. Kate glanced towards the entrance, then pursed her lips slightly.

And then they were going through security, flinging their bags into little grey plastic trays and removing their shoes. Romano forbade himself to look back, both physically and mentally. He had something *really* worthwhile to live for now, much more important than seeing his family name on a label in someone's clothes. Now he had a family to pass that name on to, and it mattered in a way he'd never thought possible.

Just as he was helping Sue wrestle her hand luggage off the conveyor belt, there was some kind of commotion behind them. He ignored it at first, too drained to spend any emotional energy on anyone but his little party, but then someone yelled, 'Do I *look* as if I'm carrying any hand luggage to you?' and all the hairs on the back of his neck lifted and tingled.

He dropped the bag he was holding and spun round.

Right there, giving the female security officer at the metal detector the evil eye, was Jackie. At least, he thought it was Jackie.

This woman had no make-up on, her hair was half hanging out of a ponytail and she was wearing an old lilac fleece and a pair of… What were they? Jogging bottoms? And on her feet were the ugliest pair of flip-flops he'd ever seen.

Kate froze to the spot beside him and Sue crowded in protectively. Jackie stopped waving her passport and boarding pass at the woman in the uniform—he didn't want to think about where she had her money hidden in that outfit—but then she looked up and saw them standing there, watching her. Multiple emotions flickered across her face. Relief. Frustration. Joy. Panic. When the woman officer nodded to indicate she could pass through, Jackie pulled herself to her full five feet six and walked through the arch with her head held high.

Even though his overriding instinct was to laugh out loud, Romano kept his face under control. She'd done well by turning up, but she still had a way to go before it was time for hugs and celebrations.

'Sorry I'm late,' she said, and brushed a tangled strand of hair out of her face. She turned to Kate. 'I need to talk to you.'

Kate was so tense, he thought her over-long teenage body would snap if she moved. He knew she was desperate for some show of emotion from Jackie, but the need to put on a good front must be genetic, because right now she was looking as approachable as…well, as Jackie usually did.

Kate folded her arms. 'So talk.'

Jackie's face fell. 'Here?'

Her daughter just pressed her lips together and nodded.

Jackie took in a breath and blew it out. 'Okay. Here it is, then.'

Where did she start? There was so much she wanted to say, so much she'd left unsaid. Which of the hundred possible speeches she'd rehearsed in the taxi did she pull out of the bag?

Then she remembered how Romano had talked to Kate. *Not so much in the words as in the delivery.* And she knew she had to start right back at the beginning. She wanted to pull Kate into a hug, take hold of her hands, but Kate's body language told her she'd better not try. The best she could do was look her daughter in the eyes and tell her the truth. No varnish. No *gloss*.

'I did name you,' she said, and discovered her knees had just gone all cotton wool-like. 'Right after you were born.'

Kate's eyes widened. 'You did?'

Jackie nodded furiously. 'But I didn't tell anyone. It was a secret name, one just for me.'

Oh, hell, her voice was cracking and she really, really needed to sniff. Kate did it first, and Sue produced a couple of tissues from her capacious hand luggage and offered one to each of them.

'I knew I had to—' her face crumpled and she struggled to get the next few words out without completely going to pieces '—give you away.' Nope. That was it. The tears fell. Her throat swelled up. Kate was staring at her, as if she were a being from outer space. Jackie decided to keep going while she was still able to croak. 'It seemed selfish to tell anyone. It wouldn't have been fair to your new parents…'

She glanced at Sue, expecting to see her normal guard-dog expression, but instead found a warm smile and a look of compassion.

Kate stepped forward and her arms dropped to her sides. 'What…what did you call me?'

Jackie had never babbled in her life. Not until now, anyway.

'That first day, when they let me hold you in the hospital…' She took a great gurgling sniff. 'It would be healthy for me to say goodbye, the social worker said. She was nice…' She paused as a mental picture flashed in her brain and she smiled in response. 'I swear her arms were as thick as my thighs. And she smelled of peppermints and talcum powder. Sorry… I seem to remember every silly detail of that day.'

The four of them were like statues. Passengers coming out of the security checks were pushing past and muttering about people getting in the way, but they didn't move.

Jackie sniffed. 'You can't laugh or hate me for it. I was sixteen and had very funny ideas about things…'

Sue nodded and glanced across at her adoptive daughter. 'Tell me about it.'

Kate blushed.

Jackie wanted to cry and laugh and smile all at the same time. She managed two out of three. 'I called you Adrina, after the lake near Romano's home. It means "happiness".'

Sue nodded. 'That's beautiful.'

'Well, she was.' Jackie looked Kate in the eyes. 'You were. And it tore my heart out to give you away. Don't ever think that I didn't care. I did. But I only let myself feel it for that one day. After that I had to make myself not care, or I never would have survived. And that's why I struggle sometimes…'

Kate frowned. Jackie could see the disbelief in her eyes. 'Because you don't care any more? Because it worked?'

'No!' Here came the tears again. It was just as well she wasn't wearing any mascara. 'Because I *do* care! I love you, Kate…so much. And I've wanted to tell you so many times, but I've taught myself to bury it deep and hide it well. And, even if I do say so myself—' she gave a weak smile '—I'm an excellent teacher. I'm sorry. It's going to take me some time to unlearn all those hard lessons and I'm afraid you are just going to have to be patient with me. One day I'll be a woman who'll make you proud.'

She held her breath and waited, then Kate, who had been looking fiercer and fiercer all through her speech, launched herself into Jackie's arms and held her tight. Jackie, who had never held her daughter since that day in the hospital, wept freely, making the most unattractive noises, and hugged Kate back.

Eventually they separated themselves. Kate reached for the tissue that she'd stuffed in her jeans pocket and decided that it had no more uses left in it. She looked hopefully at Sue.

Sue shrugged. 'I'm all out. Let's go and find some more.' And discreetly she led Kate away in the direction of the Ladies'.

Jackie turned to Romano, who had been standing slightly

to the side, and had been silent all through her outburst. He smiled at her.

'Where did you get that lovely jacket?' he said, with a twinkle in his eye.

'It belongs to my housekeeper. I found it by the front door.'

'It's a well-known fact that what a person wears says a lot about them. What do you think your clothes are shouting about you right at this moment, Ms Patterson?'

Oh, help. By the time she'd decided to try and catch them it had been too late to do anything but jump in the cab and tip the driver exorbitantly so he'd make it to London City Airport in time. What must she look like? She was standing here in front of the man she loved in cheap flip-flops, her housekeeper's dog-walking fleece and her pyjama bottoms. Whatever that was saying, she wasn't sure anyone wanted to hear it.

'That I was in a hurry?' she said optimistically.

Romano just threw his head back and laughed out loud. And then he wrapped his arms around her and lowered his head until his lips were almost touching hers. 'No,' he said quietly. 'This is the most beautiful I have ever seen you.' And he kissed her, softly, tenderly, deliciously, to drive the point home. 'Today, your clothes say that you are on the outside who you have always been on the inside—a woman of great courage, great strength and great love.'

Jackie smiled against his lips. 'Really? You got all that from an old lilac fleece? I must wear it more often.'

Romano kissed her once more. Or she kissed him, she wasn't sure which, and then he took her passport and papers from her and tucked them into his bag.

'I don't think the New York fashion gurus are ready for this look yet, so it's just as well you are coming home with me.'

EPILOGUE

NOT long after there was another wedding at the courthouse in Monta Correnti, followed by a small reception for family and friends. Tables and chairs from a restaurant in the piazza outside the church were rearranged to accommodate the bridal party and their guests.

Musicians appeared and serenaded the bride and groom, and wedding guests and locals began to dance in the piazza and the air was filled with song and laughter.

Late in the evening their youngest bridesmaid tottered over the cobbles on her new high heels and handed the bride and groom a medium-sized, slightly wonkily wrapped present.

Jackie gave her daughter a kiss on the cheek. 'You didn't have to get us anything! Just the fact that you came was enough.'

Kate just smiled shyly. 'Open it.'

Romano slid it across the table to his brand-new wife and she carefully peeled off the bow and wrapping paper. Inside was a big scrapbook. Jackie opened the cover, then instantly covered her mouth with her fingers. On the first page was a picture of a dark-haired baby, grinning toothlessly at the photographer. And after that was page after page of memories—photographs, programmes from school concerts, certificates and badges. It left the bride and groom completely speechless.

'Sue helped me put it together,' Kate explained.

Jackie picked it up and hugged it to her chest. 'Thank you,' she whispered. 'You don't know how much this means.'

'I think I do. I just wanted to say that I understand now, and that I'm sorry I didn't share these moments with you…' She paused and scrunched her face up. 'But I can't be sorry you gave me to Dave and Sue, either.'

A look of sudden horror passed over her features, and Jackie reached out and took her hand. 'That's how it should be, sweetheart,' she said. 'Of course you love them.'

Jackie stood up and pulled her daughter into a hug.

'I love you too, Mum,' Kate whispered in her ear, and by doing so she gave the bride a wedding present beyond price and compare.

They held each other for the longest time, until Kate tugged herself gently away. 'I'm going to go now.' She glanced at where people were dancing in the piazza. 'A really cute boy asked me to dance.'

Romano straightened in his seat and started to look around. Jackie just patted him on the arm and told him to 'stand down', and then they kissed their daughter again and watched her wobble her way back across the cobbles towards where the dancing was.

Later that evening, Jackie and Romano left the town partying and crept away to a little island on a nearby lake for the start of their stay-at-home honeymoon. They walked out onto the terrace, a glass of champagne each, and stared across the lake as it winked the stars back to them.

'I can't quite believe the pair of us managed to produce a human being quite as perfect as Kate is,' Jackie said softly.

'I know,' Romano replied, in that mock-serious voice of his. 'It would be a terrible waste if we didn't do it again. It's practically our duty to the world…'

Jackie turned to look at him. 'Are you saying what I think you're saying?'

Romano took the glass out of Jackie's hand and placed it on the stone balustrade with his own, then pulled her close and kissed her.

'I certainly am.'

She looped her arms around his neck and pulled him close, kissed him in a way that showed just how much she agreed. 'I love you, Romano.'

'You know what I love?' he said, surprising her by pulling back and giving her a cheeky grin.

She shook her head.

'That, although you wouldn't allow me to design your dress—and I was cross about that at first.'

Jackie let out a shocked chuckle. 'Cross? You pouted like a two-year-old!'

He shrugged her comment off. 'No matter. My father has outdone himself. I have never seen you look so breathtaking.' He pulled her close and started to kiss her neck, bunch the silk taffeta up with his hands. 'What I really love, *Signora* Puccini,' he whispered in her ear, 'is that tonight, I get to *undress* you.' His fingers toyed with the top button on a row down her spine that seemed to go on for ever.

Jackie just laughed softly and wiggled closer to give him better access.

'You're incorrigible,' she whispered back.

'Oh, yes,' he said as he gently bit her ear lobe. 'And that is just the way you like me.'

THE COWBOY'S
ADOPTED DAUGHTER

BY
PATRICIA THAYER

Originally born and raised in Muncie, Indiana, **Patricia Thayer** is the second of eight children. She attended Ball State University, and soon afterwards headed West. Over the years she's made frequent visits back to the Midwest, trying to keep up with her growing family.

Patricia has called Orange County, California, home for many years. She not only enjoys the warm climate, but also the company and support of other published authors in the local writers' organisation. For the past eighteen years she has had the unwavering support and encouragement of her critique group. It's a sisterhood like no other.

When not working on a story, you might find her traveling the United States and Europe, taking in the scenery and doing story research while thoroughly enjoying herself, accompanied by Steve, her husband for over thirty-five years. Together they have three grown sons and four grandsons. As she calls them, her own true-life heroes. On rare days off from writing, you might catch her at Disneyland, spoiling those grandkids rotten! She also volunteers for the Grandparent Autism Network.

Patricia has written for over twenty years and has authored more than thirty-six books. She has been nominated for both the National Readers' Choice Award and the prestigious RITA® Award. Her book *Nothing Short of a Miracle* won an *RT Book Reviews* Reviewer's Choice award. A long-time member of Romance Writers of America, she has served as president and held many other board positions for her local chapter in Orange County. She's a firm believer in giving back.

Check her website at www.patriciathayer.com for upcoming books.

To the Scissor Sisters,

Michele Braithwaite, Lindsay Fulmer, Amy Lawrence,
Barbara Marshburn, Karren Mitchell, Margaret
Russell, my sister-in-law, Pat Wright and Kay Yu Kim
for letting me visit your group, and answering
all my questions.

You sure aren't your grandmother's quilting bee.

CHAPTER ONE

ALEX CASALI sat atop his stallion, Diablo, as he looked at the pasture below where three hundred head of prime Herefords grazed contently. In another few months the herd would be moved again at fall roundup, and the yearlings shipped to his feedlot outside Kerry Springs.

He shifted in the saddle and looked over the hill country. With each season came the familiar routine he needed to keep order in his life. He glanced around the hundreds of acres that made up his ranch. In Texas, his cattle operation was considered average, except the A Bar A Ranch purebred steers weren't average. Casali beef demanded top dollar, and got it.

It had taken years of hard work and struggle to get a piece of Texas land. He'd hired on to several cattle outfits and saved every dime for his own place. Little by little he'd restored this once rundown ranch he'd bought at auction until it suited his tastes. After ten years and some good investments, he'd built an empire.

He leaned his forearm against the saddle horn. Yet, the Casali Cattle Company wasn't enough to satisfy him. He'd begun breeding horses a few years back. Now, another new venture. He'd soon be opening a guest ranch. He looked past the grove of trees at the dozen new cabins that would soon be open to strangers.

He had to be crazy for letting Tilda talk him into this project. Yet, his one-time housekeeper, ranch book-keeper—and now partner in the guest ranch—had come up with some good ideas over the years to stimulate revenue. It still didn't change the fact that what he liked the most about this life was the solitude, having no need to be around many people. Outside of his brother, Angelo, he preferred to be alone.

Diablo danced impatiently and Alex tugged on the reins to get him under control. That was when he caught sight of a vehicle coming down the main road toward his house.

He didn't recognize the car. That meant they had no business on his land.

Allison Cole glanced out of the window as she drove her small SUV through the large stone and wrought-iron archway announcing the A Bar A Ranch. Cedar and oak trees lined the narrow road from the hot sun. Rows of pristine white rail fences ran alongside the road as horses roamed contentedly in the grassy pastures.

"This is really something, isn't it, Cherry?"

She glanced into the rear-view mirror to see her daughter watching the countryside from her safety seat. Most four-year-olds were inquisitive and asked a lot of questions. Not Cherry. And Allison missed hearing her child's tiny voice. Outside of her cries in the night, Cherry hadn't talked since the accident. Nor had she walked.

When Tilda Emerson called her early this morning, Allison couldn't turn down her intriguing invitation. Coming here today was for her daughter, as much as for the new business she was trying to launch in town, her quilt shop, Blind Stitch. So she dropped everything, packed up Cherry and drove out here to meet Tilda.

It had been a long time since she'd taken a leisurely afternoon off. On impulse, Allison pulled the car to the side of the road where several horses and foals were grazing in the high grass.

"Cherry, you want to see a horse?"

Ignoring the silence, Allison got out and removed her daughter from her seat. Lifting the small child in her arms, she carried her to the fence.

She was encouraged as her daughter gripped the rail and looked over at the animals. There was awareness in the child's eyes that hadn't been there for a long time.

"See the baby horse?"

"What do you think you're doing?"

At the sound of a deep voice, Allison swung around. A large man was sitting atop a very large horse. The bright sunlight was behind him, making it impossible to see anything except the outline of his wide shoulders and cowboy hat.

It was hard not to be intimidated. "I'm sorry. What did you say?"

The black stallion danced sideways and blew out a breath. "You're on private property," he said. "That's called trespassing."

"No. I was invited to come here. I have a business meeting with Tilda Emerson."

Although she couldn't see his eyes, she felt his gaze locked on her.

"She's up at the house. I suggest you don't keep her waiting." With that he wheeled the horse around and took off.

"Not a friendly man," she murmured. After strapping

Cherry back into her safety seat she headed back to the narrow road. Maybe coming here wasn't such a good idea.

Allison drove past several outbuildings, including a huge red barn and attached corral. Then she saw the large, two-story, brick and clapboard home. Black shutters stood out from the glossy white siding, and the wraparound porch was highlighted by hanging baskets of flowers.

"Really something," she murmured again, recalling the luxury home she'd left back in Phoenix. Per instructions from Mrs. Emerson, Allison passed up the circular drive in front of the house and parked by the back door.

Shutting off the engine, she turned to Cherry. "We're not going to stay long, sweetheart." She reached back and brushed the strawberry-blonde curls away from her daughter's face. Those big blue eyes looked back at her, but her child didn't respond, just turned her head and stared out of the window.

Allison looked past a large oak tree and saw a horse grazing just beyond the fence.

"Look, Cherry, another horse."

Allison climbed out of the car just as a woman stepped out of the house. About sixty, she was tall and slender, dressed in a pair of jeans and a colorful blouse.

"Mrs. Emerson?"

The gray-haired woman smiled as she came down the porch steps. "It's Tilda. You must be Allison Cole. So glad you could make it."

They shook hands. "Well, you made me curious with your proposal. I'd like to hear more."

"Good. Did you have any trouble finding the place?"

Allison thought back to the cowboy. "I ran into one of the ranch hands and he gave me directions." She glanced back into the car. "I hope you don't mind that my daughter came along."

Tilda waved a hand. "There's no reason why you shouldn't bring her. Let's get her out of the hot car."

Allison hesitated, then she popped the SUV's hatch, revealing the small wheelchair. "Let me get Cherry settled, and then we can talk."

The older woman's smile wavered. "Here, let me help you."

Together they got out the chair and Allison lifted her daughter into the seat.

Tilda led them to a shaded patio area just down from the porch. "Cherry, that's a pretty name and you're a pretty little girl," she said. "Do you like animals?" Even without a response, the older woman continued on, "I hope so. We've got plenty of them around here."

As if her words were magic, a large dog wandered over, followed by another smaller one.

"This big guy is Rover." She stroked the black Labrador mix. "The little one is Pete." She also gave some attention to the Heinz 57 variety of a mutt. "They like to be petted by little girls and boys." On cue Rover wandered over and laid his head on the arm of the wheelchair.

Allison was shocked when her daughter placed her small hand on the animal. Pete soon wanted attention and rose up on his hind legs and danced around. Cherry petted him, too.

After getting her daughter some lemonade, Allison went inside to the big open kitchen.

"I should bring Cherry inside, too."

Tilda brought two glasses to the table. "I doubt she wants to leave her new friends. Relax, we can see her from the window. Rover and Pete will keep an eye on her."

With a nod, Allison sat at the table next to the picture window. With her daughter in full view, she turned to Tilda. "You have a beautiful place."

"Why, thank you, but it's not mine. Not any more, that is. When my husband died twelve years ago, I couldn't manage the ranch on my own, and I couldn't afford to hire anyone. It got pretty run-down. Finally the bank took it and sold it at auction to Alex Casali."

"I'm sorry, that had to be awful."

"It was for the best. Besides, Alex asked me to stay on. I took care of the house, helped with the bookkeeping. He's accomplished a lot in the past ten years. He's restored this house, built a new barn and outer buildings for his prime cattle operation. This ranch is a showplace again. I'd like to think I helped with that." She grinned. "Now, I'm a partner in this new project of the guest ranch."

"I have to be honest, Tilda. I might not be able to put the time needed into this project." Allison knew she was crazy to nix this chance. She could use the income. "I can't take the time away from my daughter."

The older woman nodded. "I expect we can work something out because I believe you're perfect for what I have in mind."

At the barn, Alex handed Diablo's reins off to Jake, one of the ranch hands, then headed toward the house. That was when he saw the woman's car at the back door. Great. Tilda's visitor was probably the decorator for the cabins. Who needed to decorate log cabins? He didn't want any part of picking wall colors or curtains. He'd just go inside, give a nod of greeting to the striking redheaded woman with the haunting green eyes, then go off to the office.

Easy.

He'd been attracted to women before but walked away, especially when they had commitment written all over them. This one had a child.

He started up the porch steps when he spotted an empty wheelchair next to the slatted fence. When he got closer, he saw the dogs, along with Buckshot, just on the other side of the fence. Nothing strange about that, but they had company. The little girl he saw earlier.

"What the hell?" He went over and slipped through the railings to find the child sitting on the ground next to the fence. Old Buckshot's head was down so she could pet his muzzle. This was not a good idea.

"Well, damn," he said under his breath. The little sprite heard and turned to him. Her sky-blue eyes were wide with excitement as she smiled at him, her head a crown of strawberry-colored ringlets.

"Horsey," she whispered.

His chest tightened. "Yeah, he sure is." Not wanting to frighten the kid, he made slow, easy movements. "How 'bout I lift you up so you can pet the old gray better."

He was taken by surprise when the girl raised her arms toward him. A strange feeling went through him as he picked up the small child as if she didn't weigh anything. With her secure in his arms, he took her to the animal's side so she could touch him.

"His name is Buckshot. He likes to be petted here." He took her tiny hand and placed it on the horse's head.

Alex was rewarded with a tiny giggle. Another sensation stirred in his chest.

Suddenly he heard a woman's cry. "Cherry!"

Alex turned in time to see the kid's mother running

from the house. Her long auburn hair was flying around her face as she hurried toward the fence. She ducked through the slats. Suddenly her shapely bottom became his focal point with her efforts to get into the pasture. She finally got untangled and stood in front of him. The top of her head only reached the middle of his chest.

"Cherry." She took her child from him. "Are you all right?"

He didn't like the look she gave him. "Thanks to me she is."

The woman turned her attention to him, pinning him with a jade-green stare. "I don't appreciate you taking my child in here without my permission."

"Lady, I didn't take her anywhere," he said, pointing toward the ground. "I found her right in this spot with Buckshot."

The mother glared back. "That's impossible. Cherry can't walk."

Alex glanced at the child, wondering what had happened. "Well, however she got here, I didn't bring her."

"Then how?"

Alex shrugged. "Ask her."

Suddenly tears filled her eyes. "I would love to, but my daughter hasn't spoken in a year."

"She spoke to me," he told her. But as if to call him a liar, the girl refused to say anything.

They both stared at the child. "Cherry? Do you like the horsey?" her mother asked. The child looked back to the horse, but didn't say a word.

Finally Tilda appeared, causing Alex to wonder where she'd been all this time. "Sorry, I had to take that call. Is everything okay?"

Allison continued to glare. "Seems I'm having a

disagreement with your ranch hand. Something he knows nothing about."

Alex refused to be baited by this woman. "Maybe you don't know your child as well as you think."

"How dare you?"

Tilda stepped in. "Stop! This was my fault. I'm the one who said she'd be fine on the patio." She looked concerned. "I'm sorry, Allison, I had no idea she would wander off."

Alex looked at the woman, unable to ignore her appeal. "And I'd appreciate it if you stayed with your daughter from now on. A ranch isn't the best place to leave kids unsupervised."

Allison turned to Tilda. "How do you put up with this?"

"It's hard sometimes," Tilda said as her mouth quirked as if hiding a smile. She shot him a glare. "Allison Cole, this is Alex Casali, the owner of the A Bar A."

Allison hated that the man was so smug. She also hated that she noticed he was so handsome. That was, if you liked the tall, muscular, rough type of guy with piercing gray eyes.

"At a loss for words, Mrs. Cole?"

She'd forgotten arrogant. "My concern is for my daughter, Mr. Casali." She shifted Cherry higher on her hip. "She's usually shy around strangers."

He pushed back his black cowboy hat, revealing light brown hair. "That's understandable." He glanced at Cherry and his expression softened. "She's sure not afraid of animals."

Cherry made a grunting sound and pointed toward Buckshot, then reached out toward Alex Casali.

Allison tried to hold her back, but the uneven weight

threw her off balance. Alex had no choice but to take the determined child.

He easily lifted her daughter into his arms. "Do you mind?" he asked.

She shook her head. This had been the most response she'd seen from Cherry since before the accident. "Please be careful with her."

He gave her a stony look. "I'd never be anything else."

Alison watched closely as he carried Cherry over toward the horse.

Tilda came up to her. "You don't have to worry about old Buckshot," she said. "He was my husband's horse, and a darn good cutter, too. As they say, he's been put out to pasture to live out his days. And besides, Cherry's got some pretty strong arms holding her."

"Horses are so big."

"You're right. Even though Buckshot is gentle, he's still a large animal. But Alex will make sure she's safe." Tilda nodded toward the two dogs following after her. "Your daughter has made many friends today."

Allison wasn't looking at the horse or the dogs, but at the man holding Cherry. As big as he was, he was gentle with her. And most importantly, her daughter seemed to trust him. Not that either of them had much reason to trust when it came to men.

"I know Alex is a little rough around the edges," Tilda began, "but he's got a good heart." The older woman smiled. "What's most important is Cherry thinks so."

Before Allison could say anything, the rancher turned and started back toward them. Her daughter's head rested contentedly on his broad shoulder, her eyes closed. "I think someone's tired."

"Well it's no wonder with the time she's had," Tilda said. "Let's take her inside and put her down."

Allison hesitated. "Maybe we should head back to town."

Tilda shook her head. "Why put her in a hot car? We have a comfortable bed close by. Then we can finish our talk."

Without getting permission, Alex Casali started for the paddock gate. Allison ran after him. "I didn't agree to stay."

"I don't know where you come from, but here in Texas we don't turn down hospitality when it's offered." He kept his hand on the child's back and his strides were steady and smooth. "Me, I can care less if you stay, but your visit is important to Tilda."

"It's important to me, too."

He stopped at the steps to the porch. "Then it's settled, you stay and talk with Tilda."

She fisted her hands, but kept her voice low and controlled. "My concern, Mr. Casali, is my daughter. She's been through a rough year."

"It's Alex. And I can see that, but I can also see this little one was enjoying herself a few minutes ago."

Okay, he had her there. "All right, we'll stay."

With a nod, he went up the steps and she followed behind. Tilda arrived and rushed on ahead, through the kitchen and pantry, then into a good-size bedroom containing a double bed. She pulled back the bright patchwork quilt.

Allison's heart ached, watching the large man gently place her tiny daughter on the mattress, her lifeless legs at a funny angle. When Alex stepped away, she quickly shifted Cherry's body onto her side, and draped a thin blanket over her. After brushing away a few soft curls from her baby's flushed face, she turned to find the rancher had already left. She followed Tilda out and back into the kitchen. Her daughter's rescuer wasn't there, either. To her surprise she was disappointed by his disappearance.

CHAPTER TWO

ALLISON walked across the kitchen to the table. She knew Tilda wanted to discuss business, but her mind kept wandering elsewhere. Where had Alex Casali gone? And would he be back to sit in on the discussion? More importantly, did he want her here?

Tilda brought two fresh glasses of lemonade. "We'll be able to hear Cherry if she wakes up. So sit and relax."

"Thank you." Allison took a long drink.

The older woman took the seat across from her. "I guess I'm not making much of a first impression."

"No, it's not your fault, Tilda," Allison said. "I probably should have explained the situation and asked you to meet at the shop. It's easier for Cherry."

The woman studied her a moment. "If you don't mind my asking, has your daughter always been in a wheelchair?"

She shook her head. "No. She was in an automobile accident last year and she hasn't been able to walk since."

Tilda's aged hand covered hers. "That has to be so hard on both of you."

Allison swallowed hard, feeling a growing connection with this woman. Since her grandmother's passing,

Allison really hadn't had anyone to talk to. "It was touch and go for a while. Although the surgeon repaired the damage to Cherry's spine, she needs a lot of therapy. Even then, there aren't any guarantees for a full recovery."

Tilda smiled sadly. "Well, as long as there's hope. She seemed happy around the animals."

Allison shook her head, amazed. "I'm confused. I'm usually the only one she wants."

"Alex might be a man of few words, but he's the best with animals…and it looks like kids, too."

Definitely not adults, Allison thought.

"Feel free to tell me to mind my own business," Tilda began, "but what about Cherry's father?"

"He's not in our lives anymore." And that was all she was going to say about it.

"It's a tough job, being a single parent."

"All I want is for Cherry to be a typical, happy kid again." Tears threatened. "She hasn't spoken since the accident."

Tilda sighed. "Oh, bless her."

Allison thought back to the corral, seeing her daughter reach out for Alex Casali. A perfect stranger and a man, no less.

"Today, Rover, Pete and Buckshot seemed to get a big response from her," Tilda said. "You're welcome to bring Cherry back any time. If you decide to do the quilting retreat, she can spend time with them every day."

"Oh, Tilda, I don't see how I can oversee a workshop and care for my daughter, too. And there's my shop in town."

"Cherry's welcome. She can join us and you'll have plenty of time to spend with her. And as for your shop, can't Mattie handle running it for a few days?"

Allison had been lucky to find Mattie Smyth, a widow who had time on her hands. But Tilda's offer was tempting, too. "Five days is a long time."

Tilda leaned forward. "We can make adjustments on the time if needed." She sighed. "Look, Allison, the straight talk is, the Hidden Hills Guest Ranch is a new venture for us. Let's just say Alex wasn't keen on my idea of bringing people here. He's more into his cattle and horses. Besides the money to be made in this venture, I'm going to enjoy having people around. And truth is, Alex needs it, too."

Allison would second that. The man didn't seem to have many social skills.

"So if I can make this retreat work," Tilda continued, "my plan is to eventually have several different events going on during the year."

Allison was impressed with this woman's business savvy, and also tempted.

Tilda continued, "Kerry Springs has become a popular retirement community. There are a lot of seniors who aren't ready to just sit around, including several women from my church who want to attend the quilting classes."

Allison certainly missed designing her quilt patterns and doing her weekly cable program. Yet, a demanding career had cost her the early years with Cherry. A lesson she had learned nearly too late. Never again would she get back into that rat race of long days and travel. "What level of classes are you talking about?"

Tilda shrugged. "I've advertised it for experienced quilters, but we aren't turning anyone away. Many of the women were fans of your television program, *Quilt Allie*. They've even used some of your quilt patterns."

Allison glanced away, recalling the reason she'd had

to walk away from her lucrative career. "I gave up the show after Cherry's accident. She needs me to be a full-time mom." And her ex-husband got the income from sales of all her previous quilt designs. She'd given Jack Hudson everything to get the divorce and permanent custody of her daughter. Since Cherry's care was costly, she could use some extra income.

Allison looked at Tilda. "I'll need to have two after-noons off so I can take Cherry to therapy."

"Not a problem. And you'll have your own cabin during the retreat. You won't even have to drive back to town, unless you want." When Tilda named the salary, Allison knew she had to try and make it work.

The brooding Alex Casali flashed in her head. The man didn't even seem to like her, but she doubted he'd get involved in a quilting workshop.

Allison released a breath. "Then as long as Cherry can come with me, we should be able to work something out. But first, I need to talk to Mattie about working longer hours."

"Of course." Tilda's eyes brightened and she stood. "I know Mattie will do this. Would you mind if I called her?" She left the room before Allison could stop her.

Allison got up and looked around the big country-style kitchen. It had been remodeled with maple cabinets and granite counters, but it still had a warm, cozy feeling. The aroma of spices coming from the oven made her think of her grandmother. Their home hadn't been close to this grand. It had just been a small two-bedroom rental with noisy pipes and squeaky floors. But Emmeline Cole had given her love and a roof over her head when no one else wanted her.

Later on, Allison had been just as eager for love when

she'd picked a husband. Jack had other ideas on what marriage meant.

Allison went to a window and looked out at a picturesque scene of the large ranch operation. She hoped Cherry understood her reason for doing this, remembering sitting at her bedside fifteen months ago. All the time she'd begged her daughter to wake up, she'd promised she'd be a real mother to her from now on.

Cherry had held her accountable to her words and had been possessive since the accident. Until today when she practically jumped into Alex Casali's arms.

Allison heard steps and turned around. It wasn't Tilda returning, but Alex who walked into the kitchen.

Speak of the devil. Her breath caught as her gaze moved over the man. He'd showered and shaved and, now he was minus the black hat, she got a good look at the startlingly handsome cowboy. He was getting an eyeful, too. She felt a strange tingling of awareness through her body.

"Surprised you're still here," he said, then went to the coffee pot and poured a cup.

"We'll be leaving as soon as Cherry wakes up."

He took a drink from the mug as he leaned back against the counter, his booted feet crossed at the ankles. "Makes no difference to me. It's just that Tilda wants the guest ranch to go off without a hitch. So if it's more money you want—"

So far everything out of this man's mouth had irritated her. "Her offer is more than fair. I only have to make sure I can care for my daughter."

He nodded. "Good. The little one will probably enjoy coming out here." He pulled her back to his steel-gray gaze. "That is, unless you're afraid to let her be around animals."

"Until today, Cherry hasn't been near a horse. I had no idea that she'd respond so strongly."

He put down his mug and pushed away from the counter. "Then you shouldn't deny her the pleasure of visiting Buckshot. Some say horse therapy helps kids. Maybe she'll even be able to ride someday."

She tensed. "Wait a minute. I didn't say anything about letting her ride. She can't even walk…yet."

"She may not be able to walk, but she's figured out how to get what she wants."

He crossed the room to her and she felt her breath catch in anticipation. "What about you, Allie? You brave enough to go after what you want?"

Alex couldn't figure out why this woman got to him. He should just walk away and leave this all to Tilda. Instead he kept coming back to the pretty redhead.

"Brave or not, Mr. Casali, my only concern is to be a good mother to my daughter. I'm teaching this workshop for that reason and that reason only. So don't let me keep you from what you have to do." She turned to the window. "Don't you have some cattle to brand, or round up somewhere?"

Although she tried to hide it, he could see that she was uncomfortable with him.

"Not at the moment."

"Well, don't let me stop you from your work."

"You aren't." He put his mug in the sink. "I've been up since four a.m. so my chores are finished."

"I thought ranchers worked from sunup to sundown."

"Not if we can help it. And there are ranch hands that help out, too."

Before Allison could answer him, Tilda came into the

room with the phone against her ear. She was smiling. "She's right here." Tilda held out the receiver to Allison. "It's Mattie."

She took it, then walked away. Alex turned to Tilda. "Any problems?"

"None at all. Looks like we got Allison Cole," she said.

Alex studied the petite woman in the dress trousers and leather pumps and prim white blouse. City. "You sure she's going to fit in here?"

Tilda looked at him. "Of course. Why wouldn't she? Besides, Allison is from the country, Virginia, I think." She placed her hands on her hips. "Why are you suddenly interested? I thought you didn't want any part of this project."

"I don't but I more or less got thrown into it when I rescued the kid from the pasture."

A spark lit in her hazel eyes. "Cherry is cute, isn't she? The mother's not so bad, either."

He didn't want to have this discussion, but that didn't stop Tilda.

"I don't think I've seen hair that rich auburn color before," she went on, "And those freckles across her face are cute. I think her best feature are those green eyes."

The last thing he needed to do was think about Allison Cole. "I've got paperwork." He started to leave, but she stopped him.

"Alex, don't run off. I'm showing Allison the main building at Hidden Hills and we'll need your help getting Cherry there."

"I doubt she'll take my help." He glanced at the woman in question. "She's one of those independent women."

Tilda fought a grin. "You mean instead of one of those women who fall all over you." She glanced at

Allison, then back to him. "But then again, this one just might be one who stands up to you."

Alex started to leave when Allison made the trip back across the room. "Well, it looks like Mattie can handle every day but Wednesday afternoon." Those green eyes met his. "I'll just close the shop for those few hours." She smiled, and there was stirring in his gut and lower. "It looks like you've got an instructor for the class."

Tilda grinned. "That's wonderful." She hugged Allison. "You and Cherry have to stay for supper so we can celebrate. Before you argue, I already have a roast cooking. We'll show you the new community room where the classes will be held, and we need to go over a few details before I put everything up on the website."

They were all jolted back to reality as a child's cry rang out. "Cherry." Allison took off to the bedroom; Tilda followed close behind.

Alex went out to retrieve the child's wheelchair from the patio and carried it into the house. He pushed it down the hall just as Allison carried her daughter out of the bathroom.

When the girl saw him a shy smile appeared on her face. "Looks like I got here just in time," he said. "Your chair, *signorina*." He gestured toward the seat.

Allison hesitated, but her daughter leaned down, forcing her to place her there. Once she was secured in the chair, she looked up at him.

"It seems my daughter is a little smitten with you, Mr. Casali," Allison said.

"Since we'll be working together, it's Alex. And I will call you Allie."

That got a rise out of her. He found he liked to see her frazzled.

"I go by Allison."

"Tilda would like to show you around the guest ranch." He raised a hand. "Before you ask, it's wheelchair accessible, so Cherry can go along, too." He leaned down to the girl. "You want to go for a ride?"

The child nodded and looked at her mom.

"Yes, we can go," Allison told her.

They returned to the kitchen and found Tilda checking the roast in the oven. "By the time we get back supper should be done."

"I don't want to put you out, Tilda."

"Nonsense, like I said, we have to eat. And it's not often we get company." She looked at Alex. "This one lives like a hermit." She turned back to Allison. "Maybe you'll help change that."

Twenty minutes later, loaded into Alex's crew cab pickup, they took the mile-long trip to the guest ranch through a grove of trees. Just off the dirt road several log cabins came into view, then finally a large two-story structure appeared in the clearing.

"This is impressive," Allison said.

"Good." Tilda beamed. "There are twelve one- and two-bedroom cabins, and in the main house there are another ten guest rooms. We're advertising the main house for family reunions and business conferences and retreats."

Alex pulled into a gravel parking lot in front of the main house. "If you haven't guessed, Tilda is big on public relations," he said.

The older woman smacked his arm playfully. "Well, someone has to promote us. And you get top dollar for Casali Beef because I've advertised it online."

He adjusted his hat. "Word would have gotten around."

She huffed. "By that time I'd be in my grave."

Alex grumbled something as he climbed out of the truck. Allison didn't understand the language, but with the name Casali she figured it was Italian. How did an Italian end up in Texas?

The back door opened and Alex appeared to take Cherry out of the safety seat. "Come on, little one. Want to go for a ride?" He lifted her out of her seat and into the wheelchair.

Allison got out her side and hurried around the truck as Alex pushed Cherry up the ramp to the long porch. Tilda went on ahead and unlocked the double doors, then held them open. They walked into a huge room where the scent of fresh-cut wood teased her nose. Tilda turned on the lights and the massive room came to life. A large stone fireplace was the focal point. A wide staircase led to a balcony upstairs. A bar area took up another space along the wall. Furniture was still covered in plastic, but she knew it was leather. A rustic chandelier hung over a huge rectangular table with a dozen high-back chairs.

"This is amazing," she whispered.

"We think so," Tilda said, leading them toward the hallway and into another large room. "In here is where I planned to hold your class. It should handle twelve to fifteen tables and machines comfortably."

Allison looked around the room, checking the light coming through the window, measuring space in her head when she caught Cherry with Alex. They were at the windows, her chair close as he leaned over her, pointing to something outside. What interested her was the expression on her daughter's face.

"Allison, is there a problem?"

She turned back to Tilda. "No, I was thinking about all the supplies we're going to need, especially if there are beginners."

The older woman smiled. "Well, that's your department, and more money for you since you have the shop. I'll advertise for anyone who wants to attend, either bring your own supplies, or we'll make them available for an extra fee."

Allison finally smiled. "Are you sure people are going to attend?"

"I have a nearly filled class already. My goal is to get fifteen attending for the week. I love to quilt myself, when I have the time, but it's always been more about sharing the time with friends and family while creating memories."

"My grandmother taught me when I was about Cherry's age. Emmeline Cole was the talented one." Allison smiled at the memories. "I still have some of her quilts."

"See that's what I want to create with this retreat. Mothers and daughter together, making memories, and returning here year after year."

Alex watched Tilda and Allison from across the room. Maybe he should plan to go out of town while this retreat was going on. He looked out of the window, knowing they'd planned this guest ranch far enough away from the main house so not to disturb his operation or his privacy. But he had a feeling distance wasn't going to help him.

Keeping his distance from Allison Cole wasn't going to be easy. He glanced down at her precious child and felt a tug on his heart. There had to be more that could be done for her.

"Horsey?" she whispered as she pointed out of the window and off toward a mare and her foal in the pasture.

He tried not to act surprised on hearing her speak again. He knelt down. "That's Starlight and her baby." He smiled at her. "Maybe you can think of a name for him."

She looked up at him and those cornflower-blue eyes filled with wonder. She wrinkled her freckled nose, and he felt a strange protectiveness toward her. He couldn't help but wonder who had hurt this child so much that she didn't speak.

Tilda and Allison walked over. "What are you two up to?" Tilda asked.

Alex winked at Cherry. "It's a secret," he said as the girl became distant once again. He turned his attention to Allison and saw her hurt look.

He recalled a lot of bad years with a mother who'd lied and put herself before her sons. Allison Cole seemed to show real concern for her daughter. But people had fooled him before. People he trusted, who'd claim to love him, then walk away.

Now, he made sure people didn't get close enough to do any damage.

CHAPTER THREE

"YOU old son-of-a-buck," Alex called, trying to get control of the young stallion. The horse resisted the commands, kicking up his hind legs. Whiskey Chaser was having none of it, saddle or rider. Determination won out and Alex got the red dun calmed down and he finally fell into a rhythmic lope around the corral.

Alex felt little satisfaction since he'd been working non-stop the past week to saddle break the animal. He'd had too many distractions. Ever since Allison Cole and her daughter had arrived and disturbed his peace and quiet. Worse, he hated that he'd been watching for her to return to the ranch. That hadn't happened either.

He knew every detail of what was going on. Whether he'd asked or not, every night Tilda had filled him in on the progress with the retreat, and the opening was just days away. Great, people would be swarming the place, including the pretty mother and her daughter. A killer combination.

He walked Chaser back toward the barn and was greeted by his foreman, Brian Perkins. At forty, the one-time rancher and horse breeder had lost his own place through divorce. Ten years ago, he'd shown up at the ranch asking for a job. Back then Alex couldn't afford much, so Brian had cleaned stalls and herded cattle for a low salary and a roof over his head. He'd never complained about any task.

A few years ago, Alex had made him the foreman. It had been Brian who'd talked Alex into trying his hand with breeding and raising quarter horses.

"He did well today." Brian reached for the horse's reins, but Chaser whinnied and pulled away. "I still say you should put him on a track and see how he does. He wants to run."

"There's no reason you can't give it a try," Alex relented.

That was what he liked about Brian. The foreman threw out suggestions, but never pushed Alex into making decisions. Another thing he liked was that they never got too personal. He knew that Brian had been married, and had two kids, John and Lindsey, he supported. They'd visited him here in the summer. Other than that neither man shared much about their past. But Alex knew he could depend on Brian, same as Brian could depend on him.

Alex climbed off the horse as one of the ranch hands came out and began to walk him, cooling him down. He turned back to Brian when a vehicle caught his eye. He recognized Allison Cole's SUV right off. He followed the car's journey to the house, but she didn't get out. Instead Tilda came out, climbed into the passenger side and they took off toward the cabins.

"Looks like Tilda's about ready for the grand opening." Brian turned to him. "Are you?"

Alex pulled off his gloves. "No, I'm not crazy about the place being overrun by women."

Brian smiled, causing lines around his eyes. "I guess I'll stay clear of the place, too. I'll take my chances with the wannabe cowboys coming here in a few months. That should be fun."

Alex wasn't sure how any of this would work out. He wasn't too worried; he'd made bad investments before. It wouldn't break him, and, more important, it made Tilda happy.

"Have you got a crew together for the fall roundup? With the inexperienced riders, we're going to need extra help."

Brian nodded. "I have a feeling we're going to be doing a lot more of the work this year."

Alex looked toward the guest ranch. He wondered if little Cherry had come along today.

When he turned back, Brian was watching him. "It's a shame about the girl. Tilda told me how she reacted to Buckshot."

"Yeah, she was quite taken with him," Alex said, recalling the kid's excitement.

"You know, we have Maisie," the foreman suggested. "She might get a kick out of seeing her."

The pony had been included with some stock he'd bought at an auction. Alex found he wanted to see a smile on the little one's face, wouldn't mind getting a reaction from the mother, either.

"I guess it wouldn't hurt."

Allison pushed Cherry's chair into the conference room. She quickly counted sixteen tables. They were set up with sewing machines and a large table at the front of the room. She went to the oversized shelving unit lining one wall; it was filled with several bolts of fabric.

Tilda came up beside her. "I organized everything you ordered, plus the fabric you'd sent out from the shop. The shelves are labeled in decades, the 1920s, '30s and '40s fabrics." She pointed toward the other cabinet. "And here we have the quilt kits for the beginners. We have every supply you could need, too. If the women don't bring their own, there are rotary cutters, rulers, mats, seam rippers and thread." She looked at Allison and smiled. "Did I forget anything?"

"This is incredible, Tilda. You must have worked day and night to get all this done."

"I had help. Some of my friends from church came out. I sort of promised a few of them that they could sit in on the classes. They're such fans of yours, Allison. And they want to help with Cherry's care, too, and help you go around the class seeing who needs anything."

Allison couldn't believe this. The last two years had been a nightmare. It had been bad enough dealing with Cherry's condition, but her ex-husband had then stripped her of nearly everything, including her pride and confidence. It had taken a long time before she could be creative again.

"Oh, Tilda. This is an instructor's dream." She fought her emotions. "I can't thank you enough for all your help with this."

"Well, I advertised this as top of the line, and with your name that's what it will be." She smiled. "I just want you to be comfortable. I want to make this a twice-a-year event. We might be able to get you back on cable."

Allison froze. If she did that, Jack would get half the profit. He'd gotten enough already. No more. Besides, she meant to keep her promise to her daughter. "Let's start with this retreat first." She glanced down at her daughter. "With the shop and Cherry's therapy, I have a lot to deal with."

"Of course."

Suddenly Cherry began to make sounds as she pointed to the window.

Tilda leaned toward the child. "Well, would you look at that, Cherry? It seems Alex is bringing you another friend."

Allison watched the rancher ride in on his big black stallion, leading a gold-color pony behind him. She glanced down to see her daughter sit straighter in her chair. Even her expression changed.

"That's Maisie," Tilda told her. "She's been around for a few years. She's as docile as a big old dog, and she loves kids, not that we get many around here."

Allison watched as Alex climbed off his horse, tied the reins to the porch railing. Then he walked the pony away from the stallion and tied her to another post.

He glanced toward the window and tipped his hat, then he took those long, lazy strides back across the porch and into the building.

"That's one good-looking cowboy, even if he wasn't Texas born and bred," Tilda said.

Allison had to agree. Her heart raced with anticipation as she heard his boots on the wooden floor, and he appeared in the doorway.

"Afternoon, ladies," he said and strolled in as if he owned the place. Well, he did. He walked directly toward Cherry. "I have a surprise for you, *uccellino*." He pushed his hat back off his forehead, revealing his sandy-colored hair as his gray-eyed gaze met Allison's. "May I take your daughter outside to meet Maisie?"

How could she deny him? "Maybe we can all go along."

He nodded. "Let's go." Instead of taking the chair, he lifted Cherry into those big strong arms. Seeing the pleased looked on her daughter's face, she wasn't about to stop him, especially when she realized she was a little envious.

She and Tilda hurried along to keep up with Alex's long strides through the building and across the porch toward the golden pony with the white mane and tail.

"Cherry, meet Maisie. This pony has lived on the ranch for two years, but she doesn't have any kids to visit her. So she's pretty happy that you're here today."

Allison had to bite back her emotions as she watched her daughter lean forward and her tiny hand began to stroke the pony's coat. For the first time in a long time she felt hopeful.

Alex couldn't take his eyes off his charge. Something happened to him when she was around. Those big hopeful eyes, the sweet innocent scent of hers. Maybe she reminded him of himself and his brother. They'd been about Cherry's age when they'd been shipped off to America by a father who hadn't wanted them, to a mother who hadn't wanted them either.

He glanced at Allison. She seemed to care about her daughter, but why didn't the little one talk?

"Horsey?" the girl whispered so no one else could hear.

For some reason the child had chosen him to speak to. She trusted him with her secret. He wasn't going to betray her, yet.

"It's a pony, Cherry. Maisie is a pony."

Cherry gave him a shy smile. The word, "Pony," came as another whispered response. Then she leaned forward, trying to get onto the pony's back.

"Whoa, cowgirl," he said, pulling her back. "I don't

think you're ready for that yet. We need a saddle
before you ride."

Allison came over. "Cherry, you don't know how to
ride."

The child didn't like that and began to cry. Loudly.

Alex walked her away from the pony. "Crying isn't
going to get you your way," he whispered in her ear.
"Show your mom that you're a big girl."

Cherry hiccupped, and finally stopped. He pulled
out a handkerchief and wiped her eyes. "Better? Now,
today we pet the pony and maybe go riding another
day. We have to get your mom's permission," he told
her. "Okay?"

She turned those large eyes on him. He felt his
heart melting and knew he was in trouble. He glanced
over his shoulder, seeing the beautiful Allison Cole.
Big trouble.

Two hours later, Allison and Cherry were seated at the
kitchen table sharing another meal with Alex Casali and
Tilda. She was surprised yet again when her daughter
didn't balk about eating her food. Once Alex told her to
finish her vegetables, and, although it was a slow
process, Cherry did just that.

After supper Alex disappeared, leaving her with Tilda
to discuss anything left to do before Thursday morning
and when the retreat would open.

Tilda got out her list of things to do. "I only want you
to worry about showing up. In fact, come the day before
so you can get settled in your cabin."

"You know, Tilda, Cherry and I can stay in the
main house."

"No, you need to get away from the others. I have a

feeling a lot of these women will be working on their quilts in the evenings. As long as you're available they'll monopolize your time."

"I guess you're right." She recalled her tours around the country at craft fairs. People wouldn't leave her alone even to eat. "I do need my time with Cherry." She glanced at her daughter, who had been looking through her books, but was now fast asleep.

"I think it's time I got her home."

Tilda smiled. "Oh, the little sweetheart. She's had a busy day."

Allison gathered her things. "I'll load the car, and come back to get her." She walked out of the back door into the dark night. After tossing her books on the seat, she went around to open the hatch for the chair. She started up the steps as Alex came out carrying Cherry. "You don't have to do that. I could have gotten her." It was a touching scene, seeing the big, gruff cowboy holding her baby.

"Well, I've got her, but I'd appreciate it if you'd open the door."

"Of course." She hurried back to the car and did as he asked. Alex carefully placed the sleeping child inside into her safety chair. Fastening the seat belt was a different story.

"Here, it's a little tricky." She leaned inside and immediately found how close the space was. She nearly collided with Alex when she turned his way. When their gazes locked her heart sped up as she felt his breath against her face.

"There, I got it." She quickly backed out. "I'll get the chair and we'll be out of your hair."

"Stay here, I'll bring it down."

Allison watched Alex climb the steps two at a time and went inside. Soon he returned with the chair folded and put it in the back of the car in no time. After closing the hatch, he came to her. "How do you lift that chair?"

"I'm stronger than I look."

He gave her a once-over and Allison could feel heat rush through her. "I have no doubt," he said. "But there's no reason why you can't take help now and then."

She glanced away. "I've found it safer to do it on my own."

He watched her awhile, then finally spoke. "I'll follow you into town." Before she could argue, he walked across the driveway and climbed into his truck.

She wanted to march over to him and give him her speech on how she didn't need help, especially from a stubborn, know-it-all cowboy. But the sun was setting, and she didn't particularly like going home in the dark.

Okay, she'd let him play hero this once, for Cherry.

Night had fallen twenty minutes later as Alex followed Allison's taillights past the city-limit sign. He turned in after her onto 2nd Street, the historical area of downtown. These storefront buildings had been around since the 1930s. She pulled into the alley at the back of her shop and parked. The area was dimly lit, only by the single bulb over the door. Great. Even though Kerry Springs was a good town, that didn't mean bad things couldn't happen here.

He pulled up behind her, then jumped out of the truck to get to the child, or Miss Do-It-All-By-Herself would refuse his help again.

He opened the car door and unbuckled the sleeping

child, then lifted her into his arms. The small girl curled trustingly against his chest.

He quickly shook the feelings away and followed Allison through the shop's back door. She paused to flick on a light, exposing a narrow hallway and a staircase. She turned to him as if she would take the child, but then instead she led him toward the stairs and they climbed up to a large open room that had once been an attic. The place was stifling hot. She went to the window and turned on an air conditioner.

"Cherry's room is this way."

She walked him past a bathroom and to a small room with a single bed. Allison tossed back the ruffled covering to expose white sheets.

He lowered the child to the mattress, but she opened her eyes, then started to fuss as Alex tried to step back. She grabbed onto him.

"Hey, it's okay. Let your mama get you dressed for bed and I'll come back to say goodnight." She continued to grip his arm. "Remember you're a big girl." When she finally let go, he glanced at Allison, then left.

He went down and took the wheelchair out of the car. After locking the car and back door, he carried the chair upstairs. He took his time to look around the makeshift apartment. It reminded him of one of the nicer places he'd lived in as a kid.

The large attic room had kitchen cabinets against one wall along with a small stove and, on the counter, a microwave. A sofa and chair with a bookcase and a small television took up the rest of the space. *Where the hell did Allison sleep? And why the hell were they living here?*

He turned away. Damn. He didn't want to see this place. How they lived. He didn't want any reminders of his past. It was time to get the hell out of here and forget about Allison Cole and her daughter.

Suddenly he heard his name whispered, and he turned to find Allison motioning him to the bedroom. The little girl was dressed in a nightgown and had a book in her hands. "I told Cherry you would read two pages and then she had to go to sleep."

He shouldn't have promised anything.

Allison stood in front of him and kept her voice low. "Look, you're the one who followed us home. Now, you have to take the consequences." She stared at him like a mother lion protecting her cub.

Alex walked into the room, sat down on the edge of the bed. "Show me where to start."

Cherry smiled and pointed to the exact line. It took all of five minutes before the child fell fast asleep. He put the book on the dresser and walked out.

Allison was waiting for him. "Thank you."

He only stared at her, then finally said, "Why are you living like this?" He pointed to the stairway. "And how long can you keep carrying your daughter up those steps?"

She straightened. "As long as I need to. Cherry's treatment has been expensive. So is starting up a new business."

"What about insurance?"

"There was a settlement after the accident, and I'm using that money for her therapy. We moved here because of her doctor. He's the best."

"What kind of accident?"

She glanced away. "Cherry was in the car when it was hit in bad weather."

Alex wondered about the details she left out. "Where's her father?"

Allison shook her head. "That doesn't matter."

"The hell it doesn't. It seems to me that both Cherry's parents should take responsibility for their daughter's welfare."

She shook her head. "Jack's out of our lives. I have full custody of my daughter, financially and emotionally."

Alex turned away. So her ex was a jerk. He knew all too well how easily a parent could walk away from their responsibilities. He looked at the small woman, stubborn and so determined to prove she could handle everything on her own.

He told himself to get the hell out of there; he didn't need this kind of headache. "Do you ride?"

She blinked at his question. "Excuse me."

"Have you ever ridden a horse?"

She shrugged. "Years ago."

"What about Cherry? Do you think she could sit in a saddle?"

Allison straightened. "I'm not sure that's a good idea."

"Did you see her today, how she responded to Maisie? You ever heard of horse therapy?"

"Yes, but I can't do anything until I ask the doctor."

"Then ask him," he said. "Because she's going to be at the ranch all next week." He took a step closer. "And another thing, your child is capable of talking. She's spoken three words to me. Today, she said, horsey and pony. It was barely a whisper, but she said them."

Tears filled Allison's eyes and something tightened in his chest.

"Hey, this isn't anything to cry about."

"I know. It's just been so long since I heard her speak. And she ends up talking to a stranger."

He couldn't help himself; he reached out and grasped her by the arms. Feeling her softness, he wanted so much more. "Sometimes it's easier to share things with strangers."

She looked up at him with those emerald eyes and, damn, if his throat didn't dry up as if he were a teenager.

A tear fell and he felt her tremble. "I just want to help her so badly."

He reached out and cupped her face, brushing a tear away with his thumb. "She knows that, Allie," he managed. "She'll come around."

Allison shook her head and pulled away. "No, she won't. I can't blame her, either."

"Why do you say that?"

"Because, I'm the one responsible for her accident."

CHAPTER FOUR

SHE was responsible for her daughter's accident.

Four hours later, Alex sat in his office at the house. It had always been his sanctuary, a place he'd come to work in peace and quiet after a long day. He'd chosen dark wood, with floor-to-ceiling bookcases filled with books on finance and business, many more on horse breeding. In his youth, he'd escaped into libraries to get out of the bad weather. That was when he had found he loved to read.

Thanks to Allison Cole's confession, there wasn't any relaxing with a book tonight. He went to the large picture window that overlooked the compound. Security lights lit the deserted area. He never should have followed her into town. Escorting her home had been the right thing to do, but it was staying and learning more about the woman that had been wrong. He didn't get close to people. He'd learned it was better to keep a distance, except for Angelo.

It was Cherry, he told himself. For some reason, the kid kept turning to him, pulling him into their lives. Probably because of that no-good father of hers. Tonight, Allison had mentioned the name Jack.

Earlier, Alex had done a search on the name Jack Cole. There were hundreds. He went to Allison Cole's website,

Quilt Allie, and discovered a Jack Hudson had been her business manager and, later, her husband. Most recently he had become her ex-husband. There had also been a list of items and books by Allison Cole for sale. Surely she would get any profit from the merchandise. Or did Hudson get the money and business while she got custody of her daughter? Was that how she had got rid of her ex?

Alex's hands fisted. He thought about his own father. He barely remembered the man, except for that day when Luca Casali had shipped him and his brother from their home in Italy to America.

At least Allison kept her daughter with her. He recalled the pain he saw on her face when she told him she'd caused the accident.

No way. Unless the woman was the best actress in the world, Allison Cole would lay down her life for her child. He walked back to the desk and turned on his computer. There had to be special saddles for disabled kids.

An email alert caught his attention and he clicked to see a list of personal messages. Angelo. He smiled, thinking about his famous pro-ballplayer brother. The New York Angel. Although now, their star was out for the season with an injury, and he was bored.

Alex wrote back that if he needed something to do, he could come to the ranch and work. At one time, his twin had been part owner in the operation. But Angelo hadn't wanted to be a rancher anymore than Alex wanted to be a ballplayer. They had invested in many other projects that had made them both wealthy men.

Then Alex opened an email dated over two months ago titled *Family Wedding*. He opened the saved message and began to read it again, already knowing the script off by heart.

Dear Alessandro,

Hello from Italy. I know it's been so long since you've heard from this side of your family, so I thought I would try to communicate with my long-lost cousins. Maybe the best way is to invite you to come to Italy and my wedding. It has been years and we're not getting any younger. I would love to see you both. Please, if you and Angelo would come, it would make my day perfect.

A formal invitation will arrive in the mail with the time and date.

Love, Lizzie.

Alex frowned as he reread the curt reply he had typed.

Lizzie,

Thank you for the invitation, but I have to decline. I'm too busy here to leave the ranch. Best wishes on your special day.

Alex

All of a sudden his father's family wanted him. Why was this happening after over thirty years? Where had they been when he and Angelo hadn't had a home or a family?

He shut off the computer. He didn't want to think of his family in Italy anymore. He wasn't about to ease their guilt. He wasn't the Casali who'd turned his back on the family.

Driving back from San Antonio, Allison glanced in the rear-view mirror at her daughter. Therapy hadn't gone well. Cherry had cried the whole time. Finally she'd had to leave the room while the physical therapist took Cherry through the exercises.

Allison pulled into the back of the shop, glad to be home. After retrieving the wheelchair, she lifted Cherry into it and pushed her through the back door. Hearing a man's voice coming from the front of the shop, she wheeled Cherry inside. The main room wasn't especially large, but it had enough space for everything for her business, materials, supplies and quilt patterns.

What she didn't have room for was a six-foot-three rancher. Alex Casali was dressed in his standard gear of jeans and a dark blue western-cut shirt that emphasized his broad shoulders. He should look out of place in the strictly feminine surrounding. Nope, he just looked all male.

She hadn't seen him since the night he had followed her back here. Not since she had poured out everything to him.

Allison quickly turned her attention to her part-time employee, Mattie. The older woman was actually giggling at whatever Alex had said to her.

She'd had enough of this. "Mattie."

The older woman swung around. "Oh, Allison, you're back already." She glanced down at Cherry as she walked toward them. "And you, little darling. You've had a rough morning, haven't you?"

Allison didn't take her eyes off Alex. "She had a difficult session today. She needs a nap. Why don't you take your lunch? I'll put Cherry down in back."

"Are you sure?"

Allison finally looked at the older woman. "Yes. And, Mattie, thank you for coming in early today."

The woman walked around the counter and got her purse. "It's never a problem, Allison." She looked at Alex. "It was good to meet you, Mr. Casali."

"The pleasure's mine, ma'am," he returned.

He watched the woman leave, then walked over to

Allison and gave a stern nod, then looked down at her daughter and smiled. "Hello, Cherry." The man was handsome, but now the transformation made him devastatingly so.

Even Alex Casali couldn't get any reaction from the child. "She's pretty tired."

But when she tried to turn the chair to leave, Cherry reached out for Alex. He didn't hesitate and lifted her into his arms.

"Sounds like you've had a busy morning, so you need to rest. But first, Maisie misses you. She wants to know when you're coming out to visit her again."

To Allison's shock, Cherry giggled.

Alex raised an eyebrow at the girl. "You don't believe she talked to me?"

Another giggle.

"Want to know something else? Maisie is ticklish. I'll show you where when you come to the ranch."

This time Cherry yawned.

Allison watched the exchange with envy. She stepped in. "I think this little girl is sleepy."

Cherry gave a weak protest, but went to her mother. Allison carried her to a small backroom that was an office. It also had a daybed. She placed Cherry on the mattress and pulled a lightweight blanket over her. Her eyelids were drooping, and finally closed.

"Sleep tight, sweetie." Allison kissed her, then walked out.

Alex took a walk around the shop. The old storefront was far from fancy, but everything was organized in rows of bins and up on shelves. Along the high walls were several colorful quilts. He examined them closely, realizing that Allison Cole was a talented woman. Okay, maybe he could understand why Tilda wanted her for the retreat.

Alex went to the large worktable. On top were several cut squares of cloth, stacked in neat piles. Some were sewn together. He glanced at an oversized notebook that read "Patterns." He opened it to see drawings of different shapes on the paper. One was labeled "Wedding Wishes", the next page "A Sister's Bond." He continued to the next one, "My Cherry's Delight."

He glanced up to see Allison and tried not to act as if he was doing anything wrong. "She asleep?"

Allison walked over to him. "Yes." She closed the book. "Is there something I can help you with?"

He shook his head. "I'm here to help you. To take out any supplies you need for the retreat."

She blinked. "I don't want to put you out. I'll just bring it all out tomorrow with us."

"If you were putting me out, I'd tell you. I was in town anyway."

She nodded. "Thank you. I do have two bins packed up. They're on the landing."

He continued to stand there. It was hard not to notice her striking looks. She had large emerald eyes, a creamy complexion and a sweet kissable mouth. Her hair was tied back in a ponytail, showing off her delicate jaw line. His gut tightened in need.

She looked away. "Well, if there isn't anything else, I don't want to keep you."

"As a matter of fact there is. Did you ask the doctor about Cherry going riding?"

She shook her head. "No, but I did discuss it with the therapist. She says horse therapy might be good for

Cherry as long as she uses a special saddle, and only if she wants to do it."

"I got the saddle." He saw her shock. "I guess we'll see if she really wants to ride when you come out tomorrow."

"Wait, you bought a saddle for her?"

He shrugged. "Not a big deal."

"It is to me. Saddles are expensive, and a special-needs saddle has got to cost a fortune."

"Don't worry about it, Allie. I'm not going to go hungry. Not anymore."

The next day, Allison walked into the place she and Cherry would call home for the next week. Within a group of tall trees was the new two-bedroom cabin. It had a spacious main room with a huge stone fireplace, and an open kitchen with Shaker-style cabinets and dark granite counter tops. The best feature was the hardwood floors throughout.

"How do you like it?"

She turned around and saw Tilda in the doorway. "It's amazing. I could live here forever."

Tilda's eyes lit up. "Maybe we could work something out."

Before Allison could respond, the woman went outside. Allison followed her to get Cherry. Off the deck was a ramp that connected to a concrete walkway that went all the way to the main building. That meant she didn't have to struggle with Cherry's chair.

"Thank you for adding the walkway and ramp."

Tilda picked up another box from the back and smiled. "You're welcome, but it was Alex who thought about it. So thank him."

Allison was confused. She hadn't thought he wanted

her here. Instead he'd bought a saddle so Cherry could ride, and now this. Don't you turn out to be a nice guy, Alex Casali. Then he'd really be too hard to ignore.

She went to the back to get Cherry. "Come see our new house, sweetie." She lifted her out of her safety seat, but when she turned away from the car she nearly ran into Alex.

"Oh, sorry. I expected Tilda."

"She had to take a phone call, another reservation. Here, let me carry her."

She didn't argue when he reached for Cherry; she couldn't stop the gasp when his fingers brushed against her breast. The contact sent a tingle across her skin, catching her off-guard. She quickly moved away, then went to get the chair already on the porch and followed them inside.

"Hello, *uccellino,*" he said to Cherry.

Allison found she was a little jealous of the attention that Alex gave so freely to her daughter. And it was crazy. Technically he was her employer. And she needed this job.

Inside, Alex placed Cherry in her chair. "So what do you want to do today?"

Cherry looked at her mom, giving her a hopeful look. Of course her daughter wanted to see the horses. "Maybe you need to tell me," Allison coaxed.

Cherry frowned in frustration, then she looked at Alex for help.

Alex was surprised that Allison was pushing her daughter. He looked at the little girl. "Your mother's right." He reached for the child's hand. "Tell me like you did before, Cherry. I know you can do it."

The girl gave him a stubborn look, reminding him of her mother. Those blue eyes challenged him.

"I guess you won't see your surprise today," Alex told her.

She glared harder, then leaned toward him and finally whispered, "Horsey."

Allison gasped at the single word.

"Good job, kid. And maybe if your mom says it's okay, then you can go riding on Maisie."

Allison nodded. "After lunch and a short nap."

Alex stood. "Okay, then I'll be back when you wake up." He was rewarded with a smile from both of them. He needed to get out of there. "See you later."

Before he could get away, Allison called to him as he stepped off the porch landing. He turned around to the woman in jeans and a T-shirt. Her hair was pulled back into a sloppy ponytail and she wore no makeup. She still took his breath away.

"What is it?"

She shrugged. "Just curious as to what you call Cherry in Italian?"

"*Uccellino*. It means little bird."

She smiled. "That's sweet."

He snorted. "I've been called a lot of things in my life, but never that."

She smiled and her eyes slanted upward. "I think your secret is safe." She grew serious. "Thank you for getting Cherry to talk. You have no idea how much it means to me."

A funny feeling centered in Alex's chest. He wasn't sure he did, but he was quickly realizing what her praise did to him.

That same afternoon, Allison sat on the corral fence and watched the big smile on Cherry's face. She was so proud of herself riding on Maisie. She sat secure in the saddle with a padded back brace and a strap cinched securely around her waist. A ranch hand led the pony around the arena, while Alex walked next to her, coaxing and praising the tiny rider.

"She's doing really well."

Allison swung around to find a man who looked to be in his early forties. He had an easy smile and kind hazel eyes. "Yes, she is."

"I'm Brian Perkins, Alex's foreman."

"Allison Cole." She smiled. "I'm working the quilting retreat this week."

"I know." He nodded. "And that's your daughter, Cherry."

They both watched as Alex stopped and instructed Cherry. "I never thought I'd see the day," Brian began. "A female having her way with the boss."

The foreman's words were pretty telling. Allison didn't doubt that Alex Casali kept pretty closed up. He had his own way, and she couldn't help but wonder why.

But she craved privacy, so she owed him the same. She didn't need to get personally involved with this man. Any and all men were off her list.

"She's a charmer, all right," Brian said. "Reminds me of my girl at that age. They seem to learn early on how to work us poor males."

"Oh, really? Excuse me while I get my violin out. Poor males? I don't think so."

Brian began to laugh, and she soon followed and didn't notice Alex was walking toward them.

"If you have time to stand around, I guess I don't give you enough to do."

They turned to see Alex. He didn't look happy.

The two men exchanged a long look, then Brian turned to Allison. "It was nice to meet you, Ms. Cole."

"It's Allison," she corrected. "And it was nice meeting you, too, Brian."

The foreman walked off toward the barn and Allison turned back to the angry-looking Alex. "Is there a problem with me talking to Brian?"

"None that I know of."

"I have one. You were rude."

"I run a large operation here. My only concern is that everyone does their job."

Allison smiled at her daughter seated on the pony. "If Brian Perkins is your foreman, I suspect he works hard at his job."

Alex hated that she could read him so easily. He had no reason to care if Brian was flirting with her. But he did. "Everyone who works for me does, but I pay them well." He glanced toward the barn and saw Jake bring out another horse. "How about we forget about my foreman and you show your daughter you can ride, too?"

She shook her head. "Oh, no. I haven't been on a horse since I was about ten years old."

"Good, you have some experience." The ranch hand arrived. "Jake, this is Ms. Cole. She and her daughter, Cherry, will be around here for the next week."

The young cowboy tipped his hat. "My pleasure, ma'am." He smiled at the girl. "It's nice to meet you, too, Miss Cherry. I'm Jake."

The girl smiled shyly.

Alex handed over Maisie's reins to Jake. "Here, you hold onto Miss Cherry while I get her mother settled on Honey."

"Sure thing, boss," Jake said.

Alex took Allison by the arm and walked toward the saddled horse. "Honey is as gentle as they come."

"I can see that, but I don't appreciate not being asked first."

He stopped next to the mare. "I did ask. The day at your apartment."

She jammed her hands on her hips. "You asked if I had ever rode a horse. You never asked about me about riding today."

Silently Alex counted to ten. The woman was going to drive him crazy. "Okay, would you like to ride today?" He raised a hand. "And before you answer, look over there at your daughter's face."

They both turned and saw a smiling Cherry.

"That is so unfair," she said. "Using my child to get what you want."

"No, I am trying to get Cherry what she wants." He grabbed Honey's reins and brought them back to the saddle. "Now, are you going to disappoint her?"

She wrinkled that cute nose. "Never."

He reached for the straw cowboy hat that was hooked on the saddle horn and placed it on her head. "Then let's get started. It's left foot in the stirrup."

Allison brushed back the wayward strands of hair and grabbed the reins from him. "Forget that. Just give me a boost up."

What was she up to? He finally did as she asked and locked his fingers together. She placed her sneaker-covered foot on his hands and pushed upward onto Honey's back, giving him a view of her well-shaped bottom. A short view, because she was upright in the saddle in no time. She slipped her feet into the stirrups, and tugged on the reins, causing the horse to back up.

She pressed her hat down, then with a click of her tongue the horse shot off toward the far end of the corral. At the fence, Allison turned Honey around, then kicked the horse's sides and together they shot off in a full gallop back to him.

A smiling Cherry was clapping her hands as she watched the goings-on.

Allison tugged on the reins and came to a stop in front of him. Her antics brought whistles and cheers from the men who stopped to watch her.

"You're just full of surprises, Allison Cole."

She shrugged. "I guess I didn't forget as much as I thought."

He realized that he would be the one finding it hard to forget her.

CHAPTER FIVE

THE next morning Alex stood at his office window and watched as several cars drove down the road, heading toward the guest ranch. It was opening day for the Quilters' Retreat and there would be a couple dozen women here, invading his space. His privacy. He hoped he hadn't made a mistake on this.

His thoughts turned to Allison and Cherry. Just a short time ago he hadn't known mother and daughter existed. Now, it seemed they'd pushed their way into his life and he hadn't had a thing to say about it, or a way to stop it.

Over the past couple of days he'd been around the woman and her child more than he needed. Between the horseback riding, and getting them settled in the cabin, they'd shared space and time that had disturbed his routine and peace of mind.

He shut his eyes. He could still see Allison staring up at him with those large eyes, when she got that stubborn look, telling him she had to do it herself. Fine, she could do it all by herself.

He wasn't about to let the woman tie him up in knots, but the child was a different story. Whether

Allison knew it or not, she needed help with Cherry. She couldn't do it all on her own. Was he the one to help her? And if he tried would she accept help? Probably not.

Alex grumbled as he turned around to the desk and found Brian standing in the doorway. "I called out to you, but you seemed to be thinking about something else."

Alex ignored the comment. "Do you need something?"

The foreman stepped further into the room. "The guy from Gilbert Ranch is here to pick up the bull. I need the paperwork."

Alex had forgotten all about it. "It's on the desk."

Brian found the bill of sale, but didn't leave. Instead, he came up beside Alex and glanced out of the picture window.

"So today is Tilda's big opening."

"Yeah, she's been running around like crazy getting everything ready."

"I know, the boys have been moving a bunch of boxes over there the past few days." He sent a quick glance toward Alex. "I don't think they mind helping out, especially for Allison."

"What do you mean?" Alex turned to him. "They better not be bothering her."

Brian shrugged. "I'm sure Joey and Pete flirted a little, but they're pretty harmless. They're respectful."

He tensed. "Make sure they don't hang out over there. Allison has a job to do, and so do they."

Brian frowned. "Come on, Alex, you know Joey and Pete. They're good kids, but you have to admit Allison Cole is a pretty distraction."

Alex drew a breath. "I still don't want them bothering her."

"You're mighty protective. Why don't you just admit that you're attracted to her?"

"Allison Cole is an employee at the ranch for the next week. Besides, she's not my type."

Brian raised an eyebrow. "Allison is every man's type." He snapped his fingers. "That's right, you don't get seriously involved."

Alex sent him another glare. "Look who's talking."

"Hey, at least I gave marriage a shot," Brian said. "Besides, I can't afford a woman. My kids will be going off to college in a few years."

Alex turned his focus back to the scene outside the window. "You don't have to worry. You'll have enough." He walked to his file cabinet, opened the top drawer and pulled out a file labeled Perkins. He handed it to Brian.

"I opened an account the second year when the ranch started making money. I took part of the profits and gave it to Angelo to invest. My brother's not only a good ball-player, he's good at making money. If it weren't for the bad market the last few years, there would be more."

Brian opened the file and swore. "Alex, I can't take this."

"Why the hell not?" he grumbled. "You worked as hard as I did to build this place. Consider it a bonus."

Brian stared down at the account's huge balance and shook his head. "I can't tell you how much I appreciate this. It was rough not being able to be a full-time father to John and Lindsey, but now I can give them what they need without any worries. Thank you, Alex."

Alex envied his foreman for his family. "From where I stand you did a good job with them. You never abandoned them. So don't let anyone ever tell you you aren't a good father."

Alex thought about Allison again. How could a man give her up? And their child? He didn't have to search further than his own father for the answer. Luca Casali hadn't batted an eyelid when he had put his three-year-old twin sons on an airplane and allowed them to fly off to a strange country that was not only an ocean apart, but worlds apart.

Brian interrupted his thoughts. "That little Cherry is hard to resist." He turned to Alex. "She seems to have gotten pretty attached to you."

Alex didn't want that. He couldn't let anyone get close to him. Only his brother. He'd learned a long time ago, it was safer just to keep his distance.

Allison glanced up at the clock and saw it was nearly five. Where had the day gone? Since it had taken most of the morning to get everyone set up in class, they hadn't really gotten down to work until after lunch. She'd quickly learned that most of these women weren't amateur. She liked that, knowing serious quilters would finish their projects and be ready to go to the long-arm quilter by the end of class.

Allison stood and walked around the tables, noting that the women were well under way. She stopped and commented on choices of fabrics and patterns. She even helped a beginner student choose material for their projects. The women ranged from the early twenties into their seventies. There were two sets of mothers and daughters, Trudy and Sally Monroe, and Connie and Alissa Huntington.

She glanced toward the bank of windows and saw her own daughter sitting there with her favorite doll, but she wasn't playing. Instead she was looking through the glass toward the ranch. No doubt she was searching for Alex Casali. The cowboy had been scarce today.

She hated the fact that his recent disappearance bothered her. She kept thinking about how he'd treated Cherry. The attention Alex had given her child. A child starved for a father. That was the main reason she couldn't let her daughter get too attached to him. After this was over she'd move back into town, and there'd be no more horses, or brooding cowboys.

Besides, she wasn't too trusting of men these days after her own disastrous marriage. Jack had been handsome, attentive at first, but in the end he hadn't been there for them. As a father, he'd been worse. He finally admitted he'd never wanted kids.

No. No matter how handsome Alex Casali was, getting involved would be a bad idea.

"Allison."

She turned around to see Jenny Collins, a thirty-something, single teacher from San Antonio. She was a beginning quilter. "Yes, Jenny."

The teacher smiled proudly. "I just wanted to show you my points. Are they okay?"

Allison examined the block of machine-stitched fabrics where the triangle points were sewn together on her pinwheel pattern. To an expert's eyes the points were just a fraction off. "This is wonderful. You've done a great job with your first project." Allison picked up a pair of scissors and demonstrated how to clip the back side of the fabric.

Jenny nodded, and then suddenly glanced across the room. "Oh, my, will he be joining our class?"

Allison turned around and Alex was standing in the doorway. His presence alone was overwhelming with his height and broad shoulders that filled the entrance.

"Oh, no, that's Alex Casali, Tilda's partner in the guest ranch."

The teacher's smile brightened even more. "Maybe I should have signed up for riding lessons."

Allison, too, admired the handsome rancher, then soon realized that he was disturbing her class. "I doubt that Mr. Casali gives riding lessons, but you could ask him."

Allison walked over. "Alex, is there something I can do for you?"

"I thought your class would be over by now." He glanced toward the window, then back to her. Those gray eyes locked on hers. "I thought Cherry could go for a ride."

She felt her heart accelerate at the thought of spending time with him. "Well, I'm not exactly finished here. It's going to be a longer day than I thought. It was nice of you to ask, but I can't get away."

"I could take her myself," he offered.

Allison looked at her daughter. Cherry had spotted Alex and her face lit up like a neon light. Without any hesitation, Alex started across the room and she hurried to catch up with him. She wanted to stop him, but, seeing her daughter's response, she couldn't do it.

"Well, hello there, little one. How was your day?"

Her doll forgotten, Cherry reached out and grabbed for Alex's hand.

"Has she been stuck in here all day?" he asked.

Allison reared back. "No, we had lunch at the cabin, and she's been outside. Tilda's friends, Carol and Charlotte, have been with her."

Alex ignored her again. "Well, she needs exercise. How about I take her riding on Maisie?"

"I told you I can't get away right now."

"I can take her now, and you come later."

Allison wanted to have this discussion alone, but there wasn't any way that would happen with nearly twenty women in the room. She turned and noticed most of the class had abandoned their work and were watching them. "Okay, you can take her, but only walk her around the corral."

He started to reach for Cherry's wheelchair, but Allison touched his arm. "We need to discuss this later," she said, her voice low and controlled. "So we don't have any misunderstandings in the future."

His jaw tensed as he stared at her, then he nodded and gripped the handles on the chair. "Let's go, *uccellino*. Maisie has been waiting all day for you to come by."

All Allison could do was watch as they left. She turned back to her class. "It's officially quitting time, but since we got started late today, we could work a little while longer. I want to make sure everyone is off and going on their projects."

Tilda walked up to her. "I appreciate this, Allison. Don't worry, Cherry is in good hands."

Allison nodded. That was what she was afraid of.

Later that evening, Allison eased the door to Cherry's bedroom shut. She was finally asleep. Her daughter had been keyed up since her ride with Alex, but it seemed to take that kind of exhaustion to put her to sleep.

Allison went to the kitchen table and began to look over tomorrow's lesson. She'd learned today the different levels of the students attending her class. Everyone wanted her to demonstrate something, from her hand-stitched appliqués, to her patterns and color suggestions. She'd loved every minute of it. It had been a long time since she felt this focused on anything but Cherry and she was excited about tomorrow.

There was a knock on the door. She went to open it and found Alex, with hat in hand, standing on the small porch. He looked as if he'd showered and shaved. Was he going out?

She shook away any thoughts of his personal life. "Alex, is something wrong?"

"You tell me. You summoned me here."

She tried not to be intimidated, but it was difficult. "I just want you to give me a little more warning about riding, instead of barging into my class."

He watched her a moment. "Just tell me what kind of jerk you were married to?"

Allison blinked, and then quickly closed the door behind her as she stepped onto the porch. "Would you keep your voice down? And who I was married to is none of your business."

"It is when you look at me as if I'm the devil himself. I would never do anything to hurt that child, and I'm tired of trying to prove that to you."

He started to walk off when she reached for him. "Alex, please, you're right. I haven't been fair to you." She sighed. "It's just that I've been overprotective of my daughter ever since the accident."

Alex knew he should keep going. *Walk away. Don't get involved in her problems.* "Is that because it was your fault?"

In the dim porch light, he could see her pain and sadness.

"I wasn't driving the car, but I wasn't the mother that I should have been."

He cursed. "I can't believe that."

She shook her head. "It's true. I was working all the time. As the show climbed in the ratings, I was spending more and more time away from Cherry. Then it seemed I was always busy designing new quilting patterns while my three-year-old daughter was being cared for by nannies."

"What about your husband?" He found it was hard to get the words out. "Shouldn't he take responsibility in this, too?"

She turned away.

He came up behind her. Seeing those delicate shoulders held so rigidly, he ached to reach out and touch her, to pull her back against him, to absorb her burden. "Allison…"

She turned back and looked up at him. "Jack didn't want children. When I got pregnant, he wasn't happy. Since he was also my manager, he thought it would ruin my career. Instead it brought in more viewers. Jack used that and made a deal to extend my show to an hour."

"What about Cherry?"

"In the beginning, I had her close by, even on the show at first. But as she got older, things changed. I couldn't have her on the set because she was distracting. That's when Jack hired a nanny."

"What did you want?" Alex asked.

"To take some time off to spend with my daughter, just do the show on the Internet at my own pace." Her eyes were glossy with tears. "I lost my own mother and dad at an early age. I wanted my daughter to have hers. I didn't think that was too much to ask."

Alex tried to remain calm, but seeing Allison upset made it difficult. "It wasn't. So why didn't you do it?"

"I was under contract, and Jack said I couldn't change anything, or I'd have to give back a lot of money. He convinced me to hang in for another year, and we'd renegotiate the contract. Eleven months later, Cherry was with her nanny when their car was rear-ended by a drunk driver."

He reached out and wrapped Allison in a tight embrace. Her softness made contact with his chest and he closed his eyes, reveling in it. Dear Lord, he couldn't remember feeling anything like this. He cupped the back of her head and felt her tears against his shirt.

"Allie, believe me, Cherry's accident wasn't your fault."

He thought back to his own mother. How she'd neglected both him and Angelo. How she had ignored them, blaming them for the fact that Luca had never come for her.

Alex drew back, but refused to release his hold on her. "Cherry survived, Allie. She's getting better, every day."

"Why won't she talk to me?"

"She will, and I expect it'll happen soon."

"Really?" she whispered.

"Really." He leaned closer, allowing her sweet breath to caress his face. He watched as her eyes widened, not out of fear, but desire.

"Alex…" She spoke his name on a breathy whisper.

"Damn, woman, you're making this hard."

Alex pulled her closer. That was his first mistake. The second was when he lowered his head to hers. He paused, his eyes searching hers, wanting her to put a stop to this craziness. When she didn't reject his advances, he captured her mouth. At first he just enjoyed the feel and taste of her. He released a groan of need, wanting more.

His gut tightened as she pressed against his body. He went to work on her sweet mouth, angling one way then the other to get more of her. His tongue sought entrance and she opened with a whimpering sound that nearly drove him over the edge. With the last of his resolve, he tore his mouth away and gasped for some air for his starved lungs.

He caught her surprised gaze, knowing she felt it, too. This wasn't good. "I've got to get out of here."

He turned to leave, but she reached for him. "Alex."

Alex stopped and looked over his shoulder. "Don't push this, Allie. I don't think either one of us can handle the consequences."

With that, he walked off the porch, knowing he'd kill for just another taste of her. He couldn't let that happen. He couldn't let anyone get that close.

CHAPTER SIX

"CHERRY, stop crying or you aren't going riding tomorrow."

The next afternoon, Allison loaded her daughter into the car for her therapy session. As usual she was putting up a fight. She didn't like having to leave the ranch. This struggle upset them both, but in times like this a parent had to take charge.

Slowly the crying died into a quiet sob. Allison closed her eyes and released a tired breath, trying to push away the feeling of helplessness. After a second or two, she pulled herself together and turned the key but, instead of the engine coming to life, she heard a clicking sound.

She tried again. Nothing. She sent up a silent prayer and tried a third time. All she heard was Cherry starting to fuss again in the warm car. "It's okay, honey."

Then there was a knock on the window. She gasped and turned to see Alex. He pulled open the door and leaned forward. "What's wrong?"

Since their kiss last night, she'd been hoping not to deal with him so soon, but now she didn't have any choice. "I think my battery is dead."

He glanced toward the backseat. "Hi, Cherry."

Her daughter giggled.

Alex turned back to Allison; those eyes pierced hers. "Let's get her out of the hot car."

She ignored the sensation he stirred in her.

He walked around the back and lifted the hatch to get the wheelchair. He was at the side door and unbuckling Cherry before Allison could get it together.

He lifted her child out. "You're getting pretty heavy, little one. I think you're eating too much," he teased her as he sat her in the chair. Then he reached into the car and unlatched the safety seat.

"What are you doing?" she asked.

"I'm driving you and Cherry to therapy." He raised an eyebrow. "You have a problem with that?"

Allison wanted to refuse his offer, but she couldn't. Even if there hadn't been much progress, Cherry needed these sessions. It was her only chance to walk again.

She nodded. "Thank you, I'd appreciate it."

He blinked. "That's a surprise. I thought for sure I'd get an argument."

"Not when it comes to my daughter."

Thirty minutes later, they arrived at the medical building in San Antonio. Alex planned to sit in the waiting area, but Cherry began to fuss, so he went along with her.

He wasn't happy about how the child was manipulating everyone to get what she wanted. Okay, she was hard to resist, but she also knew how to work them all.

The therapist came into the large training room. With a smile she walked up to Cherry. "Hello, Cherry." She looked at Allison. "Hello, Ms. Cole." Then to Alex. "You must be Mr. Cole."

Allison stiffened. "No, Kate, this is Mr. Casali. He drove us here today. Alex, this is Kate Boyer, Cherry's therapist."

He nodded. "Miss Boyer."

Kate looked him over, then glanced down at Cherry. "If we're lucky, Cherry might want to show you what she's been doing." Kate pushed the wheelchair to the other side of the room. "Have a seat, Mr. Casali."

"Alex."

The young therapist's smile grew. "Kate."

When he took a seat, Allison sat beside him in the row of chairs. He watched the therapist go through a series of exercises, and then ask Allison if they'd been doing them at home. Alex saw her uneasiness as she answered, "Sometimes."

He liked Kate's no-nonsense approach. She wouldn't let the child's tears or stubbornness sway her as the workout continued. But with every attempt, the therapist would praise her efforts. Then toward the end of the session, Kate whispered something to the child. With a nod, she motioned for him to come over.

"I think Cherry wants to show you something," Kate said. "This is her first attempt, but since she seems to be responding today, she's willing to try." Kate looked at Allison. "It's the parallel bars."

Allison tensed. Every time they'd even suggested it before her daughter had had a meltdown. "I thought we decided to wait."

Kate glanced at Alex. "I believe there's someone here she might want to impress."

Allison was wondering if Kate wanted to impress Alex, too. Oh, God, was she jealous?

Kate's eyebrow rose in question. "Two months

ago, Dr. Meyers wanted us to work with Cherry wearing braces."

With Allison's nod, the therapist strapped the braces on Cherry's tiny legs. Then she wheeled her over to the parallel bars and locked the chair into position. With the help of another therapist, Cherry got to her feet. Allison saw her daughter's panic and wanted to put a stop to it.

She felt Alex's hand on her shoulders. "Hold on. She can do this."

"Oh, Alex, she's so little."

She saw a flash of compassion in those steely gray eyes. "And because you love her and want her to get well again, you need to push her."

Allison bit down on her trembling lip and nodded.

He rewarded her with a hint of a smile, and she felt her heart tighten. He released her shoulder and they turned back to Cherry, who now was standing.

"Well, would you look at you, *uccellino*." He beamed at her as he made his way to the bar. "Now let's see what you can do."

Allison saw her daughter's panicked look, but let Alex handle it. She stood at the end of the bar as he coaxed her. The therapist helped move her tiny legs. A tear fell from Cherry's eye and down her cheek, but she kept going. After four hard, grueling steps, Alex swept the child up into his arms and hugged her tightly.

"I'm so proud of you," he said as he brought Cherry to Allison. "And you know who else is proud? Your mom."

To Allison's surprise her daughter reached for her. She gladly took the burden. "I love you, Cherry. You did such a good job." She held her daughter for a long time, then realized that Cherry's weight plus the braces was heavy.

Kate removed the extra hardware and settled Cherry back into her chair. She hugged her patient goodbye and waved as they left.

"I think we need to celebrate." Alex pushed the chair toward the elevators. "I'm taking you lovely ladies out to dinner and it's Cherry's choice."

Two hours later, after an hour at a children's pizza place, Alex managed to get Cherry and her mother home. He waited in the cabin's living room for Allison to put the girl to bed.

Why? Why was he waiting? He didn't need this at all. He'd already stepped into Allison Cole's business, and now he was involved in the girl's therapy. He felt a tug in his chest remembering the child taking those steps, seeing her pain, but she wouldn't quit. He paced to the door and back. Leave. Keep your distance, he told himself, but still he wasn't listening.

He turned as Allison walked from the hall. She looked tired, too. But those eyes locked with his, and he saw the mirrored awareness.

"Now that she's asleep, I should go."

She didn't answer, just kept coming toward him. Her eyes were filled with emotion, determination in her step as if she was on a mission.

"Please, not before I thank you."

"There's no need." He found himself backing up, but the door stopped his progress.

"Do you have any idea how many months we've worked to get Cherry to try and stand?" She blinked her beautiful eyes as she teared up. "She would never do it until today, until you asked her."

Hell, he didn't want to be the kid's hero, but it looked

as if he had the job. "Hey, I'm also the one who has the horses, and your daughter is drawn to them." And he was drawn to her mother. He reached out and brushed the moisture away. Her skin was so soft. He wanted to touch her everywhere. He quickly shook away that thought. "So we use whatever we can to get her to work on her therapy."

"Why?" she whispered. "You never wanted us here."

Hell, if he knew. "I'm a private man, but Cherry is just a kid. She's gotten a raw deal, so if I can help…" he shrugged "…why not?"

"I appreciate that. But I can't ask you to come to every one of her therapy sessions."

"You didn't ask, I'm volunteering." Was he crazy? Yes. The mother-daughter duo had gotten to him.

For a long time Allison just stared at him, then walked away.

"What's wrong?" he asked.

She swung around to face him. "I don't know if that's a good idea, Alex. What happens when we leave here? When she doesn't get to come here every day to ride?"

"Then bring her out. If I'm not around, one of the hands can help her. I'll make sure of that."

She still didn't look satisfied. "What about what happened last night? Between us."

"I thought that was mutual."

"I can't start up anything." Her gaze darted away. "I don't know if I'll be able to…again."

Hell, he wanted to pound the guy who'd hurt her. "There's no worry about that. But I'd be lying if I said I wasn't attracted to you. As you are to me."

"But we can't do anything about it."

He was annoyed that she could brush it away so

easily. There was a lot they could do about it. For a short time anyway.

She looked up, but her gaze didn't meet his. "You have the ranch, Alex, and I have my shop and Cherry—"

She never got to finish her denial as he captured those sweet lips with his, sending a surge of heat through him. With a groan, he wrapped his arms around her shapely body and pulled her against him. His hands moved over her, wanting to feel every inch of her. Brand her with the taste and feel of him so she would never think about another man.

But, damn, if she wasn't doing exactly that to him. He tore his mouth away before he lost it altogether.

She gasped for air, but didn't pull back. He wanted her, bad. "You're probably right—it isn't a good idea."

He released her and opened the door, feeling the cooler air, but it didn't help him. When it came to Allison Cole, he doubted anything could.

The next day passed quickly as Allison stayed busy so she wouldn't think about Alex. It didn't work. The man was interfering in every corner of her workday.

"Ladies, class is finished for today, but, as before, you're all welcome to keep working on your projects."

A few of the women stood up, walked around and went to get water and coffee. That was what she needed: caffeine. She hadn't slept much last night, not after Alex's kiss. Even knowing that getting involved with the man was crazy, and harmful to her daughter, she couldn't control her attraction to Alex.

She checked her watch and knew that Cherry was riding Maisie. What would it hurt for her to take a short ride, too?

* * *

Alex was walking Maisie when he saw Allison come out of the barn leading Honey. She had on snug jeans and fitted pink blouse that highlighted her glorious red hair. Covering her head was the hat he'd given her the other day, but the surprise was the buckskin boots on her feet.

She looked as if she belonged on a ranch.

"Mommy," Cherry whispered.

He felt a smile coming. "That's right, little girl. That's your mommy." Sexy mommy, he thought. He was still hot and bothered over the kiss they'd shared last night. He also knew he should keep his distance from this woman.

"So the teacher's playing hooky."

Allison went to her daughter. "No, this teacher is finished for the day. Hi, sweetie," she said to the girl. "I thought I'd come riding with you."

Her idea got a smile from Cherry. Alex felt the excitement, too, but refused to show it.

"It's not very exciting riding around the corral." He finally caught her gaze. That was a mistake. "But we could go to a creek not far from here."

Allison sobered, as if thinking it over. "How far?"

"About a half-mile," he told her, and then turned back to Cherry. "I guess we should reward our girl here for her hard work yesterday."

"Maybe we should," Allison agreed.

Alex pulled a ranch hand aside and gave him instructions to saddle his horse, and then he called Tilda on his cell to let her know where they were headed.

He closed his phone and turned back to Allison. "It's always good to let someone know where you are."

She smiled. "And Tilda worries about you."

He grumbled under his breath. "I've taken care of myself far too long to need anyone worrying about me."

Half an hour later, Allison was enjoying their ride through the beautiful hill country. Tall oak trees lined the path, filtering the late afternoon sun. She caught sight of a whitetail deer off in the thick foliage. She glanced ahead to see that Cherry, seated on Maisie, was pointing to the animal, too. Beside her daughter was Alex gripping the pony's reins as he led the way on a gelding named Wild Bill.

They both kept a close eye on Cherry, but she seemed to be able to sit in the saddle just fine. Allison had noticed, just in the few times her daughter had been on the pony, she'd gained strength in her back and posture. If this was what it took to get the child to improve, she would bring her out to the ranch every day to ride.

How would Alex Casali feel about that?

Allison knew that wouldn't be a good idea. She needed to stay clear of the man, before she ended up hurt again. Cherry was the catch. Her daughter was so taken with the handsome cowboy. It seemed both mother and daughter had the same problem.

Suddenly she heard the sound of water as they rode through a clearing and the wide creek appeared before them. Large rocks and boulders ran along either side. Ancient oak trees arched over the water's edge forming a canopy.

"This is so beautiful."

Alex climbed down. "It's one of many creeks on this ranch." He began to untie his blanket from the saddle. "But Lucky Creek is one of my favorites."

Allison got off her horse and went to Cherry. She wasn't sure if they were staying or not until Alex spread the blanket on level ground.

"Come on, *uccellino*. You want something to eat?"

When Cherry gave him a big nod, he worked the safety straps and lifted her off the pony, then carried her to the blanket. He set her down gently, then went back to get a bag.

Allison sat beside her daughter, then glanced across the creek and saw another deer. "Look, Cherry, there's another deer."

Although her daughter didn't react as strongly as she had with Alex, she saw the excitement in her eyes. That gave her some hope.

Alex handed her a canvas bag. "What's this?" she asked.

"Something Tilda threw together for us – it pays to let her know where we're going. I guess she didn't want us to starve out here in the wilderness." He turned to Cherry. "So we're having a picnic." He poked his finger into the child's middle causing her to giggle.

Alex looked at Allison and saw the hurt. She tried to hide it, but she couldn't. "How about if your mom looks inside and sees what we've got to eat?"

Allison pulled out containers of sandwiches, potato chips, fruit salad and bottles of tea and juice. "Boy, did you luck out. There isn't a vegetable to be found."

Cherry giggled as her mother opened the containers. The girl chose a peanut-butter sandwich, leaving ham and turkey.

In between bites, Alex told them stories about the ranch. Things that Tilda had told him since the land had been in her family so long.

"Do you know why they call the creek Lucky?" Alex asked.

Cherry shook her head.

"Well," Alex drawled. "There are a few stories out there. One is that the water makes a big turn," he said as he pointed downstream. "It's almost in the shape of a horseshoe. And we all know horseshoes are lucky."

Allison finished her sandwich. "What's the other?"

"A long time ago, I believe it was in the nineteen hundreds, there was a big flood in this area. Tilda's grandfather was a boy. He'd gotten too close to the edge and fell into the rushing water."

He caught the wide-eyed look in Allison's eyes.

"How did he get out?" she asked.

"Well, that's the mystery. It seems he was headed downstream when he landed on a sandbar out in the middle, then he caught onto a branch of these big oak trees and just hung on tight. Soon help arrived, someone tossed him a rope and pulled him to shore." He nodded. "And that's why they call it Lucky Creek."

He glanced down at Cherry, who was leaning against her mom sound asleep. "Seems I bored my audience."

With Alex's help, Allison shifted her daughter into a more comfortable position, but kept her close. "She's had a busy day."

"So have you," he told her, but didn't move away. "What made you decide to ride?"

"After sitting all day, I needed to move around." Her eyes met his. "I didn't think there was a problem with me riding."

"There isn't any that I can think of."

"Good." She stood and walked toward the water.

He followed her. "As long as that's all it is."

"What else could it be?"

"This attraction between us. This itch I feel for you and you feel for me."

She started to deny it, but he placed a finger against her lips. "At least let's be honest, Allie, especially when you're standing there looking so hot and bothered that you couldn't even sit beside me."

She blinked at that and backed up. "Well, that's no better than you saying you want nothing to do with me, then kissing the daylights out of me before you walk out."

"Hey, if you want to carry this further, I'm willing."

"You are the most egotistical man I've ever met."

"No, I'm just honest." He leaned forward. "I can tell how you've been turning me inside out. I haven't had a decent night's sleep since I laid eyes on you. Like now, when your green eyes turn all smoky and your voice gets breathy."

She tried to glance away, but he cupped her face, making her look at him. "Now, it's your turn to be truthful."

"I can't, Alex. I can't let this happen."

"It's already happening, Allie." His mouth closed over hers and after a moment of resistance she melted against him. Her surrender frightened him more, but he wasn't listening to the warnings as he felt a sizzle of heat when he parted her lips with his tongue. She sighed a murmur or moan, he wasn't quite sure over the pounding in his ears as he took the kiss deeper. His hands moved over her back, then down to her bottom, drawing her to him.

He tore his mouth away, trailing kisses along her jaw, her neck, to feel her shiver. He returned to her mouth, angling one way and another, hungry for more, needing her as he had never wanted anyone.

His hands went to her breasts, cupping her through her blouse, but he needed to feel her skin. He tugged her shirt from her jeans and made contact with her heated flesh.

"Oh, Alex," she whispered in a breathy plea, causing a passion in him he'd never known. Her hands were on him, working to free his shirt from his jeans.

He did the job himself as the sound of the popping snaps suddenly made him aware of what was happening, and how they were getting out of control, but didn't care. That was when he heard the sound of the vehicle.

He hugged Allison close against him and released a breath. "As much as it kills me to stop, someone's coming.

With a gasp, she turned around and worked quickly to pull herself together. He squinted into the dusk falling as he looked toward the dirt road to see Brian's truck.

After tucking in his shirt, he checked to see Cherry was still asleep, and then walked to the road. One of his ranch hands got out of the truck. "Jake," he greeted. "Is there a problem?"

"I'm sorry, Alex." The kid glanced over at Allison. "Brian sent me out here. He tried your cell first, but he got your voice mail."

"Okay, you gonna tell me why you're here?" he asked, knowing it better be good.

"It's Cheyenne Sky. She's having trouble with her foal. Brian called the vet, but he thought you would want to know."

Alex released a breath. They'd been watching the prize brood mare. "Yeah, I want to know." He turned as Allison walked over. "One of my brood mares is in trouble."

"Then you need to go," she told him.

"Okay. We'll take the truck," he told Jake. "Can you manage the horses?"

With a nod from the ranch hand, Alex went and gently lifted Cherry into his arms and instructed Allison to get in the seat of the crew cab truck and placed her daughter on her lap. Then with a wave to Jake they headed back.

Once back at the guest cabin, Alex carried Cherry inside and into her room, placing her on the twin bed.

Then he walked out and stood in the living room.

Man, he felt as nervous as a teenager, wanting to be with his steady girlfriend. He'd never had a steady girl ever. Never wanted one. And here at the age of thirty-eight, he was panting after Allison Cole.

In the past he'd always been able to keep his distance from women. He hadn't felt this vulnerable since he was a kid. He didn't like that. Not at all, but he wasn't ready to give her up.

He looked up as she walked out of the bedroom; her fiery hair was mussed and her green eyes still deep with desire. Unable to resist, he crossed the room and raised his hand to cup her face.

"This isn't over, Allie." Then he kissed her thoroughly to make sure she would lie awake thinking about him. He wanted to brand her so she wouldn't forget him. When he finally broke it off, she didn't look any happier than he felt. Good.

CHAPTER SEVEN

THE next afternoon, Allison finished up the class session a little early, hoping to see about fixing her car. Something she'd totally forgotten about during the past twenty-four hours.

Her thoughts went to Alex as they had so many other times in the two weeks since they met. She'd let herself be distracted by him. So much so she had lain awake last night for hours, thinking about his kisses, how his hands felt on her skin, setting her on fire. She'd finally had to get out of bed and begin work on a new quilt pattern.

She had three more days here, which meant she had to figure out a way to be around the man without turning into putty whenever he looked at her. Well, it had been easy today since she hadn't seen him at all.

She was nearly out of the door when Jenny stopped her to look at her quilt. The young teacher had been working on the traditional Wedding Ring pattern using lovely pastel colors and subtle prints.

"Oh, Jenny, I can't believe you've nearly finished," Allison said, happy at how well the class was going.

Jenny shrugged. "There isn't much nightlife and only reruns on television."

"But still, you must have been up half the night."

The pretty blonde beamed. "I wanted to get it finished before I start back to teaching." She sighed. "As much as I enjoyed this class, I may come back here when the dude ranch opens over Christmas vacation." She smiled. "I wouldn't mind passing time over the holidays with a good-looking cowboy. And what better way than coming to a ranch?" She frowned. "Of course, I'm finding that most of the ranch hands aren't much older than some of my students."

"That's true, but it can still be fun," Allison agreed. She had a feeling Jenny was looking for more than a good time. "If you do come back, drop by my shop in town and see me."

Jenny nodded, but was distracted by something outside. "Oh, my. I hope he's going to be one of the cowboys."

Allison looked toward the porch and saw Brian standing by her car. "That's Brian Perkins, the ranch foreman."

"He's handsome in a rugged sort of way." She gasped. "Please don't tell me he's married."

Smiling, Allison shook her head. "From what Tilda told me, he's been divorced for years and has two teenage kids. And they're a big part of his life."

Jenny grinned. "I teach teenagers. I love them."

"How interesting." Allison had an idea. "Come with me—I need to ask him about my car so I'll introduce you."

Allison had only an hour of free time since Tilda and one of her friends were watching Cherry. She needed to get a new battery before the therapy session tomorrow.

When she went outside, Brian greeted her with a tip of his hat. "Hello, Allison."

"Hi, Brian. This is one of my students, Jenny Collins."

Brian gave another salute. "A pleasure to meet you, Jenny."

"Nice to meet you, too, Brian."

Allison saw a flash of interest in Brian's eyes before he turned back to her. "I didn't want to interrupt class, but I need to let you know that your car is running again."

"Oh, Brian, you didn't need to do that. Was it the battery?"

He nodded. "I replaced it this morning, and it starts just fine."

"Thank you. How much do I owe you?"

He shook his head. "Alex took care of it."

She stiffened. The man seemed to take care of everything whether she liked it or not. "Well, then you can give him my money."

The foreman held up his hands. "Maybe you should talk to him yourself."

"Okay, where is he?"

"In his office at the house."

"I'll go see him, then." She wasn't going to let him continue doing this. She turned to Jenny. "Would you let Tilda know where I went?"

With Jenny's nod, Allison left the couple on the porch, got into her car and headed to the ranch house. She was going to let Alex Casali know that he couldn't have everything his way.

Inside the back door, Allison called to Alex, but when he didn't answer she headed down the hall in search of his office. She couldn't help but look at the beautiful surroundings. Each room she passed had been professionally decorated in rich green and brown tones, some too dark for her taste, but everything was tastefully done. The hardwood floors gleamed under plush area rugs. Every inch of woodwork had been perfectly restored, and a marble fireplace took the spot of the main focus in the large living room. The one thing it was void of was photos. There wasn't a single family picture anywhere.

She turned and continued to another doorway and glanced inside. Floor-to-ceiling bookcases filled two of the walls, and a huge oak desk sat in the middle of the room. Behind it was a large bay window that over-looked the ranch.

As she peered further into the room she found Alex in a high-back leather chair. Sound asleep. He didn't look nearly as hard, or as intimidating, or as Italian as his name stated. His sandy-brown hair was mussed, falling across his forehead. He had long black lashes, high cheekbones, and a nose that was a little crooked. His jaw was shadowed by a day's growth of beard. There was a faint scar beside his right eye. Yet none of it took away from his good looks.

She felt her heart race as she continued to survey his broad chest and wide shoulders, right down to his narrow waist and long legs encased in a pair of worn jeans.

She blew out a breath as her gaze went to his hands. Large with long, tapered fingers. She shivered, recall-ing his hand on her body last night. Getting involved with this man would be a mistake. A big one, but she was afraid it might be too late to heed the warning.

Allison started to turn away when he said her name in a husky voice that caused a warmth to spread through her. When their eyes met, she immediately felt the intensity of his gaze. She couldn't even manage a word as she walked toward him.

"I'm sorry to disturb you," she managed. "You probably didn't get any sleep last night. How's your mare?"

"She's fine now, after finally giving birth to one stubborn chestnut filly."

She smiled. "That's nice. Maybe I can see her. I mean I'll bring Cherry by—if it's okay with you."

"Any time." He stood and she backed away. "Can't say I blame you, I probably smell like a barn."

He smelled just fine. The real reason was she didn't trust herself. "You're fine."

He walked to the window, raking his fingers through his hair. She wanted to go to him, touch him, run her hands over his broad back, recalling the feel of his muscular body against hers.

No! She glanced away from temptation toward his orderly desk that held a computer screen. On the glass top was what looked like a wedding invitation. She wasn't trying to read it, but she did notice it wasn't written in English.

"It's my long-lost cousin's wedding invitation."

She jumped at the sound of his voice. "I apologize. I didn't mean to read your mail. I just noticed it's in Italian?"

With a nod, Alex leaned against the window frame. He wasn't in the mood to share this with her, with anyone. "My so-called family lives there."

She smiled at him. "How nice. Are you going?"

Why did she have to look so good today? Alex wondered. He'd thought about her during his long night coaxing his mare through a rough delivery.

He glanced away. "As far as I'm concerned I don't have any family except my brother."

She nodded.

"Was there something else you needed from me?" he asked. "I haven't been to bed yet. So unless you're offering to go there with me, I'd like to end this visit."

He saw the hurt in those jade eyes, and for the first time in a very long time he felt like a heel. But it was for her own good. She turned and walked out. He could handle the love-hate thing, just not the happily ever after. Whether she admitted it or not, Allison Cole wanted just that. He suddenly wished he could be the man to give it to her.

The next afternoon, Allison was surprised to find Alex waiting for her when she pushed Cherry outside to her car. Dressed in dark jeans and a starched blue shirt, he looked so good. She suddenly was rethinking her resolve to give up on men. How crazy was she?

"Well, good afternoon, Cherry girl," he said, making her daughter grin. He stood and took possession of the wheelchair.

She managed to find her voice. "I wasn't sure you were coming today."

"Why? I promised I'd help."

They headed toward his truck. "Yes, you did, but—"

"If I give my word," he interrupted, "I keep it."

"Fine. It's your time." She turned her attention to Alex's backseat where she was surprised again to see a new safety seat. She refused to mention it. If he wanted to go with Cherry to therapy, who was she to deny her daughter the help?

Thirty minutes later they arrived at the center and immediately Kate jumped into another strenuous routine for Cherry. Both she and Alex stayed close by, encouraging and coaxing her all the time. Even when the tears came, Alex just kept on making deals with the child to keep her going on.

When the session ended, Alex placed Cherry in her chair. The girl looked exhausted as she drank water.

Kate also came over. "You did a wonderful job today, Cherry. I'm so proud of you." The therapist looked at Allison. "Dr. Myers would like to talk to you if you have a few minutes."

"I'll stay with Cherry," Alex offered.

Allison nodded and stood. "Thanks. I'll be right back."

Once alone, Alex pushed the wheelchair over to a bench where he sat down. He turned Cherry around to face him. "*Uccellino*, it's time you stop this game."

The pretty blonde child didn't look at him.

"You're a big girl now, Cherry Cole. It's time to start talking to your mom."

She finally raised those wide baby blues and he felt a hard tug on his heart.

"We both know you can. So why not speak to her?"

A tear rolled down her cheek. "She'll go away," she whispered.

At first, he was relieved to hear her tiny voice, then he realized her panic was the same as he'd felt as a child himself. Those times when he had sat alone, scared his own mother would never come back. He pushed away the memory. Allison wasn't anything like Cindy Casali. He brushed at her tears. "Oh, little one, your mother would never leave you."

The child nodded. "She did before." Another tear, then another. "I want her to stay with me."

It all came clear to him. As long as Cherry refused to get better, she'd have her mom's full attention.

"You're wrong. She isn't going to leave you, ever. I promise. But you'll never know unless you start talking to her."

Then the girl glanced away.

"You're going to be five soon. Don't you want to go to school and have friends?"

She turned back to him. "I want us to live with you and Tilda at the ranch."

His chest tightened as he realized how much this little girl had added to his life. How much he wished there had been someone in his life to make time for him.

"Oh, sweetheart. You know you're always welcome at the ranch." He lifted her into his lap as her tiny arms circled his neck. Another barrier came crashing down and Alex didn't know if he could handle letting either one of them go.

The next evening, Allison finally finished up her class for the day. Earlier Tilda had taken Cherry back to the ranch house for supper so she wouldn't have to hang around and wait for her mother.

She was planning on sharing the evening meal with the women when she looked up and saw Alex standing in the doorway of the room. She paused and admired the handsome rancher in the black jeans, a burgundy western shirt, and shiny black boots. Dear Lord, she'd never seen a man look so good.

"Allison." He nodded. "I have a message from Tilda."

"Has something happened to Cherry?"

"She's fine. Tilda just wants to know if it's okay if she spends the night?"

Her daughter wanted a sleepover? "Oh, that's so much trouble."

"I don't think Tilda feels that way about Cherry. I have no doubt she's enjoying every minute of it."

Since the accident, Allison had always worried about leaving her daughter with anyone. "What about Cherry?"

"They were both working on a jigsaw puzzle when I left."

She was a little sad that she would be alone tonight. "That's good. I want her to be independent." Allison gave him a brave smile. "Thanks for letting me know."

He pulled out his cell phone and pushed a button, then placed it against his ear. "Tilda. Yeah, she said it was okay." He nodded and held out the phone to her. "Your daughter wants to talk to you."

Allison's heart stopped suddenly as Alex handed her the phone. "Cherry?"

"Mommy," came out in a tiny whisper.

"Oh, honey," she managed as tears flooded her eyes. "Do you really want to stay all night?"

"Yeah."

Every soft word spoken caused her such joy, she could barely speak. She wanted nothing more than to run over there and hug her daughter, but didn't want to overwhelm her. "Okay, I'll see you in the morning. I love you."

"Love you, too. 'Night."

"Goodnight, sweetie." She handed the phone back to Alex. "Thank you."

"Why are you thanking me? I didn't do anything."

"Okay, play tough guy, but I'm not buying it. You somehow convinced my daughter to talk again."

He shrugged. "Maybe." His steely gray eyes met hers and she felt a different kind of emotion. "Go to dinner with me, and I'll tell you my tricks."

Allison knew Alex Casali had a lot of them. One of them was making her fall head over heels for him. "Will you give me a few minutes to clean up?"

After his nod, she turned back to the women in the room who were all smiling. She let them know she wouldn't be staying after all, but would be here the first thing in the morning to answer any questions. She turned to leave, ignoring several comments about her sexy cowboy. She knew one thing for sure. She couldn't ignore her feelings for Alex any longer.

An hour later, Alex walked Allison into a small family-owned Mexican restaurant in Kerry Springs. An older couple greeted them with a warm smile.

"Alessandro, it's been a long time," the older woman said, giving him a big hug. The heavy-set woman in her fifties had black hair laced with gray pulled back into a bun.

They exchanged words in Spanish, and then Alex turned to her. "Juan and Maria, this is Allison Cole. She owns the Blind Stitch shop downtown."

A smiling Maria grasped her hands. "So good to meet you, Allison." Then she looked back at Alex. *"Muy bonita."*

"Sí, bonita."

Allison found herself blushing. *"Gracias,"* she said.

Juan stepped in. "Mama, our guests are hungry," he said. He led them through the dimly lit restaurant out to a terracotta-tiled patio edged with small trees adorned with tiny lights. They were seated at a wrought-iron table in a secluded corner. "Enjoy."

Mr. Lopez left them alone. "They are a lovely couple," Allison said.

He glanced across the table at her. "They're probably saying the same thing about us."

Allison couldn't look away from his penetrating gaze. Did he want them to be a couple? No, she couldn't go there. "I bet the food here is good," she said.

He raised an eyebrow. "I think so, but you tell me." He motioned for the waiter and they ordered dinner.

When the wine arrived, she took a sip, hoping it would help her relax. "This is very good."

He nodded. "I'm glad you like it. I don't drink much. My mother did far too much."

"I'm sorry." She released her glass. "I'm not much of a drinker, either. This is the first since Cherry's accident. It's the first time I've gone out."

Alex watched her expression change. "Hey, don't go getting sad on me. You should be happy—your daughter is speaking."

Her pretty face broke into a grin. "She is. And I have you to thank for that."

He shrugged. "Cherry would have talked eventually, but she's pretty stubborn." He took a drink of his wine. "A lot like her mother."

Her happiness seemed to fade. "Is that the reason she hasn't talked? She's angry at me?"

"Cherry isn't angry." She stared at him as he toyed with his glass. "She's afraid you'll leave her."

Allison's eyes widened. "How could she think that?"

"She told me if she got better, you'd leave her again, like last time."

"Damn Jack for all his lies."

Alex reached for her hand and gripped it tightly. "It's okay, Allison."

"No, it's not. I allowed my husband to run my life. He kept me from my own child. Worse, I let him."

He hoped he never ran into the guy. "Well, you're doing it right now. So put the past aside, and move on. Cherry's improving every day. Her therapy's going well. She'll be walking one day."

Allison looked up at him with those beautiful jade eyes. "You think so?"

His gut tightened. "I know so."

She quickly brushed away a tear and smiled. "Oh, Alex, be careful. You're turning into a nice guy."

He doubted that.

"And that makes you hard to resist."

He grinned at her. "That's my plan."

Two hours had gone by way too quickly as they walked out of the restaurant. After no lack of conversation during their meal, they suddenly grew silent during the ride back to the ranch. Alex enjoyed the quiet. He always had. The full moon overhead lit the road, adding to the intimacy. Finally he pulled up in front of the cabin as he had many other times, but tonight Cherry wasn't in the backseat. Selfish as it was, he wanted time alone with her mother.

He got out, went around to the passenger door and lifted Allison down. When her slim body made contact with his, he couldn't resist. He lowered his head and kissed her because he couldn't wait any longer for the taste of her, the feel of her against him.

When he finally tore his mouth away, they were both breathless. "Allie." He rested his forehead against hers. "You're driving me crazy."

Allison suddenly realized they were outside in front

of the cabin silhouetted by the porch light. What was he doing to her?

"It would probably be wiser if I said goodnight right here before I get into trouble," he warned her.

Disappointed, she started to step away, but he drew her close to his side and walked her inside the dimly lit cabin. Her heart raced as he pushed her back against the closed door and kissed her as if it were their last time. "I'm not very wise when it comes to you."

She wrapped her arms around his neck, pulled him down and kissed him again. "I guess I'm not either."

His gaze bore into hers. "It would be crazy to take this any further."

It was her turn. She had the choice to send him away, or have the man stay and make love to her. "Yeah, crazy," she breathed.

He closed his eyes. "I've never wanted a woman as badly as I want you."

Allison felt the same as she placed her mouth against his, sending another surge of heat through her. He groaned and wrapped his arms around her body and pulled her against him, deepening the kiss. She let him.

Alex swung her up into his arms and headed down the hall into the master bedroom. The king-size bed took center stage. The rich cocoa-brown comforter was masculine, but there were some feminine touches, too, including satin sheets.

He stood her on the floor, then turned her around to face him. His finger touched her jaw, tilting her face up to his. "Tell me to walk out that door."

Allison felt her body turn hot, her breasts grow heavy. With a moment of unexpected and reckless desire, she couldn't move and realized she didn't want to. He saw her hesitation.

"Not so sure?"

"No!" she denied, then her voice softened. "It's just I haven't been with—"

"Anyone but your husband," he finished.

She nodded.

He released her with a curse. "Look, Allie, this isn't going to work. So let's put a stop to it now."

Before she could find her voice, he'd turned and headed out.

She tried to call him back, but he didn't stop. Then she heard the cabin door close and she was suddenly alone. She curled up on the bed, telling herself it was probably best he had left. But if that were true, why did she feel more alone than she'd ever felt in her life?

CHAPTER EIGHT

AT five the next morning, Alex drove up to the house. He climbed out into the cool predawn air, glad there was no one else stirring, yet. He knew work had already started on the ranch, but he wasn't ready for the daily routine. Not yet.

He'd been driving around most of the night, trying not to think. Not to see the hurt look on Allison's face before he had walked out on her. But he knew if he'd stayed he could never leave her. He wasn't ready for that. She wasn't either.

He walked inside the house. Relieved to find the kitchen empty, he started upstairs to his bedroom. Stripping off his shirt as he went, he entered the moss-green room with dark furniture and a king-size bed.

Everything was big and masculine. Not a thing was feminine. Why would it be since there had never been a woman in here? That was the way he wanted it.

Dropping his shirt in the hamper, he went into the connecting bathroom and turned on the water in the shower. He removed the rest of his clothes and stepped inside the stall, then let the warm water begin to work its magic. He closed his eyes, and once again Allison Cole appeared in his head.

Just hours ago, he'd stood beside her bed. She had been willing. Her fiery hair draped against her shoulders, her mouth swollen from his kisses. Her body pressed against his.

Alex groaned as a strange feeling stirred in his chest. Damn, if he never wanted any more than to climb into bed with her. Make love to her and then again. The honest truth was he knew he'd never get enough of her.

He opened his eyes and grabbed the soap to wash away any thoughts of spending more time with her. He'd already broken too many rules. Number one, he'd spent entirely too much time with her, making him feel things he hadn't felt in a long time. He didn't like that. He stepped under the spray of water, trying to rinse away the soap along with all the memories of a woman who had burrowed in a lot deeper than he'd ever allowed anyone. If he let her, she might find her way into his heart. Deep down, he knew it was already too late.

It was six-thirty when Allison walked up the steps to Alex's house. She was feeling confused and insecure. God, Alex was the last person she wanted to see and he certainly didn't want to see her. But no matter that she'd been relieved nothing had happened between them, his rejection still hurt.

The sound of her child's laughter pushed aside everything else. She put on a smile and went inside. Cherry was sitting at the table as Tilda worked at the stove, singing a silly song. Her daughter was clapping her hands and Allison's heart soared. For the first time in a very long time she had hope that things would get better.

Tilda looked at her. "Well, look who's here. Good morning, Allison."

"'Morning, Tilda, Cherry," Allison greeted as she went to her daughter and kissed her. "So, did you have a good night?"

Her daughter nodded. "I did a puzzle."

Allison bit her lower lip. "How fun. What else did you do?"

Cherry glanced at Tilda. "Go on, tell your mother."

"I stayed up late." Her pretty blue eyes sparkled. "'Cause I did my exercises."

Another miracle. "That's wonderful. I'm so proud of you."

Her daughter's smile widened. "And I get to ride Maisie, too."

"Good. Today is my last day of class. Then you and I are going to be spending a lot more time together. Does that sound like a good idea?"

Her daughter nodded as Tilda carried food to the table. "I've set you a place, and if you go get Alex we can eat."

Allison would rather walk over hot coals. She stood up. "Where is he?"

"In the office."

Allison went off down the hall. All she had to do was call to him. Besides, if he wanted nothing to do with her all she had to do was get through today, and tomorrow they'd move back to town. And she could forget ever knowing the man. That appeared to be the way he wanted it.

Alex stood at the window, his phone next to his ear, listening to his brother complain about a shoulder injury that had sidelined the future Hall of Fame pitcher for the season.

"You could come stay at the ranch if you're bored."

"Thanks, Alex, but if I want to work, it won't be around smelly cows and horses."

Alex grinned. "Is the only reason you called me to complain?"

"Oh, man, I almost forgot. Did you get the email from Isabella? There are a few surprises. She sent wedding pictures."

Alex went to his desk and turned on the computer. He found the email and clicked on it.

Since you couldn't be here for the special day, I'm sending along a family picture. Cristiano couldn't make it either, but I thought I would attach his picture anyway so you can get a glimpse of all of your family that are very eager to meet you, perhaps one day soon...

The photo appeared of the large group enjoying Lizzie's wedding, and Alex began to search for anyone familiar. Then he clicked on the separate photograph attached to the email.

"Oh, sh... Who is he?"

"Cristiano Casali," Angelo said. "He's our half-brother."

Alex continued to stare at the young man who looked remarkably like him and his twin. Then his attention went slowly back to the man in the back row of the wedding shot, Luca Casali. The man who hadn't had room in his life for his sons, so had just sent them away. Had he ever regretted it? Had he ever thought about them? Suddenly emotions clogged his throat. "I've got to go, Angelo. I'll call you later."

Alex hung up, but he kept looking at the photos. All the years of pain and loneliness hit him hard. Lost in his past, he suddenly heard his name. Standing in the morning light, he saw Allison. She looked pretty dressed in her trim trousers and white blouse. His heart raced and he felt a stirring in his body that he didn't need right now.

"Allison."

"I'm supposed to tell you breakfast is ready."

All at once he felt a need for her. He got up, went to her and drew her in his arms, then captured her mouth in an eager kiss. After he pulled back, he said, "Now that's a better way to start the morning."

She still didn't smile.

"You're angry with me because I had to leave you."

She shook her head and stepped back. "You were right, it would have been bad to take our relationship any further. Since after today, when class ends, you don't have to worry about running into me. We only have to make it through breakfast."

She started to leave, but he grabbed her by the wrist, stopping her. "You think that's why I left you, Allie?"

She closed her eyes. "Don't call me that."

He leaned closer. "You didn't mind last night."

She shook her head. "Stop it," she breathed. "You walked away from me last night. I don't know how I'm supposed to act, Alex."

Hell, he didn't know how to act either. He wasn't supposed to feel like this about her. She wasn't supposed to get this close. "I left because you weren't ready for what little I could offer you."

"Did I ask for anything more?"

"Your type always wants more." When she tried to pull away, he held tight. "You deserve more."

He dipped his head and nibbled on her mouth. "But

if you're willing to settle I've got some ideas on how to spend a few hours."

She pulled back. "Not a good idea."

He agreed. "So we agree to stay away from any more trouble." He gave her a quick kiss. "Now, let's go get some breakfast." Reluctantly, he released her and went back to turn off his computer.

Allison followed him and saw the pictures. "What a lovely picture. Family?"

He nodded. "You could say they're family. They live in Italy."

Allison stared down at the large group. "You're lucky. I lost all of mine."

"You're welcome to mine."

She didn't miss the sarcasm in his voice as her gaze combed over each person, eager to know Alex better. She stopped as she saw the smaller photo of a younger version of Alex. "Is this your twin brother?"

He shook his head. "No. I believe that's my half-brother. Seems my father remarried and had another family to replace the one he shipped off."

Allison watched the pain flicker across his face. "So your mother took care of you."

"When she wasn't drinking or on drugs. The only thing Cindy ever wanted was for Luca Casali to come after her. Instead she got stuck with a couple of kids and died trying to drink away her misery."

Allison gasped. "Oh, Alex, you can't mean that."

He glanced at her, his eyes dark with anger. "At least after she died, we stopped hoping she would get clean and want us."

How could a mother not want her children? "She had a problem."

"Stop whitewashing it. If our mother had cared, she wouldn't have left two kids alone all night, or forget to feed us; she'd worry that we didn't have heat or water to bathe, or that we were living on the street. As far as Angelo and I are concerned, our mother didn't even try. No one tried."

Allison's heart went out to him. She didn't have the words to help him deal with the anguish. "You still have a family in Italy and your father is alive. Maybe you could reconnect with him now."

"That's almost funny since Luca has only contacted us once in all these years."

"Maybe there were reasons." She moved closer. "Maybe you owe it to yourself to find out."

Later that afternoon, Allison was wrapping up her class and saying goodbye to her students. She'd felt good about everything she'd accomplished on her first retreat. Several of the women had already talked about returning for her next class. Honestly, she wasn't sure she'd be back to do another one.

If she hadn't gotten so close with Alex it might be different. He'd told her that he didn't get involved long term. She wasn't about to be a convenience. She deserved more. Besides, Cherry had to be her main focus. Although she'd made such great progress, there was a long way to go.

So why was her day clouded with worry about Alex? The turmoil he had to be going through over his family. What a horrible life he and his brother must have had growing up. Her heart went out to them both.

A commotion at the door caused her to turn around to see Tilda bringing in several ranch hands to help the guests load up their things. After directing them to their tasks, Tilda walked over to Allison.

"I didn't think I'd feel this sad now that it's over." The older woman hugged her. "Thanks to you, Allison, the retreat was a great success. Any time you want to do another one, please let me know. In fact, a few of the women were asking how you felt about doing a class at your shop."

Allison thought eventually she would like to do that. "I'm not sure if I have the room where I am at right now, but I might be able to swing it two times a month, if the group stays small enough."

"Or we could meet here," Tilda added. "You and Cherry can continue to stay in one of the cabins."

That would heighten her chances of seeing Alex. "I'm not sure that's a good idea. It's a long drive from town."

"You can have it on a day Cherry comes to go riding."

Allison had forgotten about the riding. How would Alex feel about her coming back every week? "I'm not sure it's a good idea."

Tilda studied her awhile. "Look, I may be getting old, but my eyesight is still pretty good. Whatever has happened between you and Alex is your business. Just so you know, in the ten years I've known Alex Casali, he's never acted this way before with another woman. Somehow you and that sweet girl of yours have managed to get under his skin. And it's about time."

"Oh, Tilda, I never planned for anything to happen. But now that we're leaving, I won't be seeing Alex again."

She frowned. "I know Alex can be stubborn and difficult at times, but he hasn't had much love, or family, in his life. So if he backs away, or gets distant, don't give up on him. There's a pretty wonderful guy hidden inside."

Allison blinked at tears. "I have to put Cherry first."

"Of course you do, and he could help you with her. I believe that you care about him, too."

Care? She was close to falling in love with him. All Allison could do was nod.

"Good." With a smile, the older woman looked out of the window. "Land sake's, would you look at this?"

Allison turned around and saw two riders coming toward them. It was Alex on the gelding, leading Cherry on Maisie, and also Honey.

"I'd say the man's got it bad," Tilda said.

Allison ignored Tilda's comments as they walked outside. Alex climbed off his horse and one of the hands helped with the others.

"Hi, Mommy," Cherry called with a wave.

"Hi, sweetie." Her daughter had on jeans and a T-shirt. On her head she had a new cowboy hat. No doubt who it came from. "You're getting pretty good at riding Maisie."

"I know. Alex said we can all go riding. You, too."

Alex came across the porch with that lazy gait that caused her stomach to do a funny flip.

"I thought it would be nice if we all took a ride together."

That wasn't a good idea. "I can't leave everything for Tilda."

"It will be here when you get back." The older woman nudged her. "Now, go change. You can't keep them waiting."

Allison glanced at the happiness on Cherry's face. This was their last day here. How could she turn them down? "Okay, just give me a little time to change."

"Hurry, Mom, Alex's taking us to a secret place. And he says it's just for special girls."

* * *

Allison changed her clothes, came back outside and mounted Honey in record time. When she asked Alex where they were going, he refused to say, only instructed her and Cherry to follow him through the open pasture.

Allison watched her daughter, surprised how well she handled the pony. Although Alex had a lead rope, Cherry gave commands and handled the animal's reins. Allison glanced down at the child's jean-clad legs and saw a slight movement.

Allison's heart stopped and then began to race. She shot a look at Alex, who'd been watching her. He shook his head in warning, silently asking her not to say anything.

She rode up beside him. "Did you see what she did?"

Alex kept his gaze forward. "Yes, but I don't think she does. If we say something she might try too hard to do more than she can handle right now."

No matter what had happened between her and Alex, she knew he cared for Cherry. "You're right." She started to fall back behind her daughter, then stopped and touched his arm. "Thank you, Alex. Thank you for all you've done for my child."

He shrugged. "All I did was put her on a horse."

"And helped with her therapy, and took the time to teach her to ride. Oh, no, you didn't do much."

Alex watched Allison blink back tears and it nearly killed him. He regretted leaving her last night, but not as much as not being able to promise her a future.

"We'll never forget you," she whispered.

Unable to speak past the lump in his throat, he nodded, and she turned her horse around and fell back in behind her daughter. He would never be able to forget them either. Yet, the reality was she was leaving today.

Today. She and Cherry would be out of his life. It surprised him how much of his time had been filled with the two of them. How much he'd looked forward to seeing them every day.

He rode his horse through a grove of ancient oaks as they began to climb the gentle grade.

He turned back to Cherry. "Are you doing okay?"

The four-year-old nodded, concentrating hard on her task. Once again, Alex caught the slight movement of her tiny legs against the pony's flanks. He couldn't help but smile as the girl mimicked a clicking sound he'd made many times.

"We're almost there," he assured the riders. He finished the slight climb to the top of the hill. As soon as the ground leveled out, he stopped and looked at the incredible scenery. He moved the gelding into the sun for a better view of the ranch. Dense trees covered the slopes to the northwest, rich pasture land where his cattle grazed was to the east, and to the south ran one of the two creeks on the property that was lined with thick mesquite bushes. Cypress and cedars dotted the waterline.

"Oh, Alex," Allison gasped as she rode up beside him, her gaze roaming over the miles of his land. The bright hues of greens met the rich blue sky, mixing with the golden colors of the setting sun.

"Is this your secret place?" Cherry asked.

"In a way it is because I come here to see how pretty the world is. It always makes me feel better. But there is something else I want to share with you." He climbed down and came around to Cherry. After he unfastened her safety straps, he lifted her into his arms. He called to Allison over his shoulder. "Come on, Mom, you've got to see it, too."

They walked a ways back through the trees. It was almost forest-like when they came to a small clearing and a giant oak. The majestic tree reached high to the sky and its branches stretched out in all directions, shading the ground. The stocky trunk was covered with a rough bark and a hardy base with massive roots burrowing into the earth.

"It's a giant," Cherry called. "It's so big you can live in it."

"I don't know about that." Alex carried Cherry over and placed her on one of the low-hanging branches. "But it's big enough so a little girl can sit for awhile."

She giggled, balancing herself. "Wow! Mom, look at me."

"I see," Allison said, coming up next to him. "You be careful."

Alex couldn't resist. "Maybe you want to stay close by to make sure." He gripped Allison by her waist, and, ignoring her gasp, lifted her up next to her daughter.

"Alex!" she cried. "You can't lift me."

He grinned and stood back. "Looks like I already did." He reached into his pocket and pulled out his cell phone. "I think we need a picture of this day. So smile, ladies."

When both mother and daughter turned to him, smiling, he could barely concentrate on taking the photo. His chest tightened and he found he couldn't breathe, realizing how much they'd both come to mean to him. He didn't want to let them go, not yet.

Not ever.

CHAPTER NINE

IN A flash, her time at the A Bar A Ranch was a distant memory. No more rides to the creek, or to special places with amazing views. Most of all, no more rugged cowboy with steel-gray eyes and a touch that melted any resistance. Allison's heart fluttered as she recalled his kisses, his hands on her skin. His husky voice could send shivers down her spine. Then he turned on one of those rare smiles, or the gentle calming words that reassured her little girl her world seemed right.

It was past ten o'clock when Allison drove her loaded car back to Kerry Springs. She brushed away a wayward tear. Stop it, she chided. She'd known this was going to happen. Alex Casali wasn't the kind of man who would want to settle down with a woman and a kid. How many times had he said just that? He liked his life the way it was. No complications.

Fine. She didn't need him, either. All she needed was Cherry. All her attention had to be focused on her daughter to help get her well again. For the first time in a long time, she had hopes that would happen.

She drove through the alley at the back of her store and glanced in her mirror to catch the familiar truck headlights. Alex pulled up behind her. After getting out, she went to unlock the door while Alex took Cherry out of the car. Her daughter whimpered a little, but quieted with his soothing voice. He carried her inside and up to the apartment. Allison brought in two of their bags and made her way upstairs.

Alex met her halfway. "I'll get these. Go take care of Cherry."

She bit back any retort that might make him leave. "Thanks." She climbed the stairs and turned on the air conditioner, trying to cool off the small apartment before she went into her daughter's room.

"Mommy, it's too hot," the child complained. "I don't want to stay here."

"Honey, we've talked about this. This is our home." Allison bit back her own frustration, hating that she couldn't give her daughter something better.

Downstairs, Alex unloaded the boxes from the vehicles and stacked them in the storeroom on the first floor. He had to fight the urge to put everything back in the truck—including Allison and Cherry—and take them back to the ranch.

He rested his hands on his hips and looked around the cramped area. How could he leave them here? There wasn't enough room, and the apartment wasn't any better. He had to get them back to the ranch. He paused. And what? How would he keep them there? What could he offer her? To share his bed? No, Allison wouldn't go for it, and he couldn't blame her.

He carried the rest of the suitcases upstairs as Allison was coming out of the bedroom. "If you don't mind, would you say goodnight to Cherry?"

"Of course I will."

He put on a smile and walked into the bedroom. "Hey, little one. You're all tucked in."

She nodded. "But I don't like it here. I want to go back to the ranch."

He wanted the same thing. He sat down on the twin mattress. "It's not so bad. Your room is pretty." He could see that Allison had worked to decorate the small space. What made him angry was he could easily give both of them everything their hearts desired, including the best therapy room and treatment for Cherry.

Allison left Alex alone to say goodnight to her daughter. She could tell by his body language that he didn't want to stay. Well, she hadn't wanted to start anything in the beginning. He'd been the one who pursued her, the one who'd gotten involved in her life.

Made her care about him.

Alex came out of the bedroom. "She's asleep," he said as he walked toward where Allison stood in the kitchen area. "She's pretty exhausted from the ride today."

"Thank you for helping with all the boxes. Mostly for making our stay at the ranch so nice."

He shrugged. "It wasn't a big deal."

"No, I guess for you it wasn't. For my daughter, it was." Allison sighed. "I just have to figure out a way to get her to accept *normal* again."

He drew his eyebrows together in a frown. "I thought we decided that she would come to the ranch every week to ride."

"I don't know, Alex, if that's a good idea. Cherry will want more and more." She finally looked at him and wanted to shout, *It's you she wants. So do it.* She quickly glanced away. "I don't want her to be disappointed, or hurt."

He stood his ground. "And I don't want that girl to go without."

She closed her eyes a moment. "She isn't going without, Alex. I can give my daughter everything she needs."

"I know you can. I was just trying to take away some of your burden."

She fought her anger. "Cherry's not a burden."

"Dammit, that's not what I mean. But you have to work. You can't be everywhere." He reached for her. "I can afford to help you."

"In exchange for what, Alex? Are you suddenly changing your mind about taking me to your bed?"

He cursed. "I'm not asking for any strings, Allie," he said.

Hearing the endearment, she had to step back. She cared too much to let him do this. It would only be harder when he tired of her.

"Please Alex, you should go. I can't deal with this right now. Under the circumstances, us coming to the ranch is only going to complicate things more."

Alex stood his ground. He knew it was already too late, but he couldn't just walk away. "Maybe we should see where it leads."

She shook her head. "You don't want to do that, Alex. You like your life on your ranch away from everyone."

"That's not true. I have Tilda and Brian. Maybe I want to include you and Cherry in that group. I care about you both."

"And I care about you, too," she admitted. "Oh, Alex, I don't know if you can give us what we need. I'm not sure if we're what you want, either. I've already had a bad marriage. My record isn't very good."

He reached for her, bringing her close. "I didn't know we were keeping score. If so, add this in on the positive side." He leaned down and closed his mouth over hers, not wanting to give her a chance to back away from him again.

He drew back a fraction. "God, Allie, I want you. You want me, too. Nothing will ever change that."

She was breathless. "That's not the problem, Alex. But what if it doesn't go beyond that? For Cherry's sake, I can't risk it. I can't give her a taste of something so wonderful, and then take it away. She's already lost so much, including her father." She swallowed. "She's so attached to you. I can't have her lose you, too."

His chest ached. "What if I don't want to lose either of you?"

She smiled through watery eyes. "You haven't lost us, Alex. You just don't know where we fit in. You need to figure that out." She hesitated. "Maybe if you started by making peace with your past."

He hated that she made sense.

"You have a family, Alex," she went on. "It's far away in Italy, but they're extending a hand to you and your brother."

He tensed. "They haven't contacted either of us in years, and suddenly they want to include us?"

"There could have been a reason."

Alex crossed the room. He couldn't bring himself to tell her any more than he already had about his awful childhood. How abandoned he'd felt most of his life. God, he'd never do that to a child. He could never leave Cherry like that. He cared for the little one too much. He froze as he stared at Allison. He cared for her mother, too.

She came up to him. "I know this is hard for you, Alex. Good or bad, they're still your family."

He'd prayed for years someone would come for him and Angelo. To take them away from their mother, give them a home.

Allison touched his arm, making him look at her. "Do you have any idea how much I would love to have a relative out there? I was eight years old when I lost my parents. My grandmother took me in, but she died when I was in college. I only have Cherry." She blinked at threatening tears. "I nearly lost her. Now, you have the opportunity to talk things out with your father." She hesitated. "He isn't getting any younger. God forbid something happened and you'd let this chance slip by."

Alex swallowed back the dryness in his throat. Would his father even talk with him? Since he'd gotten Isabella's email and the wedding invitation, it had sparked curiosity about his family. It had also brought back feelings of hurt and despair that had been with him all his life.

"I don't know if I can do this, Allie," he admitted, his gaze meeting hers. "Not without help."

"I'll help in any way I can," she offered.

He leaned forward and brushed his mouth over hers. "If you mean that, then come to Italy with me."

Five days later, Allison was calling herself crazy as she buckled her seat belt on Alex's private plane. The sleek Learjet's interior was decorated in shades of gray and burgundy with comfortable captain's chairs and even a sleeping area for long flights.

Looking across to the window seat, she saw her daughter's smiling face and stopped berating herself. They were going to Italy. Thank goodness they'd had passports from a previous trip to Canada to see a doctor.

After finding someone to watch Blind Stitch, and rescheduling Cherry's therapy, she felt a little giddy just thinking about the trip.

In the front of the cabin, Alex was talking with the pilot. He'd left his hat and western clothes back at the ranch, replaced by a pair of charcoal dress trousers and a white oxford cloth shirt opened at the neck. Yet, he wore a pair of shiny black cowboy boots.

Once Alex ended the instructions, he pulled out his cell phone. During the call, he frowned as he nodded, then by the end of the talk his expression turned sad. She knew he'd been trying to convince Angelo to go with them. It looked as if he wasn't making any headway. He shut his phone and said something to the pilot, then he sat down in the seat next to hers.

He touched Cherry's arm. "You ready to go flying, *uccellino*?"

She nodded enthusiastically. "I want to go up to the clouds."

"Then we're in luck. That's where Captain Jason is taking us." He turned to Allison. "Are you all right?"

She nodded, too. "What's not to be all right about? I'm flying to Europe, and on a private jet."

"I'm glad you're enjoying it."

She sobered. "You're the one I'm worried about. I'm afraid I rushed you into this trip."

"I don't have the luxury of waiting. Roundup is coming in another month. I have beef orders to fill. So it's as good a time as any to get this over with."

He didn't sound happy. "Poor you, you've got to go to ugly old Italy."

He tried to glare at her, but it didn't work.

"It's all right, Alex," she began. "I'm sure Brian can

handle things. And Tilda has finally got you out from underfoot."

His glare intensified. "Did she say that?"

She sighed. "Look, Tilda loves you like a son. She only wants you to be happy. We're both hoping this will help you. So tell me about this family of yours. Are you related to royalty, or anyone famous?"

He gave her an annoyed look.

"Come on, Alex. You can't tell me you haven't investigated your roots." All she'd gotten from him was he was born and lived three years of his life in a small town called Monta Correnti between Rome and Naples.

He shook his head. "I know only what my mother told me." He looked at her. "When she'd been sober enough to talk about it."

Allison watched the emotions play across his face, knowing none of this was easy for him.

He began the story. "Seems the interesting part began with my paternal grandmother, Rosa Casali. She was sixteen when her family arranged her marriage to an older man, Roberto Firenzi, and they had two children, Lisa and Luigi.

"During the Second World War Rosa volunteered at a hospital where she cared for a wounded English soldier, William Valentine. After three weeks, they couldn't resist temptation any longer and spent the night together."

Hearing the jet engines, Allison checked on Cherry, but quickly turned to Alex, wanting to hear more. "Did William ever come back for her? Was he killed?"

Alex shook his head. "No, but it seems before he left he gave her a secret recipe for tomato sauce. That last day after she said goodbye to William, her husband

Roberto died. Just weeks later, Rosa also discovered she was pregnant with my father, Luca."

How wonderful that Rosa found love, Allison thought. "What did she do?"

"Having to support her family, Rosa sold everything she could and opened the restaurant, Sorella. My father worked there along with his sister, Lisa, but they never got along. And it got worse and after Rosa died, Luca struck out on his own. He started up a roadside food stand. That was when our mother, Cindy Daniels, came through the village on vacation from the states. Their attraction was instant and they quickly married. Soon after, my brother and I arrived."

"I bet you two were a handful," Allison said.

"According to our mother, Luca didn't help at all, he ignored her. So she divorced him, and left us all and returned home to Boston. A year or so later, Luca shipped us off to her. End of story."

Allison doubted it was the end, but she could see Alex wasn't about to say any more. "I guess you'll have to hear your father's side of the story."

Alex shrugged and scooted down in his seat. "You're hoping for a miracle."

She reached for his hand. "It'll be okay, Alex." She sent up a prayer hoping that was true as the plane headed off down the runway. She glanced at the man who'd stolen her heart.

There was no going back now, for either of them.

Sometime later that evening the plane landed in Naples. Allison was surprised that Cherry had slept on and off during the long flight. They'd played games and watched videos, even did some leg exercises, and then she finally drifted off to sleep. Allison hadn't been so lucky. Sleep eluded her, and Alex stayed busy with work he'd brought along.

Once they got off the plane and through customs, there was a car waiting for them. The darkness made it impossible to see any scenery and Allison was too tired to care. After the car was loaded with their luggage and portable wheelchair purchased for the trip, they took off to where they were going to stay.

About thirty minutes later they pulled up in front of a large villa. Even in the dark she could see the building's grandeur. Suddenly the car door opened and Alex stepped out. She heard a greeting exchanged in Italian, then he leaned in and reached for Cherry. "I'll get her."

He adjusted the child in his arms as Allison climbed out. She tried to brush the wrinkles from her clothes, but gave up.

"*Signora*, welcome to Villa Monte Vista. I hope you enjoy your stay with us. My name is Stefano and my wife is Ghita. She is preparing you a light meal."

"Thank you."

The man in his fifties bowed and motioned to the young boy to come toward the car. "And this is our son, Tomasso." The teenager nodded. "Allow me to show you to your rooms," Stefano said as his son began to load the luggage on the cart as they walked up the path.

They continued on through the tall carved doors and into an enormous entry with marble floors and rough, golden-hued walls. A huge staircase angled against one wall; the steps were partly covered by a beautiful carpet runner.

They took an elevator just under the stairs. After it reached the second floor, they stepped out into a sitting area where there was a table with a large bouquet of fresh flowers. The heavenly fragrance followed them down a wide hall until they came to a set of double doors. Stefano pushed them open and stood aside, allowing them to enter a sitting area with overstuffed sofas and a large tiled fireplace. He then took them to a room with a huge bed decorated with a rich wine-colored satin comforter. She couldn't help but wonder if Alex had planned to stay in here with her.

Stefano instructed his son to leave Allison's luggage, then he walked over to an alcove where there was a single bed. The bright yellow coverings were pulled back, revealing snowy white sheets.

He smiled. "This is for the *bambina*."

"It's perfect," Allison said. "Thank you."

Alex placed the sleeping Cherry on the mattress and Allison went to remove her shoes and took off her jeans. The child didn't even stir. In the end, Allison left her in her T-shirt and underwear for this once. With a kiss on her daughter's forehead, she turned on the night-light and went back to the sitting room.

Allison followed the voices into another doorway across from hers. This room was smaller with a cream and gold décor. She glanced at the queen-sized bed.

Alex turned to her as Tomasso brought in his luggage. "Is your room close enough to Cherry?"

She nodded. "It's perfect." She turned to Stefano. "Thank you."

He bowed again. "You're very welcome, *signora*." Another few minutes, they finished their task and left.

"Alex, you didn't need to give up your room," Allison said. "Cherry and I can easily fit in this bed together."

"I want you to be comfortable."

"What about you? This bed can't be big enough for you."

"I'll survive."

She caught his heated gaze and quickly glanced away.

"There's food in the sitting area," he said. "Some cheese, bread and wine. Join me."

That wouldn't be wise. "I think I'll shower first."

He nodded. "Good idea." Then he left for his room.

She had seen the stress etched on his face, and nearly called him back, but she was better off to keep a safe distance.

After hearing the door close, she went to get her pajamas and robe out of her bag. In the spacious private bathroom, she turned on the shower and let the water relieve the tension of her long day.

Fifteen minutes later she felt much better. She checked on Cherry, then peered into the other room, and found Alex outside the French door standing on the balcony.

She started to leave when he called to her.

"Are you afraid to be alone with me?"

She looked back to see he had on the same trousers, but a fresh black T-shirt. It outlined the muscles in his chest and arms.

She pulled together her cotton robe and came forward. "I just didn't want to disturb you. You have a lot on your mind. Does your family know you arrived?"

"Only my sister, Isabella." He shook his head. "Man, that's crazy. Suddenly I have a sister and two more brothers. How am I supposed to act with them?"

"Don't act." She felt her mouth fighting a smile. "Just be yourself."

He threw his head back and laughed. "That should go over well."

"What I mean is be your *charming* self."

Alex's gaze connected with hers. He tried not to notice how good she looked, how her red hair brushed against her shoulders, recalling how it felt like to touch. Even dressed in simple satin pajama bottoms and tank top didn't take away from her sex appeal. He could see her nervousness as she tugged on her robe to cover her enticing body.

He didn't think it was possible to miss someone so much in just a few minutes. He crossed the room and took her hand. "Come, have a glass of wine."

"I should go to bed." She resisted, but let him lead her to the table where he poured her a glass.

"You can't come all the way to Italy and not sample the local vintage." He handed her a goblet. "Stefano informed me it's from a winery not far from here."

She held her glass up, then took a hesitant sip. "Oh, it is wonderful." She nodded. "You should taste it."

Mesmerized, he watched her press her lips against the crystal goblet. He put his glass down and came to her. "I'd rather taste you." He dipped his head and caught her mouth as she gasped. Next came a soft moan and she melted against him. She felt good. She tasted good. Who needed wine?

The next morning, Allison awoke early and immediately her thoughts turned to Alex. She wasn't happy that she had nearly given into her feelings for him. The man knew how to push the right buttons. Of course, she half expected that he would take advantage of the situation. And being in romantic Italy had nothing to do with her wanting the man.

She knew he'd be a tender and considerate lover, but

she needed more than the physical side. When the trip was over where did they go from here? She was definitely in love with the Texas rancher. Late last night, they'd both been willing, but in the end they'd parted and gone off to their separate rooms.

Thirty minutes later, both she and Cherry were dressed and ready for breakfast. With Stefano's help, Allison took Cherry down to the patio. Seeing her daughter's excitement, she knew that this trip was worth it.

Allison went to the wrought-iron railing, excited as she scanned the beautiful scenery surrounding her. Lush green foliage covered miles of rolling hills. Off in the distance she could see groups of salmon-hued structures in the neighboring village. Was this Monta Correnti? Was it where Alex's family lived? Where he had been born?

A warm breeze caught her hair and she closed her eyes, praying that everything worked out for him.

"Mommy?"

She turned around. "What, sweetie?"

Her daughter was dressed in a pair of black tights and a red and white jumper-style dress. Her blonde curls were pulled back into a ponytail. "Does Alex's family have any little kids?"

Allison still got a rush when she heard Cherry speak. "I'm not sure. You'll have to ask Alex."

"Ask me what, little one?" He came through the door and leaned down and kissed Cherry on the cheek. She looked up at him with adoring eyes. She wasn't immune to the man, either.

"Do you have any little girls in your family?"

"I'm not sure. But we'll find out soon."

He walked to Allison and kissed her full on the

mouth. "Good morning," he whispered. "Just so you know, I had a restless night." His gaze met hers. "I kept dreaming of you."

Allison felt a blush creeping up her face as she glanced at Cherry's smile. "I slept very well."

With his grin, her heart raced. "You're not a very good liar, Allie Cole."

She kept watching him. Those steel-gray eyes locked on hers, and she couldn't manage any words. Afraid was more like it, that she might confess her feelings. And he wasn't ready for her. He might never be. "You don't need any distractions right now."

Stefano appeared in the doorway. "Excuse me, *signore* and *signora*. But you have a guest."

Before Stefano could announce her, a young woman came rushing out. She had long black hair, olive skin and stood a little taller than Allison and she had a curvaceous body to die for. She smiled brightly as she looked directly at Alex. She quickly closed the distance between them and kissed both his cheeks.

"Oh, Alessandro, I'd know you anywhere. Welcome home, *fratello*, brother."

CHAPTER TEN

ALEX hadn't been sure what to expect on coming to Italy. Now, seeing this beautiful woman, his sister, created feelings in him he couldn't express in mere words.

He glanced toward the patio doors, wishing Allison would change her mind and return to help get him through this. After a short exchange of pleasantries, Allison had excused herself and taken Cherry and left.

He turned back to Isabella. Even after learning everything he could about his childhood here, Alex was still thrown off seeing a family member.

And she was his sister. God, he wished he had known about her. Maybe things would have been different. But he'd been excluded.

"I can't tell you how happy I am that you decided to come home," Isabella told him.

He tensed. "This isn't my home. Angelo and I were sent away. It's hard to consider this my home. It's hard getting used to you being my family."

Dark blue eyes stared back at him, not wavering. Nearly black hair hung loose, her skin rich olive.

"Over the years many mistakes and misunderstandings have occurred," Isabella began. "Our father would have never sent you to America if he knew what kind of life you lived there. He tried to stay in touch, but your mother moved so often, our papa lost track of you, Alessandro."

Alex tensed on hearing his given name. "Seems to be a good excuse, but, to me and my brother, he just didn't try very hard to find us. By the way, my name is Alex." He'd made the change years ago when kids had made fun of his name. And when he'd been old enough to discover that he'd been abandoned by the father who'd chosen it.

She smiled easily. "I can see you are as stubborn as he is." She waved her hand in the air. "Please, this is not the time to argue about this. One of my *grandi fratelli* has come home from America."

"*Fratellastro*. I'm your half-brother."

Tears filled her eyes. "You're still of my blood, Alex. *Famigila.* Family. And everyone wants to get to know you as much as I do."

He stiffened. "I asked you not to tell anyone. I refuse to be scrutinized on my reasons for coming here."

"And I honored your wishes. It's just from the moment the secret came out about yours and Angelo's existence, we've all been eager to meet you." She arched an eyebrow. "We would also like to know Allison and Cherry. It's easy to see how much they mean to you."

Alex wasn't going to give into Isabella's speculation. It was none of their business. "She worked at my guest ranch, and I help her with her daughter."

"Oh, men. It is so difficult to admit your feelings? They are both *bellissima*."

He glared at her, then gave a nod of agreement.

She laughed and the sweet sound tugged at him. "I can't wait for you to meet my husband, Max. Then you'll understand why you don't intimidate me." She gave another bright smile. "Please, you didn't come all this way not to give us a chance to be a family." She pulled out a card. "Come to the family restaurant. Rosa."

Alex took the card. This was the hard part, finally facing his past. "When?"

Isabella released a sigh. "Tonight. If that's convenient, of course."

He'd waited years for this. Years to face his father. Maybe he'd finally get the answers he needed so he could move on. "We'll be there."

"That's all I can ask." She smiled as they walked toward the doors at the front of the villa. She rose up and kissed both his cheeks. "Please tell Allison I look forward to seeing her tonight. *Ciao*." She waved and got into her car and drove off.

Alex returned to the patio. He stood at the wrought-iron railing that overlooked the beautiful countryside. He and Angelo had been born here.

"Alex?"

He turned around as Allison walked toward him. He managed to smile.

"Isabella is lovely. But I know it had to be rough on you to see her."

"You mean all the years I missed watching her grow up?"

She nodded. "You're here now. You can share her life now."

He pulled her close, even though he didn't want to need her. "Sometimes I wonder if I'll ever belong anywhere."

"Then let's find out. You can't stay cooped up all day when there's all this beautiful country to see."

He opened his mouth to disagree.

"Don't say you'd rather be inside today. Not a man who rides the borders of his vast land."

He frowned. "How did you know?"

She smiled. "I didn't, but you're not the type of man who likes being inside for long."

"You think you know me so well?"

"I don't think you let anyone that close." She put on a smile again. "Come on, let's take Cherry into the village." She tugged on his arm. "We'll pretend we're tourists."

He found he enjoyed playing her game. "We are."

"I said we're pretending."

That he could do, since he'd been pretending all his life.

Later that evening, Allison sat with Cherry in the backseat of the town car as they headed to Monta Correnti. She glanced toward the front passenger seat to where Alex rode. They'd had fun today. They'd taken Cherry around the grounds, then into the small village where they'd bought silly souvenir trinkets.

By the time they got home and put Cherry down for a nap, Alex had pulled inside himself once again. She knew he'd started thinking about seeing his family.

She hoped that once he met with them he could find some peace. Seeing the tension on his face, she couldn't help but wonder if she'd been wrong to suggest he come to Italy.

Allison glanced out of the window at the exquisite scenery. Earlier today, Stefano had told them about Alex's birthplace, the rolling hillsides with small farms and villages that dotted the landscape. The car drove down a hill and Lake Adrina came into view. The water was a crystal-clear blue, reflecting the sun setting behind the hills.

A while later, the car slowed as they came to the edge of town. There were narrow streets and rows of stairways ran in between a maze of ancient buildings. The quaint hillside structures reminded her of an artist's painting.

Her heart began to race as she wondered how Alex was handling all this. Did he remember any of it? She wanted to reach for him, help him through it.

In the front seat Alex tried not to react as they drove into Monta Correnti. The narrow streets took him back in time, but only served to heighten his interest in learning more about his past. They came to the town square, but nothing there triggered a memory. Finally the car stopped in front of a stucco-coated building with a wrought-iron-trimmed courtyard. A sign overhead read, "Rosa Ristorante".

Alex ignored the pulse pounding in his ears. He climbed out and glanced at the people dining outside, then turned to open the back door. He peered in and met Allison's gaze.

She looked concerned. "Are you sure you want us here?"

He wanted to pull her out of the car and into his arms, but he'd always done things on his own. Besides Angelo, he wasn't sure he was capable of trusting anyone. Every time he had, he'd been the one who lost. "I'm not sure I want to be here."

She placed a hand on his arm. "Then I'm glad we're with you."

"Alex, do I get to see your papa?" Cherry asked.

Alex wasn't sure. Of anything. Isabella had been the only one he'd contacted about his visit. "He's supposed to be here. This is his restaurant." He released a breath. "So let's go see."

He helped Allison out and gave her a long look. She had on a burgundy-colored sundress that flattered her trim body. Her hair was pulled back away from her pretty face and large sterling hoops hung from her ears.

"Am I dressed all right?"

"You're perfect."

He reached in the car and lifted Cherry out. He placed her in her chair that Stefano had waiting. "And you look pretty as a princess." Her sundress was blue and her hair was pulled back in a ponytail.

As they turned around Isabella came rushing out of the entrance dressed in a white chef's uniform. "Oh, you came." She reached up and kissed his cheeks, then Allison and Cherry.

"Oh, *uccellino*."

Cherry giggled. "Alex calls me that name."

Alex's gaze shot to Allison, then to Isabella. His sister didn't miss his surprise. "And that's what our papa called me from the time I was a *bambina*."

Alex didn't want to think he'd remembered all those years ago, but the fact was he must have. Had his father used the same endearment towards him and his brother Angelo?

"Come, let us go inside," Isabella said.

Alex resisted. "Is everyone here?"

Isabella shook her head. "Heavens, no. Luca is here, of course. It's impossible to get him to stay away from this place. I also work here. Please, Alessandro, it will be okay." She gave him a sassy wink. "I will protect you if anyone treats you bad."

Alex couldn't help but smile. She probably would. He glanced at Allison. He'd already experienced the woman's strength. "I guess I have enough protection."

After walking through the courtyard filled with guests, Stefano held open the door to allow them to enter the dimly lit entryway. Alex glanced around the restaurant that had been named after his grandmother Rosa. The rustic setting had frescoed walls and terracotta floors and was sectioned off into different areas. Rosa's served traditional, home-cooked Italian food, and, by the size of the vociferous crowd, it was successful. Many of the tables were filled with people and the sounds of laughter and shouts were almost overwhelming.

Isabella stopped by one of the white-clothed tables and spoke with some guests. She then motioned for Alex to follow her. He started to push Cherry's wheelchair, but Allison stopped him.

"Alex, why don't I let you talk to your father first?" She smiled. "Cherry and I need to make a trip to the rest room, so we'll be back in a few minutes."

He wasn't convinced he wanted to do this either.

"You've waited a long time for this day. This is between you and your father. We'll be back in a little while." She nodded. "Now, go."

She gave him an encouraging smile. He started to disagree, but he could only watch as she and Cherry started off toward the lounge.

Isabella called over one of the restaurant's hostesses and spoke to her. The young girl followed after Allison. "They'll be looked after," she said as she took his arm and led him toward the back of the restaurant and into an alcove. A semi-private area in the back of the restaurant was set aside for larger parties.

He looked around, trying to picture his father. Even with a photo, he wasn't sure if he would recognize him. Would Luca know him?

Suddenly he heard voices as the kitchen door swung open. An older man walked out. His head was turned away, calling to someone over his shoulder, then he spoke to a few guests before finally looking in their direction. He saw Isabella and smiled and his steps got more determined.

Alex's heart lodged in his throat. The man he'd once called Papa was tall with a slender build. His gray-streaked hair was cut short, his narrow face showed many years of life. It seemed that Luca Casali had lived his sixty-seven years to the fullest.

Slowly Luca's gaze locked on him. His smile faded as his steps faltered. A look of panic crossed his face, then it seemed to change to sadness. At that moment, Alex once again felt like the unwanted child that had been sent away.

"Papa…" Isabella began, but she was ignored as he continued toward Alex.

Luca stopped in front of him. "Alessandro," he whispered as tears welled up his clear blue eyes. "Oh, God, Alessandro."

All Alex could do was nod, trying to ignore his own emotions, but it was hard. "I go by Alex now."

Luca seemed to freeze, not knowing what to do next. It was Isabella who stepped in. "Papa, Alex came all the way from America to see us." The noise level seemed to rise. "Come, let's move some place a little more private."

She led the two men into the alcove, then closed the louvered folding doors, muffling the outside noise. She motioned to a long table covered in linen. "Sit," she instructed the two men. "I'll get the wine." Before they could stop her, Isabella had slipped out once again.

Alex didn't speak. He couldn't if he wanted to.

Besides, he'd come all this way to hear this man's explanation. What he hated the most was that he wanted Luca Casali to have a good reason why he'd sent them away.

Luca took a long time to speak. "I've prayed for this day."

"I stopped praying a long time ago."

Tears filled the older man's eyes again as he stood there and took what Alex was handing out. "I don't blame you and your brother for hating me."

Alex felt his control slipping. "Believe me, I've had years to perfect it."

"I'm sorry, *figlio*. So sorry. There is no excuse for what I did."

Alex straightened. "How can you call me your son? For years you denied us."

Just then Isabella came through the door carrying a bottle with glasses with Allison and Cherry following her.

"Look who's joining us." His sister smiled. "Papa, this is Alex's friend, Allison Cole and her daughter, Cherry."

Luca went to Allison and took her hand. "I'm pleased to meet you," he said, then looked down at Cherry. "Aren't you a *bella signorina*? Just like your mother."

Cherry blushed. "Thank you. Are you Alex's papa?" she asked boldly.

Luca looked sad. "I'm sorry to say not for a very long time."

Alex tensed and Isabella saw it. "Please, Alex. Papa. Everyone, let's sit down and have a drink together. We'll talk."

Alex wasn't sure if he could; his feelings were too close to the surface. "What should we drink to? The long-lost son returns?"

His sister handed Alex a glass and Allison one, too.

"Yes, for one. And to hear Papa's side of what happened all those years ago." She turned to Luca. "Papa, tell him why you had to let them go. Why you didn't have any other choice."

Luca looked at his daughter. "It doesn't matter the reason. I did the unforgivable and sent my *figlios* away." He took a long drink from his glass. "I thought you needed to be with your mother."

Alex drained his glass. "You wanted to be rid of us."

"Never," Luca denied, his gaze not wavering from his son. "I couldn't afford to keep you with me. Business was bad then, and I had to work all the time. There was no money, no one to watch you and Angelo. I thought sending you to your mother would be best."

He saw Allison get up and take Cherry out of the room. He wanted to go after her, but things needed to be said. "Well, you thought wrong," Alex threw back, but kept his voice low and controlled. "Cindy didn't take care of us. She was a drunk. We went hungry, several times we were out on the streets. And when she was home, all she did was moan about you. She wanted you to come to her."

Luca looked wounded by the words and Alex wished he'd gotten satisfaction, but he hadn't. But it didn't stop him. "Cindy didn't want Angelo or me, and neither did you. You were a great pair. It's surprising you didn't stay together."

The door opened and a man came in. He was shorter than Alex, but no less muscular. He had dark eyes and hair. He sent a glare toward Alex before he walked to Luca and placed a hand on his shoulder. "Papa, is there a problem?"

Luca shook his head. "Of course not. Valentino, I'd

like you to meet your older brother, Alessandro. Sorry, it's Alex. Alex, this is your brother, Valentino."

Alex nodded. Earlier today Isabella had told him more about his half-siblings, Cristiano, a firefighter who lived in Rome, and Valentino the race-car driver who lived in town. His sister had tossed out another zinger earlier when she had also told him that Valentino wasn't actually Alex's biological brother. Apparently Luca's second wife, Violetta, had had an affair during their marriage. Luca had raised Valentino as his own child.

Yet, Luca hadn't seemed able to keep in touch with his own twin sons. With hurt and anger building, Alex turned to his sister. "I can't deal with this right now."

Isabella looked panicked. "Of course, this is difficult for you." She touched his arm. "Please, let's make it another time."

Alex wasn't sure he could go through this again. Ever. He walked out of the room, glad no one followed him. He hated the feelings that churned inside him. He couldn't let anyone see them. Then he would lose all defenses.

Maybe Angelo had been smart to stay away. Maybe he shouldn't have come here, either. How could it help to drudge up old news, old memories? He'd still had a miserable childhood, and nothing would ever change that.

He was still on the outside looking in.

Alex had managed to get Allison and Cherry back into the car, but not without Isabella coming out to assist them. She'd packed up food to take with them back to the villa.

Cherry was soon distracted by having a picnic in the car. So during their impromptu meal of chicken and warm bread, Alex tried to explain to the child about his father.

By the time the thirty-minute drive ended as Stefano

pulled the car up in front of the villa, Cherry was sound asleep. Alex carried her upstairs without too many questions. Since he'd gotten the precious child to talk, that was all she did these days.

She was one of the highlights in all this. He realized that he wasn't anything like his father; he could never abandon a child. No matter what. Cherry had come to mean too much to him. If he was honest, so had Allison.

Alex came out into the main room. After pouring a glass of wine, he walked out onto the second-story balcony. A soft breeze cooled his face as he recalled the scene at the restaurant. All the years of anger, the abandonment, came rushing back. A father that had turned his back on him and his brother. He didn't want to rehash the reasons, more likely the excuses, that they all were handing out.

He took a swallow of wine, trying to dull the pain, but it was doing nothing. Why had he even answered Isabella's message? Why had he let her talk him into coming here? All that came from this trip was that he realized he didn't belong.

Well, he didn't need to be told again. As soon as he could make the arrangements, he would head back to the life he'd made for himself in Texas and forget about anyone connected with Monta Correnti.

Alex heard the door open from the master suite. He turned and saw Allison standing in the doorway. She was still wearing the same dress as earlier, but she'd taken her hair down, the way he liked it. But then, he wanted Allison any way he could have her.

He drank the last of his wine and set his glass on the table. He crossed the patio, pulled her into his arms and kissed her. It was quick and hard, sparking his mood and need. He wasn't subtle about relaying what she did to him. He broke off the kiss. "I want you, Allie."

She placed her hands against his chest and pushed him back. "Oh, my, what every woman loves to hear. Besides, sex isn't going to take away the pain you're feeling."

"Hell, you could make me forget my name." He arched an eyebrow at her. "There's never been a doubt that I've wanted you. Even from the first day you came to the ranch. Why do you think I tried to drive you away?"

Allison was flattered and thrilled over the back-handed compliment. She was crazy about the man, but she couldn't help him do this. "That's just it, Alex. You want to drive everyone away. You can't take the chance of being rejected. Again."

He cursed. "I don't need to be analyzed by an amateur."

She couldn't back down. "Too bad about that. You wanted me to come here with you, so I get my say." She took a calming breath. "I came to support you through this time with your family. I know it's been difficult, but you aren't giving it a chance."

"There wasn't much to say. Luca shipped us to America to our mother. He had no regrets. No remorse. He said he couldn't keep us. There was no room in his life. End of story."

"Alex, there has to be more. I heard him apologize for misjudging the situation with his ex-wife."

He shrugged. "Okay, he said he didn't realize how bad things were. I might be able to understand that, but not even checking on us until we were eighteen?" He glared at her. "I thought I could handle the fact he kept us a secret from the rest of the family, that he denied our existence. But after tonight…"

It killed Allison to see his pain. "What?"

He poured another glass of wine and one for her. "It's not important."

She refused the drink. "It's important to you."

He took a long drink, then refilled the glass and paced across the tiled floor. "It seems funny to me that my father gave away his own sons, but accepted a child who wasn't even his. His second wife had an affair and he took her back…pregnant." He turned to her. "He came in after you left—Valentino Casali. He actually looked at me as if I was the outsider. Like I didn't have a right to be here. He called Luca 'Papa'." Alex nearly choked on the words. "The guy acted as if I were the threat to my own father."

"I'm sorry, Alex. I'm truly sorry."

He glared at her. "Damn it. I don't want pity. I've had pity all my life." He walked to the railing. "I'm not a scared, lonely child any more. I've handled everything that's been dealt me. I have a successful life and money. I don't need to get approval from a family that never wanted me."

Allison saw his agony and she couldn't do anything for the man she loved. "Alex, don't push this aside as if it doesn't matter." She walked to him, wanting to comfort him. "He's your father."

"No! Luca was never my father and never will be. I don't need anyone."

"Everyone needs someone."

"I guess you just met the first, then." He grabbed the wine bottle off the table and stormed through the main room and into his bedroom, slamming the door behind him. The sound was deafening, but the silence afterward was worse. It felt so final.

Once again, Alex Casali had shut her out of his life.

CHAPTER ELEVEN

THE next morning, sunlight poured through the window and across the bed as Alex rolled over with a groan, then jerked upright. He glanced around the room, quickly remembering where he was. The clock on the bedside table read 9:00a.m.

With a curse, he stood, his stomach rolled, and pain seared through his head. He was still dressed in the same clothes as the day before. His muddled brain managed to recall incidents from the night before he'd rather forget. The trip into Monta Correnti. His father. The argument. Then back at the villa, he had taken out his anger on Allison. He groaned again, recalling things he'd said to her.

He headed for the bathroom. After a quick shower, he pulled on a pair of jeans and a shirt, and went in search of the woman who hadn't deserved his wrath. Allison. He hoped mother and daughter weren't up yet so he could clear his head with some coffee before he apologized for his rude behavior. Then he'd offer to take them sightseeing before heading back to Texas.

He knocked on their bedroom door. When there was no answer, he looked inside to find it empty. He hurried downstairs to the patio, expecting to find them eating breakfast. The place was deserted, too. He was about to pick up the house phone when Tomasso appeared.

"Have you seen the *signora* and the *bambina*?"

"*Sì*. They left with *mio papa*."

"Did they go into the village?"

The boy looked confused, then shook his head. "*Aeroporto*."

His gut tightened. Allison had left him? "The airport. When? How long ago?"

The teenager spoke in rapid Italian. Alex wasn't in the mood to try to decipher the words. "I need an automobile."

The boy shook his head. "No automobile."

Alex cursed and took out his cell phone and punched the number for directory assistance. He walked into the house, where he spotted Luca Casali waiting in the entry.

Alex straightened. "What do you want?"

The older man was dressed in khaki trousers and an open-collar navy shirt. "I came to talk to my son," he said as he walked toward him. "Something I regret not doing years ago."

Alex didn't want this now. "You're right, but it's too late. Besides, I have something more important to do at the moment." He headed for the stairs.

"You're correct, Allison and Cherry are definitely worth your time."

He paused and turned around. "You know where they are?"

Luca nodded. "They're at the restaurant with Isabella and your cousin Lizzie." He smiled. "They are entertaining the lovely *bambina*." His expression grew serious. "It's a tragedy about her accident. I hear you've been instrumental in her recovery."

He eyed his father. "I might have helped some, but

until Cherry is walking again, it's not a full recovery. Now, if you'll excuse me, I have to go get them."

Luca raised a hand. "You have my word that they will not leave Monta Correnti until we've finished our discussion."

Alex was somewhat relieved. He'd have a chance to try and talk with Allison. Once they returned home to Texas he could straighten things out with her. He looked at Luca. He wasn't sure about his father. "We'll all be leaving today."

Luca only watched him a moment, then said, "You came all this way to meet family, Alessandro. Suddenly you changed your mind?"

He nodded. "I decided some things are better left alone. So give the family my regards, I'll be returning home."

The man didn't move. "*Per favore*, Alessandro. Don't cheat your brothers and sister out of their chance to get to know you because of how you feel about me."

"I don't fit in here," he blurted out.

"You are a Casali, of course you belong here. So don't let your anger at me keep you from your family." He spread his arms. "Maybe you can tell me what you've wanted to say for all the years that I wasn't there for you or for your brother. Now is your chance."

Alex's chest tightened as he felt an unwelcome pull to the man he didn't want or need. For all those years he'd had a hundred things he wanted to tell his absent father, but none of it seemed to matter now. Just Allison. "It's not important."

"It was important enough to bring you to Italy." His blue eyes searched Alex's face. "It's too many years past due that we meet again. For a father who hasn't seen his son since he was a boy."

"Whose fault is that?"

"*Sì*, it's mine. But it's also time that you know everything." He came closer. "I can…" Luca swallowed. "I can never ask or expect your forgiveness. Just know that when I sent you off to America, it wasn't because I didn't care, or love you and your brother. I couldn't afford to keep you, things were desperate here."

With a mother like Cindy, things had been desperate for Alex and Angelo, too. "I don't think you want to compare stories on who had the tougher life. But go for it."

His father shook his head. "Believe me, I had no idea how bad your situation became until years later. I admit I lost touch, but I had no idea what Cindy had done to you. What a horrid childhood for you and Angelo."

"Then you should have come to the States to find your sons." Alex glared at the man. "You owed us that. Instead you went and got another family. You claimed a child that wasn't yours." He folded his arms across his chest. "Well, damn, aren't you the noble one."

Sadness appeared in Luca's eyes. "It was because I had turned my back on my own sons that I needed to be there for Valentino. I wish I could have done more for you and Angelo, but I'd missed any chance of that." He paused. "And the things I've done, the mistakes I made over those years, will follow me to my grave."

"Is that how you've lived with yourself all these years?" Alex asked. "You put us so far out of your mind that we no longer existed to you?"

Luca ignored his words. "I wish I could take all the pain away. I can't, Alex. When I found you and Angelo again at eighteen, I called, but I let you push me out of your life too easily. I should have come for you then. I should have fought for my sons. I'm sorry, Alex. I'm so sorry for all those awful years that you and Angelo didn't have anyone to care for you, to protect you."

Alex felt the ache in the middle of his chest. He hated that the feelings he'd buried years ago had resurfaced. "Nice speech, but don't expect me to disagree, or to forgive you."

Luca shook his head. "That's not what I came here for."

"Then for what?"

"For you. You say none of this bothers you, yet I see the pain in your eyes, hear it in your voice. You have so much anger in your heart."

"Of course I have anger. You kept us a secret from the family. Were you that ashamed of us?"

A flash of hurt crossed the older man's face. "Not of you. Just the opposite. Of me. I was so ashamed that I couldn't keep you, that I couldn't be the father you needed. I'm very proud of what you and Angelo have become."

"Don't take any pride in us, because you had nothing to do with it."

"I think I did. I believe your anger for me helped drive you towards success. That's the only part I played in it. If you would like, I will sit down with you and admit to everything I did wrong, with your mother and with you and your brother. But when we finish, you need to let it go, Alex. To get rid of the anger before it kills your soul. Before you lose everything."

Alex hated the fact that this visit affected him so strongly. "I'm not losing anything."

"You're wrong, Alex. You're already driving away a family you have a chance to know. And what about Allison? You've driving her away, too."

"Leave her out of this."

Luca shook his head. "I can't. Not when she's so important to you. She's part of this, too. Yet you won't let her get close to you."

"And I'm supposed to take advice from you?" He saw the flash of hurt and regretted his harsh words. "Maybe you should leave now."

His father held his gaze. "I'm not going anywhere. At least not until we talk through this. You may not want to hear them, but I need to say them. We may never be father and son again, but I'll settle for being civil to one another."

Alex arched an eyebrow. "Isn't that aiming a little high for us?"

"Then do it for Allison. It's what she wants."

Alex didn't want to talk about Allison. "How do you know what she wants?"

Luca smiled. "She told me. The little one, too." His father's eyes locked on his. "It's such a shame, since you have the same opportunity to be a father to little Cherry. They both need you." Luca's face held sadness. "More importantly, you need them."

An hour later at Rosa's *ristorante* there was a collective gasp when the most recent family bride, Lizzie Green Lewis, opened a large box containing Allison's original quilts. One she'd already had in the shop. She lifted the blanket out and spread it on the table. The soft blue print design was mixed with ivories, spring greens and mauves.

"It's *bellissima*," Lizzie gasped. "Oh, *grazie*, Allison, *grazie*." She hugged her. Then went back to eye the quilt. "Did you make this?"

She nodded. "I didn't have time to make one with your colors. "It's called 'Forever and Always'." Allison's finger traced the linked circles. "It's one of my wedding quilt designs."

"I love it."

The tall, graceful hazel-eyed brunette was down to earth and Allison liked her right off. And a big surprise she got after Stefano had dropped them off this morning: the recent bride was very pregnant.

She also learned that Lizzie had been pregnant even before she'd met her husband, Jack. At the age of forty, she'd decided she wanted a baby and had been artificially inseminated.

"If I had known, I would have brought you a baby quilt."

Isabella showed up. "Then you would need two blankets."

"Twins?"

With a nod from Lizzie they all laughed.

The members of the Casali family Allison had met so far had been warm and welcoming to both her and Cherry. She hated to have to leave this wonderful place.

If only Alex could see what he was denying himself by not getting to know his siblings. He had two brothers and a sister. Even though he had a right to be angry, she refused to stay around while he continued to isolate himself from people. From a family he desperately needed in his life.

She turned to Isabella. "I had no idea there were all these new brides in the family. You were recently married, too."

She waved her hands. "How were you to know about all the weddings?" Alex's half-sister hugged her, too. "When the time comes, I will let you make me a quilt for my *bambino*."

Allison felt a tug on her heart, trying not to envy Lizzie's and Isabella's lives with their new husbands.

The promising future ahead of them. Something she doubted she would ever have with Alex, because he was still locked in his past.

Allison put on a smile. "Should I start on one now?"

Isabella winked. "I'll let you know. I wish you could meet Max before you leave." She gripped Allison's hands. "*Per favore*, say you'll stay a little while longer? Just ignore Alex and all the Casali men. They may be very handsome, but also stubborn."

Allison studied both women. Isabella, Alex's sister, and his cousin, Lizzie, were the ones who'd contacted Alex and his twin Angelo. Lizzie had been one of the few family members who knew of the twins' existence.

"Definitely stubborn," Lizzie agreed. "So you both need to convince Alex to stay."

Alex had come here. It was a good first step. Yet so far he'd refused to open up to the possibilities. Okay, so there'd been years of secrets and lies. She thought about the man who'd spent a lifetime closing himself off from everyone. But the Casalis were ready and more than willing to pull him and Angelo into the fold. He'd let her know last night that he didn't need her at all.

"I should go." She fought tears. "I still have to make reservations on a flight back to the States. I have a business to run back home and Cherry has her therapy."

Before Isabella could argue, Allison said, "You have to be the one to convince Alex to stay, and then you can get to know what a good man he is."

"If you leave, Alex will follow you." She shrugged. "I guess if he won't stay, then Max and I will just have to come to America. I've never been on a cattle ranch."

"You'd love it. And you can meet Tilda."

Isabella's eyes rounded. "Who is Tilda?"

"Years ago she was the ranch owner, then Alex bought it. At first, he kept her on as the housekeeper, then as the bookkeeper, and now she manages a lot of the ranch. But mostly, she's been Alex's family. She loves him as much as if he were her own son."

Tears filled Isabella's eyes. "I'm so glad he had someone in America. And you."

Alex doesn't want me, or at least he doesn't know it. Allison wanted to scream. She'd been foolish enough to involve him in her daughter's life, even come on this trip. Now, she had to get home before she did something truly foolish like confess her love for him.

"And now he has you and his family," she told Isabella.

Isabella started to speak but something caught her attention. Allison turned and saw Luca coming through the kitchen door, followed by Alex. He didn't look happy.

Her gaze couldn't capture enough of him. He was handsome in a strong, rugged way. His steel-gray eyes locked onto hers and she couldn't look away.

"Alex," Cherry cried and raised her arms. "You came to us."

Alex smiled at Cherry as he went to her and hugged her. Then he knelt down and they exchanged some quiet words. Luca waved for Isabella to come to him and quickly the room began to clear.

Before Alex's sister left her side, she said, "Seems someone is eager to talk to you." She took off and pushed Cherry out of the room.

Great. They were alone. Okay, maybe she was glad he was here.

"So you decided you couldn't handle it and are running out on me."

"No, you decided to push me away. And I didn't

want to argue anymore." She met his gaze. "I thought I could help you, Alex, but now I know it was a mistake that I came with you."

He turned away, raking his fingers through his hair. "No, it wasn't a mistake you came. And believe me you have helped me," he said as he looked at her. "More than you know. I was wrong to have acted the way I did last night, especially the way I treated you. I could blame it on the wine but—as I learned from my mother—that's just an easy excuse." His eyes held hers. "I had no right to take my anger and frustration out on you." His gaze softened. "And I swear, you'll never see me drink like that again."

She drew a deep breath and released it, inhaling his scent. It was doing crazy things to her common sense. "I'm glad to hear that." She glanced toward the table where Luca sat with Cherry. Her daughter was laughing. "You talked with Luca?"

"He showed up at the villa, and he wasn't going to leave until we talked." He fought to keep from smiling. "Seems the Casalis are known for their stubbornness."

"I think I heard that somewhere." She was surprised he would admit that. "So you and your father got a chance to talk. Did it help?"

Alex glanced away. "I wouldn't go as far to say that I'd ever call the man my father. I doubt that will ever happen. But I gave him my word that I'd stay a few days and meet all the family."

"Oh, Alex, that's wonderful news." She fought the tears, happy for him. She released a breath to compose herself, knowing that she was no longer needed here. "If you'll help get Cherry and me to Rome, we'll get a flight home."

"Why leave now, Allie?" He lowered his voice. "You're the one who convinced me to come—aren't you curious to see how things will turn out? At the least meet the rest of the Casalis."

Yes, she was curious about anything that concerned Alex, but she wasn't going to hang on, hoping things would turn out differently. "I have a business to run. Cherry has her therapy."

"We can call them, make another appointment. I'm only asking for a few days." He stepped closer. "You're running away, Allie."

She shook her head, but even she didn't believe it. "I'm not."

He leaned down and brushed a kiss over her lips. "You're scared. You made a mistake and trusted your husband and he let you and Cherry down." His gaze held hers. "I'm not him. I want to try and prove it to you. We need a chance to see where this leads. I won't let you down again. Don't desert me now."

"Oh, Alex." She had trouble keeping a clear head.

Alex cupped her face, praying that she would give him another chance. A lot of bad things had happened during his life, but seeing his father again cut into his heart. Allison had been his lifeline. He couldn't let her go.

"Then let me convince you." His mouth closed over hers, tasting the traces of her mint toothpaste. He drew her closer, holding her against him as if she would disappear. He couldn't let that happen, not now, and if he had the opportunity, not ever.

When he finally pulled back, he saw the want and need in her pretty emerald eyes. "A couple of days, Allie," he asked. "Give me a couple of days, that's all I ask. I promise you and Cherry will enjoy it."

She rewarded him with a smile. "My daughter is a pushover." She wrapped her arms around his neck. "It's me you have to convince, cowboy."

He smiled, too. "I'll do my best, ma'am." His head lowered to hers and he did as he promised.

CHAPTER TWELVE

DURING a pleasant lunch, Isabella convinced Alex to stay in town for the night so more of the Casalis could meet them. His persuasive younger sister even managed to talk him into a family dinner at Rosa's the next evening.

Before he could give her an answer, Isabella pulled out her phone and found them a nearby hotel. She then went along to help get them settled in their two-bedroom suite, and gave them ideas for sightseeing around Monta Correnti and the local countryside.

Alex hadn't spent any more time with his father, and Luca had disappeared into the kitchen. Allison worried about unresolved issues between the two men.

Once settled in the lovely hotel suite, Cherry had quickly fallen asleep after her busy day. Allison walked out of the bedroom. When she saw Alex talking with his cousin, Lizzie, she started to go back but he called to her.

"Allison, please join us." He stood and escorted her to the sitting area. "My cousin has been filling me in on the years I missed."

Allison put on a smile as she greeted Lizzie, then sat next to Alex on the sofa. At least she was happy that

Alex was willing to talk with his family about the past. "So you remember Alex and Angelo."

Lizzie sat with a protective hand over her rounded stomach. "I was telling Alex that I was only a few years older when they left." Sadness filled her eyes. "Yes, I remember a lot. For many years I was told never to mention the twins. And I was too young to not obey my mother."

Allison glanced at Alex to see his reaction. He didn't show any expression, but she could see his jaw tense.

She turned back to Lizzie and asked, "Why? Why all the secrecy?"

"I believe it was the shame. Families are supposed to stay together, but Luca couldn't support the boys. And my mother didn't help her brother at all. Maybe it was because of the circumstance of Luca's birth. Since he's William Valentine's son, there's always been friction between them. Even in business, they were competitive, and disagreed on how to run the restaurant. That's the reason Luca took his mother's maiden name, Casali, and the reason he opened Rosa."

She looked at Alex. "That's one of the reasons I came here tonight, to tell you something about my mother, Lisa Firenzi. You probably don't remember her."

Alex shook his head. "Only bits and pieces of my life here."

Lizzie nodded. "Here's a piece of news for you. Lisa is the real reason your papa had to send you and Angelo away. So any anger you have should be directed toward her."

More secrets had come out. Alex wasn't sure he wanted to deal with any more family turmoil. He took Allison's hand.

"Why is that?"

"It's no secret that my mother and Uncle Luca never got along. After Grandma Rosa died it got worse. Luca left the original family restaurant, Sorella, and started his own. When he opened Rosa's *ristorante* he worked all the time while trying to raise two boys on his own." She paused. "Your mother had already left him and gone back to America."

Knowing how selfish Cindy Daniels Casali was, he wasn't surprised.

"Luca knew he couldn't go on without help. He went to his sister and asked for a loan to get him through the difficult time." Lizzie glanced away. "Lisa turned him down and Luca had no other choice but to send you to your mother."

Alex stood and went to the window. "But why were we kept a secret?"

"I believe that was my mother's idea, too. She didn't want to bring shame onto the family, or be reminded that she had been a part of it." Lizzie stood and went to her cousin. "I only told you, Alex, because I don't want you to put all the blame on Luca. I know for a fact how much he missed you and Angelo."

Alex couldn't speak. So many emotions were stirred up.

"I should go." Lizzie stood. "My husband is waiting for me, and the *bambinos* are restless."

Alex froze. *"Bambinos?"*

She put on a smile and nodded. "Can you believe it? Twins. Boys." She wrapped her arms around him and hugged him. "I hope you're around to be in their lives," she whispered. "In my life, too. I'm glad you're home, cousin."

Lizzie released him, then gripped Allison's hand. "I hope to see more of you and Cherry. *Ciao*, Allison."

"I'll walk you down." Alex went with Lizzie to the door, but paused and went to Allison. He pulled her close. "I need to go out for a while. I can't ask you to wait up, but I'd like you to."

She nodded. "I'll be here."

Alex kissed her, wishing he could give her more, but he couldn't think about the future until he settled with the past.

The streets were almost empty at this late hour, but Alex found he enjoyed the peace and quiet. Even on the ranch, there'd always been the nagging voices from his past. Now, he knew about his past, where he'd come from. After he'd helped his cousin into her car, he'd started walking through the narrow streets, across the piazza, ending up at the restaurant. It wasn't a complete surprise; he needed to talk with Luca.

Finding the front door locked, he went around to the back and into the alley where there was an open door leading into the restaurant's kitchen. He stepped through the entry and saw the long stainless-steel counters stacked with dirty pans from the night's meals. Dishwashers were busy at the deep sinks, talking and working through the steam rising from the water.

How many years and how hard had his father worked to build this business? The long hours and days. Maybe that was where he and his brother got their work ethic. He'd never thought that he'd gotten much from his absent father. But although a world apart, they might have been similar in many respects. Life hadn't been easy for any of them.

The kitchen door opened and Luca appeared along with another employee, both speaking rapidly in Italian. When his father saw him, he sent the worker off.

"Alex." He went to him. "Is there a problem?"

"No. I was out for a walk and ended up here."

His father's expression relaxed, and a flash of Angelo came to mind. There were subtle similarities in their looks.

He motioned for Alex to follow him into the quiet dining room. "Monta Correnti must be very different than your ranch in Texas," Luca said.

Alex nodded. "Yes, but there are nice things about this area, too." He studied Luca. "Why didn't you tell me that Lisa wouldn't give you a loan so you could keep us here?"

He shrugged. "It doesn't excuse what I did. It was wrong to let you go. I still should have come to find you and Angelo. I should have known your mother…" He turned away. "She wasn't very maternal."

"That's an understatement."

Luca suddenly looked tired and older than his years as he sank into a chair. "I did send money to her for the first few years. I even called. Then I lost track of you both. I should have tried harder, I know. Cindy made it difficult. I'll always regret that I never came to get you."

"So will I."

"I'm sorry, Alex. I'm sorry I wasn't there for you." Luca stared at him for a long time. "A day never went by that I didn't think about you and Angelo. You both were in my mind, in my heart, always."

Alex glanced away, not liking the sudden heaviness in his chest. "There are some things I remember about living here. A small room that I shared with Angelo. Who called me *uccellino*?"

"Little bird." Luca's smile brightened but Alex saw tears in his eyes. "It was a story I read to you and your brother. But you, Alessandro, carried the book around all the time, begging me to read it again and again. I still have the book along with photos of you and Angelo. If you like I could show you."

Alex wasn't sure he could handle any more right now. He shook his head. "Maybe another time. I need to get back to Allison and Cherry."

Luca nodded. "You are a lucky man to have two special ladies in your life."

Yes, he was lucky. He hoped they would be patient enough to wait for him to figure it out.

Allison stood at the window in the bedroom she shared with Cherry. She couldn't go to sleep, not as long as Alex was out there. As much as she wanted to help, he needed time and some space to take it all in. And knowing Alex as she did, he had to do it on his own.

She glanced at Cherry asleep in the bed. The one thing that had made this trip worthwhile had been the change in her daughter. All the affection and attention she'd gotten from the Casalis had been incredible. Allison was also concerned about the letdown for her daughter when they had to go back to Texas, move back into their small apartment.

Allison wasn't foolish enough to believe in fairy tales. Not anymore. She'd faced too many challenges on her own to believe that someone would come charging in to rescue her. Her disastrous marriage and Cherry's accident had made her stronger; she had learnt to rely on herself.

What part of Alex's life they fit into, she wasn't sure,

but she wasn't going to be his charity case just because he had a lot of money. She loved him too much to let that happen.

A soft knock sounded on the door, but before she could answer it Alex poked his head inside. He nodded once in her direction as he walked to the bed and pulled the covers a little higher over Cherry. Studying the child for a moment, he brushed back her hair. Even in the dim light, Allison could see Alex cared about her daughter.

He glanced at her and motioned for her to come with him. Allison took a calming breath and followed him out. She stepped into the sitting area just as he pulled her into his arms.

Alex didn't wait for her protest, his need for her won out and he bent his head and his mouth covered hers. Her lips were warm and she tasted cool. With a groan, she lifted her fingers to his hair as her tongue slid over his. He liked her eagerness. The way she touched him, the way her breasts pressed against his chest. She tasted like everything he'd ever wanted and needed, but spent his life trying to stay away from. Until now.

He finally drew back, working to catch his breath enough to speak. "You waited up for me."

"You asked me to," she whispered.

He smiled, wanting her desperately. He lowered his head and rained kisses along her jaw and neck, feeling the slow, heavy need coursing through his blood. "You taste good. Really good."

"So do you," she whispered in between nibbles on his mouth, making him more aroused than ever. He plunged his fingers into her hair, deepening the kiss, wanting to sink into her so far, there was no separation between them. Instead, he drew back, and released her.

"I better slow down before I break my promise to you." He knew this trip to Italy was supposed to be hands off. But when she looked at him with those big eyes he nearly lost it.

He turned away. "I came from seeing my father."

Allison looked surprised. "At the restaurant?"

He nodded. "We talked about what Lizzie told me tonight. He wouldn't let his sister take all the blame." He went on to tell her about the photos and his childhood storybook. "Although I can't think of him as a father, I know now I want a relationship with him and the rest of my family here."

Her eyes flooded with tears. "Oh, Alex, I'm happy for you."

He blinked. "I don't know if happy is the word I'd use. I've never considered myself a family man, and now I seem to have a rather large one whether I like it or not. And you've had a lot to do with that."

She shook her head. "Your sister, Isabella, was the one who contacted you." She glanced away. "Now, you have to stay awhile and meet the rest of the Casalis. Cherry and I should go back to Texas. That will give you time to visit without having to worry about us." She put some distance between them. "I still have our tickets to return to the States. I can make reservations tomorrow."

Alex swore. "No. Don't leave, Allie." He reached for her. Heat surged through him and his lips caressed hers.

He raised his head, but didn't release her. "I'll fly the damn therapist over here," he murmured. "Whatever you want or need to keep you here. I want you with me." He touched her face. "I need you, Allie. If you believe anything, believe that you and Cherry are important to me." He tilted her head toward his. "I don't want to be separated from you even for a little while."

Allison couldn't think rationally right now. Not when she was in Alex's arms. When it came to this man she hadn't been able to think since that first day when he had ridden up to her on his horse. She wanted this man like no other.

"Oh, Alex, I don't want to be away from you, either."

"God, Allie. You say things like that and I won't be able to stop."

She raised up and kissed him. "Then don't. Don't walk away from me again."

"I couldn't leave here if the place was on fire." He swung her up into his arms and carried her into his bedroom. The place was dimly lit as he placed her next to the bed. Then he captured her mouth and she sank into him, her lips parting under his. She wanted to lose herself in him, if only for this one time. She pulled back and reached for the bedside lamp.

"Leave it on," he urged. "I don't want to miss any of this night."

Alex let out a long breath. He stepped forward and began to remove her clothes, starting with her peasant-style blouse. With a shaky hand, he tugged on the elastic neck and pulled it down her torso, exposing her bra. With her help, he continued the job, pushing her top along with her skirt until they lay in a pool on the floor. She stepped out, leaving her in only a pair of lacy panties and bra.

He stood back and yanked off his shirt, then tossed it aside. Somehow he managed to get his boots and his trousers off. "There's not going to be any more hesitation, Allie. This night is for us. Only us."

He reached for her, drawing her against him as he kissed her once, twice, soon losing count. He backed her to the bed until she was lying down on the mattress.

He paused, leaning over her. "God, Allie, I want you. For so long."

She smiled at him and cupped his face. "I don't need words, Alex, I need you."

"You got me, Allie. You got me."

She wrapped her arms around his neck, tugging him closer. She wanted this memory to keep forever. She pressed her lips to his and whispered, "Make it a night to remember."

His mouth closed over hers and he proceeded to fulfill his promise.

The next morning, Allison awoke in her own bed for obvious reasons. Of course it hadn't erased the incredible night she'd spent with Alex, but she'd needed to be there for Cherry. She wasn't ready for her daughter's questions, either.

The one thing that dampened her spirits was when she came out for breakfast and found Alex gone. Again. Yet, she had no right to feel disappointed. There hadn't been any promises. During their night together, Alex had made her feel incredibly special, but he'd never spoken a word about love. And she knew he might never do so.

It was something she had to be prepared to live with.

She glanced at her daughter while she ate her breakfast. There had been so many positive changes in her in the last month. Alex was a big part of that and the child had become very attached to him. What would happen when they returned home?

"Mommy, is Alex gonna live here?"

Where had she heard that? "Honey, I don't know, but he has a ranch back home."

"Yeah, someone has to take care of all the horses and Maisie." She ate a piece of cut fruit. "But his daddy lives here. And Luca wants Alex to stay. He said so." Cherry looked at her. "I wish I had a daddy, too."

Allison froze. This was the first time Cherry had mentioned her father since before the accident. "I wish I could give you one, honey. But remember we talked about this—Jack lives in Arizona."

"And he doesn't want a little girl," she said matter-of-factly.

It was the truth, but Allison wished it would be different for her child. "But I want a little girl, one just like you." She got up and came around to hug her. "I love you, Cherry."

"I love you, too, Mommy." She pulled back. "I wish I had Alex for my daddy."

Allison tried not to react. "I know he's been good to you. He might not be your daddy but he can be a friend. He'll let you ride Maisie."

That finally made her daughter smile. "I miss her, and Tilda and Brian."

"Well, we'll be going home soon. But remember, we'll be going home to our place in town." She raised a hand to stop her daughter's protest. "I have to run the shop. And you have therapy, so you can walk again. For that to happen, we need to go back."

Suddenly the door to the suite opened and Alex strolled in. "*Buon giorno*, ladies," he called, and came to the table. Leaning over, he kissed Cherry's cheek, then Allison's surprised mouth.

"Hi, Alex," Cherry said. "We didn't know where you went."

He frowned. "You didn't? I left your mother a note."

"What note?" Allison asked, unable to turn away. The man looked too good the first thing in the morning, in jeans especially. Of course, he wasn't bad at night either.

"I didn't want to wake you, so I left it on your nightstand to tell you I was going out for a while." When he headed toward her bedroom, she got up and followed. He pointed to her side of the bed. "I put it right there." With further searching, he found it on the floor. "Here it is."

Allison took it and read it.

Allie,
I hope I made your night memorable, because it was for me. Have a special errand to run this morning. See you in a few hours.
    Alex.

She felt her heart race. "Oh, Alex. Last night was wonderful for me, too, but we have to be realistic about this. It's going to have to end sometime."

He drew her into his arms. "I'm not very good at this, Allie. I've been alone a long time. Then you and Cherry came into my life and bowled me over and confused the hell out of me."

"Is that good?"

He placed a finger on her lips to stop her. "You and Cherry are important to me." He pulled her back into his arms and took her mouth in a soul-searing kiss, trying to convince her not to give up on him. "You stood by me, helping me get through this mess with my family. You should have given up on me long ago."

She blinked. "I'm glad we helped you."

"In more ways than you'll ever know." He blew out a breath. "I'm not where I need to be yet. But being with you last night made me realize that I don't want to let you go. I want—"

"Hey, what about me?" Cherry called. They broke apart just as the child pushed her chair into the doorway.

Allison turned to Alex. "Just so you know, she has to come first. I don't want her hurt anymore. It's not just you and me, it's the three of us."

He smiled. "I wouldn't want it any other way."

An hour later they drove into Naples for some sightseeing and shopping. Alex took the girls into an exclusive shop. With a promise from the boutique owner to take care of them, he sat back and watched the show.

Allison reluctantly tried on dresses, arguing that she didn't need anything. But Alex refused to budge and she finally went back into a dressing room and came out in a soft pink print with narrow straps and a full skirt that was short enough to show off her shapely legs. Oh, yes, he was enjoying this.

After purchasing two dresses he knew Allison loved along with a pair of sandals, they went on to a children's store where Cherry got her turn.

Who would have thought that the Texas rancher would be sitting in a too-small chair, waiting for his favorite little girl to try on a dress?

When Allison wheeled Cherry out in a pretty blue party dress and they were both smiling, he realized he was having the time of his life. He wanted them both with him always.

"Do you like this one, Alex?" Cherry asked.

"I think you're the prettiest girl ever."

She blushed, then said, "No, my mom is the prettiest girl. Do you think she's pretty, too?"

Alex looked at Allison. Yes, she was. That auburn hair and those green eyes had gotten to him a long time ago.

"Yes, she is." He finally tore his gaze away. "And you look like her."

After paying for the purchase, they walked out of the store in search of gifts to take home for Tilda and Brian. Instead, they ended up in a toy store after Cherry fell in love with a doll in the window. That was all it took for Alex to go inside and hand over his credit card to the shop owner.

On the way out, Allison leaned close to him and whispered, "You know you don't have to buy her everything. You already won her over the day you introduced her to her first horse."

He cared so much for Cherry, and it upset him that he couldn't give her a miracle so she could walk. One thing was for sure, he'd do whatever it took to get her on her feet. He would give her the best of everything.

"How about her mother?" He locked in on her mesmerizing gaze. "Have I won her over?" He meant it as a joke, but then she hesitated and he found he was eager for her answer.

She only smiled. "Let me get back to you on that."

CHAPTER THIRTEEN

BY LATE afternoon they had arrived back at the hotel so they could dress for the Casali family dinner. Cherry had fallen asleep during the ride, so she was rested for the party.

Alex got ready in twenty minutes. Being with Allison and Cherry, enjoying the day, he'd almost forgotten he had to meet up with the rest of Casali clan tonight. He hadn't run away from anything since he'd been a hungry street kid in New York. Now, he had to fight that old urge. It was time to deal with the past.

He walked into the sitting area and called his brother. He wanted to give it one more try to convince Angelo to come to Italy, or at least tell him what he'd discovered about the family.

He soon learned that nothing was going to sway his twin brother. "I guess I'm not as forgiving as you are, Alex," Angelo said. "Nothing changed the fact that our old man still shipped us off to the States."

"That's true, but things are different now. He isn't the only one who's involved. There are two brothers and a sister who knew nothing about us."

Alex turned when he heard the bedroom door open, and Allison appeared pushing Cherry into the room.

He got a warm feeling inside seeing their bright smiles. He managed to return it before he turned his attention back to the phone call. "They are family, too," Alex told his brother.

There was silence on the other end.

Alex continued, "Okay, I get the message. I'm staying for another few days, but those arrangements can be changed if you decide to make the trip. I can send my plane."

"Thanks for the offer, but don't count on me," Angelo said. "Look, have a great time in Italy. I gotta go, talk to you when you get back. *Ciao*." Then there was silence as his brother hung up.

Alex closed his phone. He wasn't going to let Angelo ruin his mood. He'd made a promise to himself that he'd at least meet the rest of the family and show his special ladies a nice evening. After that he could pack up, go back to Texas and move on with his life.

He went to them, eyeing Allison in the rose-pink print sundress with thin straps and fitted on the top, showing off her tiny waist and her other assets. The fabric looked soft, touchable. So did she. "You both look *bellissima*."

Allison blushed. "Thank you."

"That means beautiful, Mommy," Cherry said proudly. "Thank you, Alex, for my pretty dress, too."

He leaned down and kissed the child's cheek. "You're welcome, darlin'. Does this mean you'll never wear jeans again when we get back home?"

"Yes, I will, 'cause I want to ride Maisie. I miss her and Tilda and Brian."

"And they all miss you, too," he assured her. "We'll be home in a few days. But right now we have a party to go to."

* * *

Thirty minutes later they arrived at the restaurant and Alex escorted Allison and Cherry inside. Right off he was intimidated by the number of people there. It seemed they were all related to him either by blood or by marriage.

"Isn't it wonderful?" Allison said. "Look at all the family you have, Alex."

Before he could say anything, his father came up to him. "*Buona sera*, Alex and Allison." He shook Alex's hand and kissed Allison's cheeks. Then he bent down and did the same to Cherry. "I can't tell you how wonderful it is that you came tonight. There are so many who want to see you."

Alex glanced at Allison. "I told you I'd be here, but you neglected to tell me about the size of the group."

Luca's smile faded. "Yes, you kept your word. My only hope is that you will stay in touch with your new family."

Alex felt that tug again toward a man he'd never gotten the chance to know. The man he'd never called father. Luca was getting up in years and he hadn't had an easy life. Alex glanced away. None of them had. "I expect Isabella will see to that."

Luca smiled again. "*Sì*, your sister works hard to see that the Casalis stay together," he said, and then added, "And tonight, we celebrate because we are together."

A waiter came by with glasses of champagne. His father began handing them out. Once he got the crowd's attention, he held up his glass. "I have been blessed with so much over the years, but having one of my sons return home is a prayer answered. *Bentornato*, Alessandro. Welcome back." He lifted his glass higher. "*Salute*."

After the toast Allison tried to stand back as several

family members came over to greet them. It was overwhelming with all the hugs and kisses. Her once-shy daughter was eating up the attention. Allison loved watching Cherry blossom, but couldn't help but wonder how she would handle going back home.

Alex reached for Allison's hand, drawing her back to him. "Don't desert me," he said. "You're the one who convinced me having family was wonderful."

She smiled. "I still believe that. You're a lucky man, Alex."

He leaned down, his eyes locked on hers. "I know that." He brushed his mouth over hers. "If we were alone, I'd be showing you how much."

A shiver shot through Allison, but before she could answer Isabella made her way through the crowd, bringing her husband with her. The perfect description of the man was tall, dark and handsome. She introduced her new groom, Maximilliano Di Rossi. Even the scars beneath the stubble on his chin didn't detract from his good looks.

"We first met when I was trespassing on the grounds of his palazzo," Isabella confessed.

"I take it he didn't have you arrested," Alex said.

Max pulled his wife closer. "My life would have been simpler if I had." He sent Isabella a heated look. "But not nearly as wonderful."

Finally Isabella looked at Alex. "I was searching for Monta Rosa basil. It's the secret ingredient for Rosa's special tomato sauce. You need to know this since it's part of your heritage, too."

"I guess I have a lot to learn. Maybe I should teach you about beef cattle. Max, you will have to bring my sister to Texas."

His sister looked surprised. "Are you inviting us?"

Alex wasn't sure what he was doing. He normally didn't like people invading his space, until a pretty redhead had come into his life. "The A Bar A is a big place. With the guest ranch, we have plenty of room for everyone."

Lizzie appeared and introduced her husband, Jack. And soon another couple. It was his brother Valentino and an attractive brunette.

Alex eyed Italy's one-time playboy and thrill seeker. Now married, he seemed to stay close to home and family.

He extended a hand. "We didn't get much of a chance to talk the other night. I'm Alex. I hear we're brothers."

A few heartbeats passed, then Valentino took the offered hand. They shook. "Are you sure you want to claim this crazy *famiglia*?"

"It seems it's all I have."

They all laughed and Alex realized he was having a good time. Valentino drew forward a small woman with dark brown hair and jade eyes. "Alex, this is my wife, Clara. Clara, this is my long-lost brother from America, Alex Casali."

"It's nice to meet you, Clara. This is Allison Cole and her daughter, Cherry." He pointed down toward the child at the table.

"It's nice to meet you," Allison said.

"It's a pleasure."

Alex turned back to Valentino. "I apologize for leaving so abruptly the other night."

Valentino nodded. "It's understandable. This family can be overwhelming," he said, glancing at Luca. "But very protective. I'm happy you came back to visit. You've made our papa happy."

Alex studied the one-time race-car driver, who had recently married his childhood sweetheart. He'd also given her a kidney. "What about you? Are you happy about my return?"

"Yes, I am." He smiled and hugged his wife next to him. "I have family, and I'm married to the love of my life." He glanced at his father. "And we have some wonderful news, too. Clara is pregnant."

Cheers went up in the room as Luca hugged Valentino and Alex found he was a little jealous. "Congratulations," Alex said.

"Thank you. Since you're going to have a niece or nephew, you'll need to come and visit more often."

Once again Luca raised a glass. "We have another generation beginning."

His father turned around where an older woman appeared in the doorway. The crowd hushed as she locked her dark gaze on Alex. He'd never seen her before. She was attractive, her age somewhere between fifty and sixty. She had black hair, cut in a long, straight style that brushed her shoulders. Although their coloring was different, there was a family resemblance to Luca. Then recognition hit him.

Lisa Firenzi.

Luca lifted his glass once more to the woman. "Let's hope they do better than we did, dear *sorella*."

With a nod, Lisa walked in as regal as a queen, and came directly to Alex.

"Alex, this is your aunt Lisa Firenzi. Lisa, your nephew, Alex."

She smiled but it didn't reach her eyes. "*Ciao*, Alessandro. It's good to have you home. It's been too long."

He tensed, knowing she'd had a lot to do with his disappearance, too. "*Ciao*, Lisa."

The room remained quiet as attention zeroed in on them. "I'm sorry," Lisa said, "I was out of town when you arrived." She tried to smile again, but it didn't work. "As you can see, I'm not exactly the favorite person here." She took a breath. "But I had to come. For you. To apologize for my part in you and your brother leaving Monta Correnti. I had no idea that it would turn out as it did."

Alex nodded, but he wasn't sure about her sincerity. "I'm not here to place blame, Lisa. Too many years have passed to rehash all the wrong. I'm here because I wanted to meet my sister and brothers and long-lost cousins."

He felt Allison reach for his hand, giving him courage. "So let's enjoy this evening."

"Yes," Luca added as he took his place next to his sister. "It's time we put the mistakes of the past aside. We have much more to be grateful for. Your grandmother, Rosa Casali Firenzi, worked hard to keep her family together." He handed Lisa a glass of wine. "We have another generation starting, sister. With that there is always hope that things will be better.

"Everyone raise your glasses for all the blessings bestowed on our family." He raised his glass over his head and looked at Alex. "*Al famiglia.*"

Alex lifted his and repeated the words that had come to mean something to him since being in Italy. Could he forget the past? No, not all of it, but he knew now that he wanted to look ahead to a future. And not just for him and his brother. Now he knew he had room in his heart for more. He looked at Allison and Cherry. He wanted them in his future.

* * *

Hours later, after a delicious meal and far too much wine, Allison was exhausted, and so was Cherry. It had been a long day and night, and her daughter needed to be in bed. If they were just going back to the hotel, she would go alone, and leave Alex here to spend more time with his family, but they were going back to the villa tonight.

Allison thought back to last night and sharing Alex's bed. She wanted to think they'd grown closer with all the positive attention he'd given her, and Cherry. The big question was what would happen once they returned home? Would he give them a chance?

She glanced around the large room, but didn't see Alex. She asked around and a waiter directed her out to the patio area. She came to the iron gate where she saw Alex sitting with Luca. Seeing that they were deep in conversation, she turned to leave when she heard her name mentioned.

It was Alex who said, "It was Allison who convinced me to come here."

"Then I am grateful to her," Luca said. "She's a special woman."

There was a pause, and Allison found herself holding her breath, hoping for Alex's confession of his undying love.

"And she's a special mother," Alex answered. "When we get back, I plan to help with Cherry's treatment. She's going to have the best of everything. I owe them that much."

Allison didn't want his gratitude. She knew Alex cared about her and Cherry, but would he share the most important part of himself? His heart. She turned and walked back inside. It was time for her to go home.

* * *

Alex was surprised to find he was relaxed as he talked with Luca. He wanted some time getting to know his father.

"I believe you have picked the perfect woman in Allison," his father said.

"How do you know I've picked her?"

Luca smiled knowingly. "Your face gives you away. Your eyes follow her around a room. She makes you smile. And the child, she's in your heart, too."

Since adulthood, Alex had had few doubts about getting what he wanted. Whenever he set his sights on something, he usually got it, except when it came to relationships. He knew he didn't want to live without her. "But it's hard for me to trust my heart."

"She is your heart."

Twenty minutes later, they said their goodbyes to family. Alex pulled Isabella aside. "How is the restaurant really doing?"

His sister glanced away. "It's not in the best of shape, but our cousin, Scarlett, is returning from Australia. She's a financial advisor and is willing to help with Rosa."

"Do you trust her to turn things around?"

Isabella nodded. "We talked a lot at Lizzie's wedding. She has some good ideas about bringing tourism to this area."

Alex was troubled as to why he cared. "If you need anything, you call me." He pulled out a business card. "For anything."

His sister took the card and hugged him. "Oh, I'm so happy I finally got to meet you."

He returned the hug. "I'm glad, too."

"So will I get a wedding invitation so I have an excuse to come see you in Texas?"

"You don't need an excuse to visit."

Her smiled widened. "Maybe then you'll be able to meet Cristiano." She frowned. "He's gone through a bad time lately with his injuries, but he's getting better. He'll be sorry he missed you, but it wasn't possible for him to be here."

"I'd like to meet him," he said, hearing about the heroics of the firefighter. "And maybe by then Angelo will come around, too."

Isabella smiled. "And then we'll all be one big happy family."

Alex smiled, too. "Maybe that's a little too much to hope for." He glanced again at Allison. He'd settled for his own small family of three.

Earlier that evening, Alex had asked the hotel to pack up everything and put it in the town car so that they could head back to Monte Vista tonight.

What he wanted couldn't wait one more day. But what surprised him was how distant Allison was suddenly. Okay, his family was overwhelming, and she was probably exhausted from their long day, but he'd hoped to continue a private celebration with just the two of them.

Alex carried the sleeping Cherry into the villa and the stairs.

"d have taken the elevator," Allison said, fol-

alves that were heavier. And I don't sweet package."

ou to carry me," Cherry said in her

"Don't wake up too much," her mother warned. "Because you're going to bed."

"I had fun at the party, Alex. I wish I had a grandpa and aunts and uncles like you do."

He hoped she meant that. "They all adore you, too. So maybe they'll adopt you."

They went through the suite door, continuing on to the bedroom where he laid her down on the mattress in the alcove.

"What does 'dopt mean?" Cherry asked.

Alex thought a moment as Allison went to the dresser and took out pajamas. "Let's see, it means that someone loves a child so much that they want that child to come live with them forever."

The girl's eyes rounded. "I wish you'd 'dopt me."

"Cherry Ann Cole, you shouldn't say that."

"But, Mommy, I want Alex to be my daddy."

Allison's face flamed. "It's time you were asleep. Alex, if you'll excuse us."

He didn't move. Instead he leaned down and whispered, "I want to adopt you, too. For now keep it a secret. Okay?" The child smiled and nodded. Then he placed a kiss on her cheek and left.

He touched Allison's arm. "I'd like to talk with you."

She sighed. "I'm really tired, Alex. Couldn't it wait until morning?"

"Five minutes, Allie. That's all I ask."

When she nodded, he left and went straight out onto the balcony. He couldn't wait to make his feelings known to her.

After pouring a glass of sparkling water, he took out his cell phone and called Brian at the ranch. The time difference made it hours earlier in Texas. After getting updates, he gave his foreman an assignment to find an architect to draw up plans for a therapy room that included an indoor pool. He had to prove to Allison he was going to be the man for her and her daughter. He loved them both.

Allison appeared in the doorway. "What is it you need to talk about?"

She was still being distant.

"Us."

She blew out a breath. "Is there an, 'us', Alex? I mean, aren't I just a companion on this trip? Isn't that why you brought us?"

"Maybe at first, but not anymore."

She tried to look unapproachable but he saw her nervousness. "What changed?"

"Me. You changed me. You and that little girl in the other room."

"I don't want you to feel obligated to us."

"What makes you think that?"

"I heard you with Luca. You told him you owed us. You don't owe us anything, Alex. And we don't need your pity. I came here with you to Italy of my own free will. If you think I came to your bed last night because I felt I owed you, then you're sadder than I thought." She turned to leave and he stopped her.

"Hold it right there, Allie. You had your say, now I get mine." He took a breath, then released it, trying to refrain from shaking her. "First of all, you didn't hear all the conversation. I said I owed you because without you I wouldn't have opened up to my family." He raised a hand. "I'm not about to call Luca Dad, but we are talking now. And if you hadn't convinced me to come in the first place, I would have never met the rest of the

Casalis." He took a step toward her. "You did that, Allie. You made me feel things. For the first time you made me feel joy."

"Oh, Alex," she whispered.

He placed a finger over her lips as his gaze met hers. "I don't want to go back to my solitary life. I need you, Allie. If you believe anything, believe that. You and Cherry are important to me. More important than I've ever let anyone become." He cupped her face in his hands. "I never want to leave you or Cherry. So understand I will never abandon that little girl." He nodded toward the bedroom. "I love her too much."

Tears filled Allison's eyes.

"I love her mother, too. Oh, God, Allie. I love you." He took her mouth in a swift kiss, trying to convince her that he was worth the chance. "Just give me time to prove that I'm the man you need. To prove that I can make us a family."

"Oh, Alex, don't you know? You're everything I've ever wanted. I love you, too. I don't want you to change anything." She smiled. "But I could use some more convincing."

His head lowered and his mouth covered hers. He drew her against his body, trying to get her as close as possible. Things were beginning to get out of hand when he knew he had to pull back, for now.

"Hold that thought," he told her, and hurried off to his room. He dug through his suitcase, found what he needed and returned to the balcony.

His heart raced as he looked at the woman he loved so much. "Yesterday morning when I left and you wondered where I went—I knew after spending the night with you in my arms, making love to you, I couldn't let you go. Ever."

He pulled out the small, blue velvet box and opened it, revealing the pear-shaped diamond, surrounded by smaller emeralds.

"Oh, Alex."

"If it's not to your liking, we can shop for something else when we get home."

She shook her head. "It's beautiful. Perfect."

He relaxed a little. "The emeralds reminded me of your eyes. I love your eyes."

"And I love this ring, because you chose it."

With a smile, he went down on one knee. "Allison Cole, I love you with all my heart. Will you marry me and will you and Cherry come live on the ranch with me?"

Allison was choked with emotion but managed to nod. He slipped the ring on her finger. The solitary diamond sparkled up at her.

"Oh, Alex. I love you. Yes. Yes, I'll marry you."

He stood and pulled her to him. First he kissed her cheek, the corner of her mouth and then her lips, savoring the special moment with her. When he finally released her and said, "I want Cherry, too. I want her to be my daughter. I'll do right by her, Allie. She'll have only the best of everything. I'm building her a therapy room at the ranch. We'll go see the best doctors."

Allison placed her finger against his mouth and he captured her hand. "She's going to have the best, Alex. She'll have you as her father."

"No, I'm the lucky one. I have you, Allie, and as a bonus I have Cherry, too." He placed a kiss on her nose. "We're all lucky. Do you want to get married here or Texas?"

"I think we should get married at home, in Texas." She kissed him. "But that doesn't mean we can't start the celebration in Italy."

He swung her up in his arms. "Whatever the lady wants."

"You. I'll always choose you."

Alex paused as the overwhelming feelings swelled in his chest so he could barely speak. "I want to give you and Cherry everything."

"You've given us the most important thing. You." She touched her mouth to his. "That, and your love, is all a girl could ever want."

"And you're giving me what I've always wanted: love and family."

EPILOGUE

TEN months later Allison stood in the new therapy room Alex had had built as soon as they returned from Italy. The structure—including an indoor pool—was located behind the main building at the Hidden Hills Guest Ranch, which was now known as Cherry's Camp.

The reason for the close proximity was to change the place into a ranch for disabled children. Children who otherwise couldn't have a vacation. Now, they could come to summer camp to ride and be with other kids, even continue their therapy. The camp would have two therapists on staff during the summer. It was due to open in a few weeks. With enrollment filled to capacity, there were already plans for expansion by adding a gymnasium for even more activities.

Tilda was in charge of it all and there was a minimal fee for the week of vacation. Alex could afford to be generous.

"Have they started yet?"

Allison turned and smiled as her husband of the last several months came into the room. He moved with that easy gait that she'd come to love, along with how he looked in a pair of jeans and a cocked cowboy hat.

She rose up on her toes and kissed him. "Do you think Cherry would do anything without you here to see her?"

"I hope not," he said, frowning. "But she's getting pretty independent since she's started school. I love it, but I hate it at the same time. She's my little girl."

Allison knew the feeling. "Oh, Alex, you're the one who's helped make her strong so she can handle this, and make her believe she can reach for goals. From the first day when you picked her up off the ground she knew you'd be there for her."

Alex was having trouble holding onto his emotions, especially when it came to his girls. "It took a lot longer for me to win over her mother."

Allison smiled and patted her rounded stomach. "I'd say you were pretty convincing. Papa."

He loved the endearment she'd called him since the morning they'd read the positive pregnancy test results. He glanced around for a chair. "Shouldn't you be sitting down?"

"That's all I've been doing." She let him lead her to the row of chairs along the wall of the large workout room and sat down. "I'm pregnant like millions of other women."

"But they aren't my wife, and aren't carrying my son and daughter." He drew a breath. They hadn't planned adding to their family quite yet, but nature had had other ideas when he and Allie had stolen some time alone and gone riding to their special place. He was crazy about the idea.

"I still can't believe it. Twins."

She gave him a sideways glance. "We're going to have to rename your special place Double Trouble."

He grinned. "Or Double Delight."

She raised an eyebrow. "Oh, I like that. Just so you know when the time comes you'll be a terrific dad." She leaned back against him. "Just like you are to Cherry."

For years, Alex had doubted that he'd ever have enough to give to have a life with someone. Then Allison had come into his life. She'd helped him heal his past hurts and given him hope for the future. She'd got him to talk about his childhood, to share even the worst times. She cried over the twin boys who'd been left alone, who were made to feel that no one loved them. Alex knew that even during that time, he had Angelo. They had each other. Now, he had family in Italy, and his wife, daughter and two more babies on the way.

"Are you sure you're not doing too much?" He stroked his hand up and down her arm. "I mean with your quilt shop and the cable show."

It had taken time and a good lawyer, but Allison had got out of the legal agreement with her ex-husband. It had cost Alex some money, but it was worth it. Jack Hudson had no more control over Allison's life.

She smiled at him. "*Quilt Allie* is on once a week. And I'm seated most of the time. And soon Jenny will be taking over."

Alex had been happy when Jenny Collins had eagerly agreed to work on the show with Allison. The teacher was a natural for television. What she lacked in expertise, she made up for in enthusiasm. The audience loved her. Her biggest fan was Brian. The two had been seeing each other since they met at the first quilting retreat.

"At least she's moved to Kerry Springs after the first of the year. Maybe that will help with her relationship with Brian."

Alex cringed. "They're doing just fine without our help. If the two want to work it out, they'll find a way."

Those green eyes lit up and he knew she was planning something. "I just want them to be happy, too."

"They don't seem unhappy to me." Alex shook his head. "Besides, Brian will be pretty busy building a house on the east end of the ranch."

Allison gasped again. "You did what I suggested. You gave him part of the ranch."

"A few acres aren't even noticeable on this spread. Besides, he's earned them. And now, since he's bought a partnership in the cattle operation, I don't have to be away so much."

Her eyes widened. "Careful, Alex, you'll lose that tough-guy image."

"As if I ever fooled you," he said, happy she'd seen through it all.

"You have a big heart, Alessandro Casali. And I love that you chose to share it with me."

He kissed her. "We chose each other."

He pulled her against him, enjoying just being with her, sharing things. "I talked to Luca earlier," he mentioned. They'd kept in touch since the trip to Italy. "I asked him to come for a visit after the babies are born. And somehow I'm going to get Angelo here, too."

Allison raised her head up from his shoulder and looked at him. "I don't think I could love you more than I do at this moment." She placed her hand on his jaw. "I repeat, you are a nice man. And I love you."

"I love you, too."

He gave her a lingering kiss, but it still had his pulse pounding and heart racing. He pulled back and smiled. "Later," he promised as Tilda came through the door.

"Am I in time to see Cherry?" she asked.

"She hasn't even come in yet," Alex said.

The older woman rubbed her hands together. "Good, I didn't want to miss this."

Soon Brian and Jenny showed up. They had big smiles on their faces as Brian shared the news about plans for his house.

Alex watched the women chat away and he realized they might not be blood, but they were all his family. They cared for each other.

"Here she comes," Tilda announced as therapist, Kate Boyer, escorted Cherry into the room. Alex's daughter wasn't in a wheelchair much these days. As often as possible, she got around with her braces and crutches.

Nearly six years old now, Cherry Casali worked hard during therapy sessions. Alex had given her an incentive, too. The promise of her own horse. For months the girl had worked all the time and barely complained about it. They always knew that Cherry might never walk on her own and if she did, she would probably have a limp.

A lot of the time, Alex was in on his daughter's workouts, but the last few weeks she'd banned everyone from the therapy room. Until today when she'd summoned them all here.

"Hi, Mommy and Daddy. And everybody," she called. "Stay there. I want to show you something."

She made her way to the parallel bars and eased down in a chair where Kate helped her remove her braces. Alex's heart nearly stopped and Allison gripped his hand tightly.

He watched the strain on Cherry's face as she reached

for the outside of the bar and pulled herself up with one hand. Once standing she looked across the room, her gaze locked on him.

He held onto Allison's hand and whispered the words, "You can do it, *uccellino*."

It seemed as if everyone held their breath as Cherry took that first step, then another. Tilda gasped and Allison began to cry and he felt his own tears gathering as their daughter continued the hardest journey of her short life. He couldn't sit there any longer. He got up and walked to the end of the railing.

"You can do it, Cherry," he repeated. "I'll be here for you."

She smiled and continued each slow step until she made it to the end and stood in front of him. "See, Daddy, I did it. I did it."

He swung her up into his arms, and hugged her to him. "I always knew you could."

Allison joined them, giving her daughter a kiss as whistles and cheers broke out in the room.

"Don't cry, Mommy," Cherry said. "You're supposed to be happy."

"Oh, I am, sweetheart. You've made me so very happy."

Alex knew that Allison could finally move on from the guilt, stop blaming herself for her daughter's accident. This had been the one thing he couldn't help her with. But Cherry had.

"Do I get my horse now, Daddy?"

Allison looked at him, wiping her tears. "Looks like she won and you have to pay up, Casali."

"It's my pleasure to pay off this bet."

Cherry hugged him. "You're the best daddy and mommy ever."

Alex looked at Allison and Cherry, and his chest tightened with love and pride. He kissed them both. "No. It's the best *family* ever."

* * * * *

PASSIONATE CHEF, ICE QUEEN BOSS

BY
JENNIE ADAMS

Australian author **Jennie Adams** grew up in a rambling farmhouse surrounded by books and by people who loved reading them. She decided at a young age to be a writer, but it took many years and a lot of scenic detours before she sat down to pen her first romance novel. Jennie has worked in a number of careers and voluntary positions, including transcription typist and pre-school assistant. She is the proud mother of three fabulous adult children and makes her home in a small inland city in New South Wales. In her leisure time Jennie loves long, rambling walks, discovering new music, starting knitting projects that she rarely finishes, chatting with friends, trips to the movies and new dining experiences.

Jennie loves to hear from her readers, and can be contacted via her website at www.jennieadams.net.

For the gentle men in my life.
For walking with dignity and grace.
For your strength and integrity and giving.
Most of all for your love. Right back atcha!

CHAPTER ONE

'LORENZO, I sent a message requesting your presence in Luca's office for a meeting ten minutes ago. Did you not receive it?' The words were calm. Professional. They stated the facts and requested an explanation of the man's absence, nothing more or less.

Yes, Scarlett Gibson wanted to tug in frustration on the hot-pink ribbon adorning her ponytail of shoulder-length black hair and, yes, that reaction annoyed her. She hadn't seen Lorenzo for five years. For the next two months she would be working with him. Scarlett had hoped she would be able to do that without caring much about anything to do with him. After all, that was the state she had been forced to reach after he broke her heart five years ago.

Well, Scarlett hadn't become a top financial advisor in Australia by losing her control the first time something annoyed her. But she also hadn't come back to Italy to help out at her uncle Luca's Rosa restaurant, only to have her authority thwarted by the head chef on her first day at the job.

The source of that thwarting stood inside the kitchen of Rosa with his back to her. A slim, muscular back in a fitted black shirt. He wore black trousers, black shoes on his feet. Did he still wear the gold medallion?

Not that Scarlett cared, though she supposed such thoughts were bound to surface. But, surely, they were no different from her wondering if the stranger on the tram beside her back in Melbourne had her coffee made on full milk or skim!

As Scarlett glanced about the kitchen different things began to register. The scents of rich, melted chocolate blended with the warm heartiness of yeasty savoury bread stuffed with tomato and herbs, onion and garlic and olives. Several loaves of the bread were cooling on trays on a bench. Those scents probably explained why Scarlett's tummy suddenly felt a bit odd. She'd have to watch that. She didn't want to eat her way through the next two months. In any case Lorenzo certainly wasn't the reason for her tummy-consciousness.

Three kitchen hands were at work. A woman who looked to be in her thirties, and two men. Scarlett had bumped into the woman inside the restaurant as she appeared to be arriving for work, and had asked her to let Lorenzo know that she wanted to see him in Luca's office without delay.

The woman glanced up now and met her gaze. She didn't look at all guilty or forgetful, which led Scarlett to believe that she had, indeed, passed her message on to Lorenzo.

So what was Lorenzo Nesta's game? Yes, he appeared to be working with great concentration and, yes, there appeared to be quite a bit going on in the kitchen right now. Various desserts in different stages of production littered the bench space around Lorenzo in what appeared to be a very organised kind of chaos.

Scarlett registered this fact, but it was still quite early in the morning. Lunchtime diners were a long way away. Lorenzo should be able to leave his kitchen hands unsupervised at this time of day, with tasks to keep them going, and give Scarlett the time she needed.

Scarlett's sherry-brown eyes narrowed. If Lorenzo thought she would chase after him any time she wanted a few words, he needed a lesson in the order of authority in this restaurant. Scarlett's uncle Luca came first. He was the owner, though he'd told Scarlett that during her time here he didn't intend to come in, just let her get on with what had to be done.

Cousin Isabella had been managing the restaurant a lot of the time anyway. Isabella was gladly taking a step back to focus on her relationship with her newly found reclusive prince, Maximilliano Di Rossi.

Then came Scarlett in the role of business manager.

And *then* came the head chef/assistant manager, Lorenzo Nesta. In other words, where Lorenzo was concerned, Scarlett was the boss!

Scarlett gave a determined nod of her head, only to feel a recalcitrant lock of hair slip loose of its beribboned ponytail.

Confound it all.

Scarlett frowned and blew the lock of hair off her cheek, and glared at that stretch of shoulders in her line of vision.

She had every right to glare. The man was a love rat.

Lorenzo twisted his upper body and glanced over his shoulder at her. 'Just one minute more.'

'*Just one more—?*' As though she had nothing better to do than stand about and wait for him? Scarlett's brows went up even as she forced her teeth together over the words that wanted to pour out.

Lorenzo held a slender, hollow stainless-steel tube in his hands. He rotated it with long, deft fingers and Scarlett got a view in profile of a manly cheek already darkened with a hint of beard shadow, a strong nose and chiselled lips pursed in concentration, and the downward sweep of thick lashes over eyes that she knew were the deepest, richest shade of brown.

Not that Scarlett had any particular kind of obsession with dark brown. Well, with the possible exception of it swirling around in a mug with a marshmallow melted in the top of it.

'Actually, Lorenzo, I've been waiting ten minutes already.'

Scarlett uttered the words in a calm tone that nevertheless held a hint of steel within it. 'You know the way to Luca's office. I'd appreciate it if you didn't keep me waiting any longer.'

Scarlett wheeled about and made her way back through the kitchen's swing doors, through the rear of the indoor dining area past several potted plants and a nook filled with a warm colourful display of bottles of oils and relishes and sauces, and into the corridor that housed Luca's office.

Mixed feelings walked with her. This return trip to Italy was important to Scarlett for many reasons. She wanted to enjoy Isabella's company and bond with her again and maybe get in a better place with *all of her family here*. If that was even possible after so long? Helping Uncle Luca out felt like a good step towards that. She'd hesitated when Isabella had asked her, and that had been because of Lorenzo. But then Scarlett had decided if she was facing down old demons she could just as easily face down this one at the same time. How hard could it be?

'Scarlett, good morning.' Her cousin Isabella approached as Scarlett put her hand on the office door. 'All set for your first day on the job?'

Scarlett stopped, and regrouped. And smiled, because this was Izzie and they had grown up together. They'd had a lot of girlish fun together before she and Scarlett had done something incredibly silly. The ramifications of which were only now settling. Scarlett had punished herself and had moved to Australia, away from her Italian family and friends to get to know her father and his side of her family.

'Hi, Izzie. Yes, I'm ready for my first day. I didn't expect to see you in here today. You look glowing. How's your prince?'

'Princely as ever.' Isabella blushed a little, but she also smiled and held out her arms. 'I'm rather pleased that I've found him.'

'He's made you happy, so I'm pleased too.' Scarlett stepped into Izzie's hug.

There was an ache in the middle of her chest when she let go.

Coming back here always tugged at her emotions. This time she was here to try to help the family out, with a hope of reconnection hiding some place deep inside her that was perhaps unrealistic.

If it was going to make her feel all mushy whenever she came across a family member, Scarlett had better get that reaction right under control, and fast. 'I have Lorenzo coming in for a meeting. Since you're here, I'd like to speak with you after that, if possible.' Her full lips tightened before she went on. 'I'll probably have questions for you after I've grilled him.'

'Grilled? You won't upset—?' Isabella cut herself off and forced a smile back to her face. 'You're the boss. Of course you should manage things here however you feel is right.' Isabella drew a breath. 'I'm here to put together a batch of Papa's special sauce, so I'll be around for a while. I can speak with you when you're ready.'

'Let's say in about half an hour, then.' Luca's secret recipe sauce was a mainstay of the Rosa restaurant's authentic Italian cuisine. Scarlett wondered what kind of reception she would get when she wanted an accounting of the ingredients list so she could cost-base it.

A *hands-off we're-not-telling* reception, she imagined, from both Luca and Isabella. Well, perhaps they could tell her the costs, but not the ingredients?

'It's nice to have you back in Italy, Scarlett, and I really appreciate all you're going to do for Rosa.' Her cousin's expression tightened. 'The money issues are worrying. Max was prepared to invest a cash injection to get Rosa back in a strong financial position, but of course that would have offended

Papa and it wouldn't have really solved anything in the long term. I couldn't have let Max do that, either, much as I love him for wanting to.'

'Quite right.' Simply throwing money at things wasn't the answer. But with the right changes and improvements, success *could* be grasped. That was what Scarlett believed, and had proved in her own career path as she climbed the ranks to a highly successful financial advisor in Australia, advising some very respectable companies. She wanted the same for Rosa. She wanted the restaurant to run at a profit and be self-sufficient and successful.

Isabella disappeared and Scarlett stepped into Luca's office. It would be her headquarters for the time being, though she didn't intend to be the kind of manager who sat behind her desk all day and didn't watch what was going on around her. Despite her hope to not need much to do with him, she might have to watch Lorenzo Nesta very closely. Particularly if he thought he could get away with stunts like ignoring her summons when she sent it!

'Scarlett—'

And speaking of her nemesis, there he was, standing in the doorway of the office looking a little prickly beneath the surface though she could see he was trying hard to mask that. And, she supposed, somewhat attractive.

Not that he appealed to Scarlett any more in any particular way. He'd killed that reaction in her five years ago. Her heart rate *had* jumped a little just now, but that was as a result of preparing to do battle if necessary.

'Lorenzo.' She gestured to the visitor's chair on the other side of the desk. And really, wasn't she the one to have the right to some prickliness? She'd only just started here, and already he'd put her morning's schedule off centre. 'Please be seated. I want to speak with you about how things have been running here at the restaurant, and how they'll need to be run from now on. But perhaps you'd care to start by explaining why you ignored my request for this meeting.'

'I didn't ignore the request, I just couldn't drop everything and come to you immediately.' His chest expanded beneath the black shirt before he carefully exhaled. Scarlett caught sight of a glint of gold around his neck. *Was it* the chain that he'd had when they first met?

Not that you care, Scarlett.

'Why couldn't you leave your staff for a few minutes?'

'It's not always possible to walk out of a busy restaurant kitchen without consequences.' His words were respectful, but also firm. 'You gave me no notice, just a message that my presence was immediately required.'

'At this early hour of the day I would have thought you'd be able to spare some time.' Scarlett tried to keep her gaze locked on his eyes, yet it wandered to the curve of his lips, the strong nose, the very old, small scar over his left eyebrow and despite her determination, a memory stirred.

He'd held her in his arms one day after they'd made love, and had made up outrageous stories about how he got the scar as a child. Each one had been sillier than the last until Scarlett had needed to hold her sides to try to contain her mirth. The truth was that he'd fallen, not very far or excitingly, off a piece of play equipment at school.

That day, Lorenzo had said something strange to her. *Sometimes the scars you see are better. I'm happy to wear this one. At least it bears no shame.* His gaze had sobered and for a moment Scarlett had felt as though he'd pushed her away, even though she still lay snuggled in his arms. She'd opened her mouth to ask, she hadn't been sure what, but he'd kissed her again and the moment had passed…

Well, that was then, and what was she doing thinking about this now anyway?

Scarlett *wasn't* laughing now. Nor did she want to reminisce about the far distant past of her life. She couldn't afford to be distracted!

'We're very busy in the kitchen today. It's good that Isabella came in. I've asked her to supervise until I can get back.' Lorenzo drew a deep breath. 'At least that's something.'

Did he say that as though Isabella wouldn't know what she was doing in there?

'My cousin has worked in the kitchen of Rosa for a long time.' Isabella could do a just fine job of supervising the staff, or making the meals for that matter. 'Whether she has a whole lot of bits of paper to say so or not, it wouldn't surprise me if she's a more qualified cook than you are.'

Lorenzo made a sound in the back of his throat. 'Of course I trust Isabella in the kitchen. That's not what I meant.'

'Whatever you meant, we're wasting time.' Scarlett glared at him across Luca's desk. If her anger was somewhat of a shield, she wasn't about to admit it.

Lorenzo stared back and whatever thoughts he had disappeared in his eyes. 'By all means, please go on with what you need to say.'

'I will.' Another curl of Scarlett's hair slid from its moorings and lay against her cheek. Scarlett gritted her teeth and asked herself how a few minutes in his company could get her so worked up so easily. She'd just finished telling herself she would treat this in a calm, professional manner.

Lorenzo's gaze clung to her hair for a moment before he raised it to meet her eyes.

Dark brown to sherry brown.

Five years older to aeons wiser.

He'd be thirty-two now. Scarlett was twenty-eight. That extra layer of maturity…flattered him.

'Do you understand the reason for my presence at Rosa?' Scarlett didn't know what Isabella had told him. She doubted Luca would have said much. Her uncle had hidden the state of

Rosa's finances even from Isabella for as long as he could. It had taken effort to get Luca to the point where he was willing to have Scarlett come in to try to clean things up here.

Lorenzo made a 'Who knows?' gesture with his hands. 'You're here as Financial Manager for the time being. Isabella has relinquished her management to you, though she'll still be actively involved in the restaurant in other ways. In other words, you answer only to Luca himself, though he's been quite scarce here of late.'

'Good. You understand, then.' In fact he had a better grip on his knowledge of events than Scarlett had imagined.

Lorenzo examined her face. Maybe he was searching for her response to him? Or maybe he saw a different woman five years on from the one he had known? Well, he'd helped Scarlett to become that woman. Self-contained, determined, career-focused and beyond guarded in some ways. She'd been halfway there before she even met Lorenzo.

'As Head Chef and Assistant Manager you will answer directly to me. Everything you do will be under my scrutiny, and I expect your full co-operation with any changes I decide to make to improve the financial bottom line of the restaurant.' *This* was what needed to be said.

'I run a good kitchen and do my best with the resources Luca has allowed me.' He spoke the words and then clamped his lips together before he added, 'All of us have had to work within the framework of Luca's feelings about employing and buying locally and treating the staff in some ways as a big family.'

And Luca loved to be generous and giving. This was something Isabella had brought up and, though her cousin hadn't gone into much detail, Scarlett had wondered whether this had caused problems for Isabella in her management efforts. Scarlett would look into it.

'I'm accustomed to co-operation, Lorenzo. This morning,

by your actions, you communicated to other members of the staff here that I can wait until it suits you if I request a meeting.' She drew a breath. 'I don't want to have to make changes to the staffing here, but I also will not work with a head chef who doesn't respect my authority.'

Scarlett's message was clear, and clearly received if the tightening of Lorenzo's expressive mouth was any indication.

'We received a special order—' He cut the words off and shook his head. 'My apologies for not attending you immediately. It would be great if in future you could give me a little notice so I can leave the kitchen without any negative impact on the work there, but if you can't, you can't. I will still co-operate with you to the fullest.'

He held her gaze with a level one of his own. 'I value this job. Every step I take is aimed at making the best of Rosa that I possibly can.'

'Then I'm sure we understand each other and will get along just fine.' Scarlett's fingers closed over a typed list on Luca's desk. 'I'd like to discuss the current staffing policies with you. I understand from Isabella that you've been given a fairly free rein to make decisions about the number of kitchen hands employed at any given time, how you roster them, that sort of thing.'

'I have enough kitchen hands to meet the kitchen's needs. Some of them, Luca has speared into the positions when I... might not have chosen them for the work, but I do my best with the workers I have.'

It wasn't a negative statement. Scarlett got the impression it was an honest one.

Lorenzo named staff members. He explained whether they were full or part time, hours they worked and what their roles were. 'There is room for all of them to improve their skills in one way or another. I work on that on a daily basis.'

For a restaurant the size of Rosa, the staffing levels seemed appropriate. 'I'll want to examine your kitchen roster some time in the next day or two.' And the wages and staff conditions, but those weren't Lorenzo's responsibility.

There had to be reasons why Rosa didn't make a better bottom line financially. Scarlett would turn the restaurant inside out to discover those reasons and fix them.

For now she needed to know: 'How economical are you with your cooking methods? What are you doing to reduce ingredient wastage? How often do you have Isabella in to supervise the making of the special tomato sauce?'

'Within the guidelines I have to work with, I believe I'm being quite economical.' Lorenzo stared into Scarlett's sherry-brown eyes and assured himself he could and would finish this interview in a calm relaxed manner no matter how many questions Scarlett threw at him or how less than happy to see him she might appear to be. And no matter how concerned he felt about his job security with Scarlett now in a position to decide his fate.

He didn't need any more ripples in his work record, but what could he do besides work hard and perform to the best of his ability?

Regret tugged at him. It wasn't easy to look into Scarlett's lovely face and keep memories at bay. That was a problem he'd worried over since he first heard she would be coming to Rosa to act as Financial Manager. He wanted to ask how she'd been—was she happy? So many things. He couldn't ask any of those questions. It was all long gone, the mistakes and missteps were made. He couldn't fix the past. And his present.

'I maintain a high standard in my kitchen.' Best to stick to these things with her. Best not to notice her too much, and he was *trying* not to notice how lovely she looked in the prissy cream blouse. She'd teamed it with a deep crimson and cream pinstriped skirt that had clung to her hips as she stalked out of the kitchen minutes ago.

The clothes were businesslike yet still practical for Italy's summer weather. But did Scarlett think the outfit made her look severe? Remote? If so, she didn't have much idea. Her hair slipping from its moorings put paid to that, as did the bright pink ribbon that adorned the silky black mass.

That and the softness that she couldn't quite hide, deep in the backs of her guarded eyes. She might play the tough boss lady, but it was clear she still had…her softer side.

'My reputation and that of the restaurant are on the line with every meal produced.' His tone wanted to soften. He forced it to remain businesslike. His job could be on the line here, which meant he couldn't let himself indulge in memories of the past when, for a time before it all went wrong, he and Scarlett had been happy together.

He forced the words out. 'If a dish is substandard it's thrown away, but my ultimate goal is to ensure everyone on my team works hard enough and carefully enough to always produce a dish worthy of the standards of Rosa.'

'Throwing meals out at all—that'll have to stop.' Scarlett leaned forward in her chair.

'Sometimes things happen even in the best kitchens, Scarlett.' Did she really imagine that could be otherwise?

'Well, I suppose so.' Scarlett's pretty nose scrunched.

'Now and then a patron will throw a fit over a perfectly good meal, too, and send it back.' From time to time, this happened. 'It's important to maintain goodwill, even when we know the restaurant is in the right.'

'Yes, of course.' Scarlett drummed one slender set of fingers on the desk before she stopped the movement abruptly. 'I want to be brought in on it if I'm here and a diner carries on like that.'

So Lorenzo could hide behind her skirts while she took

care of things for him? Pride rose up. He pushed aside all knowledge of the edge of shame that went with it. What did they say?

If you don't acknowledge it, it doesn't exist.

His father was certainly good at that. Well, at ignoring Lorenzo's existence much of the time, now that his son had 'dishonoured the family with his behaviour'. Lorenzo wasn't in a position where he could explain himself to his family.

And now was not the time to dwell on any of that!

'I assure you I am quite able to deal with any difficult patrons here.'

'Well, I know that.' She said it as though any other option was ridiculous.

And Lorenzo realised he might have overreacted. He could thank his past with Marcella for that. Well, he could thank that past for a few things, couldn't he? 'Regarding Isabella making the trademark sauce, I keep her informed of the supply. She tops it up when needed so we make sure we never run out.'

Maybe if he made it clear to Scarlett that he had a good knowledge of the restaurant's workings, she would feel more able to work with him to achieve whatever she needed to here. Lorenzo needed to know just what her goals were and what she would expect of him.

He'd worked closely with Isabella, and she'd handed plenty of responsibility to him. That had suited him, but what did Scarlett want? 'Is the restaurant in real trouble? Are jobs secure? Isabella only said you'd be working to improve our bottom line. She didn't cover the why of it.'

Scarlett hesitated for so long, he'd almost decided she wasn't going to answer. Finally she said, 'The restaurant has been running at a loss, I believe for quite some time.' The moment the words were out, she glared at him. 'You're being trusted with that information because I need your co-operation and full disclosure from you to enable me to do my work here properly and get Rosa back in the black. If you discuss this fact with anyone, or if you hold anything back—'

'What kind of man do you think I am?' Lorenzo's nostrils flared.

But they both knew the answer, didn't they? To Scarlett, Lorenzo was a man who had let her down. The answer shone in her eyes for a moment before she glanced away.

'You won't lose your job due to financial reasons.' Scarlett uttered the words in a low tone. 'Luca and Isabella both speak highly of you and want to keep you here. I am determined to turn the restaurant around so it starts making a profit, and continues to do so. If you prove to be good for Rosa as they are saying you are, and you're respectful to me and my authority, then I'm sure your job will be quite safe, too.'

Her assurance helped somewhat. Scarlett might feel angry towards him because of their shattered past love affair. But if she said his job wasn't in jeopardy provided he continued to work well, Lorenzo *should* be safe. He wished it didn't have to matter so much to him, but it did. He needed every Euro of his wages to help him save for *his* ultimate future. That future was a long way away, years still, but he was doing his best.

So now he only had to make sure Scarlett didn't fire him for any other reason, and he hoped, over time, that she would see his commitment to Rosa.

Scarlett seemed to make an effort to centre her thoughts once again. 'I'm sorry for all the questions, but your answers will help me prioritise how I approach change here.' She drew a breath. 'What are the most popular dishes and how do they stack up in terms of profit margins? Do you buy one hundred per cent only local produce?'

'We always use local produce if possible, otherwise I shop nearby for other things.' The restaurant had a small van for that purpose. He listed the most popular dishes. Many of them used Luca's secret sauce. 'As Luca's rules about local produce have been hard and fast, I haven't looked into how much money we might be losing by buying locally but there are times when I think there would be a substantial difference.'

'I see. Well, thank you. I can see I have a lot of things I need to look into.' Scarlett got to her feet in a single, lithe movement.

Meeting over, apparently. For a moment he wondered if she would shake his hand. But she simply strode to the door in the cream pumps that matched her blouse exactly.

Lorenzo dragged his gaze upwards away from tanned slender legs. 'My history in restaurants has taught me a lot. If you want to discuss any aspect of Rosa at any time—'

'I'll keep that in mind.' Scarlett's brows drew together and she took a half-step towards him before she stopped and tugged the door wider. 'I'll let you get back to work.'

Lorenzo stepped forward too, until he was even with her. The scent of her perfume filled his senses, catapulted him back to happy times between them before the complications of his life had wrecked everything for both of them. Could either one of them hope to truly get through her working here, and just ignore all that? 'Scarlett, the past—'

'Is irrelevant between us now.' She acknowledged its existence and dismissed it with a wave of one hand, all in the space of seconds. 'I can assure you, from my perspective it is long forgotten!'

He might have believed it, he supposed. That Miss Scarlett *Gibson* quite frankly *didn't give a damn*.

Yes, Lorenzo might have believed that if he hadn't seen the burn of hurt deep in the backs of her eyes that had nothing to do with Rosa or now or here, and everything to do with that past.

'I'm glad to hear you're okay with that.' Lorenzo turned on his heel and went back to his kitchen where he at least had the hope of telling himself he was somewhat in charge and in control. He needed that. Marcella's treatment, her behaviour towards him, had left him with the need to…find self-esteem within his work. It was a cliché, he supposed, but Lorenzo was honest enough to admit it about himself.

As for Scarlett's position here as the new boss, Lorenzo wanted to believe the two of them could work together without things turning catastrophic. Surely they could.

Couldn't they?

CHAPTER TWO

'You know there'll be fallout for you once Lisa learns that you've moved yourself out of her villa.' Isabella put the middle-sized suitcase of Scarlett's set of three down in the centre of the small bedsit, and turned with raised brows to face her cousin. 'And *I'd* have loved to have—'

'I know. And…thanks. But I would have felt I was intruding.' It was the next morning, early. Max had driven them here, helped them to unload Scarlett's luggage, and had then disappeared with a promise to meet Isabella in the village later.

Or should Scarlett say the prince had driven the princess into town? The romance between his cousin and the reclusive prince *was* a little like a fairy tale. Scarlett stifled a small grin and wondered how she could be so cheerful when a part of her very much did not want to face another day at the restaurant with Lorenzo working under her nose, and making her feel uncomfortable and overly conscious of him by turns.

Not that he'd been trying to do that, to be fair. Being in contact with him had turned out to be more difficult than she had anticipated, that was all. Scarlett dumped her overnight bag and laptop case beside the suitcases. 'It's not up to Mum to decide where I stay while I'm working at Rosa.' Lisa wasn't in Monta Correnti just now anyway. 'Though I do appreciate her inviting me to stay at her villa.'

Isabella raised her eyebrows. 'You mean inviting you in a way you felt powerless to refuse.'

Her accompanying smile reminded Scarlett of girlhood days.

'Maybe Mum did sort of coerce me into agreeing to stay there. But I found a way to get out of being under her scrutiny, even if it was only the second-hand scrutiny of her house staff.' Scarlett had tugged on her ribbon before she thought about it. It was a gold and black polka-dot ribbon today, which she felt nicely offset her black and yellow A-line, knee-length linen dress.

'And anyway, with no offence meant to anyone, I prefer to be here.' Scarlett let her gaze rove over the room. It was small, simply furnished with a sofa that pulled out into a bed, a tiny dining table with two chairs, a kitchenette and a bathroom with a washing machine tucked behind a door at the far end.

Certainly Scarlett's apartment back in Melbourne had been much roomier, and her mother's villa heaps roomier again. Well, she'd sublet her apartment.

And this little bedsit tucked onto the end of a widow's house was clean and neat and serviceable. It would meet Scarlett's requirements for her stay in Italy. Most of all she could be private here at the end of the day. Scarlett wanted to reconnect with her family, but she needed *some* kind of bolt hole! 'I need my own space sometimes, Izzie. Anyway, by the time Mum turns up again I could be halfway through my stay. What she doesn't know…'

'Won't cause an outburst?' Isabella shook her head. 'Have you really forgotten that much of what it's like to be part of a big family with all the related tensions and nosiness and everything else? I know you have your father and his relatives in Australia, but have you also forgotten what Lisa can be like when she unleashes her sharp tongue? Your mamma will hear about you moving out within days, if not sooner.' A hint of annoyance leaked into Isabella's tone.

It wasn't directed at Scarlett, and Scarlett knew this. They were all less than happy with Lisa after the way she'd behaved towards her brother Luca recently.

'I haven't forgotten. Mamma hasn't spoken with my father, even on the phone, since I turned eighteen, but I remember a few of the calls before then. Mum shouting and my father looking as though he'd like to tear his hair out by the end of it.'

Dad had made a good home for her when she decided at twelve that she wanted to go to him in Australia. It had taken time for Scarlett to let herself really love Brad Gibson. She'd been an unhappy, upset child at the time, but they'd got there. Her father was a good man.

Scarlett went on. 'The bedsit is perfect, Izzie.' She gestured about her. 'It's literally less than five minutes' walk from Rosa.' Scarlett walked to the opened door and glanced out. 'In fact, you can see the restaurant from here, if you stand in the part that isn't screened by the overhead lintel and all that flowering creeper. Anyway, shall we go? I need to get to work. I'll unpack tonight.'

Scarlett reached once again for her laptop computer and purse. She perched a pair of sunglasses on her nose. With her eyes shielded from view she felt somewhat better.

'I have an errand to run before I drop by the restaurant.' Isabella gave a soft smile. 'It's just a little something I'm picking up. A photo of me that I had framed.'

'To give to your prince when you meet up later?' Scarlett asked teasingly, and smiled when Isabella blushed.

Isabella smiled, too, and while she was still smiling she said, 'Speaking of photos, Jackie's got heaps of her daughter now. You should—'

'I don't have time to look at photos.' The rejection shot

out of Scarlett's mouth before she even realised how trapped Isabella's suggestion had made her feel. Scarlett found it hard to think about the daughter her sister, Jackie, had given up for adoption.

Because she'd thought, and thought, and *thought* about it over the years and the more she did that, the deeper her guilt seemed to lodge itself. Scarlett had avoided contact with Izzie *and* Jackie for years because of this.

Now they were back in contact, and Scarlett *did* want to be closer.

But a part of her also wanted to demand to know if her cousin truly thought getting over something like that long separation and loss could be so simple for Jackie? So easy? That Scarlett's sister would miraculously have forgotten all the years of feeling as if there'd been a hole left inside her just because now she had her lover back in her life, and some contact with her daughter, Kate? After all, Scarlett and, to a lesser degree, Isabella, had caused Jackie's loss!

Before Scarlett could speak or do otherwise, the sound of a motorcycle echoed through the square.

'I didn't think he'd be in this early.' How stupid, to get all breathless just from the sight of Lorenzo across the square. It must be because he'd made it necessary for her to assert her authority yesterday.

'You recognise him from that distance?' Isabella seemed surprised.

'Who else would it be?' Scarlett dodged having to explain that she and Lorenzo had known each other five years ago, and had *more* than simply known each other. They'd kept the relationship secret and Scarlett wasn't about to reveal anything about it now. 'I mean, he's gone to the restaurant, it's a man and he *is* reasonably recognisable even at this distance.'

'I suppose so.' Isabella followed Scarlett's glance. 'Lorenzo did well yesterday, didn't he?'

Praise for the head chef wasn't quite what Scarlett had been expecting. She said carefully, 'The diners seemed happy enough with their meals.'

'Oh, I'm sure they all would have been.' Isabella waved a hand as though to dismiss this. 'But I meant with that special order for lunch for twelve people. It was *very* last minute, but Lorenzo was sure he could pull it off. I wouldn't have been able to. Not with the things on the menu.'

Oblivious to Scarlett's surprise, Isabella went on. 'The movie star was happy, though. One of the kitchen hands made the delivery and Lorenzo said at the prices he insisted on to do the catering, the restaurant will have cleaned up on it financially.'

A movie star?

A last-minute order for a special lunch for twelve people?

This was the reason why Lorenzo hadn't come immediately to yesterday's meeting?

Why hadn't he said so? Scarlett stared at her cousin as yesterday's impressions realigned themselves. 'I wasn't aware—'

'I thought Lorenzo would have explained it to you. He'd just finished tempering the chocolate rolls when he asked me to take over while he had his meeting with you. I was a nervous wreck even in that short span of time. I can cope with our regular menu, but that?' Isabella's eyes glazed over as she started listing dishes.

'Chocolate tart, limone mousse, a chocolate and hazelnut gateau, vanilla and raspberry chiffon cake, *lime*-custard-stuffed profiteroles, built into a profiterole *tree* if you please, and that was only one course of the menu.' She drew a breath. 'Even with the meeting with you in the middle of it, Lorenzo managed and got flawless results.'

'Oh.' Scarlett found herself in the rare position of feeling as though she hadn't really behaved appropriately in relation to her work, that she'd perhaps brought personal issues into it and allowed those to colour her judgement. That she'd been hard on Lorenzo and hadn't really given him a chance to explain things. That was bad management on her part, and, no matter what her personal feelings might be towards him, he'd shown dedication and commitment to Rosa.

'Well, I'd better get going.' Isabella gave her a quick hug again. 'See you in a while.' She walked off.

'Yes. See you.' Scarlett frowned and started towards the restaurant.

It appears I may have misjudged you yesterday, Lorenzo. Scarlett practised the words in her mind as she pushed open one of the kitchen's swing doors. Lorenzo might have played her false five years ago, and Scarlett wasn't about to forget that. But when Scarlett made a mistake in her work, she admitted it. Now she just had to find Lorenzo, and say those words to his face. Then she could get on with the real work of the day with her thoughts at peace.

It only took a second for Scarlett to realise that her hopes of catching Lorenzo alone were not to be. Two seconds later she comprehended that the conversation being conducted beyond a bank of open shelving was not a happy one.

Lorenzo and another male stood with their backs turned to her. They were unaware of her presence. They spoke in Italian in muted voices that seemed all the more intense for that fact. The young kitchen hand had a backpack dangling from his hand, and Lorenzo plunked two bottles of some kind of spirits down on a work surface before he turned back to the boy.

From the stiffness of Lorenzo's back, and the guilt Scarlett could see written all over the boy even from this distance, it was clear Lorenzo had caught the young man trying to steal the bottles. What was the teenager's name? Scarlett ran her mental list from yesterday's 'meet the staff' moments. Dante…

Scarlett's brows drew together. Was this where Rosa's profits had gone? *Taken by light fingers?* She wanted to wade in, and yet something in Dante's posture and expression, and the way Lorenzo was holding his emotions in, made her hesitate. And the boy was young. He couldn't have worked here all that long. Certainly not long enough to sink Rosa financially through petty theft, even though this *was* a very serious thing to have happen.

As Scarlett stood there Lorenzo's low words carried to her.

'This stunt—' He gestured towards the bottles. 'I can't believe you'd do such a thing. You're not a bad boy, Dante. Not everyone on this team is here by my choice but you're someone I've really wanted to keep. You try hard; you're keen to learn. You've always made your shifts without any problems at all. You'll take direction and you have a natural flair in the kitchen. You have it in you to become a good chef one day.'

'I'm sorry. I know this was stupid. Mamma has this new boyfriend—' The boy cut his words off abruptly and for a moment looked trapped. 'I knew taking the bottles was wrong and I've never done it before. I promise you.' The words were passionate. 'Please, don't fire me.'

'You're the only child at home, if I remember rightly?' Lorenzo said the words as though they meant nothing, yet Scarlett could see enough from the view of his profile to understand that he wanted to know more.

'Yes. I'm an only child.' The boy confirmed this.

'You took Luca's hidden spare key yesterday and came

in to steal the wine this morning.' Lorenzo made the statement flatly. 'Weren't you worried I might catch you? Everyone knows I start earlier than my shifts and often work later, too.'

'I don't know.' Dante shrugged skinny shoulders and then seemed to almost wince as he stopped the movement. 'I guess I didn't think about that.'

But Lorenzo was thinking about that.

And Scarlett thought about that.

Why would this boy, who seemed clever and capable and able to plan such a thing in the first place, plan it for this late in the morning?

If a part of Dante had hoped to be caught, then Scarlett was inclined to believe he hadn't done this before and hadn't really wanted to do it now. Was his behaviour a cry for help?

Even so, how to deal with such a thing? Should she step forward? Intervene? Before Scarlett could decide or announce her presence, Lorenzo spoke again.

'Trouble in here is the last thing I need right now, Dante. The last thing any of us needs.' He tugged his chef's jacket into order. 'Our new financial manager will want an accounting of every Euro that comes and goes in this kitchen. You couldn't have picked a worse time to try to steal.'

The boy looked stricken. 'If you speak with her—'

'She may be just as cold about this as her mother would be. Scarlett Gibson is Lisa Firenzi's daughter. Don't think for a moment that Scarlett isn't equally capable of the same level of business-minded lack of emotion.' He drew a breath. 'I don't know if I can protect you from where Scarlett might want to take this.'

Until then the boy had still maintained a small amount of youthful expectation that the 'real grown-up'—in this case, Lorenzo—would be able to fix this for him. That expectation faded to outright concern now.

In tandem with Dante's reaction, anger inside Scarlett began to bubble up. So she was the ogre of the piece now? The one who could single-handedly destroy this boy, who clearly simply needed someone to help him get back on a straight path?

Scarlett would have Lorenzo know that she had…
Never dealt with anything quite like this.

Scarlett drew a deep breath, but it still didn't help her to dispense with the tight ache in the middle of her chest that had come from Lorenzo saying she was cold.

Could he really believe Scarlett could have no feelings for those around her?

Scarlett's hand crept up to touch her ribbon, to let her fingers absorb its soft feel.

She wasn't like that. Not really. Not deep down inside herself, and Lorenzo had known her well enough to know that. Scarlett hated that this man still had the power to cause her hurt. She'd healed from that. She'd moved on whether she now happened to be back in his actual realm of existence, or not.

'You won't get another warning.' Lorenzo glared at the boy. 'I won't discuss this with Scarlett at this stage, but don't break the rules here again. Do I make myself clear?'

'Yes. We're clear. I'm sorry.'

'You've got a chance to straighten yourself out, Dante. Don't mess it up, okay?' Lorenzo reached out to lay his hand on the boy's shoulder.

They'd both turned as they spoke, so Scarlett clearly saw the flinch, quickly disguised as a shrug when Lorenzo's hand landed on the boy's shoulder.

What—?

'You're bruised. What happened?' Lorenzo's brows drew down as his gaze examined Dante's shoulder where his shirt had pulled open a little.

And Lorenzo's expression was really odd. His face had paled. He looked sick. He had an expression in his eyes that Scarlett had…seen before? Why did that expression look like concern…and some kind of shame?

'I went mountain cycling. I fell off.' The boy uttered the words in a rapid stream as he tugged his shirt back into place. 'On the weekend. I fell into a bush.'

The words were so clearly a lie. But…why?

Lorenzo's eyes narrowed before he hurriedly rearranged his face into a mask of agreement. 'Injuries can happen in all sorts of ways.'

Like Lorenzo getting bruised and scratched falling from his motorcycle. He hadn't owned it long when Scarlett met him, and he'd told her while they were seeing each other that he'd taken several spills.

But Dante—Dante was hiding some kind of physical damage that he didn't want to tell the truth about, that *hadn't* happened riding his bike in the mountains.

Dante was unhappy at home suddenly. Unhappy enough that he'd resorted to stealing with the intention of drinking his unhappiness away?

Was Lorenzo thinking what Scarlett was thinking? Was that why Lorenzo looked sick to his heart?

'You're growing up, Dante.' Lorenzo said this with a careful air of mild interest. 'Maybe you should think about moving out of home, spread your wings a little, eh?' He forced a laugh. 'You might meet a nice girl. You won't want to have your mamma looking over your shoulder when you do that.' He drew a breath. 'In fact, I know of a woman who takes in boarders. If they're willing to help her out around the place she'll board them cheaply.'

'I'd be interested, if I could afford it.' The boy all but jumped on the suggestion. 'If she didn't want too much.'

Lorenzo shrugged as though he'd already lost most of his

interest in the topic. 'She's always up early. You could see her now, before you have to come back for your shift later.'

Dante nodded. 'Yes, that would be good, if I could see her now.'

'I'll write the name and address down for you.' Lorenzo walked to the bench and took an order pad and stub of pencil and started to scribble on it.

Scarlett realised her presence would be noted very soon if she didn't move. It was too late to disappear so her best bet was to pretend she was just arriving. She gave the door a push behind her and allowed it to bump against her back.

A couple of noisy steps forward and both their heads turned. Chirpiness was beyond her. Lorenzo's hurtful words still echoed inside her, as did concern for Dante. *Scarlett* felt sick, too. If Dante was being abused, that was a terrible thing.

'Lorenzo.' She nodded towards Dante, too, but for his sake didn't make any attempt at eye contact before she turned back to the head chef.

'I just thought I'd let you know my plans for today. I want to observe, speak with employees as I see fit, and start my study of the account books.' There would be times they would have to liaise, but Scarlett had made the decision in the past few minutes to ensure those times were kept to the absolute minimum.

Let Lorenzo think she was cold and emotionless and say 'just like her mother'. Scarlett knew her heart. She wasn't about to let Lorenzo stomp all over it, though! 'Please ensure any receipts, requisitions forms and any other money-related paperwork you might have lying around is delivered to my office. Can you do that before noon?'

She'd intended to apologise for yesterday's assumptions about his work commitments. A concession to his need for time was the closest he would now get.

Lorenzo's gaze locked on her face and searched her eyes, her expression. Scarlett knew what he would see. She'd seen it enough times herself in a mirror. A somewhat different version of Lisa's facial features in full chill-mode. How else could she protect herself?

Scarlett heaved a deep breath and slowly released it.

'I'll bring you everything I have.' Lorenzo handed the written note to Dante, but his gaze didn't leave Scarlett's face. 'Did you hear—?'

'Thank you. I've only just arrived but I really need to get to work so I hope you'll understand if I don't hang about right now. Excuse me.' She walked away before Lorenzo could do a thing about it. Not that she wanted to speak to the man now.

He might have helped Dante, and Scarlett was genuinely glad this had happened. By the sounds of it the boy needed all the help he could get.

But Lorenzo had also said some cutting things about Scarlett's personality in the process.

She didn't feel like dwelling on that, or discussing it, or anything else other than getting on with the job here and ignoring the existence of one Lorenzo Nesta and his capacity to upset her.

He shouldn't even possess that capacity.

Not at all any more!

CHAPTER THREE

'THANK you all for staying back for this meeting.' Scarlett uttered the words and let her gaze travel over each of the employees present. It was the end of her second day at Rosa's restaurant. The dinner hour was over, tables and chairs stacked, the kitchen clean and tidy. For the next few minutes it would be the site of their meeting.

Scarlett's office was not tidy. It was covered with bookwork, sheaves of account invoices and receipts. Amongst it were Lorenzo's records of kitchen expenditure. He was very thorough, and in fact so far his bookkeeping was the easiest to understand of all of this.

When Lorenzo had delivered his bookkeeping records to the office, he'd apologised for his words about her that morning. He'd clearly figured out she'd been standing there, had heard it all. He'd explained he'd wanted to scare the boy into behaving better but not make him feel as if he didn't have a friend in Lorenzo if he needed one.

Scarlett had…admired him for that and realised he hadn't been out to hurt her feelings with his words. She'd suggested the police needed to be called in to try to make sure the mother was safe. Lorenzo had surprised her with his wisdom in the matter.

Let Dante get out of there first. Once he's safe, I will make the call to the police myself. I'll ask them to check on Dante's

*mother when they're certain the boyfriend won't be around,
though it's quite possible he isn't harming her.*

He had seemed extremely uncomfortable with the topic.

Well, this understanding man was part of the Lorenzo
Scarlett had known and…

Scarlett reached behind her and twisted her hair ribbon
through her ponytail before she forced her hand back to her
side. What she'd felt or hadn't felt about Lorenzo in the past
was irrelevant now.

'I know it's late and I'm sure you'd all rather be at home
now so I'll keep this as brief as possible.' When she felt certain
she had the absolute attention of everyone there, she went on.
'I'll repeat this meeting with the remaining staff tomorrow.'

Scarlett reached for a small sheaf of papers on the bench
and handed it to the nearest person. 'If you'd take one of those
and pass the rest down the line?'

While her printouts circulated, Scarlett drew a breath and
squared her shoulders. Her gaze, whether she wanted it to or
not, shifted to Lorenzo. He stood right at the end of the group
and was the last to receive his copy of her printout.

Why did he get to look not even slightly dishevelled after
a long shift at work? And why was she noticing how Lorenzo
looked anyway?

'Everyone, what you have in your hands is a new streamlined roster, and two pages outlining expectations of you as
a staff member of Rosa.' From her discussions today with
Isabella, Scarlett suspected much of the necessity for change
in these areas came down to Luca being too lenient in certain
respects.

In the end, the how of it didn't really matter. Scarlett had
Luca's agreement that she was to set things straight here, and
she would.

Her gaze fell briefly on Dante. She wished the boy *had*
got his bruises falling off his bicycle, as Lorenzo had done

taking spills from his motorcycle years ago. At least Lorenzo had worked out Dante's problem. He'd done his best to give Dante a lifeline without harming the boy's pride. That had been kind.

You mustn't soften towards Lorenzo just because of that act of kindness. He's still a love rat.

'Work conditions, pay conditions, holidays and negotiation of time off in this establishment have all been extremely generous to this point.' Scarlett made a concerted effort to keep her thoughts on the task at hand. 'The conditions have been far more generous than the accepted norm in restaurants in this country.'

If there'd ever been written employment contracts Scarlett hadn't been able to find them. She suspected Luca would have made verbal arrangements and felt those were enough. Only by studying the rosters and what people were getting paid for hours of work, what paid holidays they received and so on, had Scarlett pieced together that her uncle had indeed been giving away too much too easily around here in his commitment to 'treating his staff well'.

Lorenzo seemed to be the only one who worked properly for his entitlements, and, in his case, he kept meticulous time sheets and never asked for overtime despite working longer hours than his weekly wage suggested he should. Since starting here four months ago he'd yet to take any extra day off that he wasn't fully entitled to.

Muttering started from a few people as they looked at the rosters.

Scarlett had expected that, but it was best to make these changes now rather than later. They wouldn't salvage Rosa in and of themselves, but they were one step in the right direction at least. 'I'd encourage you to take your handouts home and examine them. I'm certain when you do that, you'll see that the conditions are on a par—'

'This roster means I have to start an hour earlier.' The woman who made the comment spoke over Scarlett's words. She was a waitress who worked lunch shifts only. Late thirties, with high-school-aged children and a husband who ran a small farming concern not far out of Monta Correnti.

The woman turned to Lorenzo. 'It doesn't suit me to be here earlier. I have to do my housework after the family leaves for school and work each day. When *you* tried to change this, Luca said—'

'Excuse me.' Scarlett said the words firmly and waited for the woman to glance her way. 'I recall speaking with you earlier today. In fact, I've spoken with each and every staff member, explained my presence here and let you all know that, for the extent of my stay, Luca has handed the reins of control of Rosa to me.'

Did this woman think she could turn to Lorenzo and usurp Scarlett's authority? It sounded as though she'd already used Luca's generous outlook to undermine *Lorenzo's* authority, too.

That can't have been easy on the head chef, Scarlett admitted silently. She held the woman's gaze. 'I am your boss now and, while you are always welcome to discuss any concerns with our head chef in his role as Assistant Manager, it's not appropriate to do so as you've just done, ignoring my authority in the process.'

'Well, I merely wanted—'

'Miss Gibson is quite right.' Lorenzo seemed to be having his own battle. His fingers were clenched about the copy of the paperwork he'd received as his gaze took in the small group of faces. 'If changes need to be made here, perhaps it's best to be grateful that you still have a job. I've only been made aware of these changes now, as you all have, but, at first glance at least, they still seem fair and equitable to me.'

His eyes gentled as he looked at the other woman. 'Perhaps

you can rearrange your schedule so you clean your home after your shift instead of before it.'

When the woman looked ready to argue again, Scarlett spoke. What was her name? 'Maria, I'm sorry, but it doesn't suit Rosa to have one of the wait staff arriving to start a lunch shift when everyone else is run off their feet already and your presence was needed an hour earlier. Are there special circumstances for why you absolutely can't make it earlier?'

The woman dropped her gaze and muttered beneath her breath, but eventually shook her head.

'All right.' Scarlett let her gaze travel over the group. 'Across the board I've streamlined the rosters to maximise staff availability at the busiest times of the day. As staff are paid on a Thursday, this new roster will start straight after pay day, this Friday.'

She drew a breath. 'Within the next week we'll be getting ourselves up to date with written employment contracts for all staff members. It's in your best interests, as well as Rosa's, to have these in place so you know things will have to go through due process if there are ever problems.

'You'll all see that I've made it part of your conditions here that you don't try to swap rosters at the last minute unless there's a case of genuine emergency. Those will be assessed if and when they arise. Rosa will function best if we run a tight show.'

That about covered the roster side of it. 'Please read the written conditions. You'll be expected to adhere to those from now on. Cuts in the number of paid holidays et cetera simply bring Rosa into line with industry standards.'

Scarlett wound the meeting up. 'If any of you wish to discuss any aspect of the new conditions after you've read them, you are most welcome to book a meeting with me to do so. Thank you, and goodnight.'

They filed out. Good staff, many of them, and possibly a

few less than great ones. Let them go to their homes, read the conditions, take the time to absorb them and hopefully realise they were, indeed, quite reasonable.

Lorenzo was the one person who didn't file out with the others. 'That was unexpected.'

Scarlett drew a breath. 'These steps have to be taken. I thought you understood that.'

'Of course.' He spread his hands. 'As your assistant manager, I could have supported your cause better if I'd known your plans. That's all.'

Scarlett had forged ahead without consulting him or asking for his support. She admitted this. Emotionally, she didn't trust him and yet, when it came to Rosa, Isabella trusted Lorenzo. Luca trusted Lorenzo. The other staff seemed to trust Lorenzo. *Could he be* a wonderfully supportive assistant manager to Scarlett? Could they work together like that, despite their past history?

'I will try to keep that in mind in future.' In this moment, that was the best she could come up with.

Tomorrow. She would force herself to totally assess all of this tomorrow. Scarlett cast a longing glance at the door. 'It's, um, it's getting late. We should be going.'

Scarlett needed to go, so she could stop being aware of the fact that they were here alone. Alone, together, for the first time in five years. She was pushing that knowledge down as hard as she could, but it was still there.

Why couldn't she simply respond to him in the same way she responded to anyone? *Only* treat him as a co-worker. Her tummy was suddenly in knots and…

'I'll walk you to your bedsit.'

He already knew of this? 'How do you know—?'

'This is Monta Correnti.' He gestured to the restaurant. 'And this is Rosa, which is owned by Luca, who is a member of your family, which makes your presence here the topic of a great deal of interest amongst staff and patrons alike. Did you think the news that you'd moved out of Lisa's villa and into your bedsit wouldn't travel all through the restaurant in minutes?'

He shook his head. 'All the family gets talked about here, Scarlett. A week ago, it might have been "The Angel of New York's" baseball career, but your presence gets its degree of attention, too.'

Scarlett had not as yet met Luca's sons, Alex and Angelo, born to an American woman. Her Italian family certainly knew how to keep life complicated, though Scarlett wasn't at all sure that *she* wanted any time under the Rosa staff's microscope!

'Actually, I hadn't thought that news would travel through the restaurant at all.' She tugged so hard on her ribbon that it came out in her hand. Scarlett compulsively threaded it through her fingers and decided it wasn't fair that she had dressed for success and got through a *big* day, only to be startled by the strength of the gossip mill right at the end of it.

'Your nose is scrunching,' he said softly. This observation was followed by a frown that seemed self-repressive before he quickly turned his gaze away and headed for the door. 'It's less than five minutes' walk to your bedsit. I'm sure you can deal with my company for that long, despite your efforts to avoid me today.'

'I did not.' She had, though, and why did a tingle go over Scarlett's skin and her breath catch in her throat at the thought of him walking her home, for goodness' sake? 'As for moving to the bedsit, it's not that I wasn't happy at Mamma's villa.'

'Happy to the degree that you chose to move yourself into a bedsit after just two days there? And that was with your mother not even in residence in her home at the time.' He shook his head. 'You left her at age twelve, preferring to move to the other side of the world and live with your father, Scarlett. I haven't forgotten that you told me that, or of your inability to feel close to her.'

He hesitated. 'I also hear plenty about Lisa in terms of her ownership of Sorella. Your mother's restaurant is our key rival for business here.'

'Well, at least this way I avoid any conflict of interest.' Scarlett dropped her guard a little. 'I'm sure Mum would understand. Working for Luca, I couldn't allow that. Really, I should have thought of it before I came over here.'

'Certainly. I'm sure your mother should understand this.' A twinkle in his eyes showed that he could see the strategy in Scarlett's outlook. A moment later his smile faded to a more serious expression. 'Scarlett, this morning I said things about you—'

'It's all right. You explained why you made me the ogre of the piece.'

He shook his head. 'I could have thought of a better way to handle that. Realising Dante's situation…threw me off. Enough that it took all my attention to not let him know what I'd worked out.'

'You allowed him to keep his pride.'

'Sometimes pride is all a man has left.' The moment the words emerged, he clamped his lips together.

There were shadows in the backs of Lorenzo's eyes as Scarlett searched them. But he quickly shielded those eyes with long silky lashes.

'Will Dante be able to move into that boarding accommodation?' She needed to focus on that, not on her rising consciousness of Lorenzo.

Anyway, it had to be a 'workers co-operating for the better good' kind of affinity that Scarlett was feeling. Anything else would be quite insane.

Lorenzo nodded. 'He did so this morning.'

'That's good.' Scarlett glanced behind her to make absolutely sure they truly were alone. 'I can get alongside him; watch him for a while to make sure he's okay. That that horrid man, whoever he is, isn't still—'

'You don't have to worry about that. I'll keep a close watch on Dante.' Oh, his voice was so deep, so soft.

As was the expression in his eyes as he looked at her. Out of nowhere a sense of affinity rose between them. Scarlett opened her mouth and spoke straight out of that fellow feeling. 'I trust you to do that.'

She realised that she did. Without any hesitation, she knew she could trust Lorenzo with that. He might have hurt her, let her down five years ago, but she just knew this.

He's a good head chef, Scarlett. Isabella had said this.

When Luca discussed Lorenzo, he'd gone even further. *I have great faith in him.*

Maybe it was the faith of Isabella and Luca that gave Scarlett this belief in Lorenzo. Or maybe it was what she had seen of his work practices and ethics in the past two days. But they didn't seem to compute with the 'love rat' image Scarlett had carried of him for the past five years.

As Scarlett really didn't know how to address these thoughts, she turned her attention elsewhere. 'You said this morning that Dante had taken a key that Luca kept as a spare? That Dante used that to let himself into the restaurant?'

'Yes. Luca had a secret hiding place where he kept a spare key in case he ever lost his.' Lorenzo drew a key chain from the pocket of his chef's pants. There were two matching keys on it. 'I knew about it, but I thought Isabella and I were the only ones aside from Luca who did. I should have thought better of that assumption.'

He shook his head. 'In any case, that hiding place is no more. Would you like the second key?'

'No, I have one from my uncle.' Luca *had* run Rosa with

a naive degree of trust in some respects. This became more and more clear to Scarlett the more she learned about the restaurant.

'Then perhaps we should go.' Lorenzo uttered the words quietly.

'Yes.' Scarlett glanced up. The expression in Lorenzo's eyes made her breath catch in her throat.

Awareness, consciousness, memory. They were all there and for one brief moment they were all inside her, too. The feelings were so unexpected, and so opposite to what Scarlett had believed she felt towards him for five years, that she froze.

He drew a breath and stilled for a moment too before he blinked and got his feet moving and led the way to the kitchen doors. He pushed one open and stood back for her to precede him.

Somehow they made it outside and somehow she managed to say something about work as they headed across the square towards her bedsit. Her landlady had told her she travelled a lot, which suited Scarlett just fine. 'I hope the staff will realise they're not being given unreasonable conditions with the changes I've handed to them tonight.'

'If you continue to make and implement all your decisions without informing me before you put them into action, you'll make your job here harder than it needs to be.' His words were a soft murmur as his gaze travelled once again over her face, her eyes, and dropped...to her mouth before he gave an almost imperceptible shake of his head.

Scarlett forced herself to breathe carefully and evenly and not allow herself the same examination he had just taken. 'You feel that, as Head Chef and Manager, we should join our forces more?'

She had wished she could avoid him as much as she possibly could for the duration, but even Scarlett could admit that

wasn't very practical when he was her assistant, and the most
pivotal employee of Rosa.

'I don't want to usurp your authority here, but, yes, I do
feel we need to work together.' His expression told her he
wanted co-operation between them. 'I believe your likelihood
of success will be better if we combine our efforts.'

He held out one hand, palm up. 'We would present a united
front to the rest of the staff, if nothing else.'

'It *would* make for smoother sailing, provided you can
accept my—' Authority? Her being further up the employment ladder than him? Scarlett didn't quite know how to put
it, and she'd never worried about that kind of thing before!

'Provided I can accept your leadership in this workplace.'
He turned, just a little turn towards her, but it made the difference between two people talking from their safe distances
as they faced forwards and walked, and something just that
little bit more intimate.

Scarlett doubted he was even aware he'd done it, and she
could have taken one step away from him in any direction to
put an end to that feeling, but instead she continued to walk
exactly as close as she was to him.

Scarlett shoved her ribbon into the pocket of her dress and
told herself to get over it.

Whatever *it* was, exactly.

Well, she supposed 'it' was this strange feeling she had
that felt like a combination of history and remembering and
becoming conscious of Lorenzo all over again in ways she
hadn't anticipated and didn't welcome.

*Except that no matter how much you tell yourself you're
not, there's a part of you that is aware of him.*

'I'm prepared to discuss things with you, but my decisions
about the finances here are still final, no matter whether you
agree with them or not.' Even so saying, she felt the need to

temper her statement. 'I can see that two heads might be better than one with some of this. I suppose we can at least try.'

She had to do what was best for Rosa. If she felt this was best, such a decision didn't have to feel dangerous to Scarlett, dangerous to her emotional well-being. She wasn't about to fall in love with Lorenzo again, for crying out loud. They could work side by side for the betterment of Rosa. In fact, doing so would be really good for her because it would prove to her that she could remain completely emotionally distanced from him.

And physical attraction, Scarlett?

These few moments this evening of feeling a little too conscious of him, well, they were probably just a couple of old memories surfacing. They didn't mean anything and would be long gone and forgotten by tomorrow morning when she met him again at work.

Scarlett drew a breath that filled her lungs with the blunted scent of his aftershave lotion and realised they were somehow walking even closer than they had been. Their shoulders were leaning towards each other. He smelled familiar and…she was far too tired for this right now. Her defences were not as strong as they should be.

'Thank you. I want to help you, Scarlett, not get in the way of what you're trying to do here.' Lorenzo drew a deep breath.

They arrived at her bedsit and stepped into the lee of the door lintel.

'Goodnight—'

'Thank you for seeing me—'

He reached for her hand, perhaps to shake it.

Scarlett took a step towards the door as he did so, and they each stepped into the other's path. Lorenzo's hands came up to cup her elbows, perhaps to hold her still while he stepped around her.

Instead she glanced up. He glanced down into her eyes and a moment later, their lips met.

CHAPTER FOUR

'GOODNIGHT. I—thank you for seeing me home.' Scarlett uttered the words through lips that wanted to deny what had just happened.

Wanted to deny a kiss that had lasted less than a second, a mere brush of lips against lips before she and Lorenzo had both…broken away. They'd each stepped back as though they'd been burnt. 'I have to—'

She couldn't make calm words come out, couldn't do anything to downplay something that shouldn't even need to be downplayed and yet, to Scarlett, the entire world had stopped and then started up again and now it was spinning strangely and nothing felt quite right because of Lorenzo's kiss…

Barely even a kiss, Scarlett.

Somehow she got her key straight into the lock, twisted it and got the door open. Her feet carried her through and she closed the door. She didn't look back, and then through the closed door she heard his footsteps taking him away in a rapid stride that went, and then half missed a step, and then kept going.

He'd hesitated.

And as that happened Scarlett had leaned her shoulder against the closed door and shut her eyes and silently willed… What? For him to stop? Keep walking away?

She should have said something. Scarlett shouldn't have

allowed that kiss to happen in the first place. And that was the problem. Scarlett didn't believe either one of them had anticipated the kiss happening. It hadn't been planned or thought about. How could she protect against the possibility of something she simply hadn't expected?

For one little blink in time, five years had dropped away and they'd simply reached for each other. That should not, even for a second, have seemed the natural thing to do.

This had shocked her.

Perhaps it had also shocked Lorenzo.

Then maybe you should ask yourself how it's affected you now that it's happened?

Scarlett shook her head and went to the wardrobe to pull out her workout clothes of knee-length fitted black pants and lime-green vest-top and trainers. She clipped on her iPod, turned the music to a mind-numbing set, and began her Pilates routine.

Forget being kissed by a man who had no right to kiss her, before they both realised the insanity of their actions, and stopped. Forget how it had happened or why it had happened or anything else about it.

Scarlett was here for Rosa and her family and she only wanted to think about those issues. She forced her brain to the tricky issue of pulling Rosa into an utterly profitable financial position, and kept her thoughts there as she stretched and twisted and limbered away the tensions of her day.

Over the next five days, Scarlett forced aside what she chose to refer to in her thoughts when she couldn't avoid acknowledging it altogether, as 'that regrettable moment'. And indeed for the most part, she did a very good job of forgetting/ignoring/not confronting the issue in a tizzy of busyness at the restaurant.

She worked hard, visited often with Isabella and sometimes

with other family members. She also co-operated with Lorenzo in terms of the running of Rosa where that co-operation was needed, and he co-operated with her. Scarlett felt quite certain that Lorenzo also didn't give the matter of that one, tiny, completely insignificant slip that had occurred outside her bedsit a single thought.

She frowned and dipped her hand through the cool, clear swimming pool water. Today was Monday and the restaurant was closed during the main part of the day while the town observed a partial religious holiday. For those so inclined there'd been church services earlier. Rosa would staff up at four p.m. and open for business for the evening.

For now, Scarlett, Isabella and Scarlett's sister Jackie were lazing in this sheltered swimming pool that was available to townsfolk who belonged either as students or teachers to the study faculty that owned it. It was a hot day, and quiet and restful here. Getting away for this had been a very welcome idea.

Scarlett dipped her shoulders beneath the cool water. Her hair was up in an untidy knot on top of her head, secured with a hair band and a thick red ribbon that exactly matched her high-cut one-piece red suit. She was *not* obsessive-compulsive about her ribbons. Scarlett simply enjoyed finding new ones and matching them to her clothing.

Lorenzo has looked at each change of ribbon. His gaze goes often to your hair. He used to enjoy sifting it through his fingers...

Oh! Scarlett pinched her lips together. She was having a rest. Thinking about the head chef of Rosa was not on her agenda for right now. For at all! She turned to Jackie and forced a smile. 'This *is* nice. Thanks for talking me into joining you and Izzie.'

'You've been hard to pin down for any one-on-one time since you came back to Monta Correnti.' Jackie's words were not accusatory, simply honest. 'When Romano said he needed to come out here, I thought why not make a little pool party of it?'

Had Jackie chosen an event where Isabella would be present to make this a little easier for her sister? Scarlett didn't know what to say. Of all the family, Jackie was the one she found it most difficult to spend time with.

Her guilt over her sister's loss of her daughter, Kate, for so many years ate at her. Scarlett…didn't know how to deal with that. And she realised now, as she looked into Jackie's eyes, that she had been avoiding her sister *because* of this issue.

Before Scarlett could speak, and she didn't know what she would have said anyway, Jackie went on.

'Romano had to come out here anyway for a meeting. He only teaches an evening class once a week, but now that he's on the board of teachers things like that come up periodically.' Her voice softened as she spoke of the man who'd been her teenage lover and also the father of the baby that Jackie had given up for adoption. 'I figured we'd all be grateful for some time in the water, anyway.'

That was true. It was a hot day.

'Do you suppose we should actually make some appearance of swimming, just so we look like we belong in here?' Isabella asked the question without moving a muscle.

'Oh, I think somnolent suits us fairly well, don't you?' Scarlett inserted this quip and was proud of her effort. She wanted…to feel closer to Jackie, and to feel comfortable with her sister overall. That would be nice, but it wasn't going to happen while Scarlett kept putting off self-protective prickle vibes every time they were near each other.

Isabella seemed to have dealt with any guilt that she felt over Jackie's loss. Why couldn't Scarlett do the same and put all that behind her?

'Well, I'm not moving an inch until Romano finishes his

meeting with the others and comes to join us.' Jackie laughed and settled her arms more firmly back against the edge of the pool.

Isabella raised her brows in Scarlett's direction. 'You never said what the phone call was about from your mother yesterday at the restaurant, Scarlett. Is it anything I should know about, or tell Papa? I know we've put you in charge but I wouldn't want you to think you have to deal with everything all by yourself. If there are any issues with Sorella—'

'No, it wasn't about either of the restaurants.' Her mother and her uncle Luca owned a restaurant each. Their rivalry when it came to those restaurants was long-standing, though from the viewpoint of the staff actually working at Rosa, at least, Scarlett wasn't really picking up that vibe. They just wanted to get on with the job. It wouldn't surprise her too much to learn that the staff at Sorella felt the same way.

'As predicted, Izzie, Mamma wasn't happy to know that I'd moved out of her home.' Scarlett shrugged. 'She wasn't pleased initially to know that I was going to work at Rosa, either. I thought, when she invited me to stay at her villa while I was here, that she'd got over that.'

'I wish she and my father could just get along.' Isabella shook her head. 'I hope her call didn't upset you too much, Scarlett.'

'No. That's just Mamma. Her reaction just concreted it in for me that I'd made the right decision in moving out of her villa.' Scarlett let her glance encompass Jackie. 'As for my working at Rosa, that's my decision. It's got nothing to do with our mother.'

Jackie dipped her chin in acknowledgement. 'That sounds very fair to me.'

It was. And Scarlett appreciated the support. 'Mamma said that Elizabeth would never move out of her own mother's home making the entire town assume that home wasn't good enough for her.'

Jackie stared for a moment and then threw her head back and laughed.

Scarlett shook her head in bewilderment. 'What?'

'Lizzie might be the one of us who gets on the best with our mother, but Lizzie is also *living in Australia!* It's not as though she's right in Mamma's pocket all the time to test the friendship, so to speak.' Jackie's smile widened. 'It's just that *you're the one* who looks exactly like Mamma when you pull that intolerant, fed-up-to-the-gills expression.'

'Oh, thanks very much!' Scarlett flicked water at her sister and received the same treatment back.

Izzie, caught in the middle, squealed and ducked right under the water, which somewhat defeated the purpose if she'd been trying to avoid being splashed.

Scarlett and Jackie grinned at each other over Izzie's head as she resurfaced, and Scarlett's grin faded as that inexplicable ache started up in her chest again. She forced the smile to return and said as lightly as she could manage, 'I spent a little time getting to know Lizzie better over the past few months. We exchanged some emails and spent some time together in Melbourne one weekend.'

Scarlett and her eldest sister had sort of bonded. 'I wish I'd connected with her a lot sooner. We were both living in Australia. It would have been nice—'. She broke off, not wanting to make Jackie feel left out.

When she searched her sister's face, Scarlett couldn't help but comment on something else she'd noticed about Jackie. '*You* have a real glow about you, Jackie. Every time you fall silent your face gets this soft look.'

It was as though when her sister disappeared inside her own thoughts, whatever she found in there lit her up like a thousand candles all burning at once.

'Romano's a big part of the reason for that, of course.' Jackie's smile was indeed soft and glowing as she spoke of him, but it wasn't…all that Scarlett had seen in her sister.

'But Romano tells me the same thing any time I've been to visit with our daughter or we've had her over to spend time with us.' Jackie's mouth softened and love and happiness poured out of her. 'We know we can't take the place of the parents who've raised her. We wouldn't try. We're thrilled that Kate has been happy!

'But Kate has such a generous heart. She's let us in, let us be a second set of people who love her. I'm so happy to finally have even a "piece" of my daughter. The only problem is one of her sets of adopted grandparents. They're having a hard time accepting me, or Romano, as part of Kate's life.'

A fierce expression crossed Jackie's face. 'I wouldn't trade anything for having Kate back in my life, and just let anyone try to get in the way of that. I'm being polite but if anyone messed this up for me now and somehow took Kate out of my life again, I'd never forgive it.'

She cast a horrified glance at Scarlett. 'I didn't mean that to sound as though I can't—'

Forgive Scarlett for taking Kate out of her life?

'It's all right.' Scarlett's tummy twisted. 'I understand what you meant.'

But why shouldn't Jackie be angry anyway? And stay that way for as long as she wanted? Maybe never truly be able to forgive Scarlett way deep down where it mattered? Scarlett was the one whom Jackie had entrusted many years ago with a letter to Romano telling him about her pregnancy. And Scarlett had let that letter go into the river and never told…

Jackie bit her lip. 'I'm so happy. A part of me sometimes fears I could lose it all again. It's just that I don't think I could cope with that.'

'It won't happen, Jackie. Of course it won't.' It was Izzie

who reached out and took Jackie's hand, who held it and seemed able to keep Jackie's words in some kind of perspective that Scarlett, in this moment, tried to but couldn't.

All Scarlett could do was feel her sister's loss, deep down inside her soul, and acknowledge that loss was her, *Scarlett's,* fault. She'd run from truly acknowledging that for a long time.

Izzie went on. 'Kate loves you way too much to let that happen. You have to remember she's a grown-up girl with a mind of her own, just like you.'

Jackie shook her head as though to shake the dark thoughts away. 'I know. I get silly over it sometimes, too protective of what I've been given back, I guess.'

Izzie nodded. 'And you've had a lot of emotional ground to cover, getting back together with Romano after all this time as well, him learning of Kate's existence.'

And Jackie having to deal with being told that Scarlett and Izzie had caused all those barren years in her life by throwing her letter away that day instead of delivering it as Jackie had asked Scarlett to do.

A part of Scarlett wanted, quite desperately, to climb out of the swimming pool, claim some urgent and only just remembered prior engagement or something, and…run away. But she'd done that once already, had run all the way to Australia.

She'd gone to see her father. To get to know her father.

No, Scarlett. You ran away from the emotional upheaval of what you'd done. Getting to know Dad, being loved by him, was an unanticipated bonus.

'I've got some lovely photos of Kate, Scarlett.' Animation swept back into Jackie's face as she said this.

Beyond them, the door of the nearest building swung open and a small group of men stepped out. Scarlett's glance caught on one of them, half hidden from her view behind the others.

She was dreaming up Lorenzo's presence everywhere. Just because whoever that was was dark-haired and had a slender build and looked about the same height. Oh, maybe she just felt too overwhelmed in too many ways at the moment. And she couldn't just ignore what Jackie had said.

Scarlett had to stop this nonsense, otherwise Jackie might start to think she wasn't happy for her and that truly would be awful. 'Izzie mentioned that you'd got some great photos of–of—Kate.'

'I'd like you to see them.' Jackie's eyes softened. 'At least that way you can start to feel as though you know her a little. Do you know, I can see Romano in her eyes and the shape of her nose.'

Jackie went on, enthusing about her daughter's physical features. To hear Jackie tell it, her daughter was the most beautiful girl ever to exist.

It hurt Scarlett to hear it, even though it made her happy for Jackie, too. 'I'd…love to see the photos, Jackie.' What else could she say?

'I'll put a CD together for you.' Jackie glanced towards the approaching men and raised her voice. 'Romano. Come swim!' She started to swim towards the other end of the pool to greet the love of her life.

Izzie laid her hand on Scarlett's arm. 'Are you okay, Scarlett? Jackie's fine, you know. She's bound to have these moments, but you heard her. Her life is so happy overall.'

'I can see that.' And Scarlett was happy for Jackie for that. Of course she was. 'But she's also dealing with old grief, and with feelings about family that you and I can only try to understand. She's got a very generous heart, to be able or even willing to brush aside my part in all that the way she is.'

'And mine.' Isabella's face tightened. 'I was as much to blame.'

'Not really. I'm the one Jackie entrusted that letter to.'

Isabella drew a breath and the tension faded from her face. She raised her arm to wave. 'Lorenzo, I didn't know you were out here. Come join us.'

Scarlett froze. She wanted to look, but she didn't want him to know that she was interested.

Excuse me, you're not *interested!*

But Scarlett turned her head just as there was a quiet splash. And there was Lorenzo slicing through the water towards them. Vaguely, Scarlett registered Romano and Jackie and another man in the water at the other end of the pool, talking. And Isabella talking.

'We should do this more often, Scarlett. I could talk to Jackie about another visit here.' Isabella's voice went on.

But Scarlett wasn't really listening. And all she could see was Lorenzo. Bare-chested, his lithe body slicing through the water as he moved with neat strokes until he surfaced at their end of the pool, a little to Isabella's left.

He seemed…more comfortable with his body nowadays. Maybe maturity had brought that to him? Because back then he'd never liked to swim publicly, or even take his shirt off in front of others. He'd hated Scarlett to even see it if he'd had one of his spills and had a bruise or a scratch. At other times he'd been fine…

'Scarlett? Did you hear me?' Izzie asked the question in a puzzled tone.

What her cousin might have said prior to that, well, actually Scarlett had no idea. 'Sorry, Izzie?' Scarlett dredged her mind. 'Oh, yes, it would be fun to come here again.' The pool was shaded with beautiful trees and the whole complex was set halfway up a quiet hillside with a beautiful view over a lush green valley.

Scarlett had to act normally. She had already seemed quite out of it to her cousin. And she *could* be normal around Lorenzo. Of course she could. He was just a man!

He's the man you had an affair with five years ago when he was still married.

Well, yes, but Scarlett hadn't known about that until it was too late.

And she didn't have those feelings about him any more. Being in his company simply made her uneasy because of past history, that was all.

'Hello, Lorenzo.' There. You see? She sounded perfectly normal.

Scarlett's hand rose to pat at the ribbon in her hair. It got halfway to its goal before she stopped herself and let her arm fall back into the water.

It wasn't helping that Lorenzo was practically naked, and look how tanned he was, and muscular, and he *was* wearing the medallion…

'It's a lovely day for a swim.' Scarlett pushed her lips up into a very, very natural and completely relaxed and not at all overly conscious of him smile. 'Do you teach classes out here or something?'

'The board wanted to discuss that possibility with me.' His eyes were narrowed.

Against the sun, Scarlett told herself, and refused to acknowledge that his gaze had followed the movement of her hand, had tracked the rest of the way to touch on her messy knot of hair before it travelled gently over her face and bare shoulders.

'Um, well, that sounds interesting.' She glanced at her cousin, whose gaze was passing from her to Lorenzo and back again.

'With what they wanted, I'd have considered it a conflict

of interest against my work at Rosa.' He gave a shrug. 'So unfortunately I had to turn the offer down.'

'I see.' Scarlett should have thought of the possible threat to Rosa straight away.

Well, it would be nice if she could think anything beyond wanting to swim over to him and speak at a much closer level, wouldn't it? One that involved ignoring the presence of the others in the pool, and preferably allowing their lips to meet...

So much for telling herself that first kiss had been some random thing, like tripping over and falling onto his mouth or something. Maybe she should have examined that first kiss and its impact on her, rather than trying to pretend it hadn't happened. Would that have better equipped her for now?

Failing that, Scarlett had another highly appropriate plan to implement. 'I must take advantage and do some laps before we have to leave.'

She uttered the words as though to Isabella, and made an odd waving motion with one hand. 'Excuse me. Do feel free to talk amongst yourselves.'

And with this obscure blessing handed to Izzie and Lorenzo, who both probably stared after her as though she'd lost her mind at the bottom of the swimming pool, Scarlett set off to do laps.

Perhaps until she swam herself into oblivion.

At least until she would no longer be conscious of Lorenzo's presence in such an *everything-else-fades-to-black* kind of way.

Izzie wouldn't have noticed anything all that odd in Scarlett's reactions to Lorenzo, would she?

Scarlett increased her pace, churning through the water as though by doing so she might somehow escape all of her thoughts.

She decided Izzie would not have noticed, and, not only

that, Scarlett didn't have to think about anything. Not Lorenzo, not family, not her guilt over Jackie, not sending herself to Australia for years and years and then coming back here with all sorts of hopes apparently tucked away inside her like unexpected add-ons that she shouldn't have stuffed into her mental suitcases.

Stroke, breathe. Stroke, breathe.

Scarlett focused one hundred, no, *two hundred* per cent of her attention on her movements through the water.

And pushed every other distraction right out!

CHAPTER FIVE

'THERE has to be an answer somewhere. I just *know* it's there, but I can't zero in on it.' Scarlett murmured the words beneath her breath, mostly in the hopes of getting them out of her head.

Her swim earlier this afternoon felt aeons away. Night had fallen outside the restaurant while she slaved away in Luca's office inputting financial information onto a computer system to bring Rosa's paperwork side of things—kicking and screaming if necessary—into the twenty-first century.

Well, it had been a big day. Scarlett had come out onto the terrace that adjoined with Sorella's terrace for a breath of air, even if that air was still quite warm and balmy.

There was nobody out here at this time of night, and in fact, though the terraces joined, there was an air of disuse about both of them.

She had to stop this nonsense when it came to Rosa's head chef. She had to stop it *right now,* if not sooner. It just wasn't right that she still could react to him that way when he'd broken her heart, let her down so badly.

Yes, but he's also been the epitome of a fabulous head chef since you've been at Rosa. He's committed to the restaurant. You saw how wonderful he was with Dante and that whole situation. Isabella thinks the world of him.

Maybe Lorenzo had changed.

And, well, five years on…

She'd heard on the rumour-mill, during her last trip over here that the new head chef at Rosa was single, so he'd done the right thing in the end and got out of that loveless relationship. That meant he was free now.

Just what do you mean by that, Scarlett? Free for you to get involved with a second time? Are you nuts?

She wasn't crazy but Scarlett *was* still somewhat attracted to Lorenzo. That didn't have to be an issue, though!

'Here you are. I thought you might have still been holed up in Luca's office.'

Lorenzo's words were low-pitched, in tune with the quiet atmosphere out here. Scarlett's reaction was for her pulse to skip before she turned slowly to face him.

'I came out for a breath of air.' She *had* been working in Luca's office for a lot of hours.

'Well, now you can have something to refresh you at the same time. Don't worry.' He pressed one of two glasses of red wine into her hand.

Their fingers brushed as Scarlett automatically took the drink from him. She tried not to notice the warmth of his fingers, the familiarity of taking a glass from him. The quiet of the night around them or how it felt good to stand here with him, just the two of them. 'Worry?'

'About the expense.' He gestured with his glass. 'I'm not costing the restaurant money. A patron bought this whole bottle, had us uncork it, and then ended up leaving without touching it.'

'Oh. Yes. Very good. Well, thank you for the drink.' She said it rather assertively and took a sip. Scarlett would *not* reach for the ribbon in her hair. It was navy blue this evening, velvet and soft and…comforting.

Not reaching.

Don't need to feel comforted.

Doing just fine holding up all by myself.

Not tempted by Lorenzo, either.

Totally not thinking about being kissed by him and how that one brief kiss only made me want—

Nothing. Scarlett wanted nothing from Lorenzo aside from good cooking. 'I thought you'd be in the kitchen. Has the clientele eased off already?'

'Not only has it eased off, the evening is over, Scarlett.' He sipped from his own glass of wine.

'Really?' Scarlett's gaze dipped to the strong column of his neck, to the bob of his Adam's apple as he swallowed the rich red.

What was she doing? Letting herself enjoy Lorenzo's company? Lorenzo's words finally got through the fog of what she decided must be over-tiredness messing up her normal thought patterns.

Scarlett frowned. 'Has the restaurant closed?'

'Yes. It's just as well I check the building thoroughly before I leave. You might have ended up spending the night out here.' He leaned one arm against the railing that edged the terraced area. 'Did you even eat the meal I sent in to you earlier?'

'I did. Thank you.' Every day Lorenzo made sure she ate. He took care of her that way, even when she had her head down for hours and hours, like today. 'I want to get Rosa into a truly successful position and keep the restaurant there.'

'You've implemented changes, and smoothed ruffled feathers of various staff members when necessary.' He sipped his wine again. 'Bringing staff conditions into a more sensible place has to be a good start.'

'A good start, yes, but it's not going to be enough.' Working on the books had made that abundantly clear. 'We need to lift our client base and keep it lifted.' She didn't notice the change in her speech from 'I' to 'we'.

As the days passed, Lorenzo had worked quietly to support

her efforts. And somehow through that, Scarlett had started to trust him and rely on him.

Only as the head chef here. Well, as the *assistant manager* and head chef.

'I've stopped you from going home. I'm sorry. I lost track of the time.' That had happened while she turned her mind inside out trying to find a larger overall solution to Rosa's financial issues.

Now all Scarlett could register was Lorenzo's closeness. She had to pull herself together!

'Maybe you should tell me what brought you out here in the first place.' He said it as an invitation, not a challenge.

And Scarlett found herself responding. 'I have to find a way to let the general public know the true value of Rosa.' She let her gaze meet his in the dimness.

His eyes gleamed with interest in what she was saying, but there was more, too, and Scarlett went on a little breathlessly.

'There has to be a way to make Rosa stand out against a neighbour like the glitzy, internationally flavoured Sorella.' She had sent out a feeler for one idea that might help.

Scarlett would have elaborated on that.

But he chose that moment to lay his hand on her arm. 'If there is any other way I can help—I can work longer hours—'

'You already give of your time and don't claim the overtime you should.' This was also something that had bothered Scarlett. Of all the staff that Rosa employed, Lorenzo was the one who should be paid *more*.

She tried not to react to the knowledge of his hand against the bare skin of her arm, tried not to want more of his touch. Yet when he finally dropped his hand away, she missed it.

'That's not important at the moment.' He turned his head

away, almost as though her comprehending his generosity had embarrassed him.

'You—you made us some money catering to that movie star for her special lunch.' Oh, Scarlett wanted to rest *her* hand against his arm, to touch him and feel his warmth.

'Maybe we need to find a way to bring Hollywood to Rosa's front door.' He smiled a little as he said it.

'Yes, why not? We'll move the entire tinsel town here. Do you think anyone would notice it had gone missing?' Scarlett returned his smile. They fell silent and finished their wine and…he was so close. She could smell the scent of his cologne, and old memories suddenly got all tangled up with the here and now.

She dropped her gaze away from him. The goal that had been to think about the future of Rosa and see if a break from the office would rattle loose any other ideas inside her mind faded in the face of her awareness of him.

Why was Lorenzo different from any other man? Surely, lots of men could kiss her and make her feel the same way he did. Or even better. Not that Scarlett had kissed a whole lot of men in the past years, and not that any of the candidates she had kissed had stacked up.

She'd been busy building her career. For that reason she hadn't involved herself in a great amount of dating.

And so what if none of them had swept her away?

These thoughts were *not* productive, especially at this time of night when she was obviously weary and not able to think clearly.

'Has it been hard for you, Scarlett? Coming back like this?' He turned and somehow their fingers were brushing, just gently touching on the railing. 'You seemed unhappy when I first saw you today at the swimming pool with your sister and Isabella.'

'I didn't think you'd see.' What *had* he seen? She searched his gaze, and somehow in the dim quietness the words came out. 'It's no secret now, that Jackie had a daughter a long time ago. What most people wouldn't know is that I all but single-handedly separated them back then. This afternoon at the pool, when Jackie was talking about Kate, I felt guilty for the way I'd hurt her.'

Scarlett felt emotion clog her throat, and she was appalled. She shouldn't have let this out. 'You mustn't say anything to anyone. That's…'

'Your business, and Jackie's business.' He shook his head. 'I won't say anything. I…understand about secrets.'

Until he said those words, Scarlett had thought he might pull her into his arms, hold her, and perhaps try to kiss those painful emotions away.

She would have let him.

In fact, somewhere deep inside she admitted she might even have wanted that.

But his admission about secrets hung between them, a thinly veiled reference to his past marriage.

'Well, I'm being a bit dramatic all of a sudden.' Scarlett made as light of things as she could manage. 'I shouldn't have brought that old history up. Jackie just wants to forget it now that she has Kate in her life again. And, it's late. We should go in. I'm sure you'd like to leave. I'm sorry I held things up daydreaming out here.'

Scarlett turned for the inside of the restaurant. She hadn't exactly been daydreaming, but he would know what she meant.

'Yes, of course we can go.' Lorenzo looked at the tight set of Scarlett's shoulders. She had on a simple light tan sheath that looked cool and comfortable, and brought out the beauty of her bone structure and the golden glow of her skin.

That glow had been in her face, too, until he stupidly brought up her earlier unease in her sister's company.

Yet he couldn't really regret it, because Scarlett had given him a gift just now. The gift of her trust for just a few moments before her openness made her uneasy and she wished she could have taken it all back.

He had wanted to comfort her but he'd drawn back from that, too. How could he do that when the guilt of his past plagued him? The guilt of his past and…the complications of his present.

'I'll see you home.' He'd walk her over and walk away. That was all he could do with Scarlett. What else did he have to offer her? Nothing. Lorenzo was not free to offer Scarlett anything.

And of course, after all this time, he didn't still want to. It had to be their past that made it difficult for him to maintain equilibrium in his thoughts where she was concerned.

'No, thanks.' She walked ahead of him through the restaurant, glanced back over her shoulder. 'By the time you finish locking up and get on your motorcycle I'll be there. I'll be fine, Lorenzo. I don't need you to go with me.'

She left him there, and he did watch to make sure she got home safely while her words rang in his head.

They didn't need each other.

That had to be the truth of it.

Didn't it?

'You'll understand if I ask you to explain your reasoning for whatever choices you make today?' Scarlett asked the question quietly as Lorenzo drew Rosa's small van to a stop outside a set of shops in a nearby larger township.

'Of course.' Lorenzo wasn't concerned to know that Scarlett would spend this morning scrutinising his work practices. He had nothing to hide.

They were on a buying expedition, and both of them were in a mellow mood.

A cooling breeze had driven the worst of the heat away. The day was clear and fresh. It was nice to be away from the restaurant for a little while. Isabella had taken charge to free Lorenzo for his expedition. He'd climbed into the van and Scarlett had joined him so she could see what one of his buying trips consisted of. When he'd turned the key in the ignition, old rock music had blared out of the van's speakers.

Scarlett had thrown her head back and laughed and he'd… laughed with her. He'd turned the volume down a little and they'd made the trip with the windows down, the wind whipping through their hair and against their faces. It had been… fun.

Lorenzo glanced at Scarlett's flushed face, and couldn't help the soft smile that came to his lips. 'You can cross-question me all you like. I want Rosa to succeed as much as you do.'

Lorenzo got out of the van to stride around the front and open Scarlett's door with a bow and a flourish. 'Shall we go?'

For a moment she froze, but then a smile came over her face and she held out her hand and lifted her nose into the air at such a haughty angle it was a wonder it didn't catch on the top of the doorframe. 'By all means let us go, but you should know, I'm not carrying the basket for you.'

'Actually, I have string bags, and I'll be doing the carrying myself.' He gripped her hand and helped her out, and their hands slid away from each other with a slow glide of fingers.

They went shopping. Lorenzo made his choices as carefully as he always did. These were ingredients and items he couldn't get for the kitchen locally in Monta Correnti.

Scarlett observed, questioned his brand choices, and nodded her approval as he carefully explained how each item would be used.

When they'd finished the shopping for Rosa, he gestured towards another small shop. 'If you don't mind me taking the time, I'd like a few things from in there for my home stores. They can wait if you'd prefer.'

'No, that's fine.' Her eyes had lit up as she realised what they were looking at. It was a chocolate wholesaler. She turned to glance at him with her brows raised. 'I know you make fabulous desserts. You were working on some the first day I started at Rosa, but I wouldn't have pictured you with a sweet tooth for it.'

'Then picture again.' He smiled and shrugged his shoulders. 'I occasionally make them at home. Partly to keep my hand in and my capabilities sharp, but mostly—' he smiled '—so I can eat the results. Maybe one day I could cook a dessert for you.'

'Maybe.'

A little silence fell. It wasn't awkward, exactly, just both of them realising that they'd let their conversation drift into something it perhaps hadn't started out to be.

That perhaps wasn't particularly appropriate, and Lorenzo tried to remind himself of this as he gathered up his purchases and the items were tallied.

He managed, sort of. Well, except for his imagination taking him to making chocolate desserts for Scarlett and feeding portions to her somewhere quiet and romantic.

You've managed not to feel romantic about anyone else for five years.

Lorenzo hadn't been celibate, but those encounters had been occasional, and emotionally meaningless.

'Lunch.' He needed to shift his thoughts away from the concepts of Scarlett and romance. 'We, ah, we agreed that we'd eat at the most popular restaurant, check out the competition.'

'My guess would be that one.' Scarlett gestured to a small,

cosy restaurant tucked into the corner of the square. It wasn't the largest, but it was clearly busy. 'Shall we go there?'

Lorenzo tucked their purchases into coolers in the back of the van, and they made their way on foot to the restaurant.

'The demographic they're getting is different here from Rosa.' Scarlett leaned forward to say the words quietly, so they wouldn't be overheard by other diners. So no one would know they were being studied and picked apart. 'We get some tourists, but not as many as we have locals.'

To be fair, she and Lorenzo were picking apart the food, table service, ambiance and everything else as well. That was why they were here. To examine all of it.

She took a small sip of her wine. 'It's a decent red. Nothing outstanding, but I don't think you'd do better for a table-wine price.'

'Yes. The wine is good value.' Lorenzo's lids drooped and his gaze stilled on her lips.

Scarlett was trying hard not to be too aware of him, too conscious. And yet with each moment that passed, her awareness seemed to increase.

They'd laughed together this morning as they drove here. Played silly old music in the van and let themselves relax. Scarlett had let her guards down. She couldn't seem to get them back up again.

'They're catering to at least a fifty-per-cent tourist clientele here.' Lorenzo leaned in a little closer. 'These are people who *won't* be back again and again. They just want to eat and leave.'

'It can be a tricky one, the tourist versus locals issue.' Scarlett tried to give the issue the most careful thought she could manage.

That wasn't a full hundred per cent, she had to admit. How could she fully concentrate on business when all she could hear was his voice? When all she could feel was the fact he was so close she could raise her hand and touch his face?

And he was looking at her as though, regardless of their purpose here, he saw only her.

Scarlett cleared her throat. 'You, ah, with your shopping earlier—the Rosa part of it.' Yes, that was good. Rosa was what they needed to speak about, even if Scarlett now had an almost compulsive need to be in a kitchen with him somewhere and watch him create a chocolate masterpiece.

For her?

No. Of course not.

Well, it would be rather special.

I repeat, Scarlett, no, of course not!

It would not be special. It would be dangerously intimate.

'Um, where were we?'

The liquid brown of his eyes darkened as he gazed at her through a screen of silky black lashes. 'We were discussing my shopping for Rosa.'

'That's right. We were.' Scarlett forced a nod, but all that did was make her ponytail bounce and the forest-green ribbon brush against the skin of her back. A sleeveless sundress in a matching green had seemed a good choice this morning, but now Scarlett wondered if maybe she should have dressed in something more workmanlike. Well, work-womanlike, if she wanted to be exact about it.

Maybe a suit that buttoned up to the neck. With tights. Boring, sensible ones. And low-heeled pumps. And no ribbon in her hair. Definitely no ribbon from her collection of ribbons that Scarlett anticipated wearing each day now for that moment when Lorenzo let his gaze wander to her hair.

'I've studied the way you run your kitchen, Lorenzo.' She drew a breath that she hoped would help to steady her before she forced herself to go on. 'From this morning's shopping, the only noteworthy issue was that we could purchase a lot of our goods from here on a regular basis and get them for less than we're paying to local producers from Monta Correnti and its surrounds.'

His fingers lifted as though he might attempt to smooth the puckered expression from her lips, but he dropped them back to the table and instead gave a nod of agreement. 'You're quite right, but Luca's policy has been to support local business.'

'Yet recently I saw you in a heated discussion with a local olive supplier when he brought a case of olives to the restaurant.' Scarlett had meant to follow up on that, but had become immersed again in account records and, truthfully, had forgotten. She shouldn't allow issues to slip away from her that way. Everything counted!

It was Lorenzo's turn to frown. 'The olives that grower brought wouldn't be fit to put on a cheap mass-produced pizza from some foreign country that doesn't have a clue!'

Scarlett grinned. She couldn't help herself. 'Are you having a go at *my* country's food-chain pizza makers? I'm sure the last time I had an olive on one of those pizzas, it was quite satisfactory. But then, Australia produces some good olives.'

She was teasing him.

And he was looking all affronted but with a twinkle in his eyes, letting her.

Scarlett was shocked at her own behaviour, and thrilled and happy and a little giddy from his company, all at once.

Oh, she had allowed herself to relax too much with him today. That was the problem. Relax and unwind and for a little while, though the entire purpose of her presence with him was to dig into yet another aspect of Rosa's doings in hopes of finding another edge she could trim off their bottom line, she'd simply had fun.

'Why can't I still loathe you, 'Renz?' The old pet name for him slipped out without her even realising it. The question slipped out, too, straight from her confusion and interest in him. It also came from a degree of caution and the belated realisation that she really had let this day get out of her control. 'You hurt me so much.'

'That is something I have regretted every day for five years.' He didn't say that he wished he could have fixed the situation, made it better. That he wished he could have done things differently back then.

Scarlett noted that. Oh, she heard that fact loud and clear. And even then, she still couldn't.

Had she *ever* hated him? Or had she only thought that she did, because being angry had been easier to deal with than the pain of losing him? The pain of him not caring for her enough to leave his wife and give Scarlett the future with him that she had hoped for?

A future that Lorenzo had promised and then not followed through on? She hadn't known he was married at first. She'd let herself fall in love with him before he told her. He'd been going to leave Marcella. He'd done that since. Why couldn't he have done it then? 'It was a long time ago and maybe we both have grown up since then.'

Maybe growing up was what allowed Lorenzo to finally get out of a marriage that had made him unhappy. At least he'd done that for himself.

And Scarlett had moved on, too. Perhaps they just hadn't been meant to be together.

When she searched his eyes she thought she would see agreement. Perhaps softness. Maybe still that hint of teasing. She didn't expect to see shadows. Such shadows that her breath caught in her throat and she uttered his name with a question in her voice. 'Lorenzo?'

What is it? What's brought that hurt into your eyes?

He swallowed and opened his mouth and for some reason her breath stilled as though she was bracing for something.

But he just shook his head and gestured to her plate. 'Are you finished? If so we should probably make our way back. There's a lot of work still to do before the day is over.'

'Y-yes. I'm finished.' So, apparently, was this conversation if she didn't try... 'If you need—'

'I'm fine, Scarlett, but we do need to head back.' He didn't reject her care. The gentle expression in his eyes made it clear that he appreciated it. But he shut the conversation down, just the same.

Scarlett nodded. She wanted to think about his reaction, what it could mean, but he gestured for their bill and then there was that to settle.

They were on the road again in minutes and he talked about the pros and cons of paying more for local produce, and did it with enough commitment and interest that Scarlett had to throw herself into the conversation with him.

Really, he was only being sensible, doing what Scarlett should have done from the outset today. He was trying to keep them on a business footing.

So why did Scarlett feel that with each moment that passed the tension and consciousness between them, rather than lessening, became stronger until everything between them seemed to be exaggerated a hundredfold?

She could *hear* each breath he took. The radio was silent. Her own breathing sounded loud to her ears. Each of Lorenzo's words felt like the brush of his hand against her skin. When they fell silent, Scarlett remembered times in their past that they had shared such silences. Companionable, sweet silences.

If she thought this was only affecting her, maybe she would have had a good chance of squashing it back, but it was in his eyes each time he glanced her way. It was in the clench of his hands around the steering wheel and the tight set of his shoulders as he tried so hard to keep their conversation moving and work-focused.

And safe.

When Lorenzo drew the van to a stop in the parking space at the back of the restaurant, Scarlett turned and gave him a subdued smile.

She was trying. She wanted to be wise. If he could try for that then the least she should do was meet him halfway.

Anything else was sheer madness anyway, even if her mind all but refused to consider this fact right now. 'Thank you for the trip, and for letting me bounce all my thoughts off you. That was really helpful.'

Scarlett was proud. The words were coming out and making sense. Later she would be able to really and truly examine all the things they'd talked about. For now she said, 'There are clearly some things I still need to address.'

In fact, she could even think of one of those things right now. 'I need to speak with Luca about these issues with purchasing local goods. What happened with the olives in the end, by the way?'

And see? A sensible, interested question to arm herself with knowledge about that issue, too.

'The grower replaced them with a decent grade and got a warning not to pull a stunt like that again.' Lorenzo stepped from the van and, again, came around it to open her door for her.

His words were clear and to the point and if she hadn't looked into his eyes Scarlett might have believed they could just be friends.

'Good. The grower had better do the right thing next time.' Lorenzo would see that he did. Scarlett felt quite confident of this. Confident enough that she didn't feel the need to manage the situation herself. 'I'm learning to trust you again.' She uttered the words without forethought.

Perhaps they surprised him enough that he didn't think to step out of her path.

Because Scarlett stepped down from the van and all but into his arms. They ended up practically chest-to-chest there in the rear area behind the restaurant. It was quiet and still out here, the van parked close to the back of the building. They stood between the van and a windowless section of wall.

She looked up into his eyes and he looked down into hers and…that was the end of it. The end of days of working with each other and suppressing all sorts of things and today not managing to suppress them.

Scarlett didn't know who kissed whom. She didn't know who made that first infinitesimal move or whether they both did.

All she knew was their lips pressed together in the seclusion of the back area. Lorenzo made a soft sound in the back of his throat.

Their hands rose and arms locked around each other. This wasn't a one-second press of lips against lips and a hurried and startled breaking away. This was the rest of that first kiss. The completion of that first kiss. A giving and taking and offering and receiving that seemed to touch on so much more than a shared attraction or a past closeness.

Scarlett kissed Lorenzo and completely forgot where she was. She forgot her position as Financial Manager of Rosa, forgot that potentially someone could happen along out here. She forget everything except the taste and the touch of him as they held each other close and he kissed her as though he had starved for the taste of her, had needed this intimacy with her. *Had to have it for the sake of his soul.*

Oh, these were dangerous thoughts for Scarlett to have. Dangerous, wanting-to-leap-to-conclusions-that-she-shouldn't-leap-to thoughts. They dissipated anyway into pure sensation before Scarlett could do more than feel the drift of them through the recesses of her mind. Her hand rose and her fingers cupped the nape of his neck. Strong muscle shifted beneath her fingertips as she stroked them softly over his warm skin.

Lorenzo's hands firmed at her waist and their kiss deepened, became an expression of urgency and need that felt more immediate and necessary than ever before.

'I have missed your taste, the touch of you, the scent of you.' He murmured the words as he pressed kisses to the column of her neck, the side of her jaw and across her cheek. Finally, before his mouth closed over hers, he added, 'I have missed *you,* Scarlett. More than I understood. More than I understand now.'

'Lorenzo.' His words were beautiful to her ears and Scarlett gave herself up to kissing him, to the belief in his need for her. She gave and gave and Lorenzo gave back to her, worshipping her mouth with his lips, gently caressing her arms and back and shoulders until she wanted to stay in his arms and never leave.

Would Scarlett have *ever* thought to stop that kiss?

It wasn't a question she could answer because a sound nearby broke them apart like…guilty lovers. In that first moment, Scarlett realised it was only a bird rustling through the branches of a tall bush at the edge of the area.

And then her mind began to function again and she became truly aware once more of their surroundings. She'd kissed Rosa's head chef in plain view of anyone who might have happened out the back door of the premises. She'd kissed Lorenzo and Lorenzo had kissed her right back, as though all of their past hadn't happened and she hadn't been forced to navigate her way through the pain of him totally betraying her back then.

What on *earth* had she been thinking?

'I—I need to work on the books.' Scarlett uttered the words

without any real idea of what she was doing or saying. She needed to escape. That was all she knew.

From what had just happened, from dealing with how it had made her feel, from addressing the issue of…this, whatever 'this' was, altogether.

She didn't wait for him to argue the point or question her or anything else. Something told her he wouldn't have. That he felt just as surprised and taken aback by their actions as she did. They were actions they might have taken five years ago when stealing kisses and being together had felt so exciting to her. And then she'd had to deal with his revelation that he was married, his explanations about the broken state of that marriage.

His promise to make all things right in his world so he and Scarlett…

Not now. You're not thinking about that now.

Scarlett glanced every which way about her to ensure as best she now could, after the fact, that they had indeed *not* been observed in that compromising few moments, and she hurried into the restaurant by the rear door and shut herself in Luca's office, where she proceeded to bury her head in bookwork.

Deeply!

To the point where she had no space to think about anything else whatsoever!

And can you continue to ignore all your thoughts and hope that will be a true answer to anything, Scarlett?

To not only the issue of Lorenzo, but of family, too? Do you want to be close to them, or don't you?

Yes, she did, and Scarlett was trying. These things took time!

CHAPTER SIX

'OH, NO!' Scarlett stared at the e-mail she'd just dug out of the spam folder in her Internet mail program. 'How could this have ended up in the mail trash? What date was it sent? Why didn't they contact me when I didn't respond? What if I've missed out on the opportunity?' As these questions popped out another question followed. She opened the e-mail and started to scan its contents. '*What date* have they said they want to do this?'

It was Friday evening. She'd been just about to pack up in Luca's office and to be honest she had felt a true sense of achievement.

She still didn't have all the answers for making the restaurant completely self-supporting and guaranteed to always run in the black, but the changes she'd made were starting to pay off and she wasn't at the end of her stream of ideas by any means.

This was only the beginning of what Scarlett could do. One of the things she'd tried was to canvas the local promotional body for Monta Correnti to see if she could interest them in granting publicity and media coverage to Rosa for a weekend cook-up. The body had a budget for community-related events, and Scarlett had hoped she might be able to interest them.

Scarlett had logged onto her e-mail account at the last moment just now to check for a response. Because she'd asked about it and time had passed with no answer, she'd all but given up on the possibility. But she had found her answer, sent almost a week ago and hiding out in the mail program's trash file!

She quickly skimmed the contents of the e-mail. The promotional group not only loved the idea she'd put to them, they'd taken it further and brought in a second restaurant so the two could run a 'friendly' cook-off contest. 'Oh, please tell me it's not—'

Sorella.

But of course it was, because they were side by side in the square. The local co-ordinators couldn't imagine anything more exciting or convenient. They anticipated a high degree of interest, advertising would commence… Scarlett read the date and her eyes widened. Advertising would commence *today.* And the contest itself would run *next weekend* with *TV and newspaper coverage*!

'That's only seven days away.' A lump of panic lodged itself in Scarlett's throat, and doubled in size when the remaining implications made themselves felt. 'And they've set us up to compete against Sorella.'

According to this e-mail, Sorella's owner had been more than delighted to front up for a contest to see which restaurant could prepare the best dishes and be declared better than the other.

Oh, Scarlett, what have you got Rosa into? And the family into by letting this come about?

Scarlett's mother would thrive on this kind of competition. It didn't surprise Scarlett that Lisa had agreed to the contest. That was enough of a problem. Scarlett could imagine Lisa hustling her restaurant staff by remote control over the phone from wherever she happened to be at the time, to ensure they did a good job in the contest. If Lisa didn't have other more important engagements, she might even turn up for some part of the weekend.

Unfortunately, Luca might be a little more enthused about the possibility of 'beating' Sorella in a cook-off than anyone in the family would want as well.

Isabella, Jackie, Lizzie and some of the others had all been trying to get things on a better, less confrontational footing between the various branches of the family and specifically between Lisa and Luca.

More rivalry was the last thing they needed and yet now Scarlett had single-handedly set the family up for a cook-off war.

Scarlett dropped her head into her hands where she sat at the desk. 'I can see it now. Front-page news. *Rabble-raising Restaurants in Fantastic Food Fight.* There's no way this can work out well. Either one restaurant loses the challenge or the other one does.'

'If you have a moment.' The words came from the office doorway.

They were tight, low, spoken in a very familiar male voice and they held a decided edge of 'unimpressed' about them. The words were Lorenzo's, but they didn't come from the relaxed, helpful Lorenzo she'd worked with in recent days.

Days in which they'd almost felt as though they were in some kind of holding pattern to Scarlett. They'd kissed beside the van after parking it behind the restaurant. Scarlett had melted into his arms and he'd seemed to need their kiss as much as she had. Since then she hadn't been able to get those moments out of her mind. But nor had she been able to draw any conclusions about them, decide what she should do about them.

In fact, Scarlett had asked herself whether there might be some way that she and Lorenzo could, perhaps, pursue these feelings now.

The thought wasn't an easy one for her to have. He'd broken her heart five years ago. Scarlett had never expected to feel anything again for him other than contempt and anger. But working with him here at Rosa had changed that. They'd developed a mutual respect for each other. Scarlett might have wanted… If Lorenzo had seemed to want to pursue…

Well, so far he's done a good job of not pursuing anything. Maybe he's forgotten all about the kiss. Maybe he kisses women like that all the time.

And maybe her head chef was a little upset right now and Scarlett had better deal with that. He stepped into the office and slapped down a copy of today's newspaper.

One brief glance showed her the feature piece.

Restaurants will break out their competitive spirits for a weekend cook-off next weekend!

'Um, about that.' She really could have done with a few minutes to try to figure out how to present this to him in the best light, now that there was nothing she could do to change the course of events.

It was the end of the day. Why couldn't she have discovered this earlier? Had Lorenzo known about it earlier? 'When did you find out?'

'Just now. None of us had time to look at the paper today.' His gaze held an accusing edge. 'I don't know whether to say it's just as well a patron didn't tell one of us earlier in the day, or wish that they had. At least there'd have been a *bit* more notice.'

Scarlett forced a smile to her face and hoped it was a placatory, calm, very professional one. 'Would you mind if I took a look? I didn't know this was going to be in today's edition of the paper so I haven't actually seen it yet.'

That sounded suitably under control and not totally panic-stricken. Didn't it?

Lorenzo silently pushed the newspaper her way with the

tip of one finger. He still looked ready to pitch a fit over the topic. She should feel defensive about that. No, she should be *aggressive* about it, in an 'I'm in charge here and this is just another aspect of performing your tasks for the restaurant so don't bother complaining about it' kind of a way.

Instead, she kept thinking how strong and manly he looked with his muscles locked that way and irritation and displeasure stamped on his face.

'Right, well, let me just take a quick look.' Scarlett had never skimmed a piece of print quite so quickly. As she did so she felt Lorenzo glowering down at her. She finally forced her gaze up, to meet stormy brown eyes. 'Um, maybe you'd like to shut the door while we discuss this.'

'Shutting the door isn't going to make a bit of difference, Scarlett.' His words weren't shouted, but they were strong enough that they would carry. 'I'm done here for the night, anyway. If you want to maintain some privacy on the topic of an article that *I hadn't even heard about,* I suggest we take this elsewhere.'

Right. Well, that seemed like an eminently sensible idea. Scarlett shot to her feet. That was, *she rose gracefully,* and calmly gathered her laptop into the all-purpose carry bag that housed her room key and other necessary items a girl couldn't do without, and stepped confidently towards the door.

And through it.

Without revealing even slightly that her heart was racing in a highly unprofessional way.

Oh, she wasn't scared of him.

She just hadn't had time to absorb the implications of this arrangement, and therefore didn't exactly have a plan in mind for dealing with Lorenzo's feelings about the whole matter. And she had this compulsive and extremely unprofessional urge to offer to rub his shoulders or in some other way un-ruffle his clearly ruffled feathers for him.

'We'll go to my bedsit. It's close and the owner is away so I know we'll be quite private even if you need to express your sentiments…' Loudly? Vociferously? With gusto? Scarlett decided it might be wiser not to finish that sentence.

Instead she strode through the restaurant ahead of Lorenzo, and they walked in silence across the square to her bedsit. She let them in quickly, set her laptop down carefully against the wall inside the door.

Lorenzo drew a deep breath and advanced two steps into the centre of the room.

Which also brought him two steps closer to Scarlett who happened to be standing just shy of that same centre of the room herself.

'Why is this the first I've heard of a cook-off that's to take place between Sorella and Rosa? What do you hope to achieve from this? Have you thought of the possible ramifications?'

He was unapologetically irritated. And yet his eyes stayed gentle.

Scarlett frowned. Not at Lorenzo, but at her own thoughts. Now was not the time to take stock of Lorenzo's eyes, *or* to feel that she wanted such gentleness from him.

'The response from the local body handling my application ended up in my e-mail spam folder almost a week ago and I didn't find it until today.' Scarlett would contact them to find out just why she'd received no follow-up when she had failed to respond to the e-mail. It really wasn't appropriate for the matter to be settled upon and advertised when one of the restaurants hadn't actually agreed to the terms!

'And don't you think that as Head Chef I might have been made aware that such a cook-off event was a possibility in the first place?' His hands came up to perch on a set of lean hips. 'What if I didn't want to participate in a cook-off?'

'Well—'

'And not only that.' He paced from one end of her very

small living area to the other and back again. 'I've effectively got six days to get ready to do this, and try to make sure that when I participate, Rosa wins. It's not going to look great if we don't, for the restaurant or for my career. I can't afford to lose another job, Scarlett. I'd hoped this job would be different, that I'd have a chance to prove myself and not be judged by rumours spread by Marcel—' He broke off and turned his face away for a moment before he whipped it back. 'This whole thing—'

'Is going to be just fine, despite the fact that I messed up by not following up on my approach to this local body, and by only finding the e-mail in my spam file tonight.' Scarlett owned her mistake without hesitation, and injected all the assurance and confidence into her tone that she could possibly muster.

But in relation to his past jobs, had he been about to speak his ex-wife's name? 'What do you mean—?'

'That's not the point now. Not relevant.' He chopped a hand through the air. 'How long have the Sorella staff known about this event?'

'I'm guessing, from before the date of that e-mail.' Scarlett still wanted to know what Lorenzo had been about to say. Why would Marcella still have anything to say about him after so long?

'So at the least, the Sorella staff have known about this for a week longer than we have.'

Scarlett tried for a conciliatory nod. 'Well, yes, I'm guessing so. This truly wasn't intended as a sleight to you, Lorenzo. I meant to mention the possibility when I first sent the feeler out. In the flurry of other things, I admit I forgot to follow up on that. To complicate matters, I didn't expect to be informed by merely an e-mail that I almost didn't see at all.'

'All right.' He sucked in a deep breath and slowly blew it

out again. 'Things happen. And knowing it wasn't a deliberate decision on your part to not discuss it makes a difference.'

'Thank you.' Scarlett acknowledged the level of her relief wasn't only in relation to keeping him happy in terms of work. She didn't want Lorenzo to be upset with her. Period.

Oh, Scarlett. Don't start to need his approval or need him too much. You mustn't let your emotions get involved with him a second time.

Well, of course she wouldn't do that. Certainly she wouldn't fall in love with him again or something equally silly. But liking. Liking him was okay.

Wasn't it? 'The approach that I made was actually for Rosa to do a weekend cooking demonstration by ourselves, but somebody has apparently decided it would be more interesting and exciting if we cooked against another restaurant. And they chose Sorella. I didn't look for either of those things to happen, and I didn't anticipate not being given a chance to turn the idea down rather than my agreement on behalf of Rosa being assumed the way it has been.'

'But if you turn around now and refuse to participate, Rosa will look bad.' He nodded his head. 'Well, that means the choice is made. I've seen events similar to this on television.' He frowned. 'Not entirely similar, I suppose, but I can understand how the body would have thought a cook-off between two restaurants would be more exciting than a sole performance.'

Scarlett nodded. 'And with the two restaurants side by side, diners will be able to observe the goings-on from their tables. I'm guessing the judging will take place outside in the square, between the two restaurants. 'In fact, it will make a fabulous outside event,' Scarlett murmured as the possibilities began to register. Yes, she could see pitfalls, too many of them, but she was also starting to see real potential.

Excitement started to bubble and she hurried on. 'You're

so good at what you do, 'Renz. I didn't get to see the full end results of that special lunch you prepared the first day, but you proved that day that you can work under pressure. I've seen everything that's come out of the kitchen since, and tasted a variety of the meals you prepare on a regular basis. The one thing I'm not worried about is what you can do with food to give Sorella a run for their money in a contest.'

She stepped past him to retrieve her laptop, opened it and set it on the small kitchenette bench top. 'Let's read the e-mail through properly. I may have missed something the first time. The newspaper article…?'

'Is right here.' He picked up the newspaper from her sofa where he'd dropped it, and for the first time seemed to actually look around him.

At a small room, with the two of them inside it and, aside from the tiny table and chairs, the only piece of furniture was the sofa that was her lounging area by day, and her bed by night.

Suddenly *Scarlett* felt a little too aware of this confined space, and their isolation together within it.

Not going there, Scarlett.

'The, uh, the newspaper article says that the two restaurants will be cooking against each other in…' Lorenzo bent his head and seemed to force his attention to the printed words '…"A spell-binding weekend of fabulous food, speed-cooking, and excitement galore. Table bookings commence as of Monday. Don't miss out, this is going to be amazing."'

'It's good advertising.' Scarlett had leaned in to read along with him.

Not because she wanted an excuse to be closer to him. She proved this by stepping quite calmly away and moving the two steps to the kitchenette bench and bringing the laptop out of sleep mode. Since it hadn't been shut down, the e-mail appeared on the screen straight away and Scarlett read it with complete attention.

Silently.

While Lorenzo also read silently over *her* shoulder.

So close that she could turn her head just the tiniest bit and their lips could meet.

'It—the e-mail says right here…' She pointed at the screen, as though that would help anything.

Well, it helped her to force her attention to that screen. Somewhat. If she didn't count the portion of her interest that refused to step away, metaphorically or otherwise, from Lorenzo's nearness.

He radiated consciousness of her in the same way she was radiating consciousness of him. '*The e-mail says* that the restaurants will compete in several events over the weekend, starting on Friday night, and that for one event at least each restaurant will cook to its strengths using established meals from its regular menu.'

'So authentic Italian for us, and international cuisine for Sorella. That gives them a lot broader range.' His breath brushed across her cheek as he spoke.

'Which gives them more to work with to make mistakes, choose dishes the judges may not approve of, and to second-guess themselves on what's going to be the best for the contest.' Scarlett turned her head, met his gaze, acknowledged how close they stood to each other and how far this had now gone from their initial discussion when she'd been concerned about smoothing his ruffled feathers.

'Rosa may have a less diverse menu, but every item on it is authentic cuisine for this region and for Italy. I'm seeing that as a good thing for us.' She hoped her words made sense; that they came across as focused and alert. Because a part of her could only focus on him.

How had they progressed to this point with each other in

what was really a short space of time since they met again? How had *she* progressed? From the bitterness of the way he had hurt her, to a part of her wanting to…go back to that place with him again?

If that happened, it would be different this time. Lorenzo was a free agent. Yet he'd mentioned Marcella as though she had some kind of ongoing impact in his life. When had he left his wife? How long had they been divorced? Had it been very acrimonious? Was that why Lorenzo didn't seem to want to speak about it, and perhaps why Marcella was a little bitter or something?

Well, of course his ex-wife would be bitter.

And Scarlett was *not* seriously considering a rematch with Lorenzo. That would be a hundred times worse than a restaurant war, and more dangerous to her emotional health.

'It *is* a good plan, Scarlett.' He said it with commitment. 'If it's handled right, maybe we can use it to our advantage.'

'Can you prepare adequately in the time frame? What can I do to help you get ready for the event, and to handle it next weekend?' She *had* to force her thoughts and focus onto these things. 'If you need time off before then, consultation about menu choices, extra shopping done for you?'

'I'll need an extra kitchen hand for the entire weekend. At least one.' He watched as she shut down the laptop and, without thinking about it, Scarlett led the way to the sofa, sat, and gestured for him to do likewise, which he did.

The thing dipped in the middle. Like one of those love seats made especially for cuddling. Made so you couldn't *avoid* cuddling. She hadn't actually sat on it with another person since she rented the bedsit.

Scarlett's face heated as her hip brushed against his. She moved a little away, but their bodies still leaned in towards each other. 'I'll find you a kitchen hand.'

'They'll need to be willing to take orders, and to know

enough about Italian cooking to not need to be instructed over every little thing.' His fingers shifted over the fabric of the sofa cushion. 'Cooking on a deadline, I'll want every hand available and even that may not be enough. Not if we're catering meals for patrons at the same time.'

'I'll make sure you have what you need, Lorenzo.' Scarlett made him the assurance, and then became lost in eyes that silently let her know there were other needs. Needs that matched hers. For touch. For the brush of skin against skin that could turn the simple stroke of fingers over the back of a hand from simplicity to desire.

What did he want of her? Really? What did Scarlett want of him? What was there about Marcella? 'Please, will you tell me about the past?'

'I must go.' He got to his feet and strode to the door.

She'd uttered her words softly, and he'd spoken at the same time. Scarlett didn't know if he'd heard her request and probably it was better if he hadn't. To start digging around in that now...

But there were things she wanted to know. Maybe she could ask Isabella without making it appear that she was particularly interested for her own sake.

Scarlett followed Lorenzo to the door. 'I'm glad we were able to discuss this calmly and work things out, and I do apologise for the way it all ended up coming about.'

'I'm sorry I let myself make assumptions before you'd had a chance to explain what happened.' He turned the knob and opened the door, and glanced back at her over his shoulder. 'I'll give you a menu list tomorrow morning so you can think about the costs that will be involved.'

'Yes.' She nodded her head. 'We'll get full into planning first thing tomorrow. At Rosa.'

As opposed to here.

Because *here,* with its closeness and privacy, was not a

good idea for them. They needed to concentrate on their work, didn't they? Lorenzo seemed very determined to do that, and only that. In fact since the moment he'd half mentioned his ex-wife, his attitude had seemed to focus on getting out of here, getting things back to a working footing.

'Goodbye, Scarlett. We'll speak tomorrow.' He stepped through her door, closed it after himself, and disappeared.

And Scarlett told herself to be very pleased with the outcome of this meeting. They'd discussed the necessary issues, kept it away from the other staff at Rosa while they sorted out their differences about the upcoming event.

They were in accord now. They would be able to not only cope with the cook-off, but she was certain Lorenzo would do a great job and she would make sure he had the support staff around him to make success as easy as possible for him to achieve.

Overall, it was a great outcome.

Even if he hadn't kissed her.

Particularly because he didn't kiss you, Scarlett. Being kissed by the man who broke your heart and let you down five years ago is the last thing you want!

He *had* let her down.

But Scarlett was beginning to think about the fact that she hadn't exactly been without blame in that situation, either. She'd expected him to leave his wife for her. What if she hadn't understood how difficult that might have been for him at that time? Maybe there'd been reasons?

Oh. She couldn't believe she was thinking that!

With a shake of her head, Scarlett pushed the thoughts aside and went back to her laptop. If she and Lorenzo were to make a success of this cook-off and do it well for Rosa, she'd better get cracking to figure out how to ensure he had enough staff and everything else he would need. *Those* were appropriate thoughts.

She took her mobile phone from her pocket and phoned the restaurant to speak to Isabella. Her cousin was busy in the kitchen so the conversation was brief, though Scarlett promised to fill her in about upcoming events first thing tomorrow. 'Come here for a coffee, Izzie.'

If Scarlett also hoped to grill Izzie about Lorenzo's past, well, a good financial manager *needed* to understand where her staff were coming from so she could best deal with them.

Right. Sure. That was what it was all about.

Scarlett thought about Luca and Lisa and their long-standing rivalry, and where this cook-off could put everyone in the family.

She had better figure out how to discuss *this news* with the family at large, and quickly, and hope they didn't feel she'd thrown Lisa and Luca at each other's throats.

Because that wouldn't exactly look like an attempt at helping the two to get along better!

CHAPTER SEVEN

SCARLETT stood to the side of the courtyard dining area of Rosa the following Friday and asked herself where the time had gone between her decision to grill Isabella about Lorenzo's past, and now.

The cook-off was about to start. Lorenzo had worked so hard all week, preparing for it, thinking about dishes, working things out. Scarlett had worked equally hard to get him the extra workers he'd need, to get as much advertising out as she could to augment what was already out there and yet without costing Rosa too much in doing that. The focus was to bring diners in for the event, because diners meant money, and money helped Rosa's bottom line. They couldn't really afford for this weekend to run at a loss.

'Visitors, diners and friends, what you are seeing here tonight is the beginning of a very exciting Monta Correnti event.' The head of the local entertainment body spoke into her microphone with just the right edge of dramatic effect to ensure she had the attention of everyone in the square.

Every seat, indoor and outdoor, at both Sorella and Rosa was taken. That side of the hard work *had* paid off.

Lorenzo had been focused and really supportive about the event. He might not have been impressed with the short notice at first, but once the idea was on the table, he had got one hundred percent behind it.

His attitude, well, it made Scarlett proud. And then, of course, there'd been dealing with the family. It hadn't been easy to try to convince everyone that first of all she'd meant no harm, secondly the die was cast, and thirdly if they all tried to get along this could still be okay.

'I hope this event turns out to be worth the trouble, Scarlett.' Her mother's words sounded behind her. 'Since I've flown in especially for it.'

Scarlett dragged her gaze from where Lorenzo was setting up his outdoor workstation. She hadn't even realised she'd been watching him with avid eyes. Hopefully no one else had noticed that. There literally hadn't been a moment of privacy between Scarlett and Lorenzo all week. Not one where they'd been alone for any length of time, had any opportunity…

To what? Talk? Catch up on old news? Kiss each other silly? Did Lorenzo even really want that any more? Maybe he'd decided that them mixing business and personal issues, at all in any shape or form, was a really bad idea.

Which of course was exactly what Scarlett herself should have decided long before now, and *had* decided before she came to Monta Correnti. She just hadn't managed to hold on very well to that conviction. Scarlett didn't know what to do about that, and…her emotions were a little raw anyway from dealing with a week of trying to smooth tensions within the family while simultaneously trying to be as supportive as possible to Rosa's head chef as he prepared for this weekend.

And while carrying on with the necessary work of studying how Rosa ticked in every way conceivable, studying the various staff members. Scarlett had her doubts about the suitability of a couple of them, though at least the woman whose shift had been pulled forward by an hour appeared to have accepted the change and knuckled back down to concentrating on her work.

Well, now there was Mamma to deal with.

And Uncle Luca standing over there, glaring in Mamma's direction. Scarlett pushed back a sigh.

'Mum. It's nice to see you.' *Sort of.* 'Actually, the cook-off developed out of quite a different idea. It wasn't initially intended to be anything more than—'

'A chance for you to try to convince the world that Rosa is up to Sorella's standards of excellence and can provide the same kind of international cuisine?' Lisa shook her head. 'Oh, I heard about your chef stealing the show with that meal he cooked for the movie star.'

'Rosa was approached to do that work. Nothing more.' Scarlett stopped before anything more could be said on that topic. She wasn't about to bring on an argument with her mother. 'I'd like to hope this cook-off can be a positive thing for both Sorella and Rosa.' Scarlett chose her words carefully. She didn't address her mother's assumption that Rosa was about to start trying to cook international cuisine.

It might be silly, but what if Rosa one day did want to add some international dishes to its menu? Scarlett didn't want to rule out that possibility in discussion with her mother. 'Both restaurants can really benefit from this weekend. I hope you'll look at the cook-off in that light. Not so much as a contest, but as a means for both restaurants to display their strengths.'

'Well, I guess we'll see what transpires. Excuse me for a moment, Scarlett. I want to touch base with my chef before the contest actually starts.' Lisa walked away and spoke for a few moments with her head chef.

As she did so the camera panned across the square. The woman at the microphone explained the outdoor cooking set-up—provided by Sorella because their chef had a relative able to get access to the equipment cheaply.

In fact, the local body and the two restaurants had managed an excellent level of co-operation when it came to the nuts and bolts organisation of the event. Because of those cameras, Scarlett pinned on a professional smile.

In fact, when she glanced at her mother she saw some of her own expression reflected on her face.

Scarlett wasn't entirely like Lisa. But there were parts of her mother in her, and sometimes their minds worked similarly.

With that in mind, when Lisa returned to stand at her side Scarlett tried to sell the idea to her mother in a way Lisa could, hopefully, respect. 'This event has already shown that the staff of the two restaurants can co-operate to reach a common goal, and the event itself has increased business for Sorella *and* Rosa.

'We're getting some free media advertising out of it. You didn't have to come back for the event, but now that you have I hope you can at least see that this is a good thing.'

'Good in some ways perhaps.' Lisa's gaze moved to the front of Rosa where Luca stood. She murmured, 'Of course, Sorella will win the contest.'

'You and Uncle Luca—' Scarlett bit her lip before she faced her mother squarely. 'No one in the family wants this to turn into anything unpleasant. The purpose of the weekend is to promote *both* restaurants. Please promise me you won't start any conflict with Uncle Luca about it.'

'I have no desire to fight with your uncle.' Lisa's words were a little sharp. After that she excused herself with a brief nod and returned to Sorella.

Scarlett noted the fact that she had been given an assurance of sorts, but not a complete promise. She pushed back a sigh and her gaze returned to Lorenzo. Almost as though he sensed her unease, he looked up and caught her glance on him.

Even from this distance Scarlett saw his eyes soften and the slightest hint of a smile touch the corners of his mouth before he checked everything one last time and stood waiting at his workstation.

Izzie had cancelled coffee the other morning, and Scarlett hadn't got her opportunity to ask her questions. There hadn't been time since. But that look just now hadn't seemed uninterested.

'Gentleman chefs, are you ready?' The MC glanced at each of them. 'Everyone, please focus your attention on the time because this amazing cooking marathon will start in five, four, three, two…'

The countdown ended with a cheer from the dining crowd. Lorenzo and the other chef glanced at each other and got to work. Scarlett watched with her heart in her throat. Her level of nerves was ridiculous, and she wasn't even the one up there.

Oh, but she wanted Lorenzo to succeed. For Rosa, yes, but most of all because he was an excellent chef and Scarlett realised she wanted to see his talent recognised. The other chef was efficient and moved quickly. For tonight they had a low-range budget, two hours only to prepare and plate their dishes, and they were preparing one meal and two side dishes from their restaurant's existing menus.

Oh, Scarlett wanted to be up there at Lorenzo's side, cheering him on. She had to get her nervous energy under control or she'd be a wreck before the night was over!

For a moment Scarlett wished she could follow in Isabella's footsteps for the night, and hide out in Rosa's inside kitchen. But Isabella was needed there to supervise the production of those meals while Lorenzo was otherwise occupied. Scarlett's job was to pitch in anywhere if she saw a need, but mostly to be Rosa's representative to media and anyone else interested for the evening.

Scarlett tore her gaze from Lorenzo's efficient and appealing workmanship. Truly, she couldn't see how he would do other than come out as a favourite in terms of how much the media would like him. Not that this was a man-judging contest, of course. It was a *food-judging* contest. Totally and utterly, and Lorenzo's good looks had nothing to do with it.

Where was she?

Oh, yes. Scarlett forced herself to step through the crowd and start hustling for Rosa. There were people here tonight, diners who didn't come here often, and people from out of town, and others of note whom Scarlett should meet and greet.

It was Scarlett's job to help them appreciate the beauty of Rosa so they would come back soon, bring their families and friends, tell their co-workers. Tonight was about food and contest and media attention, but it was also about word-of-mouthing a commodity so more people would try it, and come back to it again and again.

Scarlett kept Lorenzo in the corner of her eye while she went about winning over Rosa's diners.

'You're frowning, little sister.' Jackie's voice sounded beside Scarlett.

It was one hour and fifty-three minutes later, not that Scarlett had been counting or compulsively checking her watch.

There was no need now. Their MC for the evening had commenced a verbal countdown for the final ten minutes and was asking questions of Lorenzo and the other chef as they put the finishing touches to their dishes and prepared to serve them.

The crowd was enthralled. Everyone wanted to know which dishes would be the winners. The whole event was on show on large screens erected inside and outside both restaurants so that all the diners could see.

'I've asked a lot of Lorenzo.' Scarlett uttered the words to Jackie.

Scarlett *had* settled down somewhat from her earlier state

of feeling totally nerve-racked. But those nerves were back and fluttering about inside her again now.

For tonight Scarlett had dressed in a plain black sleeveless dress with black pumps on her feet. Her only concession to colour was a cream ribbon in her hair to match the pearl drop earrings and necklace she wore with the dress.

She'd wanted to blend in if she felt like blending, but still look professional. Scarlett's hand rose to the pearl drop necklace. It was a step up from fiddling with her hair ribbon, she supposed. And tonight she *had* used mousse. Enough to keep her hair in place no matter what! 'He looks so calm, but cooking in this kind of environment under the eagle eye of so many diners, let alone the dignitaries who'll do the judging, has to be really stressful.'

Jackie cast a thoughtful glance her way. 'I suppose you'd have spent a considerable amount of time with Lorenzo since you started working at Rosa, but you sound almost—'

Half in love with him? Overprotective? Too interested? 'Stressed? Yes. Yes, I have been. It's been a big week.'

Scarlett would have blabbed on further, but her sister didn't let her.

Instead she gave Scarlett a very direct look. 'I hope you aren't falling for him or anything, Scarlett. He keeps to himself, but you do know—'

'And we're into the final few seconds now, people, so let's count them down.' The MC began a backwards count, and whatever else Jackie might have planned to say gave way to the surge of excitement through the crowd as they counted down the final seconds of the two-hour block of time.

Scarlett felt she had been saved by the bell. She had to be more careful about what showed on her face. It would be mortifying for people to start to see that…

What? That she was half in love with Lorenzo again?

Not that. Of course not that. But…attracted to him. She

didn't want people to notice that she was attracted to him.
Work needed to be work and only that. Business and personal,
those two things shouldn't be mixed.

Maybe she should have thought of that before kissing him
so thoroughly that day. It was only luck that they hadn't been
seen at that time.

The other chef fussed until the final second, straightening
a garnish on one of the plates while Lorenzo checked his meal
one last time for standard of presentation. They stood back as
the MC called, 'Time is up.'

Most of the diners were at the coffee stage of their meals
now. The staff had done a good job of looking after everyone.
Isabella had clearly done a good job supervising in the kitchen,
because Scarlett had been receiving compliments on Rosa's
cuisine all night.

No doubt the same had occurred for her mother as she
strolled between tables at Sorella, stopping at this one and
then that to offer a few words. Lisa did this well. Scarlett also
did this well. Not that she was being competitive in thinking
such a thing.

As the judges took their seats to taste the meals, Scarlett
turned to Jackie. 'Will you excuse me?' Her gaze returned to
Lorenzo. 'I need—'

To be there with Lorenzo while this round is decided.

Not because she felt the need to offer the man emotional
support. Certainly not because she felt the need for some
herself, right now. Scarlett glanced again at her mother, and
Luca, who were at this moment casting quite open challeng-
ing stares towards each other. 'I need to position myself to
handle it if our mother and our uncle decide to blow up when
the winner is announced.'

Most of all Scarlett wanted to be at Lorenzo's side, because
if they didn't win she didn't want him to feel as though he
hadn't made a great achievement for the evening.

'I'll go and get ready to speak with Mum.' Jackie made this announcement with a determined glint in her eye. 'If nothing else, I may be able to distract her from having words with Luca, depending on the outcome of this round. We all want peace within the family. I'm not prepared to let Mum and Luca mess that up at this event.'

'Thanks, Jackie.' Scarlett made her way towards Lorenzo. As she approached the dais he gestured with his hand.

It was the slightest thing, but it showed he wanted her company, and for some ridiculous reason this made Scarlett feel…wonderful.

'The meals and side dishes were all of excellent standard.' One of the judges had taken the microphone and now complimented both Lorenzo and the other chef.

As Scarlett came to Lorenzo's side he dipped his head to whisper quietly, 'From the judges' reactions I think Sorella might have a slight edge over us.'

This *was* the consensus of the judges, and Rosa came in second for this round, though by a very small margin.

'Tomorrow our chefs will cook all day in their kitchens rather than outdoors. You'll be able to watch on the big screens again.' The MC smiled and raised her brows. 'At the end of it, there will be five wonderful desserts prepared for *all* our patrons to taste if they so desire, whether they be guests of Sorella or Rosa. So do come back and have another wonderful meal, and cap it off with a fabulous dessert of your choice!'

A round of applause followed.

Lorenzo waited to speak until the applause had finished. He turned then and congratulated the Sorella chef and they exchanged a few words about the evening before Lorenzo turned back to Scarlett. 'I need to get cleared up here, now that the pressure is off.'

'What you need to do is eat and rest for a while and regain your strength after that marathon effort.' Scarlett said it rather bossily, and yes, she was the boss, but that wasn't the point. 'That is, I mean to say that you must be tired. I know it's been a draining night for me, and I was only worrying about how you would do and whether you'd be okay with it if your dishes didn't win.'

And Scarlett had worried whether they would make a profit for the night, and whether Lisa and Luca would get in a fight.

Scarlett glanced about them. She'd completely forgotten her mother and uncle in the past few minutes. She hadn't even looked to see how either of them had reacted to the results. So much for positioning herself!

'Oh, damn—drat—*dash it all.*' Lisa and Luca were discussing the outcome, all right. With the media. 'Lorenzo…'

'Shall we go together?' He used his hand to give her a gentle push in that direction. A few moments later they were at Luca and Lisa's sides.

The Sorella chef joined them.

Sorella staff members efficiently cleared away after their chef. Scarlett wished she'd thought to ask Rosa's staff to do the same. She glanced over her shoulder and discovered Jackie supervising exactly that. Her sister didn't normally work at Rosa, but she and Romano had both helped out tonight. They'd spent the evening replenishing supplies of wines and topping up carafes of water, clearing dishes and generally helping however they could.

Scarlett drew a deep breath and pasted on a smile, and waded straight up to her uncle and mother. She kissed both of them on each cheek. 'Tonight has been wonderfully successful and fun for both restaurants.'

The interviewer murmured agreement and asked Lorenzo and Sorella's head chef how it felt to cook on a time crunch like that, using different equipment and with a live audience watching their every move.

Lorenzo and the Sorella chef opened up, discussing the challenges of the evening and both agreeing that they wouldn't mind a meal now and a soothing glass of wine. But neither of them wanted to eat the meals they had just cooked. Something else would be nice, preferably cooked by *someone* else!

Everyone laughed and their interviewer wrapped things up, thanked them for their time and moved off. That left five people standing about, and the Sorella chef quickly excused himself. 'It's an early start tomorrow and a big day. I want to check on things in my kitchen and then get some sleep.'

'Lorenzo, you should also get your rest.' Did Scarlett sound like a training coach? Or...a little too possessive of him?

For some inexplicable reason, there under the watchful eyes of her uncle and mother, Scarlett felt suddenly guilty and felt warmth amass at the base of her neck and try very hard to climb into her cheeks.

Scarlett forced the blush back and rubbed her hands together. 'Well, it was a fabulous night. Mum, are you staying for the full weekend or heading off first thing in the morning?' Scarlett would be happy to see her mother to the airport herself. She didn't mean that unkindly, but with Luca and Lisa both present the potential for an explosion was definitely greater.

'If you were staying at my villa,' Lisa said, 'you'd know the answer to that already.'

'Um, well, yes, perhaps that's true.' Scarlett didn't want to address that topic. They'd covered the ground already.

'I'm staying,' Lisa declared. 'This is my restaurant, after all.'

And oddly enough, when Scarlett glanced at her uncle he seemed to be quite pleased by this news. In a real, genuine way rather than a competitive one? Luca turned away a moment later with some muttered comment about speaking with Isabella before he left for the night.

A Sorella guest approached Lisa and wanted to introduce her to his dining companion, and Lisa, too, disappeared.

Scarlett's hand rose to the back of her head. She resisted the urge to tug on her ponytail and dropped her hand back to her side. 'Come back to the kitchen, Lorenzo. They'll still be working in there, but only on clean-up.'

In the time the media interview had taken place, all but a couple of guests had cleared from Rosa's dining tables. 'We'll get some food. We can eat in Luca's office.'

Her uncle was already on his way out of the kitchen as they stepped inside it.

Isabella glanced up and gave a quick smile. 'That was a good effort tonight, Lorenzo. I kept meals for you and Scarlett. We're clearing things away here now. The kitchen will be pristine for your early start tomorrow. We served a lot of meals tonight, too.'

Her eyes glowed as she turned to Scarlett. 'Between my father and your mother, I was worried about this, but it's definitely been good for business. I'm glad you thought of it.'

'Well, I thought of something a bit different and we sort of landed ourselves in the rest of it whether we felt ready or not.' Scarlett cast a glance towards Lorenzo as she said this. 'I'm fortunate that our head chef can work well under pressure and has been very supportive.'

This was true, and Scarlett wanted and maybe *needed* to say it.

Isabella handed meals to them, and poured them a glass of wine each. 'Go eat.'

They went into Luca's office. Scarlett pulled her chair around and Lorenzo pulled the other one in, and they sat side by side and enjoyed exceptional authentic Italian food.

'Isabella did a great job tonight.' Scarlett offered the words as she took a sip of her wine. With the office door pushed across, not closed but it might as well have been, it felt quiet and isolated and somehow…intimate in here.

Because of that she felt the need to fill the silence with words, and went on. 'You did a great job, too. I still think you should have won.'

He took another bite of the meal before he smiled and answered. 'I didn't see you tasting any of the meals.'

'Well, no, I wasn't on the voting panel.' She shook her head. And then she shook it again. 'You were only teasing me. I must be more exhausted than I think, if I can miss something like that.'

'We're both tired.' His hand lifted to tug gently on her ponytail.

It was the silliest thing but she'd pushed the memory from her mind, of him doing that years ago when they were together. Now she remembered and her feelings melted. Maybe Scarlett *was* really tired because she felt as though her defences were down. Her body froze into place, not wanting to move, not wanting him to lower his hand. Craving contact, craving his touch, his attention.

Oh, Scarlett, what are you thinking?

But Scarlett couldn't really think, because suddenly both Lorenzo's hands were there, and he murmured, 'Your ribbon's half falling out.'

His gaze locked with hers and his fingers gently retied the ribbon. It was just his fingers touching her hair, brushing for a moment against the nape of her neck.

So why did he lean in and she lean in? They came so close to kissing. They were almost there with his hands still lifted to her hair and their bodies close and their mouths moving towards each other until someone called out a goodbye from the kitchen.

Someone else answered and Scarlett remembered they were here at Rosa, and what on earth was she doing? Thinking?

Maybe he remembered, too, because he dropped his hands.

'Tomorrow.' Scarlett half turned from him and her hands busied themselves gathering their dinnerware, needlessly fussing over the task. 'It'll be a big day for you and you'll be working around the staff while they prepare the regular meals.'

'It'll be fine.' He got up and held the door open and Scarlett carried the dinnerware while he carried the wineglasses.

They took it all into the kitchen and got pushed out again firmly and quickly by the few remaining staff, headed up by Isabella.

Scarlett's cousin clicked her tongue and made shooing motions with her hands. 'Go home, both of you.'

So Scarlett and Lorenzo went. There were still plenty of local people milling about outside, saying farewells to each other, discussing the evening.

'I should go, too.' As though Lorenzo had invited her to stand around talking to him. Scarlett cleared her throat. 'Thank you for all that you did for tonight's event. It was a really good start to the contest.'

'I hope I can get a win for Rosa tomorrow.' Lorenzo walked with her a few paces. 'This weekend *is* something that can be of real benefit to the restaurant. I'm glad it came about, Scarlett. Your initial idea was good, and, with the way it has now developed, there's probably even more potential to get Rosa a bit more attention and hopefully ongoing patronage.'

'Yes, it's been an interesting experience so far.' Scarlett's glance roved the area. Guests from Sorella and Rosa mingled in groups, chatting. Here and there Scarlett heard snatches of discussion about the meals. One couple said they'd have liked to try foods from both menus. Scarlett's gaze narrowed and she tipped her head to the side.

When she returned her gaze to Lorenzo he was stifling a yawn.

Scarlett snapped to attention. A weary one admittedly, but attention just the same. 'Thanks again. I'll be here first thing tomorrow morning to support you in any way I can. If tonight's event hits any papers tomorrow I hope the coverage will be positive. Hopefully they'll keep it all in a good light.'

If Lisa and Luca played by those rules, too, the whole weekend might actually achieve a lot of good things. 'The family did all pull together, mostly, to try to make tonight a success.'

'Yes.' Lorenzo glanced towards her temporary home across the square. 'I'll see you home.'

'Oh, no, please, don't worry.' Scarlett gestured around them. 'As you can see, there are still plenty of people about and it's only a skip and a jump. You go home and get some rest. I want my head chef to be bright and well rested in the morning.'

If she placed any particular emphasis on the word 'my' it was purely incidental.

Scarlett turned and forced her feet to take her swiftly away from him.

She had to remember he was exactly that, an employee at Rosa and nothing else to her. Whether he'd kissed her in the back parking area behind the restaurant or not. Whether they'd once been so much more to each other, or not.

It wasn't as though they could wind back time and be together as they had been back then. That whole relationship had turned out to be an utter disaster in the end and Scarlett had got really hurt.

So remember that, Scarlett Gibson, and don't set yourself up to get hurt again.

Scarlett tipped her face up and stuck her chin out at the most in-control-of-herself-and-her-life angle she could manage. She strode purposefully to her bedsit where she proceeded to enter, get ready for bed, and then lie and stare at the ceiling while she didn't think once about Lorenzo or replay every nuance of the evening over and over in her mind, with her emotions swinging this way and that way right along with that mental journey.

Non-existent mental journey, Scarlett corrected silently, and rolled onto her tummy and gave the pillow a whack with her hand before she buried her nose in it.

Sleep.

All she wanted to do was sleep.

When she woke in the morning everything would feel much clearer and she'd be totally focused in all the ways that she needed to be.

Scarlett flipped over and squashed the pillow between her hands. She tried burying her nose in it that way and tried equally hard to force her thoughts to blankness.

They weren't making any sense, just going around and around without ever coming to any conclusions. She couldn't think about the evening without always coming back to Lorenzo. On a personal level.

No, they are not doing that!

Oh, yes, they are!

Scarlett gave up on trying to make the pillow into a slumber-inducing shape, flipped onto her back and stared fixedly through the darkness at where the ceiling was, not that she could see it. By the power of her determination if nothing else, she *would* sleep.

And no, she was *not* avoiding any issues by wanting to do only that. She was being a sensible restaurant manager and family liaison.

Yes. That was how it was!

CHAPTER EIGHT

'WHERE is Rocco? Shouldn't he be here for his shift by now?' As Lorenzo asked the question Scarlett stepped into the busy kitchen.

A frown formed between her brows and she walked swiftly towards him. She looked neat as a pin today, fresh and lovely in a simple white sleeveless blouse over a tan skirt.

On her feet she wore closed-in shoes with good support-ive soles, and Lorenzo had the passing thought that only his Scarlett would be able to don shoes like that and look sexy in them. But of course Scarlett was not 'his' anything, other than his boss here at Rosa. He'd been trying to remember that. Trying not to still want her, desire her, be attracted to her.

It's not only those things. There are emotions involved in this for you, at least to some degree. You should admit it, be honest about it to yourself, anyway.

As he'd been honest with her five years ago? Hiding, at first, the fact that he was married? He'd fallen hard for Scarlett. There'd never been anyone in his life who'd affected him the way she had. Making sensible choices had given way to need and love. And for him, that all had happened at a vulnerable time of his life.

His relationship with his wife had been unspeakable at that time. Emotionally torturous for him because of Marcella's... debasing behaviour. The love had been over, and yet Lorenzo had been trapped. He'd craved an escape that wouldn't come. Marcella had trapped him in that way, too.

He had his share of regrets. Loss of a meaningful relationship with his parents thanks to the difficulties with Marcella had been part of that. He'd only come back to Monta Correnti for the position at Rosa. There wasn't much here for him now where family was concerned. A father who'd told him he had dishonoured the family name by leaving Marcella. Lorenzo's two brothers were a little more understanding, but they didn't live here.

One thing Lorenzo did know. He couldn't become emotionally involved with Scarlett again. He was not in a position to do that.

Scarlett joined him and glanced down at the large bowl he held in one hand as he plied a whisk through the contents with the other. 'Can I talk without distracting you?'

'Yes, it's fine.' And it was fine on two counts. They weren't being filmed right now. The technicians needed short breaks occasionally and were on one now, so they could speak without their words being broadcast to diners.

'You asked about Rocco. I know the rosters for this weekend off by heart. He was due here twenty minutes ago.' Scarlett's glance roved his face as she spoke, lingered on his mouth and quickly snapped back up to his eyes. She drew a rapid breath. 'I thought he must have slipped in and I hadn't noticed his arrival.'

No one seemed to know why the man was absent, but Lorenzo wasn't too surprised. Rocco had skipped more shifts in the last month or so than he should have. He always had a handy excuse, but Lorenzo had warned him twice already to pull up his socks.

'I don't want to judge him, but I can't say I was entirely impressed with Rocco when I first met him.' Scarlett turned back to the door. 'Excuse me. I'll try to phone him from the office now.'

Lorenzo watched her leave. He couldn't afford to feel distracted, but nor could he fail to be, it seemed. He wanted to hug Scarlett and assure her that it didn't matter if the kitchen hand was absent. They would get by. It wasn't ideal to be one short but he knew the rest of the staff would pull together and do well if it was necessary, even a person down.

These protective and co-operative feelings that he experienced towards Scarlett would be fine if they were a married couple running their own small restaurant together. To a degree the feelings were half acceptable in terms of their co-management positions here, anyway.

He just happened to know that, for him, his feelings were now a lot more complicated than those of a fellow-employee with Scarlett. There. He had admitted it.

Complicated but still very manageable, he immediately added.

As he thought this Scarlett returned.

Lorenzo glanced up as he poured the whisked dessert mixture into a setting tray. He covered it and placed it carefully in the refrigerator. 'How did you get on?'

'I can't raise a response by phone.' Her teeth tugged at her lower lip. 'Can you have one of the other hands instruct me to do his chores? Or rearrange things so I take care of chores I can't get wrong, and the others cover his duties between them?'

'You, too, have other duties.' Lorenzo looked into Scarlett's lovely eyes.

And discovered a dose of determination staring back at him.

She stuck her chin out. 'The most important duty is ensuring that my head chef has all the help he needs.'

And the truth was that Lorenzo *was* hard at work on

his dessert preparation. The other staff were hard at work on lunchtime meals for a restaurant floor that was rapidly filling.

It wasn't a good time to be a staff member short, and it wasn't a good time for Lorenzo to be distracted by other aspects of the kitchen. Not if they wanted to win this round of the contest, and trying to do that was important for Rosa, too. 'All right. You can don an apron and get the others to show you what they most need you to do, but only while you're really needed in here.'

'Isabella won't be here until mid-afternoon.' Scarlett bit her lip. 'I could try to get her to come in earlier but I spoke to her on the phone this morning and she said that she and Jackie had invited Mum to have lunch with them. It wasn't really based in…social intentions.'

'A little bit of distraction.' He nodded. 'And we don't want your mother to think we're not coping in here.' That was something Lorenzo could completely understand.

Scarlett nodded. 'If I call Isabella, she and Jackie might both feel obligated to leave their lunch and come in, and that leaves Mum on the loose, um, I mean…'

'You mean *on the loose.*' Lorenzo grinned, a completely spontaneous outright grin as he watched a lovely little rush of colour leach into Scarlett's cheeks. And then his smile faded, because she was so beautiful. All he wanted in that moment was to kiss her. He shut down the response, but he suspected it would have been all over his face for the entire kitchen staff to see, if any of them had happened to be looking.

'It is best to keep your mother happily occupied for as much of this weekend as possible.' He forced the words out, and forced his attention back to his dessert preparations. 'And Isabella is handling the closing at night. She can't do everything.'

Scarlett nodded. 'And you need to get on with what you're doing now. Take a break to eat, 'Renz. Promise?'

'Yes, I promise.' It would happen later, when the rush was over and before he needed to put in his final effort on his meal prep. He would take Scarlett with him and make her eat, too.

Or maybe you should focus on your work and forget all about Scarlett, who is no doubt capable of ensuring that she eats food, all by herself.

With a stifled sigh, Lorenzo got back to work.

'They're ready for you out front. Right now the cameras are on the MC while she counts this down to the entry of you, and Sorella's chef, out there.' Scarlett spoke the words in a quiet, almost awe-struck tone as she looked at the five finished desserts Lorenzo had before him. 'You've done an amazing job, Lorenzo. I don't see how those can't win tonight's part of the contest.'

Lorenzo was pleased with his efforts, too, but still cautious. 'That will depend on what the Sorella chef has prepared. I've tried for things that I'm guessing he wouldn't risk making, and yet I've stuck to traditional Italian desserts. Every dessert could be offered on our menu at any time. I think that's a good standard to stick to.'

'And a great way to get our guests trying some new dishes that we *can* add to the menu if they prove popular.' Scarlett was impressed, and didn't hesitate to show it.

The man behind the camera called for Lorenzo to get ready to take his desserts out, and counted down to the roll of the camera.

Three staff would carry the desserts. Lorenzo took up the first two, Isabella the second two, and Scarlett the final one and they all made their way through the restaurant and outside to the dais area again where the Sorella chef was also approaching.

All Lorenzo wanted, once he'd served the various desserts for the panel of judges, was to stand at Scarlett's side to wait for the results to be announced. He joined her, and Isabella excused herself to return to the kitchen.

Lorenzo let his gaze drift out over the crowded square. For a moment he thought he caught sight of a familiar figure, there at the back. His breath caught in his throat and his hand reached automatically to close around Scarlett's wrist. The protective urge that rose in him was swift and encompassing.

As he searched again, and couldn't see Marcella anywhere, he told himself it couldn't have been her. She might have interfered with his employment in the past, but she'd never visited any of the restaurants in person.

But this was Monta Correnti. She had family in this region.

You expected you might see her around the village sooner or later.

Lorenzo drew a deep breath and tried to shake the unease aside. Marcella couldn't do anything to him. He'd been as open as he could be with Luca when he had applied to work here. Luca would not sack him on Marcella's say-so, no matter what rumours she tried to set into the older man's ears.

Yes, but what if Marcella crossed paths with Scarlett? Used words to try to hurt Scarlett? Verbally bullied her or...worse? What if Marcella approached him while he was with Scarlett, and...shamed him with one of her...attacks?

But it was equally likely that Marcella was *not* in the crowd, and, if she was, how likely was it that she would make a scene here, in the midst of her family's hometown?

Lorenzo told himself it wasn't that likely, but his fingers still slid to Scarlett's hand and tightened protectively over it. She squeezed right back and he realised she probably thought he'd taken her hand due to suspense over the outcome of this round of the contest.

Within the crowd, people were oohing and aahing over the desserts as the judges tasted each one. Lorenzo released his hold on Scarlett's hand and did his bit to describe the dishes into the microphone when asked.

He tried to concentrate on the judges' comments, but all he could realise was that he was getting way too attached to having Scarlett around again. She'd stepped up to replace his missing kitchen hand, and had worked tirelessly all afternoon, stopping only once to force him to take a break and eat. Lorenzo had wanted to be successful, not only for himself and for Rosa, but also for her.

'And we're pleased to announce that the winner of tonight's round is chef Lorenzo Nesta, of Rosa restaurant.'

Scarlett made a pleased sound beside him and impulsively hugged him.

His hands automatically caught her, held her close. It took all of his focus not to dip his head and kiss her. Not because they'd won a round, though that was great and a reward for a lot of hard work, but because Scarlett was in his arms beaming from ear to ear and looking into his eyes, not only with happiness and relief, but also with affection.

'Well, done, Lorenzo.'

'You have done Rosa proud.'

The words came from Isabella and Luca. Lorenzo released Scarlett and received a kiss on each cheek from a beaming Isabella, and the same again from Luca, and then their MC was talking the crowd through what would follow for the final day's festivities.

The next half-hour passed in a blur that turned into another hour as Lorenzo returned to the kitchen with Scarlett and they both pitched in again to take care of their dinner crowd, many of whom wanted to try the winning desserts.

'It was helpful to us for the panel to make this a bulk quantity event,' Scarlett said. 'We can put the dishes on offer for all our patrons.'

That one comment of Scarlett's rang in Lorenzo's ears and then more time passed until finally the last meal was served and it was only coffees remaining, and Scarlett came to him with a bossish glint in her eyes. 'You're finishing now. There's nothing that needs doing here that we can't all manage without you.'

There were smudges beneath Scarlett's eyes. Lorenzo guessed if he looked in a mirror he'd see the same. It *had* been a big day, but for both of them, not just for him. On a night like this, he would get on his motorcycle—

'I'll go now.' He murmured it quietly. 'But you should leave, too. You also need to rest.'

He didn't give Scarlett a chance to argue the point. Instead, Lorenzo turned to Isabella and caught her attention. 'Are you okay to finish up?'

'Oh, yes. You've done enough.' She gestured around her. 'We're fine here, though I'm guessing Scarlett will want a good explanation for why Rocco didn't turn up for his shift.'

'Yes, but Scarlett covered for him very well.'

And Isabella had kept Scarlett's mother occupied, and they'd now got through two events without Luca and Lisa aggravating each other.

Lorenzo led Scarlett away, not through the front, but out of the rear door. His motorcycle was beside the restaurant van.

'Are we dodging the crowds?' Scarlett tipped her face up. 'That breeze is nice. It gets a bit stuffy in the kitchen after a while.'

'I was going to offer to drop you home, but come for a ride with me. It will be a chance to blow the cobwebs away. We don't have to go far.' He drew the helmet from the handgrip and raised his brows. It was an impulsive suggestion, perhaps born out of his tiredness, and yet the idea of a late-night motorcycle ride really did appeal, and he'd like to share that with her.

Scarlett hesitated. 'You've only got one helmet.'

'There's a spare in the van.' It was Lorenzo's previous one, a little aged. He'd tossed it behind the seat there when he replaced it with this one. He quickly unlocked the van, retrieved the helmet.

'All right. I will.' The start of a smile broke over Scarlett's face as she put the helmet on. She left the visor pushed up. 'I want to feel the breeze.'

They climbed onto his motorcycle. Scarlett tucked her skirt about her legs. Her arms came around his waist and he glanced over his shoulder just as she spoke in a jesting tone. 'I hope your skills have improved since I first knew you. I'd rather you didn't tip us off into a ditch.' The skin around her eyes crinkled as she smiled. 'You were a bit clumsy, always getting scratched and bruised from taking spills on your bike. I used to worry about you really getting hurt one day but I haven't seen a mark on you since I've been back, not even that day at the pool.'

She seemed to realise that her words might sound a little too aware, a little too intimate, and fell abruptly silent.

Lorenzo fought for a calm response. Those scratches and bruises—God, he didn't want to think about it. 'I'm good on the motorcycle. Ah, now, I mean. You'll be completely safe, I promise.'

Lorenzo fired up the motorcycle and rode them away. Away from Rosa, away from crowds, away from all of it including his thoughts. He rode them out onto the hilly roads beyond the village. He rode and the cooler evening air whipped at his chef's shirt while Scarlett's warmth pressed against his back and after a while she let out a yell of pure delight, and dark memories left him and he laughed aloud.

The roads were deserted and he drove for ten minutes until Scarlett tugged on his arm and gestured for him to pull over. He came to a stop on a grassy area that led to an elevated outcrop.

Scarlett pulled her helmet off and blinked hard. 'Sorry. I think I got some dust in my eye. It's stinging. I suppose I should have put the visor down, but that breeze was worth it!'

'Let me help you.' There was a moon overhead. He drew a clean handkerchief from his trouser pocket and gently wiped her eye with it.

'I think you got it.' Scarlett blinked again.

He glanced at the white handkerchief. 'I see a black smudge.'

'Well, I'm glad we got it out. Thanks.' Scarlett turned to look out over the grassy knoll. 'It's beautiful here. You can see right out over the valley. And it's so quiet.' Her gaze rose to the sky and she drew a deep breath. 'I'm lucky. I've lived in two of the most beautiful countries of the world.'

'Australia and Italy.' He nodded. 'From when you were here…before, I think you found both countries felt like home in their ways.'

'Both did, and sometimes neither did.' Scarlett's brows drew together as she fell silent. After a moment, she went on. 'It can be hard, feeling the pull of two countries. Well, of people within two countries. I'm not sure it's the land so much, as—'

'As family.' All of Lorenzo's family lived within Italy. His parents were still in the village, holding their heads up and pretending their son's marriage wasn't a farce reduced to a useless piece of paper and Marcella's long-term bitterness. Their pride and judgement hadn't helped in his situation, though he couldn't blame them too much. They only knew half the circumstances. Lorenzo could never tell them all of it.

'Yes.' Scarlett bit her lip. 'Well, I'm trying to get along with all of the family this time. Sometimes I feel like Mamma doesn't make it easy, but we've never been close. Jackie says we're too similar, but I don't want to be just like my mother. I want to be me.'

As Scarlett uttered these words to Lorenzo she acknowledged that there had been long stretches of time in her life when she would have seemed cold even to those closest to her.

Her time with Lorenzo had been different. She'd let him right into her heart, had opened parts of herself to him that she'd never trusted to anyone else.

Tonight, standing here beneath this moon with Lorenzo's gaze on her, Scarlett could almost believe—

A leaf rustled from a tree and fluttered into her face. Lorenzo reached with gentle fingers to brush it away. His hand lingered, and somehow Scarlett's cheek was pressed into the palm of his hand and, oh, she just wanted to stay like that. Her eyes drifted half closed.

'What are we doing, Lorenzo?' She whispered the words.

'I think we're doing this.' His head bent to hers until their lips met softly, so softly.

A gentle kiss in the moonlight. That was all this was. Scarlett told herself this and gave into the moment, denying everything. All her fears and worries, all of their past.

How did this happen to her? How did she yield to him in her life where she had stood firm, stood alone very often and refused, oh, so totally refused to allow anyone all the way into…her soul? Yet with this man, who had hurt her and whom she shouldn't be able to trust at all, Scarlett…let go.

And she did, and this gentle kiss became another and another until senses and yielding were all that Scarlett could feel or comprehend and somehow they were lying on the grass and

Lorenzo's breath fell on her neck before he pressed kisses there and murmured low words to her in their native language.

He murmured of his need for her and that he had missed her touch, missed her, and then he cut those words off and his mouth came to hers once again and this kiss was different. The thought crossed her mind to wonder if Jackie had felt like this when she gave herself to her young lover, and Scarlett pushed aside guilt and family too and her hands rose to clasp the sides of Lorenzo's strong neck. Her fingers splayed through the hair at his nape as he deepened their kiss and she went with him. Scarlett just…packed away everything and went with him.

The tensions of today, and yesterday, left her while she was in Lorenzo's arms. When they drew back a little and she searched his face, his eyes, there was such desire and need there and she felt it, too, deep within herself in parts of her that Scarlett had thought she had lost to love five years ago.

When her body became boneless and pliant against his, chest-to-chest, arms about each other, how could anything else happen but for them to nestle closer and kiss each other again?

Legs tangled, mouths meshed. The sky was so vast over their heads and so she blocked it out and only looked at Lorenzo's face above hers, and when even that was too much Scarlett closed her eyes and thought she should regain some control, some grip.

But then she simply felt more. Felt every sensation as their tongues brushed, as his fingers threaded into her ponytail and somehow her hair was loose about her shoulders and he'd taken her ribbon and tucked it into his shirt pocket over his chest.

Scarlett felt the warm solid press of his medallion against *her* chest, and knew there would be a faint mark there. Lorenzo held her hair in his hands and she *felt* his sensual pleasure in the touch of that silky mass through his fingers as he sighed and kissed her again.

Again and again and again.

Scarlett could have stepped over the edge into lovemaking so easily with him in those moments. She wasn't sure what stopped her, what made her thoughts come back to her, take hold of her once again so that she surfaced enough from this, from wonderful sensations and warmth and rightness to *question* that rightness.

'Lorenzo.' The word was acknowledgement, withdrawal, regret rolled into one. And self-protection. 'This can't happen.'

She eased away from his mouth, away from his arms. Oh, it was the most difficult thing Scarlett had done in a very long time.

He sat up, too, and they shared one long, silent glance before Lorenzo's expression seemed to clear and change.

Scarlett searched those changes, wanted, no, *needed* to know what they meant, what he was thinking. And she felt panicked, because why did this matter so much to her? Why did Lorenzo matter so much to her when she had fought so hard to get over him mattering, to forget him mattering? To never let him or any other man ever matter to her to that same depth again?

Scarlett didn't want that kind of hurt again. Her sister had suffered hurt. Scarlett wasn't dealing with that very well. And now she wasn't dealing with this. She felt trapped by her own tangled emotions. Trapped and yet deep inside herself she had known she needed to come back.

Not only to Italy but to Monta Correnti, to the heart of her family and to the heart of where she'd fallen for a man, and been hurt by that love, and walked away and taken herself far away and sworn not to trust again.

How did she reconcile trust with keeping herself safe? Was

that even possible? And…could she be falling back in love with him again?

You could if you wanted to. It wouldn't have to be the same now. 'You're free now.'

She didn't mean to utter the words aloud.

And she saw him stiffen. 'Scarlett—' For one moment, he looked tortured.

And Scarlett felt uncertain again for nebulous reasons, ones she couldn't pin down, and it was late and suddenly the exhaustion was all there again, only more so now because of this.

Scarlett felt scared of her own emotions. 'Please, can we go back? I'm so tired.'

Emotionally drained, physically weary. Uncertain in heart and head. For Scarlett, who needed to feel in control to feel safe, these were not good things.

No, they really were not. She got to her feet and walked on shaking legs towards Lorenzo's motorcycle.

He followed, and he opened his mouth to speak again but Scarlett just couldn't.

She shook her head and he frowned, but he got them organised and took her back into town. The square was quiet now. Scarlett refused to wonder how long they'd been gone. Lorenzo stopped his motorcycle a little away from Scarlett's lodgings and she climbed off and he put her helmet away and they walked the remainder of the way.

When they stopped outside her door she tried. Maybe it was ridiculous, almost farcical, but she had to try. 'The contest part of tomorrow shouldn't be quite as demanding for you.'

Work. The goals of Rosa. 'I appreciate how hard you've worked for Rosa, Lorenzo, and that you've been a good sport about something that started out as a small suggestion and has turned into something a lot more demanding.'

'The restaurant is fully booked again for tomorrow night.'

He seemed to want to regain that normality, too. 'It's good. What's happening for Rosa is good.'

And yet he also looked unhappy and…uneasy?

'Goodnight, Scarlett.' He stepped back from her, stepped back and turned on his heel as though he had to. 'I'll—I'll see you tomorrow at the restaurant.'

He walked away, and Scarlett went inside, and wondered if maybe she *should* have stayed at her mother's place, because at least then she might not have felt so comfortable about coming and going with Lorenzo and might have saved herself from tonight, and the questions it had raised that she had been trying very hard not to hear.

One question above all others.

She couldn't be falling for him all over again? Really falling? As in, giving-her-heart falling?

Could she?

CHAPTER NINE

'Scarlett—' Isabella drew a breath and her hand came to rest on Scarlett's arm. 'I've been talking to Jackie and, well, I think… I think we need to talk. Will you come into Luca's office for a minute?'

It was Sunday. The restaurant was crowded with diners inside and out. Lorenzo and the Sorella chef were back at their outside cooking stations. Less than an hour from now the overall winner for the weekend would be decided, one way or another. The challenge was five authentic Italian main meals. Scarlett was convinced that Lorenzo would win this.

There hadn't been time today for even a moment alone with him, and Scarlett admitted that she had wanted, had hoped for that.

Last night…they could have ended up making love. Oh, the way she felt when she was with him! The way everything within her longed—

After five years of not seeing him, of telling herself she was over him, that the hurt he had done to her could never be forgiven and would never be forgotten. After all that, for her to still feel like herself, but also part of a bigger whole that was not just made up of her when they were together.

Surely that feeling must be rare? Surely it must mean something that was worth looking at, worth reaching for?

Scarlett had needed to look into his eyes today and see there the same expressions she had believed she saw last night on a moon-limned hilltop. Scarlett needed to feel reassured that she wasn't the only one experiencing this pull towards him. She needed to know that Lorenzo felt this, too, that he was equally involved in whatever these feelings were.

'Is it urgent, Izzie? There's a lot of patrons to look after right now and the contest is drawing to a close.' She glanced again at the packed square.

Normally Scarlett wouldn't think of anything but the work. She was a good financial manager, she knew her stuff, and she knew the importance of being aware of everything that went on in any establishment she worked in, from the ground up. Yet right now Scarlett could have turned her attention from all of it and simply spent that time looking into Lorenzo's eyes.

Well, he was busy trying to win the cook-off for Rosa. The last thing he needed was Scarlett distracting him and with that in mind she *had* stayed out of his way as much as possible so far today.

It just might have been nice to get more than one brief glance, loaded with suppressed passion and awareness though that one glance had been. Scarlett needed his touch. The feel of his arms around her, the press of his lips against hers. Words, to hear soft words spoken in her ear, pouring out his need for her as he had done last night.

You are in so deep, Scarlett. Have you thought about that?

'It's important enough.' Izzie's words were restrained. But also tense.

Scarlett searched her cousin's face and truly became aware of that tension within Izzie.

'Is this about the restaurant, Izzie? Work? The contest?' Scarlett had thought about the contest, about where it had taken Rosa and where Rosa needed to get in order to truly stay financially viable. There were possibilities nipping at the edges of her mind. She just hadn't had the time to really work them through in her thoughts.

Izzie shook her head. 'It's not really about any of those things. It's, well, it's about you. In a way. Scarlett, can we just talk? Please?'

'Yes, of course.' Scarlett's tummy did a big, uneasy flutter. 'I'm sorry, Isabella. I was distracted.' *Thinking about Lorenzo and a future I should not even be hinting at, not even in the darkest recesses of a mind that should be focused on problem solving during these working hours.* 'By, um, I was distracted by the final leg of the contest. I'll come now. Lead the way.'

It took minutes for them to make their way through the crowds. A couple of times people stopped Isabella for a short conversation. Izzie showed perfect professionalism, listening, chatting, but also winding things up quickly.

Scarlett's unease hiked with each passing moment, even as she appreciated the rapport that Isabella had with many of the diners. That rapport had to be worth something. The familiarity of a locally owned and run restaurant.

Had Luca hired Lorenzo as chef with that in mind when his previous chef moved out of the area? Knowing that people would appreciate that they were being catered for by a local man? Lorenzo had worked in other places, but he'd grown up here. His parents still lived here. Scarlett had seen them in passing though she hadn't ever met them.

Lorenzo didn't seem to speak about his family. In fact, Scarlett somehow guessed that his personal life was something that *didn't* get discussed here at Rosa.

You were his guilty secret five years ago.

That could be very different now.

Last night as she lay unable to sleep, Scarlett had finally asked herself, truly, was she falling in love with Lorenzo again? She'd tried to look at the question rationally, to examine it and assess it the way she would anything in her business world.

Instead she had simply longed for him with an ache that seemed to come right out of her soul. And when she did try to look at the whole picture, their past, the hurt, she kept coming back to… She had changed, and Lorenzo had changed. Didn't that mean that their lives were not the same now as they had been then? And if he truly made her feel this way then why should she hold back?

No, she couldn't say she was falling in love with him again. That would be a huge undertaking, would involve so much trust and she wasn't sure if she could give that trust ever again. But a part of Scarlett no longer ruled out…something?

Did she want a second affair with him now, while she was here in Italy working at Rosa? Was that the conclusion for these thoughts? These feelings? And if so, what happened after that? What happened when Rosa was back on its feet and/or Scarlett had done all that she possibly could for the restaurant and perhaps Luca said thank you, that's enough now and let her go?

Did she return to Australia and pick up the threads of her life there and forget about Lorenzo for a second time?

Like you forgot the first time?

Scarlett wasn't sure she could let herself think about the alternative, that her emotions might be on the way to getting deeply involved again. Could a woman fall in love with a man twice? And have things work out better the second time?

Well, right now she needed to deal with Isabella. Scarlett turned to face her cousin inside this small office with the door closed for their privacy. 'What is it, Izzie?'

Whatever her cousin had to say, Scarlett would rather hear it and deal with it. 'If this is about family—Jackie's photos—' Scarlett had planned to look at those, truly. At the end of tonight she would look at them. She just…

Had been avoiding doing that, and had blamed their busy work schedule for it.

Nothing was simple, was it?

'It's not about Jackie or…Kate.' Isabella's brows drew together. 'Though that's another issue that has been on my mind, Scarlett. You do need to look at Kate's photos. I think that will help you to let her be a real person to you.'

'She is real!' Scarlett bit the words off while her heart said that was the whole problem. Kate had always been a real person, first a child and now a young woman who'd had feelings and a heart and who must have spent years wondering why she'd been given up by her birth mother.

Whether she'd been happy with her adopting family or not, Kate must have experienced those thoughts, and Jackie must have longed for the daughter she lost. Scarlett's actions had forged that young woman's life path, and a lot of Jackie's, too.

'What do you need to say to me, Izzie?'

Sounds of the restaurant's busyness carried through the closed door, and the MC for the event had started the ten-minute countdown! They shouldn't stay in here for even five more minutes so whatever this was, Scarlett would rather hear it now. In an action that was perhaps reminiscent of her mother, Scarlett tightened her shoulders and stood very straight and waited to take this, whatever it was, squarely on the chin and deal with it. 'Spill, Isabella.'

'Scarlett, I saw you…looking at Lorenzo earlier.' Isabella wrung her hands once before she caught Scarlett's glance and gave a slight shake of her head. 'Looking at him as…a lover would. If I misinterpreted I hope you'll forgive me, and I know it isn't my business anyway, but it's not the first time I've intercepted something between you both and Jackie noticed it, too.'

'Well, it isn't your business, really.' The words emerged

before Scarlett had time to think about them. They emerged out of her surprise that Isabella would comment on such a thing. This was so far from what she had expected, and, really, so what?

Why would Isabella feel worried or concerned or upset about that, and enough that she would pull Scarlett out of a busy restaurant and away from the end of the contest to talk to her? 'Is this because I'm the financial manager here? You're concerned about something happening between me as I stand in that position, and another employee here?'

Fair enough if Isabella *was* concerned. Scarlett herself would have frowned on it if she'd discovered a similar situation between two staff members. And Isabella had worked with all her heart and effort for Rosa for a lot of years up to the point when Scarlett had stepped into the role of Financial Manager. But again, surely that could have waited a little?

Scarlett drew a breath and told herself to tread carefully. She and Lorenzo hadn't actually done anything that could be in any way construed as inappropriate. Well, they'd kissed beside the van, but she was confident no one had seen that. Even so, Isabella had noticed Scarlett's interest in Lorenzo and must have been truly confident in its existence to bring this up.

'It's not really about that.' Isabella shook her head. 'It's probably not the most advisable thing for two people who work together to become involved but that's life. It happens. Of course you can do whatever you want to in terms of personal relationships, Scarlett.' Isabella bit her lip. 'I'm doing a bad job of this.'

She paced away a few steps and swung around to face Scarlett again. 'It's just, I don't want you to get hurt.'

Scarlett didn't want that, either, and opened her mouth to say so, or reassure her cousin somehow, or something. 'It's kind of you to care, Izzie. I appreciate it. I truly do. But in the end, isn't it my—?'

'He's married, Scarlett.' Isabella blurted the words and fell abruptly silent. She drew a breath. 'He's married. It's just, he lives here now and his wife has a home in another, larger village and maybe they haven't actually lived together for a long time. But some couples do live apart yet are still together, if you know what I mean. Lorenzo is a great guy, but he's close-mouthed about his personal life, but I do know that much. That he is a married man.'

'Married.' The word reverberated through Scarlett's mind, echoed in her ears and…brought a tight pain to the centre of her chest. *Still married?* She struggled to comprehend.

Her gaze locked with Isabella's. She wasn't sure if she was looking for reassurance, an anchor, or some way to prove that Isabella had this all wrong.

Married.

Lorenzo Nesta was still *married.*

The fact of it started to penetrate. And a rush of memories came with her beginnings of understanding.

He'd told her five years ago that he would leave his wife. That he wanted to build a life with Scarlett. It had taken time for him to confess his marriage in the first place and by then Scarlett had been deeply in love with him. She'd made the commitment to stick with him and he had made the commitment to leave his wife and divorce her so he could…marry Scarlett.

Oh, she'd had such dreams and Lorenzo had stomped all over those dreams and now she'd come back and he'd let her care about him all over again. Let her give her kisses to him again. He'd allowed her to let him into her emotions again. Anger started somewhere deep inside Scarlett. Hurt welled, too. She tried to stopper the hurt back.

'I put it off. I didn't want to say anything—' There was

utterly no judgement in Isabella's expression or tone, just care. She wasn't accusing Scarlett of anything. She wanted to keep her cousin safe from hurt and so she'd crossed a line, risking being told it was none of her business.

Scarlett understood all of this, felt it go into her heart as an offering even as she battled to comprehend the rest and that boil of feeling continued to build.

How could Lorenzo still be married? He'd allowed her to reach out to him, to develop affection for him a second time when he'd *known* how much the last time had hurt her.

She shouldn't have let herself care. Not about him. Not… again. Had he thought she knew? But even if he did think that, she'd said out loud, 'You're free now.' He hadn't corrected her.

For a moment Scarlett felt as though she'd been thrown back through time. Except this time Scarlett hadn't fallen in love with Lorenzo. Oh, no, she had not. The anger welling up, drowning out everything else, proved that. *Anger.* Any pain was from…feeling embarrassed at being caught making a mistake like this, even if Izzie didn't know the half of it!

No. There was no love for Lorenzo. Oh, she had wondered whether she was developing *some* feelings again for him, but Scarlett was too smart to have let that happen again. And… too good at protecting herself from caring to that degree.

Stick to the point, Scarlett. 'You know this for a fact, Izzie?'

Scarlett had to make certain of that, because when she confronted Lorenzo—

'Yes, I know.' Isabella's face softened as she stepped forward and briefly touched Scarlett's arm. 'Please don't be offended that I brought this up.'

'I'm not offended, Isabella.' Scarlett could have wished that her cousin hadn't noticed her interest in Lorenzo, but she couldn't do anything about that now. All she could do was go forward and the best way to do that was to be armed with facts. 'I presume you know this from a reliable source?'

'His parents speak of the marriage as though it's only a matter of time until there'll be a full reconciliation.' Izzie gave a shrug that didn't manage to hide the careful way she examined Scarlett's face. 'I'm not at all sure that will be the case, but the fact of Lorenzo's marriage also came up one day when I was speaking to Papa. It was soon after he hired Lorenzo. He said that Lorenzo told him of the marriage himself when he applied for the job here.'

Isabella paused. 'Papa didn't say much about it, just to take Lorenzo on his own merits.' She shrugged. 'He's been a good chef, good worker, easy to get along with and fully behind the restaurant.'

And for that reason Isabella probably didn't want any waves between Scarlett and Lorenzo, either.

She wouldn't get them. Not on restaurant time, anyway. Scarlett would do her duty and be utterly professional about it, no matter if it killed her. But Lorenzo—

Yes, the issue of Lorenzo would have to be dealt with, but first there was the issue of a cousin who stood watching her and looking worried.

Scarlett took her turn to pat Isabella's arm, and gave her a smile that she hoped appeared calm. 'Thank you for telling me this and I want you to know that I'm fine. I will take care of myself. You don't need to worry about a thing, but it means a lot to me that you cared.'

And it did. 'Now, we need to get back out to the restaurant and see the rest of this evening through, and don't forget there's a celebration for the staff when we've got the dinner patrons all squared away. Everyone's worked so hard this weekend and we got a great result for Rosa. It's important to acknowledge that whether it's an overall win in the end, or not.'

Scarlett stepped ahead of Isabella out of the office. She took each step in full management mode. As she reached the dining area her gaze scanned tables, checked faces to gauge mood, contentment, looked at meals and checked the performance of staff.

This, Scarlett knew how to do, and would do with all of her might.

Never let them see your pain.

She'd heard her mother say that to a friend on the phone many years ago in a moment Scarlett had later looked back on and realised had probably shown a rare depth of honesty and introspection from Lisa.

No person was made of total stone. Not Scarlett's mum. Not Scarlett. But Scarlett could make a damned good effort at keeping her focus on her work and *acting* like stone until she got her anger under control and could face Lorenzo calmly and tell him calmly, just what she thought of him.

Yes, that was how Scarlett wanted to handle this issue. Her discussion with Lorenzo would have to wait until the end of the night. So be it. Scarlett had other things to focus on now and, anyway, it wasn't as if she was heartbroken over Lorenzo like the last time. Oh, she was not. She was so, totally not!

And if she remembered that he'd been trying to tell her something last night, and wondered if he'd intended to confess about his marriage, well, even if that was the case, it was rather late in the piece, wasn't it?

Scarlett glanced towards her cousin and opened her mouth to announce…something businesslike. Anything, really. But Isabella was staring with her eyes narrowed into the outdoor Sorella seating area. A moment later Isabella's hand closed over Scarlett's forearm.

They spoke simultaneously.

'*Rocco.*'

'It looks like he's out for a party night,' Scarlett observed quietly.

'I'll give him party-mode,' Isabella declared with a snap of her teeth. 'How dare he miss his shift and then turn up eating and drinking at Sorella the day after without a word of explanation?' She charged forward through the tables.

Scarlett, perforce, followed her cousin. She didn't even glance towards Lorenzo's workstation. And Scarlett was proud of *that*.

'You're on probation for three months.' Scarlett's words to yesterday's missing kitchen hand were calm, but firm.

She caught Lorenzo's glance on her as she uttered them. Lorenzo's expression suggested he wasn't quite sure of Scarlett's mood. He should be thankful that she could fake a level of self-possession for moments like this. She didn't exactly want to deal with Rocco right now, but, by God, she would do what she had to.

'But I told you I had a headache. A terrible headache. I still have it.'

'I don't doubt you have one *now*.' Scarlett shook her head. 'I told all the staff here when I first took over as Financial Manager that this restaurant needed to function as a team with all team members doing their utmost to support the overall effort.'

She let her gaze rake the man. 'You were needed this weekend, you made no effort to contact the restaurant to explain your absence, then we discover you in the crowd eating at Sorella, without so much as an explanation of your absence yesterday. One more misstep will result in you being fired. Are we clear?'

Scarlett stared at the man and he glared at her.

To her left, Lorenzo seemed to bristle with tension. The contest was being decided even now, but the judges had explained the final deliberations could take a while and Lorenzo had obviously spotted the situation with Rocco and come to offer his presence in the way of some reinforcement.

Not that Scarlett and Isabella couldn't have got Rocco into Rosa by themselves, Scarlett told herself, and utterly disregarded the fact that Rocco had been recalcitrant until Lorenzo had walked over to join them and backed Scarlett's request for a few words with the man.

As it was, Rocco had barged into the kitchen rather than going to the office.

'Whatever you say.' The hand spoke the words sarcastically and turned away.

Unfortunately as he walked towards the doors of the kitchen Scarlett heard the rather pointed curses he uttered. They were about her, and vile enough to drain the blood from her face for a moment before she pulled herself together.

Lorenzo also heard, and he came forward before Scarlett could move.

'You just stepped over the line.' He addressed the man and gestured to the doors. 'I've warned you about skipping shifts twice before, but this…is beyond tolerable. Scarlett has been too generous to you and I don't mind stepping in to say this, to save her from wasting her breath on you. You're fired. Leave, and do it through the rear doors away from the patrons. If there's pay owing to you, it'll be mailed.'

The man looked disbelieving for a moment. He swayed on his feet. He was more inebriated than he'd looked.

Well, if Lorenzo hadn't uttered those words, Scarlett would have. Yet she didn't want to see Lorenzo's strength right now. Scarlett didn't want to be conscious of him at all in any way, but…at least Rocco was being dealt with. Scarlett stifled a sigh.

'Fine, I'm going.' The guy shoved the doors open and stumbled out. 'I didn't like working here anyway. I'd rather be in one of the big cities where there's actually some life!'

As he left, Lorenzo glanced at two of the other hands. 'Make sure he leaves, please.'

The two hands walked out behind Rocco.

Scarlett drew a deep breath. 'Well, that's done.' She glanced at Lorenzo but didn't let herself meet his gaze. 'You need to get back to your station. The results could come in at any moment.'

Lorenzo hesitated before he said, 'After the contest I think we need—'

'To speak. Yes. After the contest, when this night is over.' There would be a reckoning. Perhaps Lorenzo understood that. Scarlett hoped she could pull herself together a little between now and then.

And Scarlett tried.

And to a degree, she succeeded.

Enough that she felt genuine excitement and happiness when the announcement came that the contest was over, and Rosa had won!

The staff finished serving everyone, and cleared the restaurant out. Scarlett was thrilled for the restaurant, grateful to Lorenzo for his work, and still furious at him and hurt, so hurt, all rolled into one.

But she had a job to do, and she pitched in to help with the final clean-up, and once it was done she gathered the staff together in the kitchen and gave her congratulatory speech to everyone. She could do this. She would do this. She wasn't Lisa Firenzi's daughter for nothing, and right now Scarlett was claiming every bit of her mother's strength and using it to keep herself afloat. 'Thank you all. You've made a wonderful effort, I'm so proud.'

She hesitated and then forged on. 'We've had our moments this weekend and I know some of that has probably been a bit off-putting for you all, too. I appreciate your professionalism and that you all just got on with your work.'

Lorenzo listened to Scarlett's words and felt such a mix of emotions. He pushed back the healthy weariness of several very busy days, and focused his attention on Scarlett. He couldn't pin down all of what was bothering her, but he knew her and his need to be private with her and, he wasn't sure, *find out what was amiss,* was roaring at him. It was more than Rocco missing a shift and being rude.

Taking that situation into account and whatever else was upsetting Scarlett, she had gone on to work professionally. Her ability to handle herself so well in such management issues showed her strength, and yet hers was a very different kind of strength from…Marcella's.

He pushed the thought aside, but unease remained. Scarlett *was* too calm. As though beneath the surface something bubbled and all her attention was focused on controlling it, not letting others see it.

'So a heartfelt three cheers for a magnificent effort this weekend to our fabulous head chef, and to all of you who worked so hard to help him achieve this win!'

Scarlett applauded. The other staff members applauded and cheered and beamed. Luca was here, too, though he'd missed the drama earlier and perhaps that was for the best. He also applauded and cheered and beamed.

'Speech, Lorenzo.'

'Yes, speech, speech!'

'Thank you.' Lorenzo let his gaze drift over the group. There was only one gaze he wanted to meet but she didn't want to allow it right now and in truth now wasn't the time. He went on. 'This was a team effort and whether we ended up winning or not it still would have been a highly successful weekend. It was great to see the square packed and our tables packed.'

'Yes, and let's keep up the good work.' Scarlett added these final words before she said, 'First thing tomorrow. For now, we deserve a glass of wine before we all go home to rest!'

There was cake, too, baked by Isabella and brought in especially. While Isabella handed pieces of that around, Scarlett poured wine with a rock-steady hand.

Even now her face was pleased, encouraging, appropriately proud of the staff and their work—including Lorenzo's. On the surface, nothing looked amiss. So why did Lorenzo feel so concerned?

But he was. Last night, he and Scarlett had almost made love. He had needed her with such depth within himself and yet his life was not the uncomplicated thing that he wished it could be.

Luca knew about Marcella. Oh, not all of it. Lorenzo would never, ever tell the truth of that, not to a soul. How could he when his shame burned so deep even now? But he had explained about past job problems from his wife, that they lived separately, the bare minimum for a man who had wanted to know how Lorenzo would fit back into the Monta Correnti community.

Mostly Lorenzo had tried to do so quietly. He'd rented a small home and got on with it.

Lorenzo remembered last night. Holding Scarlett in his arms. Had it been their surroundings that had affected him that way? The darkness, the time of night, the moon shining over them or the quietness and rest of that moment that had made him long so much to make her his once again?

Or perhaps it had simply been Scarlett, and him, for hadn't the two of them always been like that? Hadn't he needed her with a need that had surpassed everything? Wasn't that why things had ended up as they did? Because he had wanted her, needed her, despite every complication? He'd made promises and not kept them and Scarlett had gone back to Australia hurting. If Marcella again discovered he was seeing Scarlett, Lorenzo didn't know what harm she might try to do.

He *had* to tell Scarlett. About Marcella. How things were for him now. The thought made him sick. To admit to Scarlett that Marcella had used her vicious tongue against him to the point that he had been let go from other restaurants would be bad enough. What kind of man let that happen to him? And that was the least of it.

The pride of generations warred inside Lorenzo with the need to be fair to Scarlett, to try to find some way with her, and yet he hadn't found a way the last time and in the end what had changed? Nothing, but if he told Scarlett, then at least she would know and maybe not feel hurt—

And there he went, imagining that Scarlett would willingly *want* a second chance with him. She might have been experiencing a resurgence of an old attraction, and maybe last night had made her realise that wasn't what she wanted at all.

'Goodbye. Thanks again. See you tomorrow.' Scarlett waved the last person out of the restaurant. They'd cleaned up after their little celebration and now it was just her and Lorenzo.

'You haven't seemed yourself tonight.' His words were quiet.

She would have even said gentle.

But also uneasy somehow. Had he guessed what she had found out?

The question was enough to bring back a surge of emotion that twisted into a thick knot in her chest. A knot of anger, Scarlett assured herself, and, for the first time since Isabella had taken her into Luca's office, she let her face reveal that emotion. Well, it *was* anger and he'd earned it. She squashed any knowledge of other feelings.

He drew a breath. 'Scarlett, there's something I need to tell you. I started to last night, but—'

'Isabella told me—' She snapped her teeth together and narrowed her eyes.

Lorenzo stopped speaking, too.

And Scarlett finished it. 'You're still married. You *never* left her. Not only when you said you would back then and didn't and broke my heart, but not any time since. I had a right to know that, Lorenzo. You kissed me. We almost made love!'

'I did leave her.' He cast a tortured look her way. 'I left... as soon as you were safely back in Australia.'

Safely! She drew a sharp breath and her voice rose. 'As though you couldn't get rid of me fast enough!' Scarlett was losing her self-control and couldn't seem to do a thing about it.

'No. No!' He raised his hands, palms up. 'Please, Scarlett, if you'll let me try to explain.'

'How can you possibly explain?' Scarlett shook her head. She'd thought she needed this, to have her say, to tell him she was onto his duplicity, his deceitfulness, that she wasn't going to let him get away with hurting her all over again, but...

Scarlett was tired and her emotions were tired and she was confused and she wasn't sure she had quite the level of strength that she needed to manage this. 'There's no need to explain because the truth is out now and that's all that matters. Just stay out of my way until I'm finished here and can go back to Australia, that's all!'

She would focus on achieving the two goals that had brought her back to Italy. On making Rosa viable and successful, and on connecting with her family. Why, only this morning Izzie had said that Luca's second American son, Angelo, had been talking to his twin, Alex, and was considering a visit to Monta Correnti to meet the family. These were the things Scarlett needed to care about!

She turned to make her way to the front of the restaurant.

Let Lorenzo close up. He had to go out the back way anyway, she remembered, because one of the hands had collected him in the van today. They'd wanted some last-minute ingredient and that had made more sense, so Lorenzo was to drive the van home tonight.

None of which mattered a marinated olive to Scarlett!

'All right, then let me at least see you safely home.' Lorenzo took a step towards her.

'No, thank you!' She opened her mouth to tell him all the reasons she did not want his company.

Just as a shattering crash sounded at the front of the restaurant.

CHAPTER TEN

'WHAT was that?' As the sound of splintering glass echoed through the front part of the restaurant Scarlett caught her breath and started forward.

Lorenzo touched her arm and swore. 'That sounded like a brick or something coming through one of the windows. Wait here while I go look.'

He flung the kitchen door open and started to stride forward without waiting for a reply.

Scarlett didn't give him one. She simply started forward at his side. Upset or not, she wasn't about to let him go out there on his own.

They were both just outside the kitchen swing doors. There was a shout outside. A second missile flew through the broken window.

A bottle, a burning wick. The smell of petrol. The sound of footsteps running away.

'Oh, my God!'

'Get back, Scarlett!' As Lorenzo spoke he grasped her arms and shoved them both through the kitchen doors. The bottle exploded and there was a whooshing sound. Shards of glass hit against the doors behind them.

Lorenzo's arms were hard about her, his back to the doors.

He'd placed himself directly between Scarlett and the danger, and she didn't know—

'Are you hurt?' She pulled at his arms to try to get him to turn so she could check his back. 'Did any of it get you?'

'No, I'm not hurt.' He drew a breath. 'You're all right?'

'Yes.' And she was, and later she would have time to think about how safe he had made her feel, how utterly protected even as she had feared for *his* safety. But now—

'Stay here.' Lorenzo pushed the door enough to see flames licking all over the room. He grabbed the fire extinguisher off the wall and rushed out of the door and into the restaurant area, spraying with determined, focused control.

Scarlett grabbed the other extinguisher and followed. The fire spread so fast, balls of it everywhere where the bottle had shattered and its contents had poured out and caught fire from the burning wick.

'Be careful. Leave me to do this!' Lorenzo shouted the words at her.

'I'm not leaving you,' she shouted back.

Lorenzo cast one lightning-fast, worry-filled glance at her before he redoubled his efforts and so did she and minutes later there was foam everywhere and spattered on their hands and arms and clothes, but the fire was out.

'*Polizia* and the fire brigade! I want both.' Lorenzo barked it as he stormed into the kitchen and snatched the phone off the wall. A moment later he had someone on the line. He explained, firing off the words in rapid Italian before he slammed the phone back into its cradle.

'I have to check outside, Scarlett.' He drew a sharp breath and the look on his face…

Scarlett wanted to hold him, but instead *she* drew a breath. 'I'll come with you.'

'No, please. Not until I make sure we're safe here. Truly, Scarlett. Stay here where I don't have to worry about you.' He walked briskly away from her.

And because of the tone of his voice, the protectiveness in

it and…so much more that Scarlett couldn't find the thoughts to describe, she nodded her head. 'I have the phone. If you're not back very fast—'

But he checked, and there was certainly not anybody hanging about. They'd run, just as he and Scarlett had heard.

Even so, when he stepped back inside she started to shake and her hands reached for him. 'Wait for the police, now, and the fire brigade. They can do the rest. Don't—don't leave—'

Me. The safety of here.

'Scarlett.' He looked into her eyes for one short moment before he made a deep sound in the back of his throat and crushed her into his arms.

Where was her anger now? All Scarlett could do was hold on, hold on so tight.

Outside a siren sounded, and they broke apart to go out and meet the authorities.

The next minutes passed in a blur. Family arrived and rapidly amassed until Scarlett felt certain they must all be there. Lorenzo had called Luca. Others had come. Izzie, Jackie, Max and Romano, and some of the restaurant staff, too. Lisa was also there, a sombre, concerned Lisa who hugged her daughter and went to stand beside Luca as he frowned over the messy restaurant dining room.

Scarlett heard them speaking quietly, saw Mamma lay her hand on Luca's arm. She knew she should wade in, start planning for tomorrow, do something, but she couldn't seem to get her feet to move her away from Lorenzo's side.

'This makes me think of Cristiano.' Isabella uttered the words as she paused beside Scarlett and Lorenzo for a moment. 'The thought of my brother fighting huge blazes for a living—'

'Yes, it would be brave work.' Scarlett's glance moved to

Lorenzo. *He* had been brave, throwing himself into saving the restaurant and trying to protect her at the same time.

'Isabella?' Luca called to his daughter.

'Excuse me, Scarlett.' Isabella hurried away.

'We have to give the police formal statements, Scarlett.' Lorenzo turned from where he'd been speaking quietly with one of the officers. 'But he says tomorrow will do for that. We've given them as much information as we know for now.'

'Good. That's good.' She drew a breath. 'I should speak with Luca.'

But her uncle was already on his way to them. He wrapped Scarlett in a bear hug before he drew back. 'The floor is damaged and some of the tables are badly singed, but it could have been so much worse. Thank you both for your swift actions and I want you to go now. We can't clean up until the police have finished examining it, and they've heard your thoughts including the sacking of the kitchen hand and his anger as he left. Go and rest. Scarlett, your mamma thought you might go to her villa—'

As Luca uttered the words Lisa joined them. 'Yes, Scarlett. I was out…visiting when I got the call regarding this, but that can…wait. You're more than welcome to come. Please.'

'I appreciate it, Mamma.' Scarlett shook her head, and softened her words. 'But I'd rather go back to my bedsit. It's been…an exhausting day one way and another.'

'And my independent niece needs to handle that her own way?' Her uncle seemed to understand.

Lisa's mouth tightened and her gaze searched Scarlett's face before she seemed to relax. 'You are too like me sometimes, my girl, but if that's what you need, I understand.'

'Thanks, Mamma.' Scarlett took the brief hug her mother gave her, and squeezed back, and a moment later Lisa excused herself, got on her cell phone, and began to speak softly to someone, explaining that she would be 'back there soon'.

'That tone… Mamma must be dating someone. I wonder if he's local.' Scarlett uttered the thoughts out loud before she clamped her mouth closed.

Luca looked intrigued before he cleared his throat. 'Well, it's late. We can't do any more. My sister…' His face softened. 'Lisa has offered us as many of Sorella's outdoor dining settings as we need until this can be fixed. It's generous and so we will be fine to open tomorrow, just working around the mess until we can get that sorted.'

'I was going to speak with you about how best to manage that.' Scarlett was relieved for Rosa. And pleased to hear of this olive branch between brother and sister, too. No pun intended, she thought with an edge of slightly uncontrolled humour. Scarlett frowned. She had better not start getting hysterical! 'Is there truly nothing I can do now?'

'Nothing.' Luca shook his head. 'And I want to shoo everyone else, too. Why don't you and Lorenzo go now? Maybe that will make it easier to get others moving as well.'

Scarlett gave in and nodded.

When Lorenzo led her around to the rear of the restaurant she went without question.

He helped her into the passenger seat of the van as though she were very fragile, climbed behind the wheel and drove the short distance to stop outside her bedsit.

Her landlady was away visiting her daughter again, so the place was in darkness. Scarlett turned. She knew she had to let him go and yet she was loath—

'I know you refused your mother's offer to stay with her, but I can't let you stay here tonight, Scarlett.' His words emerged on a low tone. An unhappy tone, and one that he followed with more words as she hesitated with her hand on the door of the van ready to open it. 'We speculated with the police that it was possible this crime may have happened as a result of sacking that kitchen hand.'

He drew a breath. 'That's a guess, but whether it might be true or not, I don't want you to stay here by yourself until this is resolved. There are people who know you live here alone. I can't bear the thought of any harm coming to you.'

Scarlett drew a breath. Not because she felt frightened, but because of his care. She felt overwhelmed. She didn't know what to think any more. Right now Scarlett wasn't sure if she *could* think.

'Scarlett, please.' He drew a breath. 'I want…I need…'

Scarlett waited and for some reason her heart was in her throat. 'You…?'

He blew out a breath. 'Will you please pack a bag? I could drive you to your mother's. *I will drive you wherever you choose to go.* But…I'd like you to come to my home first. I'd like to…go over all the possibilities of who might have been behind tonight's attack on the restaurant. There are some other…options that…should be discussed, I think. I didn't know whether I should bring them up to the police, or not.'

Scarlett hadn't thought about being unsafe in her home. She wanted to say she would be just fine and yet she still felt shaken. Most of all, she didn't feel ready to let Lorenzo out of her sight yet. Scarlett had feared for his safety, too. 'I'll pack a bag. It will only take a few minutes.'

She slipped out of the van and into her bedsit without waiting for him to answer. Gathering things took even less time than that. Scarlett simply stuffed what she might need into the carry-on travel bag she'd brought on the plane with her when she first arrived from Australia, securely locked her door and rejoined Lorenzo in the van.

Why did she have this compulsive need to reach across the van's interior and clasp his hand with hers? The hug they had shared earlier had been filled with relief and yet Scarlett did not feel relieved enough. Her reactions to those events were only beginning to register and as they did so they built up inside her. She tried to push them down, to keep them all nicely and neatly tidied and under control.

She'd been so angry with him, and hurt. Fearing for his safety had stripped all that away and left only…

'I rent a place here.' As Lorenzo spoke he slowed the van and turned it into the driveway of a modest home. It was a small neat place painted white and with a garden all around. A mellow light shone on the small front porch. He glanced at her as he turned off the van. 'Ready?'

'Yes.' She clasped her travel bag and climbed out of the van. He came to join her, closed and locked the doors, clasped her hand and led the way to the door of his house.

Scarlett didn't know Lorenzo's thoughts in that moment. He might have taken her hand simply to guide her through the dim area to the door. She only knew her reactions. She felt thrown straight back through time to other occasions when he had clasped her hand in his, had held her even just in that way as though she was…his world and he never wanted to let go.

Emotion rose to clog her throat. God, it had been a bottle bomb, not really all that dangerous.

Oh, yes? If you hadn't still been there, the restaurant would have burned to the ground.

But they *had* been there and so there was the possibility that someone had hoped to burn the place down with them inside it?

'It's all right, Scarlett.' Lorenzo let them inside his home. They stepped into a small foyer and he led her straight from there to a cosy living room, flicking the light switch on as they stepped into the room.

A moment later, he'd turned, taken the bag from her hands and tossed it onto the nearest leather lounge chair, and his fingers were gently tipping up her chin. 'It's all right. You're safe.'

'I didn't need to bring my bag in.' She uttered the inanity, and then responded to his statement. 'Yes, we're safe now, and what if *you* hadn't been?' The words burst out of her and… that was the end of it.

Scarlett didn't know who reached. He did, or she did. What difference did it make? All she knew was she had her arms tight around his middle. He tucked her in against his chest, his chin resting over the top of her head as he rubbed flat, open-palmed hands over her shoulders and upper back. She felt the imprint of his medallion against her, its comforting press.

'I was the one who got that kitchen hand angry. Maybe I could have handled the conversation better.' Scarlett released her hold on Lorenzo enough to look up into his eyes as she faced her concerns, as she finally allowed all of what had happened to rise inside her. 'If I'd handled him better maybe this wouldn't have happened. What if I'd gone and you'd still been there and maybe you hadn't noticed what was happening or the fire spread differently and you couldn't get out to safety? I not only let something bad happen to Luca's restaurant while under my management, but I put you in danger.'

'No, Scarlett. No.' His fingers wrapped around hers and squeezed and he…looked tortured. 'You handled that situation exactly as it needed to be handled, and I was the one to sack him. When he spoke to you that way—'

'And now we don't know if he decided to give the restaurant what he thought *it* deserved.' Scarlett shook her head.

'It is possible.' Lorenzo drew a breath and let her hands go. He gestured behind them and they took seats beside each other on the sofa.

Scarlett was surprisingly glad to get off her feet. Her legs felt shaky! 'You say that as though you have your doubts.' It took effort to draw her thoughts together to focus on this, but it was very necessary. 'We do need to really discuss this, dig around in any possibilities. The police need whatever leads we might be able to give them.'

'I don't know what to think.' Lorenzo rubbed his hand through his hair and his mouth tightened into a flat line. 'The timing is right for this to have been done by him, but in truth it could have been any person for any reason.'

'But more than one person.' They'd heard two sets of steps running away, and something about those steps... 'One of them sounded like a woman in heels. I didn't think about that until just now!'

'But you're right.' He drew a breath.

'What is it?' Scarlett searched Lorenzo's face. There was torture there, guilt, so much guilt, just as there had been five years ago when he told her he couldn't leave his wife.

Is it guilt, Scarlett? Are you sure that's exactly what you're seeing?

Even now, she wanted to hold him even more than she wanted and needed to be held by him. Something deep inside Scarlett responded to whatever hid in the backs of Lorenzo's eyes. She needed to...comfort him. Was she being silly? Had the night's events got to her and made her over-dramatise this? Was she seeing things where there was nothing to be seen?

Lorenzo swallowed and leaned forward. 'I'm concerned that my...wife may have been behind that attack. That's part of the reason why I don't want you to go back to your bedsit tonight. If it was Marcella, she would have to be in a deep state of rage, and I can't stand the thought that she might—'

He was concerned for Scarlett's safety. That was the first thing to register. Scarlett's emotions unfurled within her, letting him back in where she had tried to lock him out when she discovered he was still married. She just couldn't seem to help that. 'Why would…Marcella do such a thing? Are you saying she might do something like that to get at you?'

'I've…lost several chef's positions thanks to Marcella's poisonous tongue. Each time I found employment, sooner or later she found out where I was working and started her campaign to undermine my employer's confidence in me.' He admitted this in a low tone. 'I don't know whether she would go this far, and I don't know whether I should tell the police of such suspicions!'

Scarlett drew a sharp breath. 'Employers shouldn't have judged you on her say-so.'

'No, but sometimes all it takes is a few hints…' He swallowed before he went on. 'I did go to her, Scarlett, five years ago. I told her about you and asked her to set me free. We still lived in the same house but our relationship was already over, had been over for some time. She knew it. She knew that, for me, there was never going to be any chance for the two of us.'

'You didn't tell me that.'

'No. You were so hurt, and I…could barely think straight at that time, either.' He went on. 'Marcella refused to release me from the marriage. She threatened recompense to me but also to you if I didn't remain with her and play the good husband to the outside world, even as we were living separate lives behind closed doors.'

A picture was forming in Scarlett's mind. A picture that didn't entirely make sense but that explained some things. He'd said he did that *soon after Scarlett went back to Australia*. 'You waited for me to be safely out of the picture and then you left her, but you haven't divorced her. That doesn't make a lot of sense.'

He got up from the sofa and took three jerky paces away from her before he swung about. 'Yes, I did walk out on her after I lost you. Her response to that was to get me fired from my job.' He'd worked in a nearby village at that time. 'For months I was scrambling to get another position and hold onto it. I was worried about money, Marcella's family *and mine* were putting the screws on me on the one hand to let her have our house, and on the other to go back to her, to make it all look right.

'I had my father and mother telling me it was all my fault because we hadn't been able to have a baby as well.' He sucked up a breath. 'All I wanted to do was—'

He stopped abruptly. 'Well, that doesn't matter now. By the time the dust settled you were gone. But Marcella has gone on with those tricks. When Luca interviewed me for this position I told him about Marcella. It was the first time I'd... admitted that to anyone and I didn't want to tell him, but I couldn't afford to keep losing jobs. I asked him to judge me on my merits, to let me prove myself at Rosa no matter what he might hear about me.'

'And then I came along and you didn't know if I would fire you out of anger over our...past.' Scarlett felt shamed now to know that the thought had gone through her mind, and that she had let Lorenzo know that she had the power to make that happen.

He'd said he and Marcella had tried to have a baby and hadn't been able to. For such a proud man, that must have been a difficult matter to face, too. 'Not everyone can have children but there are other options.'

'Maybe one day Marcella will accept that. At the time it was just one more thing she wanted to blame me for, get... angry at me about.' As he searched her face perhaps he saw something in her expression that exposed her thoughts because he said quietly, 'As far as I'm aware I'll be able to father children. It was...Marcella who had the difficulties, and even with the help of a fertility clinic she wasn't able to conceive.'

'All that must have happened—'

'Before you came into my life.' His gaze softened as he looked into her eyes. 'Marcella and I...married young. It pleased our families and I didn't see her in her true colours at first.'

What he had endured at Marcella's hands reminded Scarlett of the hurt that *she* had endured at *Lorenzo's* hands. Yet she could see now that many of his decisions back then hadn't been as simple as she had imagined them to be.

Even now, Scarlett didn't understand all of his motivations, what had driven him. Just what he'd had to deal with when it came to Marcella. 'Life is complicated, isn't it? I had no idea about any of this.'

'I don't think you would have sacked me from Rosa, Scarlett. Not on the strength of our past. I admit I was concerned about it at first, but if it had come down to it I don't think you would have been prepared to do that without a fair cause.' He stopped and his hands dropped to his sides as his gaze roved over her. 'The woman who stood at my side tonight fighting a fire to save Rosa and getting herself messed up in the process isn't someone who would be vindictive, or unfair.'

His faith humbled her. Their conversation, though it had been uncomfortable perhaps for both of them and had covered ground that *still* made Scarlett uncomfortable and clearly made him uncomfortable, too, had changed her view of past events.

Scarlett had thought mostly of herself when that all went wrong. She'd been hurting and she hadn't stopped to think of what Lorenzo might have been facing.

Life *was* complicated. People did behave in certain ways for certain reasons. Lorenzo's pride had been pricked as he spoke with her about these topics that were, to him, very personal indeed.

They had *both* suffered, and maybe she hadn't really considered that until now.

Her emotions felt shaken in that moment for altogether other reasons than the threat of a fire to Luca's beloved Rosa.

And because she did feel shaken and didn't quite know how to deal with that feeling and was only now beginning to really notice the fact that the two of them were alone in his cosy house in the middle of the night, Scarlett glanced down at her clothes and forced a grimace that she hoped would hide her deeper feelings. 'At least we got the muck off our hands.'

'Yes.' He drew a breath and his gaze caught on hers and everything she had thought and all her defences and ideas were nothing anyway.

Totally nothing.

Scarlett's breath stilled in her throat and her entire being seemed to still, to be waiting for something. Waiting…for Lorenzo? 'I think you should wait before you voice any suspicions to the police about Marcella.'

His mouth tightened. 'I *thought* I caught a glimpse of her in the crowd this weekend–not tonight–but in the end I wasn't even sure it was her.'

'Leave that until tomorrow. See what the police say, first.' Scarlett felt this was the right decision. Why expose his history to all if that turned out to be quite unnecessary?

'All right. It can wait for now.' He took a small step forward. A small step closer to her. 'We both smell of fire.'

Scarlett nodded. 'It's been a huge day.'

They were words. But with the words came a change in expression, a change in the atmosphere.

In that moment they somehow moved from trying to find answers to the crux of *all* their unanswered questions. To something that felt deeper than questions, even more necessary in this moment than answers to questions.

Finally, as though Scarlett had waited for it since he had

hugged her after they put the fire out—or perhaps she had been waiting for ever—Lorenzo's hands rose to her shoulders and gently shaped them.

Blame it on tiredness or the fears of that fire or emotional exhaustion, Scarlett didn't know. But she melted into the caress of his fingers. Her thoughts and worries and concerns all melted right along with her.

She didn't *want* to stress about any of this any more, not tonight, and something inside her just…gave way. She swallowed and her gaze fell on his mouth, and then his lips were on hers and her hands rose to his chest and she closed her eyes and took this kiss that was what she needed whether it was the worst thing she could have done, or not. Scarlett didn't know the answer to that question, either.

He kissed her gently, his lips brushing over hers again and again until Scarlett melted against him, soft feminine curves to strong, muscled male. As she melted their kisses deepened.

Scarlett surrendered and her eyelids drifted closed. 'I've needed this. I've needed it, 'Renz.'

'To hold and be held.' It was a statement, not a question. 'With *you*, Scarlett. I've needed it with you. I don't know what I'd have done if you'd been hurt tonight.' His words whispered against the side of her neck, and he sounded so torn, so worried for her, and his voice was deep and the warmth of his lips even now filled her thoughts.

Her head tilted, exposing the soft skin of her nape, silently inviting… 'We're both here. We're here, Lorenzo.'

And they were, and kisses turned to touches and caresses as they stood in the centre of that room and, one after another, softly discarded all the things that had held them apart. Their history, the hurts, all of it drifted to the floor as they removed each other's clothes. It had been so long and yet it felt like yesterday. Every touch was new, and yet familiar, awaited and already known.

When the last piece of clothing fell away he took her hand and he led her to the bathroom and that felt exactly right, as though in this moment they could also wash away the past along with the scent of the fire. Wash it aside and take this, take this moment now.

The shower ran warm and they stepped beneath the spray and Scarlett looked into his eyes until it was just them and wet hair streaming down her back and Lorenzo drying her with a fluffy towel. Finally they lay in each other's arms on soft sheets that he had slept in, that held his scent.

'Are you sure, *tesoro mia*?' At the last moment, he hesitated, seemed uncertain of his ground and of this. 'I *am* still married to her.'

'I'm sure. Tonight there's nothing, only this.' There was something else. There was the question: *Why is he still married to her?* Pride? To keep their families off his back? Because she had threatened more trouble if he divorced her? Because he'd already left her, and how much worse could a divorce be?

Scarlett did want to know, but for now he'd called her his treasure while soft brown eyes looked into hers and Scarlett had a feeling that her gaze would be equally unguarded because she was sure about this moment.

And then she just didn't care about any of that at all because all Scarlett could do was feel as he loved her with his body and the touch of his hands and a soft, giving gaze that didn't leave her, didn't waver.

He loved her and Scarlett loved him, with a unity that was as remarkable now as it had been five years ago.

No. That wasn't right. This was even more, deeper, stronger than even that had been. Scarlett, *this Scarlett,* gave all of herself to this moment with a man who was like no other in her life. He had always been…Lorenzo.

As their passion built Scarlett's heart reached for him and

her senses embraced him and all that she was needed him so, so much. It wasn't a calm and rational choice, or even a decision. This just *was*.

Scarlett was so beautiful, so completely giving of herself. Lorenzo looked into her eyes and everything inside him that had been locked away, set aside, stifled and muffled and not allowed to live since the day she left…broke free and made its way to her in each touch. In each moment of possession and of giving of himself to her.

Only with Scarlett could he give and trust, give of his heart and his body equally. This was a gift that he could give to Scarlett, could trust to her. Was he still in love with her? He didn't know, but he knew the need to love her and so that was what he did until he brought them both to the edge of completion and Scarlett shattered in his arms and he shattered with her, and words of praise and affection poured out of him and his arms wrapped deep around her.

His hands pressed against her shoulder blades so he could hold them heart to heart while their breathing first rushed, and then eased, and Scarlett slumped in his arms.

He'd waited for that without realising, for that one final moment of surrender that she had always given to him. Lorenzo rolled gently onto his back then, his arms still around her.

Her head rested against his chest. Her body was soft and warm against him. He had missed her so much and not even realised.

'I'm sleepy, 'Renz.' She murmured it against his chest. 'So sleepy.'

He stroked his hand over her hair, brushed it away from her neck so he could kiss her there, kiss the warm saltiness of her skin and keep the taste on his lips as he whispered, 'I know. Sleep. No one's expecting you tonight. We have time.'

To take this.

To let themselves have this.

Scarlett drifted into sleep and Lorenzo held her and if this had been another time he would have slept, too, but not this time. He wanted to treasure every moment of this, not lose any of it.

He needed to hold Scarlett while he thought about…the future.

Lorenzo pressed a butterfly kiss to the top of her head and faced one of his answers. He hadn't fallen back in love with her.

He'd never stopped loving her. To the depths of his being.

Where did he go with that? How could he give Scarlett all the love in his heart when his past was what it was? When his past still trapped him, even now? He hadn't told her all of it. Shame burned deep inside him, burned until Scarlett sighed in her sleep and burrowed her face into his neck and, in her sleep, murmured his name.

Lorenzo closed his eyes and the big weekend and tonight's problems and the time they had spent together here, *and* his shame, all caught up with him.

Tomorrow he would have to face all of this, figure out what to do and say and how to go forward, if going forward was even possible.

He drew a breath and he, too, slept.

CHAPTER ELEVEN

'Scarlett, I'm sorry to wake you. It's still before dawn but I thought we'd better talk.' Lorenzo's soft words woke Scarlett. 'I brought coffee for you.'

The bed dipped as he sat on its edge.

She opened her eyes to the sight of him, fully dressed in a fine white linen shirt and black trousers. His hair was still damp. He must have taken a shower while she slept.

Scarlett remembered their shared shower last night and all that it had led to. He turned his head and their gazes met and, through eyes still blurred with sleep, she looked into familiar features.

Though she knew that she was vulnerable and her instincts were starting to warn her that she needed to do something about that, that she had *made* herself vulnerable last night, and where had that got her because he was *still*, when it came down to it, a married man? Despite these thoughts, her heart swelled.

While Scarlett lay in Lorenzo's bed and he looked down at her with gentle eyes that only as he had loved her last night had come anywhere near close to losing all their shadows, love coursed through her until it filled every part of her.

Love for Lorenzo, this man who had broken her heart and loved her so gently. Scarlett didn't want him to break her heart again and yet…

Scarlett Gibson was still in love with Lorenzo Nesta. She still wanted and needed him. Her emotions were still entangled in him. She hadn't got over him as she had thought she'd done. Rather, she was more in love with him now than she could ever remember being.

How could Scarlett feel this way when she *knew* he was still married, even if he hadn't lived as husband and wife with Marcella for over five years?

Uncertainty started to come to Scarlett then. Uncertainty that the events of last night had stifled and overruled. What did she know of Lorenzo now that made any difference to the way things had been last time? He *was* still married, and if things had been so bad with his wife why hadn't he divorced her as he had told Scarlett he would before he went back on his word?

Why leave but not get a divorce? What more could he possibly have to lose?

Maybe he hasn't felt the need. Maybe if he did, he would take care of that straight away now.

But Lorenzo had lost employment because of his wife's campaign to blacken his name each time he got a new position. What more could she do to him if he asked for that divorce?

'Drink your coffee, Scarlett.' He drew a breath and handed her a T-shirt that he held in the fist of his hand. 'You can put this on if you'd like and while we have that coffee, maybe we should…talk. I can see that, like me, you're starting to think about what happened last night. Both between us, and at Rosa.'

Did he plan to blame the one for the other? Say that the stress of fighting that fire had driven them into each other's arms?

Well, hadn't it?

In some ways, Scarlett supposed, it had. Her need to connect with Lorenzo after that fright had been strong.

But now…they had to sort themselves out. They had to deal with 'What happens next?'. Scarlett didn't have a clue what the answer was to that question.

Scarlett looked again at Lorenzo. 'We need to discuss strategy for a few things. Where the restaurant can go from here is one. And we need to contact the police and find out if they have any news to tell us.'

Yes, these things were important. And yes, Scarlett had somewhat used them as a way of avoiding other matters. Scarlett shrugged the shirt over her head beneath the sheets, and sat up. All she really wanted to do was reach for him and yet it wasn't going to be that simple.

If she hadn't fallen asleep the way she had last night, Scarlett would already have started to assess that fact.

She had to assess it now, and yet how did she do that with any kind of clarity when all she could acknowledge was how much she still loved him?

Oh, Scarlett. You've placed yourself in an even more potentially hurtful state of heart and mind than the one you faced five years ago. Did he tell you that he's in love with you still? Did he tell you that anything about his situation has changed or will change?

Last night Scarlett hadn't wanted to think about it, but Lorenzo's attitude to his marriage…

'There has to be more of a reason for why you haven't divorced her.' Scarlett uttered the words and her business brain did click into place for a moment to let her see that this had to be so. Nothing else made sense.

'What do you mean?' He uttered the words in a tone that drew her gaze immediately to his face.

A tone that seemed defensive? *Yes.* Scarlett set her coffee cup down on the bedside table and looked him very directly in the eyes. 'Lorenzo–'

'I contacted the police before I woke you.' Lorenzo also set his coffee aside. 'All they could tell me was that they were still processing on the case. They will phone the moment they have anything they can tell us.'

His gaze roved over her hair and face before he seemed to recollect himself.

Scarlett drew a shaky breath and resisted the urge to tidy that hair, to raise her arms and try to check her appearance. 'I hope when you hear from the police again, they'll have something solid to tell you.' She hesitated. 'You didn't tell them that I was—?'

'Here? No.' His response was immediate, firm. 'And it's still very early. There's time for me to get you home before dawn breaks. I didn't bring up Marcella with them either. Not yet.'

So no one would know of their night together, because Scarlett had yet again given herself to a man who was not free to be given to. Just as she had given herself to this same man five years ago. And he was still avoiding the issue of his wife. Not by not discussing her with the police. But by not discussing her with Scarlett.

So where did that leave Scarlett?

It left her reaching inside herself for strength.

'I won't have an ongoing affair with you a second time.' The words cost her. The thought of never being in his arms again cost her more than Scarlett could have thought imaginable. But she had pushed them out. They were said. She needed to be respected, to have her needs respected. 'There's a gap in the things you told me last night. I'm guessing you didn't want to have to tell me the things that you did—'

'Does any man want to admit that he's been manipulated? That his career and life have suffered because of the vindictiveness of a woman he married as a childhood sweet-heart and found out he didn't know at all?' The words burst out, seemed to shock him as they echoed in the quiet of the room.

Scarlett understood pride. Oh, she understood that. Her family was full of it. She'd wrapped it around herself when she went back to Australia after their affair.

For a time pride had been the only thing that enabled her to lift her head and stick out her chin and face down the world until after a while she started to be able to do it by herself once again.

'You *are* a proud man.' This, she knew, and even understood. 'You're also a strong one, and that is why I don't understand why you haven't divorced your wife in all this time. I don't see why, for example, you would let family expectations keep you locked into a situation that is clearly causing you harm and making you miserable. It doesn't make sense. Even Dante took the chance to get away from his bad situation the moment he saw a way out. And he's happier. He's no longer trying to make up excuses for his bruises.'

Lorenzo made an odd sound and turned his gaze away from her.

Scarlett froze.

Time seemed to freeze.

Things dropped together in Scarlett's mind like pieces of a puzzle. One that Scarlett hadn't known was there, and that... made her feel ill.

Lorenzo had made excuses for having a scratch on his face one time, a bruise on his chest another. For lots of scratches and bruises. He'd said they happened from taking spills off his motorcycle and yet he was a confident rider and he'd seemed to be that back then too, and he wasn't at all clumsy in any way that Scarlett had ever observed. The man worked with kitchen knives and never cut himself, and performed intricate tasks in the kitchen and always produced flawless results.

Dante had stolen and Lorenzo had talked to him, and had looked so sick when he realised Dante was being physically abused. Lorenzo had easily comprehended that whole situation. He'd so quickly agreed that bike riding could result in such accidents.

Oh, my God. Could it be? Could one horrid woman who would go so far as to cost him job after job even years after he had walked away from her... 'Was Marcella physically abusing you in your married life?' Scarlett whispered the words in an appalled, disbelieving tone.

He stood and stalked away from the bed in one angry movement. Then stopped. Shook his head. 'You were never to know this. No one was ever to know it.'

His words were low and filled with...shame.

Scarlett got out of the bed and took a step towards him.

His words stopped her. 'Do you think I want the world to know that my wife...abused me? I could never hold my head up. I never planned to let you know. I'd hoped if I explained the rest, that would satisfy you.'

He swung about and all his defensiveness *was* nothing but a front for a shame so deep.

'Oh, Lorenzo.' Tears pricked the backs of Scarlett's eyes. She forced them back. She couldn't let him see them. He might misunderstand her empathy and think it was pity.

'She was volatile. From the day we married she began to be verbally aggressive, to blame me for all sorts of things.' Once he started, he seemed determined to spit the words all out. Maybe they needed to get out. 'Nothing I did kept her happy. Because of her volatility I had doubts about trying for a baby but I thought it might be what she needed, a chance to bring out her maternal instincts, to soften her with that kind of love for her child.'

'But she couldn't conceive.' How long had Lorenzo dealt with this? Scarlett was so shocked, she could barely think!

'And as she faced that disappointment her aggression climbed until it reached the point of…'

He couldn't seem to make himself say it.

'Of attacking you?'

'I never retaliated, Scarlett.' His gaze was strong and truthful as he finally sought hers once more. 'I promise you, I never ever—'

'Of course you wouldn't have.' Her words were soft, accepting, equally truthful. Scarlett shook her head even as her heart ached to the depths for him. 'I know you, 'Renz. Of course you wouldn't have retaliated.'

His shoulders seemed to relax slightly as he absorbed her words. 'I tried to avoid arguments. I asked her to go to counselling. This wasn't something that I could take to family, or discuss with friends. I couldn't get her to seek help. Things got so bad that all I wanted was to get away from her. We'd been sleeping in separate rooms for months when I met you. I fell for you before I knew what had happened to me. I knew I needed to tell you, but I couldn't.'

He blew out a breath. 'I was afraid I'd lose you. It was hard to think straight. Finally I went to her and told her I loved you and asked her to release me. She threatened harm to you as well. I couldn't let that happen to you. In the end I lost you, but I knew you were safe at least and then…I left her, but she continued to hold power over me by impacting on my job future, by getting at me financially.

'I found her behaviour so disgusting that I couldn't go anywhere near her. The thought of trying to fight through for a divorce…' He paused and finally went on. 'What was the point? I no longer wanted to remarry so I left it.'

'She must have hurt you so much.' Scarlett didn't mean the strength of the physical attacks, and he seemed to understand this.

'If you told her she either has to agree to a divorce or you'll go to the police, tell them everything—'

'I could *lose* everything.' He glanced around him. 'I've worked hard to get back on my feet. I've been saving to try to start my own restaurant somewhere one day.'

When Scarlett came back to Monta Correnti, there'd been the problem of getting Luca's restaurant into a better place financially. Scarlett was working on that, and during their weekend cook-off she'd had a rather unorthodox idea about that. She thought it might work. In fact, Sorella offering to help out while the fire damage was fixed was almost like a sign. That situation just might be fixable. If Scarlett handled it with enough care.

But she did not know how Lorenzo's situation could be fixable. He wouldn't want to risk exposing what had happened to him, and yet his wife's behaviour had been so wrong.

Scarlett didn't know how to help him overcome any of this.

And while she searched her heart for answers, Lorenzo's face closed down and he seemed to draw deep into himself. 'I never wanted you to know this, Scarlett. It is a badge of shame that digs deep into my soul. Last night, what we shared. That shouldn't have happened. There's nowhere that we can go from here. Not…together. I shouldn't have taken that night with you.'

Even as his words cut through the secret hopes that Scarlett hadn't even realised had built themselves up so strongly within her, Lorenzo went on.

'No matter how we felt last night, now matter how much either of us needed…' He seemed to struggle to know how to go on. 'Five years ago I ignored the facts of my life and reached out for you. I learned then that I can't give you the things that you deserve, that I would want to give you. That…'

It hadn't changed.

That was what Lorenzo was about to say.

And Scarlett dug down inside *herself*. If she didn't take control of this conversation, and do it right now before this went any further, she didn't know if she would be able to keep herself pulled together.

Everything inside her hurt. She felt as though she'd been offered something so amazing, had been offered a second chance only to have it snatched back out of her hands. 'I came to Monta Correnti with certain goals in mind.'

Those goals hadn't included falling for Lorenzo a second time. That had happened, she couldn't undo that now, but she could get over it, just as she had done the first time. And she would. Scarlett felt numb inside, but she told herself she could do this. She could! He was rejecting her, and she *could* cope with this second rejection and not let it utterly crush her.

She patently ignored the fact that she hadn't seemed to do much of a job of getting over him the first time!

'My goals—' Were clearer now. 'My goals revolve around the way I relate to my family, and making a success of my work. Once I've achieved those goals I'll return to Australia and pick up my life there. Yes, that's what I'm going to do.'

That, and only that. She wouldn't remain here, torturing herself over him. 'I've got an idea that I think is what the restaurant needs. If I can get the relevant parties to agree on it, it should really ensure the financial security of Rosa for now and for the future. I'll have achieved that goal, and I'm going to achieve my family goals, too, so I can go back knowing that I've done the things I came here needing to do. I won't be here much longer.'

She would leave. That was all Scarlett could think. She would go back to Australia and not have to deal with these feelings. First she had to get through this day of realising she still loved him with all her heart, and knowing deep down that he did not love her in the same way.

Because if he did, he would find a way. Or ask her to help him find a way. Scarlett had a really good brain. She could help him figure out strategies to outsmart his wife and get himself fully free of Marcella. There had to be a way. But Lorenzo wasn't asking for that.

All he was saying was that they couldn't be together again in the way they had been last night. So it was hopeless, wasn't it? Hopeless and she was better off to cut her losses and walk away as quickly as she could.

Scarlett would start cutting those losses as of right now. She headed for Lorenzo's living room and the carry bag she hadn't touched since her arrival. 'I need five minutes to shower but after that I'd like you to take me back to my bedsit. If I don't feel safe later I'll stay with my mother or another family member, but this…'

She shook her head. She couldn't think. All she could do was feel far too much hurt, and so much more, threatening to consume her because in the end he couldn't give himself to her.

What did that leave except a great well of nothing?

Lorenzo's telephone rang.

Scarlett left him to answer it, and closed herself into the bathroom.

Whatever came, whatever happened next, she had to bear it, be a professional. Most of all she had to bear the knowledge that he cared, but he didn't love her the way she loved him. He didn't, or he would work with her to figure this out. She wanted to help him get past his feelings of shame.

She'd told him it wasn't his fault, and that he had acted honourably. She understood a man wouldn't be able to accept that easily. She wished she could help him find that acceptance.

Scarlett had her limits, too. She couldn't let herself be crushed and broken by a love that he couldn't give back to her in the same measure. She'd struggled to survive the last time. She didn't know if she could survive a second time.

It was time for Scarlett to get herself organised, get Rosa fully and finally organised and sort out her issues with her family, and…leave Italy.

Before her love for Lorenzo destroyed her.

CHAPTER TWELVE

'I WONDER if Scarlett realises what she's achieved by getting Lisa even to the point of being prepared to consider this idea,' Romano said to Lorenzo as they stood outside Lorenzo's home.

It was Wednesday morning. Lorenzo had been leaving Lisa's when Romano had dropped Jackie and Scarlett there, before taking Lorenzo home. The last two days had been busy with police reports. The restaurant, despite or perhaps in part also because of the arson attempt, was doing great business, and working in co-operation with Sorella's to ensure they could seat everyone and get on with things.

Scarlett was forging ahead with family and work. Romano had boasted just now about his beautiful daughter, Kate, and said that Scarlett had spent hours poring over Kate's photos with her sister Jackie.

Scarlett seemed to be finding forgiveness for herself for her part in Jackie losing her child for so long. Soon Scarlett would have resolved all her issues with family, and, with her work done at Rosa, Scarlett would leave.

So why let that happen when you're deep in love with her and don't want to lose her? Why let your pride—?

'The indoor dining will be back in business tomorrow, so I hear?' Romano took the newspaper Lorenzo handed to him that featured an article about the fire at Rosa.

'Uh, yes. Yes, it will.' Lorenzo couldn't concentrate, because he'd fought these thoughts for two days, fought them since he and Scarlett made love.

He'd fought for the sake of…his pride and because he felt such shame that he had somehow ended up being abused by Marcella. And maybe he never could have Scarlett and maybe he never would be good enough for her, but didn't he owe it to her to at least let her know that he loved her? That he had never stopped loving her? Couldn't there maybe, somehow, be a way for them?

If Lorenzo could figure out how to ensure Scarlett couldn't be hurt by it, couldn't he finally break the ties with Marcella and be free? And if Scarlett *was* prepared to give him even a chance to love her, maybe they could go back to Australia together and start over there where Marcella, even if she wanted to, couldn't cause them problems?

Or they could stay right here and…face it out together? 'I can tell Scarlett. I'm at least going to tell her!'

Romano raised his brows but, perhaps wisely, said nothing.

And as though Lorenzo's thoughts had conjured her, a car drew to a stop on the street outside his home and Scarlett stepped out.

Romano murmured some words that Lorenzo didn't really listen to, something about it looking like Scarlett had borrowed one of her mother's cars. He nodded to Lorenzo and left.

Lorenzo only had eyes for Scarlett. Love welled inside him and it took a moment for him to realise that Scarlett appeared…upset?

'Did you say yes?' She walked right up until they stood just a hand's reach away from each other. 'Did you say yes when my mother offered you a better-paid position working alongside her other chef in the Sorella kitchen?'

'Did Lisa tell you she made that offer?' He was surprised. He'd got the impression that Lisa had thrown out the hint about that more as if she felt she wouldn't be doing her business-related duty if she didn't than anything.

She'd invited him to the villa, told him he was a great chef and Sorella would benefit by having him on board as a second chef in their kitchens, and then she had waited.

So, in point of fact, she hadn't exactly *offered*. 'Your mother threw out a hint. I told her how happy I am at Rosa and how good Luca's been to me. If anything, Scarlett, I came away with the impression that I'd passed some kind of test by not trying to pick up on her hint about changing jobs.'

'Because you have no right to just turn around—' Scarlett broke off. For a moment her mouth worked and no sound came out. And then her gaze narrowed and she drew a deep breath. 'So you're not leaving Rosa to work at Sorella?'

'No.' He lifted his hands, palms up.

'Maybe Mamma really is considering *my* suggestion to her, then.' Some of the heat seemed to leave Scarlett and she cast one deep, torn glance at him before she dropped her gaze.

'Your idea to combine the two restaurants so both of them can function with greater success and stronger profit margins?' When she seemed shocked, he held up a hand. 'Romano mentioned it just now. I understand this is something that needs to be kept under wraps while you all work on Lisa, and that you're not telling Luca about it yet so you don't raise any false hopes in him.'

Scarlett slowly nodded. 'And so we can figure out how to put it to him without him having an implosion.' She drew a breath. 'My sisters are both behind the idea. Jackie and I have talked with Elizabeth about it by phone conference. Isabella supports the idea, too.'

'And Lisa?' If Scarlett had come storming here to accuse him of letting himself be headhunted by her mother—

'Didn't know why I excused myself as abruptly as I did.' Scarlett sighed. 'I don't want to be at loggerheads with anyone in my family. I…love Mamma. I see myself in her and her in me, and I'd like to think we could be a bit closer as mother and daughter. I. need to be closer to the Italian side of my family. I need to let them all in, to stop shutting them out and shutting myself away. Jackie and I talked about that. And then she took me to meet Kate yesterday. That…really…'

She couldn't seem to go on and she turned her head away, but Lorenzo saw her throat work and he decided they'd had quite enough of standing around outside. 'Come into the house, Scarlett.'

He didn't wait for her to agree or give permission. Rather, he gently clasped her hand in his and took one step, and when she looked up and into his eyes he took another, and led her into the house and sat side by side with her on the sofa. 'What happened when you met Jackie's daughter?'

'My sister shone all over with happiness, and Kate is a sweet girl. Kate's other mother was there and…it was all fine.' Emotion brought a bright sheen of moisture to her eyes. 'Jackie is so happy now. Her happiness *is* allowing her to let go of past hurts. I thought she might never really be able to forgive me but, instead, she only wants to share her happiness with me. The two of us came away from that meeting with Kate closer than we've ever been.'

'That's a good thing, Scarlett.' He drew a breath and gently stroked his thumb over the back of her hand.

And Scarlett seemed to realise where she was and what she was doing. She drew her hand away and looked at him. 'I came here on a burst of anger. I thought you'd walked away from your responsibilities at Rosa, or that you were going to.'

'You don't want anything to go wrong there. You're working to put the restaurant in a great place. I have no desire to abandon ship there. One day I hope to have my own restaurant, but that will be many years from now. Though…I would leave to…forge a new start with—'

But he was getting ahead of himself. Way, way ahead. He searched her face and wished that he could see more of what was inside her. Maybe that would come. All he knew for now was that he had this opportunity and he didn't want to lose it. 'I'm glad you came here, Scarlett. I'd decided that I needed to seek you out. I don't want to let you leave, go back to Australia, without telling you…'

Scarlett looked into Lorenzo's eyes and told herself she shouldn't have come looking for him. She could as easily have brought this up with him at Rosa, during working hours.

Had she seized on any excuse to have contact with him? She'd tried so hard to keep her distance emotionally, even as they had worked side by side for the past two days in the aftermath of the arson attempt on Rosa. 'What did you want to discuss? The arson? The clean-up? Rosa's indoor dining should be back to normal and useable tomorrow.'

She was dodging. She knew it, but she wasn't sure if she could take anything more.

'And the police are dealing with the kitchen hand and his girlfriend.' Lorenzo straightened his shoulders. 'It's good that they've admitted to the crime, and I'm pleased to know that Marcella didn't do it.'

'But she *could* do such a thing. You can't predict how low your…wife will stoop to continue to make your life miserable.'

'That's in a way, what I want, and need, to say to you.' Lorenzo said the words in a low tone.

Scarlett searched his face. 'I don't really understand. What else is there to say?'

'I don't want to lose you a second time, Scarlett.' The words burst out of Lorenzo and he drew a deep breath.

Scarlett's heart started to thump in her chest. She wanted to leap up from the couch and run and keep on running. But she also wanted to stay right here and hope for things that she couldn't afford to hope for.

Before she could do anything, Lorenzo went on. 'For the past two days as you've gone about your work, making sure Rosa continued on, working to convince key family members to embrace the idea of combining the two restaurants, I've watched you moving towards leaving and…'

He shook his head. 'You're amazing. You've come up with a plan that would benefit both Sorella and Rosa, if it can be implemented. I doubt there'd be many things that you couldn't make happen, if you set your mind to them. You're a strong woman, Scarlett. Strong *and* gentle *and* giving to your family. You've done all of this…for them.'

'In a way I guess I have, but I did it for me as well.' She'd wanted to find ways to draw closer, to feel a part of them.

They were still a volatile and diverse bunch of people, but Scarlett did feel closer. 'The fire, even though it was a rotten thing to happen, drew us all together too.'

'It drew *us* together that night, as well. You and me.' Lorenzo turned to face her, and when he reached for her hand again he looked so serious as he searched for words. 'I told you of the shame of Marcella's treatment of me. And of her threats. I couldn't see a way to get fully free of her, without her causing further harm to my career, or without the truth of her behaviour coming out and…my pride didn't want to deal with people knowing.'

'She's the one who should feel shame!' The words burst out of Scarlett. She couldn't hold them back. 'There's never an acceptable reason for physical violence in that kind of situation. *You* were strong, Lorenzo. You showed your strength and your character by refusing to retaliate and by trying to get help for her.'

'I've thought about that since we discussed it.' He cleared his throat. 'Thank you for your faith in me. It means more than you probably realise.'

His eyes looked into hers with such…love?

Scarlett's breath caught in her throat. ''Renz?'

'I still love you, Scarlett.' His words switched to Italian. Scarlett guessed he didn't even notice that he'd done it as he went on. 'Even more than I did five years ago. I never stopped loving you. It stayed inside me. I think it would have for ever. I love you with everything. I don't expect you to feel the same but I need you to know that you have my heart. It's yours. It always will be.'

What did he mean? Were these just words again? Words that would go into *her* heart, but wouldn't change anything? Scarlett choked back a sob and *her* words burst out. 'I love you, too, but I can't walk that path a second time. I can't give myself into your hands again and only get crumbs in return.'

'Will you give me one day?' He asked the question in earnestness. 'Please, Scarlett? One day to get my life in order and come to you with my heart in my hands? Just say you'll give me that chance?'

Two parts of Scarlett heard his words. Heart and head. Her head said take care of herself, don't run the risk, don't hope, don't trust.

But her heart…

'I'll give you your day.' She stood from the sofa on shaky legs and forced herself to walk to the door. 'You'll need to ask Isabella to cover for you at work while you take care of what you need to take care of.' She wanted to help him, but she understood that this was something he was going to need to do by himself.

Lorenzo nodded. 'I'll speak to her.'

Scarlett left the house.

And Lorenzo…set out to take back his life. His life, and his freedom.

And his future.

CHAPTER THIRTEEN

'THIS is lovely.' Scarlett uttered the words around a stampede of butterflies that were doing hob-nailed cartwheels in her tummy. They seemed to be fluttering around in her throat, too.

It was the following day, late lunch time. She and Lorenzo were sitting on a blanket at the same quiet mountain knoll they'd visited in the middle of the night.

Isabella was covering for Lorenzo back at Rosa. The Sorella chef was helping.

Scarlett wasn't sure if she should be pleased about that co-operative effort, or embarrassed, because apparently the chef seemed to think he was helping the course of love for Lorenzo and Scarlett. The man apparently had a soft romantic streak.

'This has been a long time coming and I wanted to do it right,' Lorenzo said as he uncorked a bottle of wine and poured some into two glasses. He placed one glass in her hand.

His fingers shook slightly, and somehow that small sign of uncertainty helped Scarlett to relax a little. He took the lid from a wicker picnic basket and drew out fresh strawberries and tiny heart-shaped chocolate tarts in a crystal basket. Tied to the handle of the basket was a cream hair ribbon that matched pearl earrings and a drop necklace. A ribbon that Lorenzo had tucked into his pocket against his heart…

'When did you get time—?'

'I haven't slept.' His fingers caressed that ribbon with gentle reverence. 'How could I when I was waiting for this? And…I wanted to spoil you.'

So he had cooked for her. He'd made beautiful chocolate desserts and teamed them with fresh fruit and a light red wine that tasted just right, and tied his gift together with her hair ribbon. Scarlett sipped. She couldn't eat just now. Her tummy was in too many knots! Instead she swallowed and tried to smile. 'Thank you.'

'Yesterday, I saw a lawyer. Then I warned my family that I intended to have the divorce I've wanted for years whether they can ever approve of it or not, and…I went to see Marcella.' His lips pressed together.

'Did you take your lawyer with you as a witness?' Scarlett set her wine down and gave him all her attention.

'No.' He shook his head. 'That confrontation with her was something that I had to do for myself, and…I did it. I chose a public place. When I told her I *would* divorce her she tried to…grab hold of my arm. But I just got up from the table and made it clear if she tried again I would consider it an assault and report it to the police as such.'

He drew a breath. 'It was a coffee shop in her village. People heard the altercation. Some of them may have seen the way she tried to dig her nails into my arm, and that I had to…remove her touch. Some may have heard me say I would bring the police into it.'

'That gossip could filter back to Monta Correnti.' Scarlett bit her lip.

His smile was a little forced, perhaps, but it was also determined. 'If it does, I will hold my head up. I've realised *I* know that I did no wrong and didn't deserve her treatment, and, that I tried to be understanding and help her.'

'In the end that's what really matters.' Scarlett was so glad that he'd realised this!

Scarlett wasn't sure how it had happened, but she realised that *her* hand had reached for Lorenzo's and she had clasped his fingers in hers. His hand wrapped around her fingers, too. She said quietly, 'What happened after that?'

'I laid out my terms. I told her I'd already had legal advice, that I would not tolerate her interfering in my life ever again, and made it clear that I would no longer try to hide from her behaviour past or present.' He shrugged and he made that shrug look as though that hadn't been difficult at all, and taking that action had been easy. 'I walked out while she was still gaping.'

Scarlett laughed.

Oh, not because it was funny but because... 'I'm so proud of you, Lorenzo.' And as quickly as she laughed, emotion clogged her throat. She blinked fiercely. 'I'm really, really proud of you.'

'I'll have my freedom, Scarlett. After this length of separation, my lawyer says there's no way she could fight it when I file for divorce.'

Scarlett's heart started to thunder all over again. 'That's—that's good.'

Sunshine dappled over them through the leafy shade of trees as he drew both her hands into his. 'I'm still struggling not to be ashamed of what happened with her. It's something that may continue to raise its head now and then for a long time, I think, but I'm prepared for Marcella to do her worst. If she pushes me, I *will* go to the police. Also if she tried to cause *you* any harm—'

'I would go to the police right along with you.' Scarlett

squeezed his hands. 'For your sake I hope it doesn't all come out and I hope she doesn't attempt to come anywhere near either of us. But if that happens, will you please try to remind yourself that you were the strong one? You refused to harm her or lower yourself to her level.'

He drew a shallow breath. 'I might not have a lot else to offer, but, Scarlett, if you would take it, I would offer you… my heart. I want to love and cherish you for the rest of my life, be at your side, wake up with you, fall asleep with you.' His gaze dropped to the chocolate tarts and in the midst of the emotion one corner of his mouth turned up. 'Cook for you. I am a chef. I will always be that, no matter what.'

And his voice deepened. 'I want to marry you. If there is any way you can find it in your heart to give me a second chance, I want to marry you and spend all the rest of my days loving you. I'm hoping, if you'll give me that chance, that love can grow within you for me again. That I maybe haven't completely ruined any chance of that with you.'

He drew a slow, deep breath. 'I've made some mistakes. The situation with Marcella seemed to get further and further out of control as time passed. I felt helpless to address it and I let pride and shame get in the way of seeing clearly. I didn't want to upset my family either, or hers, but in the end they're not the ones living my life. I am, and I want my chance to be truly happy. There's only one person I can ever have that with. She's sitting here with me right now.'

Lorenzo had humbled himself for her sake. He'd faced a situation that had taken him to the depths of shame, had been prepared to make all of that public if he had to, in order to buy his freedom to ask her for this.

Scarlett's heart melted. All of her melted in love and acceptance for him. And Scarlett knew that she, too, had to be completely truthful and open with him. 'I didn't handle myself well, either, when we separated. I didn't handle myself well for a long time, long before I even met you.'

She'd run, run all the way to Australia to her father and that side of the family, but Scarlett had never addressed what sent her out of Italy. 'I knew I'd done something bad to Jackie when I threw that letter away. As time passed and I grew up and realised the full extent of my actions I hid the guilt behind ignoring the family.'

'But if you were only a child—' Lorenzo wanted to forgive the issue. That fact was written all over him.

Scarlett loved him for that generosity, but if he wanted to be able to move on in his own life and to move on with her he needed to hear that no one was perfect and that *Scarlett* was far from perfect. 'The time came when I should have addressed that issue with Jackie. I dodged doing that. Even when I came back here this time and Jackie wanted me to look at photos of Kate, at first I didn't want to do it.'

'But you did, and now you've met your niece.' His fingers tightened over hers.

Scarlett drew a breath and felt the squeeze of Lorenzo's fingers, and squeezed back and smiled. 'It went really well. Jackie only wants to look forwards, I think, not behind her now. She says I need to do the same. I needed to feel resolved with my family, to let them back into my life. I didn't want to stay shut away from them, and them shut away from me.'

'I think your sister is wise.'

'A lot of people think I'm like Mamma, and that Mamma is very cold, but I don't think even Mum is really that frozen inside.' Scarlett drew a breath. 'She's done some things. Maybe we all have. But I've started to see the chinks in her armour, too.'

She leaned forward and said confidentially, 'Maybe it's a time for the women of my family to revisit first loves, because

I learned today that the man Mamma was with the night of the fire was Rafe Puccini.'

'Didn't he help launch your mother's modelling career years ago?'

Scarlett nodded her head. 'Yes, and he opened up his family palazzo for Lizzie's wedding. He and Mum were flirting then, but I didn't think anything would come of it.' Scarlett shrugged. 'And maybe it won't. I guess we'll have to wait and see, but…Mamma's voice changes when she speaks his name.'

'Would you mind if she found love with him?' Lorenzo stroked his fingers over the back of her hand.

Scarlett absorbed his touch, felt the love within it. Turned her hand and clasped his. 'No. I'd be happy for her. Love is worth being happy about.'

'It is.' He smiled, and Scarlett smiled, and they both fell silent.

Finally she said, 'My life has been far from perfect, too, Lorenzo. You don't have to ask me to grow to love you. I already do. Deep in my heart I don't think I ever stopped. I love you now more than ever before. So if *you* can accept me with all my history and my flaws and shortcomings, but knowing that I will give all of my heart to you and not hold anything back, I…want to try. *I want to marry you.*'

Relief and joy and happiness and love, all washed over his face and straight away she was in his arms, crushed close while he rained kisses into her hair and over her face and neck and finally their lips met and it felt as if it really was a promise for their future.

When they drew apart, Scarlett looked into rich brown eyes that she had grown to know and love so much. She saw no shadows whatsoever, just happiness. Her own happiness burst forth inside her then as she truly knew that they would indeed have their lives together, a happy future. 'If Marcella causes trouble I'll help you. Though the need will never arise with Luca. He said you're an honourable man and anyone could see that, and he was right!'

Maybe Scarlett had always known that, too, deep down inside. She'd just needed to work it out. And now she had.

She hesitated as she wondered about the logistics of their future. 'If it would be better for you, we *could* go to Australia and live there.'

In truth, Scarlett wasn't sure now if she wanted that or not. A part of her wanted to stay in Italy and another part did want to return to Australia. She loved both sides of her family, but most of them were here.

'I'm trying to get to know all this side of my family, but it's not a quick job.' She shook her head. 'I have cousins I haven't even met that are children of Luca's.'

'Don't stress too much about it, Scarlett.' Lorenzo's hands gently rubbed over her shoulders as he held her against his chest. 'It doesn't matter to me where I live. If Australia is better, we can live there. If here is best, I'm happy to stay. Now that I've finally confronted Marcella and insisted that she completely release me, I have a feeling that she'll be forced to realise she truly has no hold over me any more.'

'And *your* family?' Scarlett would stand by him through anything, and she smiled as she said, 'I've had some practice dealing with stubborn family members.' She hesitated and added sheepishly, 'And, I guess, *being* one.'

He laughed before his expression sobered. 'I've yet to decide whether to tell the truth to my parents. I'm not sure if they'd ever be able to understand. I'm going to tell my brothers, though. They're good men. I'm looking forward to you meeting them.'

Scarlett would cope with meeting his parents, too. 'I want you to meet my dad. You'll like him. He's a good guy.' She gave a teasing smile. 'Even if he does eat mass-produced Australian pizza now and then.'

'I'll enjoy meeting him.' Lorenzo brushed his knuckles over her cheek. 'I don't want to leave Rosa in the lurch, either, though I know I'm not irreplaceable.'

'You are to me.' And they would support each other through whatever came their way, whatever choices they needed to make and actions they needed to take. 'We'll sort it all out, 'Renz.'

Something told Scarlett that this big, boisterous family that had been through so many ups and downs would also support them when they found out that she and Lorenzo were in love, and planning to get married.

She wrapped her arms around Lorenzo's middle. 'We're going to be part of a big family.' Scarlett would need to get to know Lorenzo's family, too, and that might not be easy at first but they would get there.

He squeezed back, loving her with his touch and his gaze and his heart. His expression sobered. 'And we will be our own family, too, and maybe one day…'

'Have children of our own.' Scarlett swallowed as she thought of it. Bearing Lorenzo's child. 'I would like that. When we're both ready.'

'Until I get you a ring, will you wear this as a sign of my love?' Lorenzo removed the medallion from around his neck and gently closed the chain behind her neck. The gold disc settled between her breasts. It was still warm from his body. 'I don't think I ever told you, but the medallion was a gift from my late grandmother. I loved her, and…it would please me for you to wear it.'

Scarlett swallowed hard and her fingers rose to touch the chain. 'I will wear it with all of *my* love.'

'Thank you, Scarlett. Thank you for the gift of *you* in my life.' Lorenzo laid her gently in the soft grass, and they rested in the dappled shade of the tree and gave themselves time. To whisper and talk and kiss and think about the future.

To eat chocolate tarts and strawberries and sip a little more wine.

And to dream and know that, this time, their dreams were *going* to come true!

A sneaky peek at next month...

By Request

RELIVE THE ROMANCE WITH THE BEST OF THE BEST

My wish list for next month's titles...

In stores from 17th May 2013:

☐ The Hudsons: Luc, Jack and Charlotte –
Leanne Banks, Emily McKay & Barbara Dunlop

☐ Bella Rosa Proposals – Jackie Braun,
Barbara McMahon & Barbara Hannay

3 stories in each book - only £5.99!

In stores from 7th June 2013:

☐ The Spaniard's Summer Seduction
– Kim Lawrence, Cathy Williams, Maggie Cox

Available at WHSmith, Tesco, Asda, Eason, Amazon and Apple

Just can't wait?

Visit us Online

You can buy our books online a month before they hit the shops! **www.millsandboon.co.uk**

0513/05